# QUEEN OF BLOOD

# QUEEN OF BLOOD

Book Four in The Cross and the Crown Series

by

## SARAH KENNEDY

www.penmorepress.com

ISBN-13:-978-1-950586-75-2(Paperback)
ISBN    :-978-1-950586-74-5(e-book)

BISAC Subject Headings:
FIC014000FICTION / Historical
REL053000RELIGION / Christianity / Protestant
FIC031020FICTION / Thrillers / Historical

Cover Illustration
The Book Cover Whisperer:
ProfessionalBookCoverDesign.com

Address all correspondence to:

Penmore Press LLC
920 N Javelina Pl
Tucson AZ 85748

Such writing! Sarah Kennedy brings a lost world blazingly to life. — *Lee Smith*

Sarah Kennedy reanimates lost perspectives of Tudor England in her second story of Catherine, a former nun displaced by Henry's dissolution of the religious houses. With a scholar's imaginative sympathy, Kennedy restores humanity to Mary Tudor and the vulnerable women sheltered by Catherine. With a poet's sensual worldmaking, Kennedy conjures up the textures, temperatures, aromas, and emotions of daily life in a country undergoing dizzying upheavals of beliefs and convictions. In City of Ladies Kennedy takes her place with Daphne du Maurier, Anya Seton, Rosemary Sutcliff, and Hilary Mantel as writer of superb historical fiction. — *Suzanne Keen*

**Praise for *The King's Sisters*: Book Three in The Cross and the Crown Series:**

Sarah Kennedy opens magical windows into the world of Tudor's England and brings it to life in vibrant colors and unforgettable reverberations. She reinvents the genre of historical fiction of that period giving voice to women of all ages, social classes, and economic standing. She writes with astounding detail of material culture and deft psychological insight about the experiences of women from the royal sisters to maids and confidants amidst whom the feisty protagonist Catherine Haven sparkles in the full richness of her empowered self, in the delicious shades of her moods, intelligence, warm motherhood and sensuality. This third novel in the series soars to new heights and we follow the heroine breathlessly on her suspenseful, sometimes reckless, always riveting journey. — *Domnica Radulescu*, author of *Train to Trieste* and *Black Sea Twilight*

"[A]n excellent novel" *Minneapolis Star Tribune*

# CHAPTER ONE

London: October 1553

On the same day that Mary Tudor was to be crowned Queen of England, a letter arrived at the Davies House in London. Catherine Havens Davies had travelled back from Yorkshire earlier than she had meant to, in order to see the unlikely event—a Catholic placed back on the throne, a woman ruling England—and, still dazed from days on muddy, leaf-smeared roads, she thought the message must be from the court. An invitation to attend a special Mass, maybe, in celebration. The Roman Catholic Church would be the Church of England again, after all. The priests were already poised for reinstatement at their altars. Silver chalices and dusty statues of the Virgin were being dragged out of vaults and false-bottomed chests, and the butchers at various shambles were, no doubt, sifting through their piles of discarded bones, looking for possible relics. The Bishop of Winchester was now the Lord Chancellor, because he had got it from the mouth of God Himself that Mary was the legitimate heir of Henry VIII and must rule their island. They would have a woman at their head; a city of ladies, at last. It was all that Catherine had ever hoped for.

Catherine laid her hand on her lap. Her flat belly felt hollow, but she could still recall, after all these years, the delight, and fear, of knowing a new child swelled there. The last had been a baby conceived out of wedlock and the cause of much shaming, mostly, she had to admit, among other women. But after all these years, Mary had surely forgiven her for marrying the baby's father and keeping the child. All would be well now. Her past sins and errors were behind her, and Catherine would live in peace with her daughters and her queen and her God, for the rest of her days.

She considered the fine, thick paper and let her fingers slide over its surface. She might have remained chaste and alone, like other former nuns. Chaste and bitter, and old, now. How many convents would be opened again, to welcome them back in? She knew that her first marriage had been approved because money had changed hands, but the slick passage of gold from one hand to another had smoothed the passage of others to the places they wanted to go. Why should she be different? She hadn't chosen the convent, after all. That had been another's doing, as was the case for so many women.

Catherine turned over the letter, and in the buttery candlelight of her private chamber, the Wittenberg seal blazed. It was not from the queen. This could only have come from one person. She almost tore the missive itself in breaking the wax. Rubbing the grit from her eyes, she squinted at the familiar, tight script, and she must have called out, because her husband Benjamin, still in his night shirt, appeared in the doorway. "What is it?" he said.

"My son," said Catherine, still reading. "Robbie says that he will return to England." She handed it over.

"As soon as this? And at this time? He surely knows that we'll be Catholic again?" Her husband scanned to the signature and set the letter aside. "Maybe the air of religious reform smells less sweet when it blows through a university instead of a king's chamber. I hope he's been studying his Latin." Benjamin, from behind, wrapped his arms around Catherine's shoulders and laid his cold palms against her bare chest. She gasped and pushed backward, into his belly.

"Let's back to bed," he said. "It's too wintery today for crowning queens."

"He is coming through Kent. My son, I mean." Catherine leaned away from her husband and dragged a brush through her hair, letting the long strands settle onto Benjamin's arm, and when she set it down she saw a white one wound into the bristles. "Look here." She held it to the window light. "I am almost thirty-nine years old. I grow ancient." She wrapped the silver thread around her finger and cast it toward the fire, listening for the whisper of a hiss. "Do you think Robbie has really had enough of the Lutherans?"

Benjamin urged her backward. "To bed."

She shivered and let him pull her up, into his arms. Benjamin had thickened in the ten years of their marriage, but so had Catherine, a little. He swung her around and laid her on the sheets, then lumbered over her and grinned down. "You will never be too old for me."

She knew his body, and his ways, and they were playful in bed, unhurried and relaxed, Catherine growing giddy in the stomach. They spent themselves without fear or shame, and when Benjamin lay afterward on his back, one arm behind his head, he said, "I will ride to Dover and meet him, if you wish it. He will stay here, with us."

Catherine turned onto her side and propped her head on her hand. "Will he, do you think?"

"Where else? I promised you I would try to be a father to the boy, and I will."

"I will send him a welcome from us both. Perhaps they have heard over in Wittenberg how kindly the queen has spoken of her Protestant subjects."

"Let us hope she maintains that generosity of spirit."

"She will. I'm certain of it." A wet leaf smacked against the pane by Catherine's side, and stuck to the glass like a dead hand. She yawned and a giggle caught in her throat. "I should dress. Let the girls stay at home this day. The sky threatens rain."

Benjamin rose and poked at the fire. Then he lifted the letter and looked at it. "Let that be the only threat we feel."

When she was alone again, Catherine put on her clothes herself. The maids were probably all downstairs gossiping about the coronation parties, and she didn't want to hear it. Few people mentioned the convent to her anymore. She had almost forgotten what it felt like, to be the subject of sideways smirks, the half-finished speculations about fortunate times for a former nun and having two husbands and Jesus as well. She'd only been a novice, after all. And now she would be a good Catholic woman, as she had tried to be in the convent, and if she was married now, who could dare to be her judge?

Her queen. And suddenly, her son. Catherine covered her head and peered into the mirror, stretching back the skin of her cheeks. She had not had so much as a word from Robbie since the summer, when he had sailed off without a backward glance. His Protestant king Edward was dead, and when Guildford Dudley had been hauled to the Tower with Jane Grey, he had fled, claiming that he would never put his neck under the foot of a queen allied to Rome. Or any queen, for that matter.

And yet, he was coming back. And the queen was speaking of mercy and peace. All would be well, and with her son at home, the world would be an Eden again. Catherine took up the letter again. The boy knew no one in Kent. Did he? The leaf at the window lost its grip and fell. Its damp shadow faded, and Catherine rose, rubbing her arms. Her son was coming home. She shuddered in the cold and tried to feel again that fluttering in her stomach. She was happy. She told herself that she was sure of it. Today could hold nothing but good news.

# Chapter Two

London was a swarm, and Catherine ducked her head as she and Benjamin pushed through the crowds. They had left their horses behind, and as they approached Westminster, she could hear the buzz of Spain in the people's words. The Spanish king would be the English king. England would be servant to Philip, and Mary Tudor would be his handmaid. One man muttered that the queen was a Roman whore and would hand them all into the pocket of the Pope. The woman beside him said, "Hush." There were priests in the crowd, and women wearing prayer beads, openly, at their sides. A couple of boys fell into a fight, rolling on the ground, and when one of the priests hauled the bigger one up by the scruff, the lad spat on him and ran off. Someone mourned aloud for Queen Jane, shouting that she should be released from the Tower, and another scuffle broke out amid curses and shrill "Long live Queen Mary"s.

Catherine would not see the queen through this crowd, nor hear her words, and she tugged on her husband's jacket. "Benjamin, take me home. We can sit by the fire and wait for the reports. I am too old for this."

They finally achieved the door of S. Margaret's, where Catherine's friend Ann was supposed to be waiting for them.

Benjamin said, "We know the news already. I want to see how the people respond to it."

"You have seen it," said Catherine. "I want to go home."

A woman's voice said, "You will not desert me, not after you've dragged me all this way." Catherine turned. Ann was behind her, with her husband Reginald Goodall beside her. "We have beaten you here by an hour, and I intend to hear what the woman has to say for herself after all these years."

"I have a letter—" Catherine said, but more people crushed in against the door behind them. Mary Tudor was coming. The hum from the friendly corners of the crowd rose to a cheer, but Catherine could barely breathe. She was glad for her superior height, and raised herself onto her toes to get some air. Elizabeth Tudor rode by, inside a carriage. Even through the small opening, she looked spectral and thin. And behind her rode Anne of Cleves, eyes on nothing at all. Catherine almost lifted her hand in greeting, but no one would have noted her. Now everyone's hands were raised. Caps were being thrown, babies lifted to the sky. And then came Mary herself—heavier now—still with that pasty complexion, but warmed in the cheeks by triumph. She waved and the crowd cried out for her, drowning out the nay-sayers.

"Queen Mary!" a woman called. "True to the true faith!"

"England will have God again!" shouted a man in front of Catherine.

"And Philip the Spaniard," said Benjamin softly into her ear. "I wonder if they will cheer so heartily for him."

"She will free Jane and Guildford now," said Catherine, but the well-wishers were nearly shrieking and Benjamin had been shoved aside by a couple with a baby that was covered in sores. Nobody marked Catherine's words. Someone had opened the door of the church behind her, and more people flew out. A man with a crutch was trying to beat his way through, toward the queen. Bells tolled.

Benjamin fought his way back to Catherine's side. "They think she's Jesus," he said.

"The Virgin Mary, more like," said Ann.

A hive of the stronger-limbed petitioners surged forward to surround the new queen, to touch her, and a space opened beside them. Catherine put her head into it, pulling her husband along. They were the only ones moving away from the mob, and when they found a street with enough room to stand together, Catherine leaned against a tavern wall and found Ann and Reg beside her.

Ann said, "She means to bring her mother back to life. She should have married the Englishman while she had the chance." A boy bumped Ann from behind, almost knocking her down, and ran on. "I am on Catherine's side. Let's go home." She cut into a side lane, and Reg followed.

Benjamin hooked Catherine's arm and steered her after Ann. "The whole city's gone mad," he said.

Reg tried to hold Ann's elbow, as though to guide her along, and she said, "Let me go. The next one who touches me will get his ears cuffed." Reg grinned, and she put her hand into his. "All right, man. You may touch your wife."

They walked, Catherine grateful enough to be on her feet instead of in a saddle. They passed bonfires and public houses sparkling with music. A pair of riders clopped by, sloshing their clothes with mud. Someone inside a shuttered alehouse yelled, "No foreign marriage!" and a small roar of agreement went up around it.

"They had better keep the windows covered all day if they are going to give their tongues such liberty," said Ann.

"She is too old to have a baby," said Benjamin. He stepped around a drunken man and walked on. "And she cannot keep Jane and Guildford locked up forever. Do you hear these people? She will have to cut off their heads."

"She wouldn't," said Catherine. "She won't. The plot was all Guildford's father, and he's already dead. Jane is a little girl. She's not even eighteen years old."

Benjamin said, "Will someone silence the damned bells?"

"She must try," said Catherine.

"Try? All she has to do is sign the order," said Ann, "and it's off with their heads, young or not."

Catherine said, "I meant to say she must try to have an heir. She will let Jane go free." Her head was muddy. They could not discuss anything in this noise.

"If he will stay in her bed long enough to give her one," said Benjamin. "This Philip is a confirmed lecher, and he will bring a houseful of mistresses with him. Or he'll get him new ones."

"She should have married the Englishman," repeated Ann.

"And make him bend his knee to her Pope?" Benjamin shook his head.

"She has London with her," observed Catherine, "in their hearts."

"Most of it," Benjamin said. "And you. She has always had you."

"She has never done me wrong. Wherefore should I speak ill of her?"

Ann said, "She's never done you any good, either, for these ten long years. A body would think you'd murdered a man, not married one. If the boy king had turned out to be more of a tyrant, she would likely have never spoken another word to you. Better a fallen nun than a raised-up brat, I suppose."

"Shh," said Catherine. She could not follow the course of their words and her head was beginning to ache.

They stopped at a crossroads and waited for a troop of armed men to ride by. One of them stared down at Benjamin until he gave up a "God save Queen Mary." The man nodded and rode on. Benjamin muttered, "And God save my horned ram, who has fathered many a good lamb."

Catherine jabbed him with her elbow, and Ann said, "Has she called you to her? You spoke of a letter. What does she want of you now? It's been an age since she called on you for anything."

Catherine said, "No. It's from Robbie. He's coming home."

Ann looked at Reg. Reg looked at his feet.

"Did you hear me?" asked Catherine. "My son is coming back. Of his own free will."

"Now?" said Ann. "Why now, of all times?"

"It's almost Christmas."

"Does he know that Guildford is still in the Tower? And Jane?"

"People have come out of the Tower before. Mary has no reason to hold them anymore."

"The Tudors and their reasons. I have heard this tale before," said Ann. "Why would he come now? He hates Mary Tudor like the devil."

"She is not her father. And perhaps he has changed his views."

Ann said, "It's true that parents and children sometimes scarcely know each other."

"He is coming home," Catherine said. A laughing band of men spilled from a door, and a wayward dagger caught Catherine's side and tore her skirt. "My son is coming back. Can you not feel some joy at that?"

"I'm happy for your happiness," said Ann, but Catherine saw her cast another dark glance at Reg, before they walked on.

# Chapter Three

They were home before dark. The Davies House in London was shallow but wide, with only a scrap of yard around and behind it and just enough outbuildings to keep the family in decent city style. But the courtyard in the front was showy, impressively graveled and set with pots of flowers and small trees, now dropping their leaves, to the annoyance of the gardeners. Catherine's introduction to the place had been at the side of William, her first husband, and she had scarcely noticed its splendidly compact design. Now it was hers, and she had chosen the plants, adding a knot of herbs among the blossoms for her pleasure, though she seldom put her hands to them these days.

Tonight, the courtyard was a shambles of discarded chicken bones and apple skins, a couple of dirty jackets and one unexplainable pair of women's thick-soled shoes. Someone's horse had left a pile on the stones near the wrought-iron front gate and it steamed into the chill air. The servants had already bolted the doors and shutters, and Benjamin resorted to shouting like a tinker for someone to open up. A small girl looked down from a window above and said, "Father!"

The front was opened, and they stumbled inside. Down the stairs came the daughters, Benjamin's Diana, slim and brown-haired, first. She had recently turned twenty-five and still showed no desire to marry. She smiled often but never showed her teeth, though they were suitably clean and straight. She was leading Alice, the youngest girl, by the hand. Alice—the child for whom Catherine had given up her place with Anne of Cleves and her loving friendship with the woman who was now their queen. Alice, at ten, was fair-haired and blue-eyed. Mary would have loved her, if she had gotten to know her as she had once known Veronica, Catherine's elder daughter. And Veronica was becoming a woman with the same blue eyes as her sister, but a blaze of red hair that she did nothing to tame. She teetered behind the others, in her first heeled shoes, calling "Mother, did you see the queen? Was she all trussed up?"

Diana ordered food in her quiet way, directing the servants with a few words, and the family gathered around the long table in the dining gallery. Reg dismissed the men to bring more logs and worked on the fire himself, while Catherine and Ann ridded themselves of their sodden shoes and the younger girls assembled around them.

"Is she fat and pasty?" asked Alice. "Vere says she looks like an old sheep."

"I never did!" said Veronica.

"You did," said Alice. "You even went, 'Baaaa.'"

Veronica snorted at that, and Diana came in and touched her shoulder until she quieted.

"She looks like Boudicca of old, riding in triumph," said Catherine. "Every inch a warrior." She pushed the hair out of her younger daughter's eyes. Her two girls were different in looks but both fiery in temperament. Diana was more a second mother to them than a step-sister, and she sat silently beside them, in shadow, her hands folded.

Reg settled beside Ann, near the fire, and she leaned on him. "Will you seek her out?" he said.

"If I have not been summoned, she has no wish to lay eyes on me," said Catherine. "I will wait."

"What of the land?" said Benjamin. "She may take it."

"What will she take?" asked Veronica. "Our land?"

"He means the old convent land," said Ann.

"We keep our sheep there," said Veronica. "She cannot have it."

Catherine shrugged. "She can if she means to have it. And what am I to do if she does? I have been little more than a traitor in her eyes. But that is in the past. It's a long time ago, now, Benjamin. She surely has greater plans in her mind than a pile of old buildings."

Alice said, "It is my fault, is it not, Mother? She thinks me a disgrace." The girl's eyes were set wide, like Benjamin's. Intelligent eyes.

A perfect child of love, Catherine thought. But to Mary Tudor, a child of sin. "No. Who has put that into your head? It was my fault for keeping secrets, but I would not undo it or unmake you for all the land in all of Yorkshire." She looked at her husband. "She will not take our property. She wants God in England, not property. And it would take years to restore."

"Her God seems to like a big house," said Benjamin. The kitchen maids brought in roasted lamb and bread, and laid out jugs of wine. When they curtseyed their way out, he said, "Girls, upstairs with you. Diana, will you take them?"

The young woman nodded and herded the younger ones out. Benjamin said, "Will she divorce us, do you think?"

This possibility had not occurred to Catherine, and she was struck through with a cold bolt of fear. But she raised her hands to the fire and said, "I cannot imagine it. Not after all these years. No. She would not. She could not, in good conscience."

"She could, as sure as she could set every one of her brother's counsellors on the water and shove them from the shores of England. As sure as she could divorce Jane Grey from her head."

"Stop," said Ann. "I can't hear that anymore."

"I only say what everyone is thinking," said Benjamin. "Even if we  had gotten permission, it would have been from a Protestant. We didn't even have that."

"You were married by a priest in a church," said Ann.

"A priest who had turned Protestant. And a marriage without permission." Benjamin shook his head. "All those priests. They'll have to burn their English Bibles now and try to dig up their Latin ones. Poor dogs. I wonder what will happen to them."

"They have families, too, some of them," said Catherine.

"God help them," said Benjamin, "because your Mary will not."

"Tell us about Robbie," said Ann.

"It's a short letter," said Catherine. "He says that he will return by way of Kent. He doesn't say if he knows where we are. Benjamin, you don't think he will try to make Yorkshire? It is such a long road in this mud."

"I know no more than you do," he said. "I know very little at all right now."

"Why?" asked Ann. "Why does he come now? He left because of the queen and now he comes back when she is crowned? No. That's not the Robbie I know. There is something else."

"Sick for home, perhaps," said Catherine. "Maybe he misses his sisters."

Ann blew through her lips. "He barely knows his sisters. He wants something, Catherine. Do you hear me?"

"He's my son," said Catherine. "I will give him what is in my power to give."

Ann said, "This cannot come to good, Catherine. Not now. You mark me, it cannot."

# Chapter Four

England seemed fully changed. Again. Mary met with her Parliament, and the island was Catholic once more. The marriage of Henry VIII and Katherine of Aragon was made valid for a second time, and the reforms of the boy king Edward VI were repealed.

The Spanish marriage was formally offered and formally accepted. No one spoke a word against it aloud now, at least not in the markets. Not loud enough in the taverns to be heard from the streets. The house maids cast down their eyes when Catherine asked if they'd heard gossip and said they had not. A beggar who called herself Old Moll came to their door and asked for charity in the new queen's name. She could clean chamber pots, she said, and Catherine took pity and gave her a pallet in the larger of the storage rooms. The woman had a following of stray cats that Benjamin frowned on, but the cats remained outdoors and Moll, dipping an awkward curtsey and thanking Catherine, retreated to the lower floor.

Catherine penned a short message to her son that her husband would meet him in Dover and accompany him to their home in London, but no letter came in return. And no letter came from the queen. The days grew short, and the grey sky closed in on everyone.

Catherine ordered the house to be made ready for winter. Firewood was purchased and stacked in the back. The cellars were packed with cabbages, carrots, and apples. Wine was bought and the barrels were laid just down from the kitchen. Every day, Catherine stood for a while at the door, watching for a messenger, but no one came. No one from Lady Anne of Cleves, who had probably not even seen Catherine among the onlookers and had probably long forgotten her. No one from Robbie. And no one from Queen Mary.

Diana, as had been her habit for years, instructed the girls in their writing, and a tutor came to teach them French and music. Ann oversaw their embroidery. The house trilled with singing while Diana practiced her lute, but Catherine's voice had never been fine enough for their complicated intervals, and she remained below, listening to her daughters. They spoke of the Yuletide in tight, excited whispers. Benjamin had always dressed up for the holidays and delivered gifts to them at the New Year, as though they could not recognize him. Diana smiled and nodded when Veronica and Alice spoke of new clothes and shoes and little luxuries: stockings so fine that they slid through the fingers, oranges from Seville.

Benjamin and Reg took a short hunting trip to the Davies country house, hauling home two fat deer and a pig they claimed was wild. "Ferocious," Benjamin insisted. "It almost gored us as we fell upon it." But the animal was fat in the flanks, and Catherine knew it for a barrow from the Davies stock.

"You have always been an excellent huntsman," she said. "I am sure he never stood a chance of escape."

Reg and Ann walked out together in the afternoons, listening for news. The talk on the streets had begun to turn back to the royal marriage, as though the short days had narrowed their conversation to the direst of possibilities: the age of the queen, how difficult it would be for her to conceive, and the cost of a stranger, a Spanish man, at court. A foreign king for England. Old Moll returned in the evenings from her haunts and denied having heard anything at all about anyone's marriage.

"She cannot make him the king of us, can she?" Ann asked one night, as she and Catherine lingered with their husbands near the great fire in the dining hall. The girls had gone to their beds, dreaming of midwinter celebrations. "Catholic or Protestant, he sounds dangerous. Or so people are beginning to say."

"She surely will not make such an attempt," said Benjamin. "A Spanish queen was enough of a problem. No one wants a Spanish king. He will have to be a prince. Or a consort."

"So that is settled," said Catherine.

"But she is old to have a first child," said Reg.

"And too ugly," said Benjamin. "I doubt that our Virgin Mary can hope for an immaculate conception."

"Benjamin," admonished Catherine, disliking the cruelty of his words.

"She could get her a healthy one from the country," said Reg. "Wear big dresses and put it in a royal cradle when the time comes. We saw plenty of plump ones out there, and their parents seem to have enough on their hands already."

"And who named you the counsellor to the queen?" said Ann, but she put her hand on his knee as she said it, and Catherine could see that they would not quarrel. It would be well, in the end. Her son would come home, and England would have an heir. The queen would get one, however necessary. And if she had the man she wanted, Mary would do no harm to the Protestants. They would accustom themselves back to the old religion in steps. In reasonable steps. This year they would have a true holiday. She felt gracious and expansive. She would send a note to the court, containing her sincere wishes for Mary's prosperity.

The weather turned cold in December, and one morning the snow blew in, thick and frothy, and the girls ran out, squealing, into it. Veronica was too old for children's games, but she spun with her sister, under the sky, catching flakes on her tongue, while Diana and Catherine stood huddled in their cloaks, keeping watch for child-snatchers. Diana lifted herself onto her toes and said, "Mother, I see someone. Just there."

A head showed over the front wall.

"A man on a horse."

Catherine dashed to meet the rider as he turned into their gate. He wore a heavy coat and a hat shadowing his eyes. But she knew him before he raised his head. It was her son, Robbie. He was in England. He had come back to her on his own.

But he had not come alone.

Four horsemen rode in behind Robbie Overton, and, behind them, a couple more horses pulling a wagon, borne down by chests. Robbie rested his wrists on his pommel and waited for the others before he signalled and dismounted, dusting his snowy hat against his thigh. He looked older than his sixteen years. He pointed to the back, and the servants toiled forward with the wagon.

The girls fluttered to Catherine's side, but she ran forward and tried to embrace her son. "Robbie! I have waited and waited! God smiles on me," she said, "to have you with us again. I would have prepared something for you."

He stepped away and bowed. "Mother," he said. "I trust you are well?" His eyes took in the girls. "And your household?"

"Come on, then, and greet your brother," said Catherine. Her arms moved into the air, as though to take in all of her children, but the girls hung back, clinging to Diana, and Robbie remained where he was. "Diana, won't you bring your sisters?"

Diana steered the younger ones across the stones, and Robbie took Veronica's hand. "Sister, you are taller."

"And you are thinner," Veronica said. She put her arms around Alice. "You see how our little one shoots up. She will be the tallest of us, Robbie. And you remember Diana? She is an excellent musician. Diana, will you play for us tonight?"

Diana nodded, and Alice approached Robbie. She was tall indeed for her ten years, and she pushed herself onto her toes. "My father was to meet you at Dover."

"I can ride by myself," said Robbie. "I do not need an escort into my own country." The girl started to speak again, but the boy had turned away, and she sank onto her heels. Diana picked up Alice's hand. Robbie said, "These are my guests, Mother. I suppose there is room in the inn for them?"

Catherine's heart was hopping, but she said, "Yes, Son. There is always room for you and yours. Bring in the chests and I will have your chambers swept. The cold has likely frozen the windowpanes. We will have fires lit."

Alice looked up at her mother, and Catherine warned her with the slightest of headshakes. Diana said, "I will order more food." Veronica was scowling at Robbie, but he had eyes for nothing but the other men, who still had not said a word.

# Chapter Five

At dinner, Benjamin studied the young men who occupied one side of the long table. The four newcomers, guided by Robbie, helped themselves to the roast lamb and bread without assistance, and they finished off five bottles of French wine among them. They had been introduced simply as Tom, John, Edward, and Peter, and they laid into the custard with a vengeance, not waiting until the dirty plates had been taken away. Diana had taken a low seat, across from the newcomers and away from the others, and Veronica appraised the strangers more than she ate. Alice kicked at Catherine under the table until her shin could withstand no more abuse and she squeezed the girl's knee. Old Moll peeked around the corner of the doorway once, and backed away.

"Have you brought your books home with you, Robbie?" Catherine finally asked.

"Books will be burned in England," her son said. "And I am called Robert now."

"Who has said anything of burning books?" said Catherine.

"Books. Men. It will be all the same. I have brought my necessities and no more."

Benjamin said, "And what is necessary for a young man these days?"

The two at the end exchanged a sideways glance and dug into their sweets. Robert said, "Men will need their consciences more than anything else now."

"Yours must be very heavy," said Benjamin. He rose and turned his back to tend to the fire.

Robert spoke to his mother. "The reformed priests will be forced to divorce their wives. The lands will be seized for the Pope. Some of those lands are mine."

Catherine coughed into her hand. She scanned the four feeders. "The lands are held in my name, Robbie. Robert. Until my death. The properties that will be yours were Overton land, never the Church's. They're safe enough."

"The church lands will be mine, will they not, Mother?" added Veronica. She cast her brother a glare. "If anyone must worry, Brother, I am the one, not you."

"Anyone who is the child of a priest should worry," said Robert. "Anything owned by a person who holds old Church property will come under the scrutiny of this new court. That may mean my land."

"You're chasing ghosts, boy," said Benjamin, sitting again. "England is ruled by law, and even the queen must follow it. Is this what you came back for? To raise a rabble like the drunks in the public houses?"

Again the furtive meetings of eyes.

"I'm not worried," said Veronica. "The queen has always been a great friend to me. And the queen's sister, as well."

"The queen's sister?" said one of the four. "She will need friends. She has had too few."

"What do you mean by that?" demanded Benjamin. He leaned onto the table, and the daughters all leaned back.

"He means that the Lady Elizabeth is reformed and the new queen is not," said Robert. "She has been ill-treated by this Roman Mary and someone must defend her rights." He pushed himself away and stood. "This is no time for wrangling and debate. We are weary and will retire." The others all shoveled in last bites and wiped their faces. They bowed stiffly at Catherine and crowded out.

"What a pack of hounds he's gathered," said Benjamin. "And what a large set of cases they carry about with them, for men who need nothing more than their consciences."

"They're young, and young men are often angry," said Catherine. "They want the world to turn on them."

"It will turn on them, in truth, if they don't mind their mouths," said Benjamin. "And if they are so angry, what are they doing here? Why didn't they stay in Wittenberg, where they have allies?"

Catherine said, "He didn't say that they came from Wittenberg. Did you not hear them speak? I think these friends of his are all Englishmen."

# Chapter Six

Catherine's chamber was down the hall from the two rooms where the young men slept, and she lay awake, listening for talk. She would not lower herself to put her ear to their doors, though her feet itched to creep that way, and she heard nothing. Benjamin had sat up with Reg, to drown his irritation in the rest of the wine, and Ann came in and sat on the edge of the bed.

Catherine said, "What news from downstairs?"

"Nobody among the servants knows them," said Ann. "Their horses are fat, though, and the grooms say they have not travelled on any boat. Their servants are as tight-lipped as they are and have taken beds above the stables. I hope they've brought blankets in those chests." She threw a stick on the fire and returned. "Robbie is not here to see you. That's my settled opinion. He has barely said hallo to me or the girls."

"Or Benjamin. He will never accept him."

Benjamin pushed open the door, and Ann said, "Speak of the devil."

"You must have been talking to the boy," said Benjamin.

"He hasn't a word to say to me," said Ann. "I might as well be Old Moll, for all he cares. I might as well be a stick of wood."

"Has anyone checked those chests?" said Benjamin.

"I looked at them," said Ann. "They're tied up with straps and locked, and the servants are sleeping within watching distance." She stood. "I will say good-night." She slipped around the man and was gone.

"They're all hunkered up together, in Robbie's room," said Benjamin. He undressed himself—he was never a man for complicated clothes—and slid in beside Catherine. "They're talking. I can hear their voices but not their words. I agree with you. These are Englishmen, and their servants are English. And they're older than Robbie. I need to know what they've brought with them."

Catherine nodded, and he blew out the light. But after he was snoring into the dark, she was still alert, listening to the hollow hours. There was no moon, and she could hear needles of sleet picking out a pattern on the window glass. A beam in the ceiling snapped once as it cooled and then settled into silence.

In the morning, Catherine was up in the dark before her husband, pulling on a skirt and covering herself with a shawl. She tiptoed into the hall and tapped at Ann's chamber with her fingertips. Ann would know it was her. She listened until she heard the bed ropes squeak, then the padding of feet. Ann opened the door a crack.

"I want to go to the stable," Catherine whispered.

Ann yanked off her nightcap and yawned. "Give me three shakes of a cat's tail."

No one else had stirred, not even the chambermaids. Ann put on enough clothes to be decent and they sneaked down the back stairs and out. The stable boy was carrying hay to the mangers, but, still half-asleep, he barely nodded as they went past him.

The wagon stood in the center aisle, still loaded with most of the wooden chests. They were locked and bound with thick leather straps. Catherine tried to pry open one of the lids, but it wouldn't budge. She shoved it, but it would not slide.

"They're heavy as coffins," said Catherine.

"Mm-hm." Ann lifted and dropped one of the locks. "They must be valuable. Did he say whose they were?"

"No." Catherine pushed again. No movement. "Maybe they're moving gold or silver. Maybe one of those boys is a rich man's son."

"Those are not boys, and if they're rich they're foolish to leave their money out here."

They walked a circuit around the wagon, then back again. The chests had no holes, no cracks. The leather was new and waxy. The stable boy back came through with a bucket of grain and said without enthusiasm, "Will you ride, Madam?"

"I think not, thank you," said Catherine. "The air is too brisk." She produced a plausible shudder for the relieved boy, and they returned to the house.

Catherine left Ann to start the kitchen maids, who had appeared at the noise, tying their aprons on, and returned to her room. Benjamin was still sleeping, and she lay beside him until he rolled over and kissed her. But before they could rise together, they heard boots in the hall. Men's voices. Laughter. "Wait," said Catherine. "I don't want to have another dead meal with them."

Within the hour, they were gone, Robbie with them. Benjamin had business with a wool merchant who was in the city for the Yuletide, and Catherine walked out with him to get his stallion saddled. The wagon remained in the stable, and Benjamin hesitated, looking it over. He smoothed the surface of the chest in front. Lifted and dropped the lock, just as Ann had. Tried the strength of the straps. Catherine saw him consider cutting them and decide against. Robbie's servants descended the ladder, and he stepped away.

"Do you men hunt?" he said.

They looked at each other. One said, "When we are able."

"We have good hunting in the next county," said Benjamin. He was watching them, and they were watching the wagon. Benjamin turned to Catherine. "Our son is a hunter, as well. Is he not?"

Catherine said, "He has been."

Benjamin looked back at the servants. "A dangerous exercise for any man. A man wants to take care, especially when he is on strange ground." He waited for the servants to bow their agreement, and then he was gone.

The men were left with no one to give them orders, and Catherine said, "You are welcome in the house."

But they shook their heads. They would remain in the stable. They thanked her for her kindness.

Catherine went about her day, ordering the making of new soap and showing one of the younger kitchen maids, who was in tears trying to pluck a dry chicken, how to dunk the carcass into a bucket of hot water to loosen the feathers. Alice came stomping downstairs, having been rapped on the knuckles by her French tutor for a mispronunciation, and Catherine sent her back up to try again. One of the manservants had fallen with a load of wood and smashed his hand, and Catherine sat by the window in the kitchen to examine the bones, then boiled up a mess of chickweed and wrapped the angry skin. She kept one eye on the stable, but the wagon remained where it had been.

Everyone gathered again for dinner as though it was no oddity to find a silent quartet of guests sitting at table. The girls had learnt a new song, and Diana smiled as they chattered to Catherine.

"They say this is an old tune, Mother," said Veronica. "Do you know it? It begins, 'There is no rose of such virtue / as is the Rose that bare Jesu.'"

"I know it of old," said Catherine. Her sisters in the convent had sung it at Christmastime, and the sound rolled her back to her childhood. She smelt pine boughs and sweet wine.

Alice tried out a few notes to match her sister's, but Benjamin hushed them. "No singing over the meat, girls. You might scare it from my plate."

"You might scare the whole town," said Veronica. "Your intervals are flat."

Alice shoved her, and Veronica laughed. Catherine said, "That is enough, girls."

Robbie said, "That is a Papist song."

"It is not!" said Veronica. "It is a lyric about Jesus's mother. Diana's lute-master taught it to her. He has been at court."

"As I say," said Robbie. "Let us eat in peace. Our Lord was born of a woman, and she was a vessel like any other female."

"Where did you ride today?" asked Catherine.

"Here and there," said Robbie. "Around the town. Getting the news. All the talk is of this Spanish king. He will put his boot on our necks until we vow to kiss it, if we allow him in. And then the Pope comes after."

"That is just idle gossip, Son. You may rouse the very talk you say is already abroad and that can do none of us good."

"I think you are not dispassionate in the matter, Mother."

"That is no tone to take with me, Robert."

"Then give me leave to be silent."

Veronica stabbed her bread with her knife and frowned. Alice chewed her lip.

Catherine could not stop herself from looking down the table at Ann. Ann was staring at her plate. But she was not eating. She was flicking the end of her knife with one finger.

## Chapter Seven

The next morning, the men were gone again. Robbie was gone. And the wagon was gone. Catherine was in the kitchen, showing the maids how to take down the bunches of dried herbs and lay the stems between sheets of linen without breaking the leaves, when Benjamin returned from the stables and slapped his hat onto the table.

"They stood with their mouths open and let them ride off with it." He picked up a cup and slammed it down again. "In the middle of the night, like a band of thieves. There's your son, Catherine, and how much he wants to come home. Not so much as a good-bye."

The maids stood motionless, and Catherine said, "Go on now. You see how it's done." She hooked Benjamin's elbow and led him upstairs. "Let us see what he's left."

The room Robbie had slept in still held a small case of men's clothing. Robbie's English Bible. A Book of Common Prayer. A dagger. Moll was in the corner, squatted with the chamber pot between her knees. But she was not using it and she certainly was not cleaning it. She was digging through its contents with one forefinger, and Catherine said, "Leave off that, Moll." The woman shouted as Catherine pulled the stinking thing from her grasp. "You must go out and pet the new kittens. They're lonely. Take this with you, if you must, and give it a wash."

The woman went, glaring and muttering to herself, and Benjamin said, "Why do we keep that woman? She is mad as a rabbit. Why does she do that?"

"She is convinced that someone is hiding riches," said Catherine. "She is good with the animals. And she would be in the prison if we did not keep her."

"I will not be having any of those cats in the house," said Benjamin.

Catherine said, "Robbie has left his personal things. He has probably gone off for another ride. Boys like to ride. They want to boast and complain about the queen."

"With a cartload of chests behind them?" He opened the Bible, read a few lines, and set it back. "Hmph. Maybe."

"Those chests might not have been Robbie's at all. Maybe they're one of the other boys'. Maybe they're on their way home, too. They could be full of nothing but young men's doublets and the new fashion of boots."

"They might have said so, don't you think? A word, even, of explanation?"

"They're boys. They don't think."

"They're not boys, except for Robbie. Those are men. They've each got ten years on him, at least. Running home to Mother, at their ages?"

"Some boys love their mothers," said Catherine.

"And some love themselves more," said Benjamin. Ann peeked in. He said, "They're gone."

"So I have heard," said Ann. "And the wagon with them. The stable men are glad not to have to put a watch on it anymore."

"The whole house is delighted," said Benjamin. "Come, I feel like a spy in here, in my own home. Where's Reg?"

"Here, Sir." He was in the hall. "Robbie is coming back. He told the boy who cleans the stalls to keep one fresh for his horse."

"Oh, that's fine," said Benjamin. "He orders my servants now?"

"It means he's coming back, that's all," said Catherine. "What about the others?"

A maid came up behind Reg. "Madam, there's a gentleman outside. He wishes to speak with you."

"Who is it?" asked Benjamin.

The maid shook her head and backed off. Catherine went down and found the front door gaping, a man shadowed within its frame. His horse was held outside by a servant. He stepped inside and scanned the painted ceiling. The carpets. He sniffed and removed his soft hat. His clothing was almost clerical in its darkness, and it made the chain around his neck look cold. When he saw Catherine, he arranged his features into a formal appearance of deference. But he did not bow.

His head inclined slightly to the right. "Catherine Davies?"

"Yes. I am called by that name." She knew Benjamin was behind her and she sidestepped to let him come up beside her. "And this is my husband."

"I know of your husband. Benjamin Davies." Now the man bowed, a little too elaborately. "A merchant by trade, or so I hear. A profession for the delicate." He straightened and stepped forward. Taking their hall for his own. "But this message is for you in particular, Madam. Her Majesty wishes an audience with you. Today."

He bowed again, more abruptly this time, then turned and walked back to the horse.

"I must go," said Catherine. "Come with me, Ann, and get some clothes on me."

Upstairs, Benjamin said, "I should go with you. He was pacing while Ann dressed Catherine, and he kept tripping over her skirt. "If she means to divorce us, she must say it to my face."

"She will not do it," Catherine said. She turned her head to reach for him, and Ann stuck her ear with a pin.

"You will both be too bloody to leave the house if you don't sit still," Ann said. She fixed the head dress again, "Face forward," and reinserted the pin. "I will go and take notes for you, Benjamin."

"You can't write."

Ann tapped her temple. "Every word will be right here."

"'Merchant.' The word might as well have been a turd on his tongue. I'll 'merchant' him. I'll 'delicate' him. I will batter his brains with an account book and see how delicate that feels upon his head."

"Benjamin," said Catherine. She shifted, and Ann boxed her on the arm. "He is just feeling his position. No one is accustomed to the new ways yet."

"No, the old ways," she thought, but she could barely remember what they had been.

The dark man waited below, and he nodded when Catherine came down and said, "I must bring my woman." She saw Ann wink at Benjamin, who scowled, fists stuck in his pockets, as they went out. Their horses were already saddled to go.

He led them out of their courtyard and down through the city to the river, where a barge swayed near the dock, for them only. A sea of men and women parted to let them through. "Leave your horses," he said. "They'll be here when you return."

A reckless wind troubled the waters of the Thames, but the bargeman coaxed them along. When they passed Richmond Palace, where she'd spent her months of shame before Alice was born, Catherine would not look at its pale face. Ann said, "That time is past. No one even thinks of it." But Catherine recalled every moment when she'd seen the contempt fall around her from the other women, from Anne of Cleves herself, like a grey sky, as her belly grew. Her marriage was ten years old now, the child a few months older, but Jane Dudley had never let her forget that it had been done in secret, without permission from the king. And now, that king was dead, and the king who followed him. And now, Jane Dudley's husband had died a traitor's death, and her sons were in the Tower. Anne of Cleves was probably at one of her other houses, playing cards with some new, more pliable lady-in-waiting.

"Don't dwell on it," said Ann. "It's done and gone. Your queen is on the throne and you will have everything you've wanted for so long."

"What do I want?" said Catherine. She tried to imagine her young self, restless for something, the convent first, then a husband. Then another husband. She'd wanted a household of educated women, women of genius, around her. She'd wanted to speak her mind. She'd wanted a queen. It all ran into a smear, until all she saw was the face of her daughter, Veronica, almost a woman herself now. And then the late autumn sky, bright, like an ocean above them, into which she might rise with her empty dreams, and drown.

Ann laughed. "Mary Tudor has a crown on her head, the Church will be restored, and you still have your man and your children. Smile, Catherine. The world has turned your way."

"And so it has." Catherine let her hand split the ripples of the dirty water. Her fingers came up dank and smelly. "Why am I so afraid of it?"

"You had better twist your courage to the sticking place," said Ann. "I think we have arrived."

A servant held out his hand as the barge pulled up to a private dock, and Catherine followed him. The dark man shadowed them. It was a short walk, and Catherine halted for a moment when they turned a corner, and she laid eyes once more on Hampton Court Palace. It was a great red lump, and even the long approach and the bright stripes of paint could not disperse the bloody glow that came from its stones. Catherine imagined it haunted by the screams of the girl queen, Catherine Howard. And by the heart of Jane Seymour, which people said lay somewhere in the chapel, still as fresh as the day it had stopped beating. Anne Boleyn had danced the king out of Katherine of Aragon's bed here. But then, there was Elizabeth, so much like Catherine's own Veronica. She could not bring herself to wish those years undone.

The two servants led Catherine and Ann to the first gate and turned them over to a group of women, who led them through the interior courtyard and inside. Dozens of men and women, stinking of sweat and perfume and gossip. A little dog had gotten loose, and a man kicked it viciously and sent it squealing and snapping. A glossy woman slapped the man, and he covered the offended spot with his hand, glowering but unmoving. "Stay here," said one of the women to Catherine and Ann. She went through a door, and Catherine leaned against a fat tapestry. The wool warmed her and she wanted to yank it from the wall and shroud herself.

Ann said, "We will be hours waiting here. Everyone is finer than we are."

Catherine nodded, but before she could respond, the lady had returned. "Follow me in."

The room was smaller than Catherine had expected, an ambitious, gilded closet rather than a grand receiving room. Anne of Cleves had had more imposing places than this for playing cards. Catherine expected her heart to clutch at her ribs, but it sat quiet within her. Almost against the back wall, Mary Tudor perched on a defiant, single throne, and when Catherine approached the chair and knelt, Ann drew back. Catherine uttered a simple "Your Majesty" and waited. She could see the specter of her own breath.

"Catherine Davies," said the queen. "On your feet."

Catherine obeyed and faced her monarch. Mary's skin hung from the bones in soft pouches, but she was fatter. She wore a severe headdress and a more severe smile.

"How does your family?" said the queen. "Growing?"

"Not growing, Your Majesty. Not for many a day. My husband is well. We have our three daughters about us, and they take lessons in writing, music, and languages. I have much to thank God for."

"God. You have much to thank us for. It was our hand that formed your family. You will recall that. It was this hand that stayed our father's wrath. The king's." The queen extended five knobby fingers. "We will not see sundered what God has joined together, however ill-conceived was the joining." A smirk wrinkled her lip. It looked painful. Mary Tudor was not famed for her wit.

The walls breathed cold. Someone's skirts whispered. Catherine said, "I am in your debt, Your Majesty, and will ever be your loyal servant." She did not know whether she was expected to return to her knees, and no one was nearby to provide an example, so she dipped her head in a compromise.

"Do you still practice your art?"

"My art?" Catherine's mind skittered about. Safer to let the other woman say it.

"Your healing. Your herbs." A high note of irritation, in discord with the undertone of threat.

"I tend my household these days, mostly." It was true enough. "The younger girls help me. I keep a small garden, but I would want the countryside to grow herbs. We depend on the merchants in the city."

"Yes, yes." Mary waved her hand and laboured from the seat. "Come. We will walk. Do you recall our walks?"

The women behind Catherine swept backward. Catherine stood her ground. "Yes, Your Majesty. Those times stick in my memory."

"Like nettles?"

"It was a difficult time," Catherine said.

"I have something to show you." Mary linked her arm through Catherine's, as though they were still girls, chaining themselves together against the king. They turned, and Ann busied herself with her shoe, not wanting to be noticed at all. She wasn't. Mary led Catherine out and down a hall, where courtiers plastered themselves to the walls, "Your Majesty"ing themselves into a blur of noise. She turned into an enclosed courtyard. "This will please your eyes," said the queen. It was a garden of herbs, still mostly green in the aging autumn. Here, the red walls burned, and the plants, laid out in raised beds, lifted their rusting leaves to the sun. Some exotics that Catherine had never seen before. She touched a familiar rosemary stem and put her fingers to her nose to remind herself that she knew this woman, this world. The scent brought water to her eyes, and she closed them.

"You have a son, as well as daughters," said Mary.

Catherine wiped her hand against her skirt. "Robbie. He prefers to be addressed as Robert now." She allowed herself a shadow of a laugh. "Young men want to be men before they have worn out their boyhoods."

"So he lives?" Mary strolled down the center aisle, and Catherine followed.

"Lives and breathes."

"Breathing the air of England lately, or so I hear." Mary's fingers grazed the top of a stem and snapped off the head.

"He has unexpectedly returned. I hope he means to celebrate the Yuletide with us."

"Here is one that you will enjoy." Mary walked to a small tree. "An orange. Sent to me from Spain. Isn't it delicate?" She took it by the trunk and squeezed. "If this were a man's neck, how easily it would break."

Catherine said, "From Spain? It is a gift for a queen indeed."

"Yes." The hand relaxed. "And why has your son come back to this island? We thought that he abjured our policies. Our religion."

Catherine stepped into a soggy spot and almost lost her balance. "My husband thinks that he has tired of his studies and longs for home. We have not sounded him on the matter. He is too lately arrived."

"Your husband. And how do you like your husband, Catherine?"

"Right well, Your Majesty."

"Once, you claimed never to think to see yourself outfitted with a husband." Mary sniffed and her face puckered. Her nose was red. "But that was a long time ago."

"I am a mortal woman, and I hope God will forgive me for my sins. I pray for it."

"As do we." Mary moved on, and they reached the wall. "Feel of this stone."

Catherine put her palm up to the heat. "This place must give you great comfort. It holds the sun."

"More comfort if it held a son."

"Yes, Your Majesty. You will marry?"

Now Mary Tudor smiled, and looked like a woman. She fished in her pocket and produced a miniature. "Have you seen him?"

The portrait showed a dark prince, posed in arrogant red.

"He is as handsome a man as befits your station."

"He is." Mary gazed into the slick surface, and Catherine thought she might giggle. Then she popped him away, into the folds of her skirt. "He must get me a child."

"I will pray for it," said Catherine. "Children bring great comfort. A child of yours would comfort an entire people."

"You will study upon it. You know of women's bodies. How to improve the chances of conception."

"I must consult my books. I have only dealt with my own people of late."

"Your son will inherit a great deal of land."

"God willing."

"Those lands. They belonged to the Church, did they not?"

They had made their way back to the center of the garden, where the alien tree grew, and Catherine stopped to admire it. "His name is on the Overton lands, once Havens lands. The convent and church are in Mount Grace, miles away."

"And who has his eyes on that?"

Catherine examined the bark and stroked the branches. "My daughter is named for those."

"Which daughter?"

"Veronica. The elder. The little one, my Alice, will get half of her father's lands."

"The Davies property. It is extensive."

Catherine nodded. "Benjamin has raised it all with his own hands. The country house was his mother's, but it was almost fallen into the dirt when he took it over. You should see how he prospers. He has a great head for business."

Mary walked on, and Catherine resisted the temptation to pluck a leaf before she followed. She wondered idly if a cutting would root, then scolded herself inwardly for allowing her curiosity to overtake her.

"Let us hope that he can keep those lands. What do you hear of your sister?"

"My sister?"

"Sister who was. Sister-in-law." The queen examined the sky, but Catherine knew she had the name on her tongue. "Margaret, wasn't that it?" She shook her head. "A precipitous fall. What has become of her?"

"I have had no word of her, Your Majesty," said Catherine. "She has disappeared like the snow in spring. It has been nigh ten years, and not a letter or a message. I did hear that she lost the child."

"Very provident for the child. Yes, a great fall indeed. A woman might take it as a warning that heaven does not smile on misguided marriages. She had a maid, did she not? A bastard of your husband's."

Catherine's ears burned. "Not my husband's. My first husband's brother. Her name was Constance."

"I recall that she had the same looks as your first daughter. That red hair. And she hung on Margaret like a plague."

"A plague and a pestilence, to me and my daughter." Catherine waited until the storm in her head blew through. She was being unfair, and she knew it. "She followed Margaret right close."

"Mm, bastards. The land is full of them. A plague indeed. What do you hear from Jane Dudley?"

Catherine stopped, surprised. "I hear nothing of her. I have laid eyes on her perhaps once in these five years."

"I see. That is well enough. And what of your father?"

"Dead these six years, God rest his soul."

"You will have to light many a candle to ensure that. But he is perhaps the more fortunate."

"He is with God."

"He may be, in time. The others will lose their benefices."

"The others?"

"Priests who once were. The ones who have broken their vows and taken wives. We shall see to the lands in time. But yours," she said, claiming Catherine's arm again, "will remain your daughter's."

"You are most generous."

"I am just. I have a justice in me that burns like these walls." They had achieved the doorway back into the palace, and Mary slapped the stone. She faced Catherine, blocking their entry. "Your son. A mother must direct her son to goodness. Sometimes back to goodness. We hear that he runs with a pack of malcontents. This displeases us."

A cold bolt from the heart of the palace enveloped them, and Catherine, sweating inside her heavy clothes, shivered. "They are young, and young men often try out their strength before they have their wits."

"And they sometimes find themselves up against strength mightier than their own."

"Indeed they do. They are like young stallions, eager to leap and kick. I will endeavor to correct it in him."

"Do, Catherine, do. We should like to see you keep your family." Mary Tudor waved her hand, waded through a pile of kneeling women, like enormous pillows with heads; just inside she turned right, away from Catherine, and walked on alone.

# Chapter Eight

Catherine was directed to the left, where she found a shivering Ann in the outer courtyard. Grey clouds occupied the western sky, and Ann scowled at them. She stomped her feet and blew on her hands as Catherine came to her side.

"Not a meal. Hardly a cup of ale. Where are the serving women?" Ann pointed at the storm. "More rain, mark me."

"The women all follow the queen," said Catherine.

"They wear beads again, as well. Did you see them? And the chapel has its icons on display again. I wonder where they were hidden."

Catherine considered it. "All over England. Perhaps I should take the altarpiece out again, the next time we are in Yorkshire, if it hasn't dried to kindling."

"In the laundry room? It's probably water-logged. Come, let's find us a barge and go home."

They walked back to the river, where the man who had come to fetch them from home was waiting. He hailed the bargeman, who pulled up and offered his hand, to help them board.

"Have you frozen nearly to death?" asked Catherine.

"I don't mind the weather," he said. "The queen's orders keep me warm enough." He crossed himself broadly, as though the very sky were watching, before he stepped on behind them.

"So we are Catholic again," said Ann to no one. "I don't know if I remember my prayers rightly."

"You'll learn," said the bargeman, "quickly enough."

They said nothing more as they pushed through the river. The twilight followed, a great black cape coming over them from the west, and by the time they'd reached London Bridge, drops were pimpling the Thames, and the bargeman pulled his hat down as he handed them back onto land. London already looked sodden, the shutters clamped tight and the roads beginning to soften. The rain pelted down. The horses slapped their hooves in resentment, and Catherine's shied against a chamber pot's contents, tossed carelessly from an upper window. Her face was splattered as the muck flew by, and, having no handkerchief, she resorted to wiping her mouth with her sleeve. It was full night when they arrived at their own courtyard again.

"A happy Christmas we'll have, if this keeps on," said the man as they turned into Davies House. "At least the churches will be warm again."

"And glad we are of it," said Catherine. She jumped down, before the stable boys could get to her, and examined her skirt. She was mud to the knees. Her court shoes were slabs. She gave the man money and scraped her soles on the gravel as she made her way to the front door, Ann at her heels. The horses of their companions had already turned away as a maid opened up for them.

Benjamin stood inside, clouded in the candlelight of their front hall. "Have they hooked you up to a plow, to prove your faithfulness?"

Catherine pulled off her hood and let it drip onto the pavers. "The sun shines on the queen. The rest of us get the storm."

Ann kicked off her shoes and threw her hood to the maid. "And hungry bellies to enjoy it in. Is the dinner cooked?"

"Cooked and served and eaten," said Benjamin. "But we will feed you. Get into dry things first, though. You both smell like a ditch."

The daughters were already at table when they came back down. Diana had taken her place at the bottom of the table, and the younger girls sat on either side of her. They had already finished their suppers, but Alice stuffed a wad of the fresh bread into her mouth. "Did you see the queen?"

"Do not talk with food in your mouth," said Diana. She winked at Veronica. "Alice has been on fire all day to hear the news. It was all we could do to keep her from riding after you."

Veronica said, "We almost tied her down."

"You did not!" said Alice, and Benjamin said, "Girls."

"We did see the queen," said Catherine.

"You saw her," said Ann. "I stood outside, counting the bricks and practicing my *Ave Maria*."

"Your what?" asked Alice.

"A prayer for deliverance," said Ann. "That's not altogether true, though. I saw her, but I looked away to preserve my eyes from her brilliance."

"Where is Robbie?" asked Catherine.

"Not returned. No word, no sign," said Benjamin.

The fish was cold, and Catherine picked at the dry husk. Her stomach seized like a fist, and she forced in a bite. Made herself chew it. Let a gulp of wine wash it down. "The queen asked after him."

"Only him?" asked Benjamin.

"No. But particularly him. She seemed much interested to know why he is with us."

"She knows, then."

"She knows something. She knows he has others by his side and she thinks ill of them. She tells me that the priests who have married will lose their pensions. Perhaps their lands. She wondered about all of you, how we prosper. She promised that our lands are safe. And then she asked about Robbie."

"Robert," said Alice.

"Yes. Robert. His things are still in his chamber?"

"Things are as they were. He's not returned," said Benjamin. "Is there trouble?"

"None that I know of," said Catherine, "yet." She drank the wine and let it warm her breast. "She will make the foreign marriage. She seems much enamoured of Philip. She carries his picture."

"She needs an heir," said Reg.

"Indeed," said Catherine. She nibbled a bite of the pork. It was also cold, but sweet and tender. It, too, lodged in her throat and she pushed the plate away. The rain slashed at the windows, and the fire behind Benjamin spat and complained. "The wood is green," she said. "Green as a boy. And just as noisy."

Benjamin ordered a man to bring logs from the covered pile in the back. Reg poked at the flames, but the chimney was wide, and the downpour found its way in. The wind hummed against the walls, and the candles flickered. Catherine said, "I must bathe more thoroughly. My bones feel rotted." The girls watched her rise, and she said, "It was a long day. Mostly on the water, then in the water. That's all there is to tell." Diana nodded, patted Alice's hand, and Catherine was free to escape.

She was sitting, undressed, at her basin when Benjamin came in. He took the clout and stroked her back with it. The warmth loosened her neck, and Catherine let her head fall, her hair trailing in the warm wash. She swayed, watching the black ends, threaded with white, curl through the water. "I am a striped woman," she said. "The darkness and the light now contend for me."

"What troubles you so?" asked Benjamin. He rinsed out the clout and lifted her hair, piling it up and fixing it with a comb from the table. He kneaded her neck. "Did she threaten you?"

"No. Not in so many words. Her questions about Robbie were pointed. And her words about his companions frightened me. They seem to carry suspicious reputations with them. She doubts them." Catherine dried herself and pulled on a shift. Turned to her husband, who knelt before her and put his head in her lap. His hair was parti-coloured, too, and she sifted it, soft as a child's, with her fingers. "Where can he be, do you think?"

Benjamin murmured, "I don't know. He is full of secrets."

"He is," Catherine said. "And Mary is determined to know what they are."

# Chapter Nine

Catherine's son returned to Davies House as they were setting up a manger in the front courtyard. Benjamin had lugged Diana's old crib down from an attic room, and the younger girls had fashioned wise men by stuffing some of Reg's cast-off clothes with straw. Ann had embroidered faces onto linen and was helping them set up the figures. But the rain came in with Robbie Overton and it would not relent, so they hauled the figures back inside, propping them against the windows to watch for fair skies.

"You have ruint our Christmas," said Alice. "You have dragged in the clouds behind you."

"Hush, girl," said Catherine. "The rain comes when it comes. Your brother is soaked through and needs some rest. Robert, your chamber is as you left it."

"It is nothing," said Robbie. He pulled off his boots and carried them upstairs.

Benjamin said, "I will have a shelter built for the Christmas dignitaries." He and Catherine found a couple of their men who were handy with hammers idling inside the stable, and they set to work, glad to have indoor labour. They sang old carols as they sawed the boards, and Catherine leaned against the back doorjamb, listening. Benjamin came running through the rain, and he joined her, silent for a few seconds.

"Where has he been, do you think?"

She knew he meant Robbie. "Nowhere that will keep him safe."

Old Moll crept around them, hugging a pot to her chest, and scurried out, into the downpour. She turned and said, "Boy shoves me from the room like he owns the place. I been sleepin' there and never no one to mind. Moll's got a right to lay her head, same as any of God's children."

"Yes, Moll," said Catherine. "Is that Robbie's chamber pot?"

"Mine. It's mine. Been usin' it; it's mine. Old Moll got a right to it; been usin' it. Nobody got a right to say me nay." She clutched the smelly thing tighter and ran off.

"That woman's mad," said Benjamin. "I've never seen a soul so burdened with a love of filth. We should turn her out."

"She upsets my stomach, but she hurts my heart," said Catherine. "She must have a soul, just as we do. We are supposed to love the unfortunate and to heal the sick. It's almost Christmas, Benjamin. I can't turn her out onto the streets."

"If you can get anyone to lay a healing hand on that one, he's a better Samaritan than I." The men in the stable lifted another song, and he stopped talking.

Robbie Overton said, behind them, "That is Papist. No, it is worse. It is pagan. You should control your servants, sir."

"So harsh, Son. Let them celebrate," said Catherine. "It is the birth of our Lord. They want to feel some joy. They do no harm."

Benjamin said, "It is my house while there's breath in my body, and I will have them sing." He shook his head and went through the kitchen and upstairs, where the music would not carry.

"They desecrate themselves and the time," said Robbie.

"The queen has asked after you," Catherine said without looking at her son.

"You told her of my arrival?"

"She knew of it before I spoke. Perhaps she means to mend the breach between us, at this holy time of the year."

"And I suppose you will send an offering to the court to encourage her?"

"I will," said Catherine. "Ann and her maids have made a tablecloth, as we used to do, back in Mount Grace."

"Don't speak of that place," he said, and turned away. Catherine remained, but the melody had gone out of tune for her, and she closed the door.

Upstairs, the cloth had been brought out, and Ann was unrolling it on the big dining table to show the tiny leaves and blue flowers around the edges. They'd placed birds, in silver thread, in the corners, and, at the center, a Tudor rose in ruby and gold. The girls stood back, admiring their own stitches, and Ann's three laundry maids held the edges while Catherine traced the images.

"This is as fine a piece as you have ever laid your hand to. My mother would have wanted to keep this for herself. Do you remember the Yuletides we had?"

"Yes," said Ann. "Take care, Maggie. Don't pull out the stitches." She lifted the corner away from the servant girl's probing fingers and folded it under. "Do you think we shall have mystery plays again, now that Mary has her throne? I would like to see a good Herod once more. Do you remember that time they all gave him a thumping at the end?"

Catherine laughed, and Benjamin came inside from the front, shaking the rain from his hat. "What's the jest? Is that my New Year's gift?"

"It's for the queen," said Catherine. They opened up the cloth again and Benjamin whistled.

"We could use that for our own feast. It fits the table right nicely."

Now Ann laughed. "Catherine, your mother is not the only one who prefers to get gifts than to give them. Benjamin, this is too fine for the likes of an old sheepman like you."

"It goes to the court," said Catherine.

"Ah, well. You will give me something better, then. Bring more wood. I want fire for my holiday!" And two servants scuttled off, followed by the maids bearing the queen's present.

Catherine had ordered three geese that morning, and while she saw to the roasting, Benjamin brought in pine boughs and rosemary that had been delivered from the country house, and they spread them over the sills themselves, enjoying the work. Reg had found some red silk ribbon in an old chest, and he threaded it through and around the greenery, taking three long sprigs of the rosemary and tying them with a bow. He hung the bunch over the doorway to the dining gallery, and stepped down from the stool to admire it. "It's been a long while since we had a proper Yuletide in this country," he said. Ann came up then, and he caught her with a kiss.

"Old man," she said, "you will scratch my tender cheeks with those whiskers. You have a face like a badger." But she put her hands around his neck and kissed him in return. "The girls have penned one of the old ewes, and they are determined to tie it out front, and you will have to get some hay so that she doesn't rebel. The Magi look well enough, except for their shabby garments. Old David says he will sit for Joseph during the day if he can have a fresh loaf of bread and jug of ale and a blanket. We can make a Mary from that cloak of yours, Catherine. It's blue enough."

One of the workmen tapped on the door, saying that the shed was complete, and they all went to look. It was neat and kept out the water, though they would have to crowd the holy family in one corner to keep the wise men dry. "Be the star of the night and take them on their journey," Benjamin said, and the men hoisted the straw men onto their shoulders, threw blankets over them, and escorted them to their destination.

Robbie Overton had come to the top of the stairs, but before Catherine could warn her, Ann had said, "Now, what will we do for a Christ child?"

"This is a heresy," he said. More man than boy, but still with a boy's temper, he stomped one foot. His fist hit the railing. "You outfit this house like the nunnery, while Cranmer, a good and holy man, sits in a cold cell and prays. They have racked him already. They will break him with their torture machines. Your queen will have his head on London Bridge for her Twelfth Night gift because he believes in the reformed ways, because he holds his conscience dear as you hold yours. And you. You go about, down there, making a mockery of God's dignity with idols and dolls."

No one spoke. Benjamin walked out, following the wise men. Reg and Ann linked their arms and went for the back stairs. The girls followed them. The rosemary bouquet swayed in the doorway, and Robbie fastened his eyes on it. "That weed. This is all an invitation to whoredom." He ran down the stairs, leapt onto the stool that Reg had left behind, and swatted the decoration to the floor. It lay intact, and he kicked it until it gave up a few leaves. He was almost halfway through the dining gallery by this time, and he scooped up the tattered remains and heaved them into the fire.

The flames gushed into the soft boughs and the entire thing dissolved with a sigh. Catherine took up a torn bit of the ribbon that Benjamin had laid on the table, and tossed it in after. Will you beat the sheep for sitting beside the cradle, as well?"

"You shame me, Mother. Will you go about with your beads again and pretend that you are the bride of Christ?"

"In order to play that game, I would have to go about without my children. And that I will never do," said Catherine. "My husband is Benjamin, and it does not shame me for the whole world to know it."

"You once kept it secret enough." Robbie walked within striking distance. He was fully Catherine's height now.

"The time and the circumstances were awkward. You know this. We let it be known we were married, almost at once."

"You lied to me. You came to me with that man by your side and his bastard in your belly and said nothing."

Catherine's palm ached to slap him, but she crunched the nap of her skirt instead. "You were a little child."

"Even a child can count."

"Robbie. Robert. That was years ago. Let's not contend over the past. We sin and we work to repair our souls. All mortals do. Don't be so hard, Son. Not at Christmas. We are a family, all of us. Together. Let us be forgiving of one another, as we are taught to be."

He gazed up, and Catherine could see that his eyes were on the empty string in the doorway. He said, "Mother," and she thought he would embrace her. But he said, "I am sorry," and pushed past her, heading back up to his solitary chamber.

# Chapter Ten

"Let me speak to him," said Benjamin. He'd come in to find Catherine on her toes, pulling at the sad, empty string that had held the rosemary. Ann had returned, after the talking stopped, and was glaring up the stairs.

But Robbie pled exhaustion and a spirit of melancholy and would talk to no one. They finished the manger out front, and Diana supplied an old doll for Jesus. The sheep was dragged by a rope to her position, and consented to sit only after she'd nosed the fresh straw protruding from the bottom of one of the wise men's breeches. Reg tossed in a flake of hay to distract her, and she seemed, indeed, to wonder at her splendid fortune. They pronounced it good.

December was an old dream of Christmas. They attended Mass, the girls looking to Ann and Catherine to show them what to say and how to pray. Alice, after hearing a sermon on damnation, became excited and insisted upon being baptized again, in the real faith. The priest, who had re-converted from the Church of England, tutted and said that God could see through a bit of water to the soul, but he finally relented and baptized all of the girls, including Diana, who knelt before him with her hands clasped. Wearing a blue cloak, she looked so much like the Holy Mother that Catherine could see that he almost forgot to speak over her. Benjamin waited patiently, nodding at their joy. Yes, he had been baptized as an infant, he told them. Yes, in the old church. But in bed that night he said, "One church is as good as another, as far as I can see. One hand on your head and the other in your pocket."

Catherine shushed him for a cynic, but when he said, "I see more of God in the sunrise over our fields in Yorkshire than I've ever seen at an altar," she had no plausible answer and rolled over to watch the stars flicker on, outside their window.

Robbie Overton came and went, declining, with a mild sneer, the invitations to Mass but appearing most evenings for dinner. Ann slid a pair of new gloves down the table to him one evening. "I have bought these off a merchant today. They looked like the thing a young man might use about the city. If you will be out, then you should be warm."

He picked them up, caressing the soft brown leather. "I thank you, Ann." He set them on his lap and picked up his knife, but before he cut his meat, he added, "You have always had my heart."

Catherine thought he would weep, but he did not. Just sawed into the loin of beef as though a silence had not erupted around him.

On the Eve of Christmas Day, Benjamin and Catherine travelled to the court to deliver the queen's gift. It was too early, they knew, but the New Year would bring the revelers and they wanted to be sure that their gift was seen before Twelfth Night. The rain had begun spitting again, and they wrapped the fabric in three layers of linen before they set off.

But when they arrived, the throng of supplicants bearing silver goblets and elaborate jewels was so large that they could not get as far as the hallway leading to the receiving room, and, after standing for an hour getting drenched, they handed over the tablecloth, with its note of good wishes and loyalty, to a lady-in-waiting, and departed for home. "I suppose we are not the only ones who want the queen to remember their gifts." As they stepped onto the loaded barge, Catherine spied Jane Dudley, also wet and disappointed, trudging along the path. She was alone.

"Look there." Catherine pointed.

"She's already lost her husband and now she hopes to save her sons," said Benjamin. "A bad day to ask for it, especially Guildford. They'll be dead before she ever comes face to face with Mary."

"It's a pity," said Catherine, "to bend and sue to the woman who has killed her husband. By my soul, I cannot think that Guildford had any part in his marriage but the saying of 'I do.'"

"A body must take care what he says he will or will not do," said Benjamin. "Even boys. And accepting the marriage is not the reason he is in the Tower. He might have taken Jane Grey and refused the crown."

"Perhaps Mary will have mercy in the holiday and set them free. She could send them away, to Jane's father's house. Get them out of her sight. They have surely suffered enough."

"Perhaps," said Benjamin. Then the thunder shattered their words, and they hunkered for the rest of the ride.

They spent the evening preparing their clothes and overseeing the children, who filled the clay piggies with coins for Twelfth Night alms. Old Moll reappeared at the front gate from somewhere, sodden and covered to the knees with mud, and Catherine ordered a pallet to be made for her in the kitchen. The sheep was taken, unwilling, back to the less luxuriously outfitted stable for the night and settled in resentfully with one of the small ponies.

Catherine, after reminding the kitchen maids how to prepare the next day's meal and seeing that the fires were covered and that no sparks had flown out, fell into bed with her husband, and they made love as the rain drummed on the windows. There had been no more pregnancies after Alice, and they enjoyed each other's bodies freely, unafraid of queens or laws or the future. Some late carolers contended drunkenly with the dismal weather, and Catherine fell asleep to their old songs.

The next morning was bright and cold, and as they piled on extra cloaks to go out, Ann came down to say, "Your son is fled again."

"No! It's Christmas Day," said Catherine.

The girls were ready to go, and Alice pulled at her mother's hand. "We will miss the singing."

"And so will your brother," said Catherine. "Has he left his things?"

"Most of them," said Ann. "He's taken his books."

"He's sulking," said Catherine. "He wants to prove he is too big for a mother. He will return."

They took pocketsful of money and handed out coins as they went, Diana and Veronica guiding Alice, Catherine and Benjamin behind them with Ann and Reg. The congregants overflowed onto the porch of the church, and Benjamin lifted Alice onto his shoulders so that she could see. The priest had felt the day descend on him and was a priest once more, and Catherine felt herself pulled backward in time, so that the hour blurred into her girlhood and she felt a little faint. And when the host was raised again and the people cheered, her mind skidded, and she almost lost her balance. Was God more in the fields than here? She felt it to be so, and yet she could feel her soul again now, high and frightened, like a winged thing skittering about the underside of her skull. Trapped or freed, she could not tell, but it made her head ache and her breastbone swell.

Two men pushed past her, too violently it seemed to be accidental, and she fell against Ann. They walked on out, and Benjamin turned to watch. Ann muttered, "Villains," and Catherine put herself back onto her feet and did not look behind her.

Veronica and Alice chattered and laughed all the way home, but Benjamin hung back with Reg. They arrived to the scent of roasted goose and were ferried into the dining gallery by the kitchen girls, proud to show off their skills, but Benjamin had hardly eaten a plateful when he threw down his napkin and went upstairs.

"What do you find?" Catherine said when he reappeared.

"Nothing." He waited until the girls had finished and run off to add their ponies to the group around the Holy Family outside. "He should be here, with us. He must needs be careful, Catherine. We hear the laughing in the churches, and the people saying we will have a new country for the new year and all will be as it was in the old days, but I heard those men today, those rough ones. They were talking about the Spanish marriage."

"They will surely not make trouble during the Yuletide," said Catherine. "Robbie will grow weary of his anger. He will grow up."

"The celebrations light a fire under these malcontents and make them burn the hotter," said Benjamin.

"Whether the world runs forward or back, someone wants to set a torch to it. Can they not shake hands and be friends, at least on Christ's birthday? Can men not drop their arguments for a little while and watch for the Epiphany?"

"Some of them can. Maybe most of them. But I see the heat in Robbie's face. And there are others. There's an Epiphany coming, I grant you. But we won't see a saviour in it. Mark me, Catherine. There's trouble brewing."

# Chapter Eleven

The twelve days of Christmas passed in merriment enough, and no one heard a word against queen or church. The servants were allotted extra ale and sweets, and Catherine and Ann distributed the coin-stuffed clay pots with their own hands to anyone who came to their door. The girls exchanged scented soaps and handkerchiefs. Catherine and Benjamin had had a new lute made for Diana, and they listened to her play before the fire. Veronica was given a new saddle for her pony and a pair of pearl earrings, and Alice, a new blue cloak, woven from Yorkshire wool, and an illuminated prayer book with her name in the front. Catherine put a cake of soap into Old Moll's hand, but she bit into it and cast it away. No talk of rebellion reached their ears, and Catherine began to hope that all would be well in the end. Mary Tudor might even bear a child, she said once over dinner, though Ann replied, "That would be a birth more miraculous than the one we have just celebrated," and Benjamin snorted into his ale.

Robert Overton did not return to Davies House until after the greenery had been swept away, into the dead kindling, and the shed in the front hauled around back, to be used as a shelter for firewood. Catherine was standing at one of the tall front windows, mourning the onset of real winter, when he rode in. Alone. Even bundled against the cold, he looked thinner, and he hunched over his hands like an old man. Benjamin was behind her, at a table, looking over the accounts from the Mount Grace draperies, and she allowed her heart time to quiet its leaping before she said, "There's Robbie. He will at least be here for his birthday."

Benjamin looked up. "Who is with him?"

"No one."

"Then we will start again, he and I. Maybe his attendants have deserted him. And good riddance to them." He closed the book and disappeared down the back steps that led to the door facing the stables.

Catherine would not allow herself to sneak after, but her ears could not stop listening. She heard the door close. She waited. Then it opened and closed again. Trilled greetings from the kitchen maids. She granted herself three steps closer. They were talking. No words came up, but the tones were friendly. They might have been any father and son, catching each other up on the news. Benjamin's big laugh, and then Robbie's, slighter and higher-pitched. She hadn't heard it in months, and she thought at first it must be one of the servants. But there it was again. Her son was laughing. She trotted back to the dining gallery to hide as they came up. Benjamin called her name, and she appeared, adjusting her face to look surprised.

"Robert, we have missed you among us." She embraced him and he held her, like any prodigal son, happy to be home. "Your gift is upstairs, in your room." She'd had a new pair of heavy breeches made of the best wool, and a cape to match it. She rubbed his arms. "In this cold, you will need it."

"Thank you, Mother." Robbie bowed. "I will go admire it now." He took the stairs up two at a time.

"He is in high spirits," Catherine said. "Where has he been?"

"In Kent. With Wyatt."

A green memory wound its way through Catherine's mind. No, not memory. Tales. Springtime. There had been stories about the court. Anne Boleyn and a Wyatt. The elder Wyatt. She said, "Thomas Wyatt?"

"The very one," said Benjamin.

"The poet's son?"

"You know him?"

"I know of him. Everyone knows of him. He is Protestant, through and through. A most militant Protestant. Does he write verses, as his father did?"

Benjamin pulled her into his arms and held her, tight. "Not that I have heard. I think he does very little. Shall I make you a poem?"

"No." Catherine wriggled to push him off. He was embracing the air out of her. "It would need to be a winter poem, and I hate the winter."

Benjamin rubbed his face against hers. "I am like a sausage, preserved by the cold." He leaned back. The smile had dropped away and he shook his head. Pulled her close again and whispered, "Your son, however, seems to carry a fire in him. I think he has been too much with the son, that young Wyatt."

"You jest, like the queen," said Catherine. But he shackled her waist again, and she whispered into his ear. "Does he still rail on her?"

"Not a word. He laughed when I told him of the men who walked out of the church. His holiday was apparently spent in more sober contemplation. God and his own sins and the like." Benjamin swung her into the dining gallery, all the way to the far end, and set her on a bench.

She said, "When did a Wyatt ever meditate on his sins, except to gain him some followers?"

Benjamin took a chair across from her and set his elbows on his knees. He took out a knife and began paring his nails. They might have been discussing the number of beeves the household needed. "Perhaps the younger is not like the elder. I have promised Robbie to ride out with him tomorrow. I may learn more then."

The boy himself halloed from the top of the stairs then, and they ran out to greet him. He was outfitted in his new garments, and Catherine said, "You look splendid, Son. Come down, and let me check the cut."

He obeyed, and stood before his mother with arms lifted outward. She smoothed the seams and tugged the cuffs. His hose were torn, and she stuck her finger through a hole. "I will have new ones ordered for you on the morrow." She stood and faced him. "You look a complete man."

He smiled. "I feel one, as well, Mother. I thank you. It's a most thoughtful present. A man mustn't ride to his destiny in rags." He put his arms around her. He was hot as a young stallion and smelt like a man, all saddle-sweat and pungent skin, like a wet summer hayfield going slightly to rot. His hair needed a wash, and though he'd tied it back at the nape of his neck, the scent of old soap still hung in it. But beneath it she smelt the boy, the skin that had always carried a sweetness. She'd thought when he was a baby that he smelt of strawberries or green apples, and she put her nose against his neck.

"I will have hot water brought up to you," Catherine said. "You must be nigh dead on your feet."

He kissed her cheek, bowed again, and ran back up. He was stroking his thigh as he turned the corner. She would order him a hundred pairs of breeches, to see him so content.

It mattered nothing what at altar he knelt. He was already almost an angel.

"You've done well," said Benjamin. "A woman's trick, appealing to his vanity."

Catherine smiled. "And if men did not have the vanity, we could not appeal to it, could we?"

"You say true. Now let me play my hand with him and see if we cannot win him back to our side. If the holy water burns his skin, perhaps we can at least convince him to kneel before his queen as a subject of her realm without believing he's sold his soul to Beelzebub."

Alice squealed upstairs. She must have seen her brother. Diana's voice, from down the hall, scolded, "Do not maul him before he's et, Alice," but the boy's voice growled like a bear, and the girl shrieked with delight. Veronica called out, "Robbie, you have finally graced us with your royal presence," and he laughed.

Catherine turned to her husband. "What is our side, Benjamin?"

# Chapter Twelve

Benjamin and Reg took the boy out to the country house for a hunting trip before dawn, and Catherine and Ann stayed in bed together until the sun had crawled above the housetops to the south. They broke their fast in their old clothes and lounged by the fire while the girls worked at their letters upstairs. Diana was practicing her music, and the notes of the lute sweetened the air.

"We will remain in the nest, like two mice," said Catherine, propping her slippers on the hearth, "and let the winter blow by."

Ann was looking out the window. "I think the winter has just blown into the courtyard."

Catherine clutched her collar to her neck. "Who is it?"

"I don't know, but he looks high and mighty."

Catherine cursed softly and ran to change while a manservant went for the door. Ann was behind her, already holding the finer skirt as she dropped the old one, then twisting her hair up as Catherine fixed the fastenings. "Give me some beads," she said, and Ann pushed a small set into her hand. She put it over her head as the call came, and they went.

A man with a curdled face stood in the front hall, squashing his hat in his hands. Clerical dress. Quite grand. His line of attendants loitered behind him, snaking from the door into the courtyard. He wiped the edge of his shoe on the pavers and lifted it to examine the result. He said, "Catherine Davies?"

"Yes," she said, still on the stairs. "My husband is not at home."

"A man of business," he said, "and of industry. How admirable."

"He is," Catherine said, wary now, "except on holy days." Her fingers touched the cold Christ against her chest.

"My name is Stephen Gardiner. I am here to speak to you. About your son."

The name fluttered around Catherine's brain. She knelt. "Archbishop. Lord Chancellor. I am honored. I would have better prepared if I had known of your coming. Forgive me. I am unready for such a presence."

"Get on your feet," he said. "I'm not here to be entertained, and I don't care what you're wearing."

Ann tore away, headed for the kitchen, and Catherine stood. He had put the crown on Mary Tudor's head, she had heard. She looked at his hands, porky and spotted, but thick with power. "I am at your service."

"So Her Majesty assures me. But is your family?"

The house was suddenly hollow with silence. The music had stopped. The girls were probably around the corner above them, listening. Catherine's heart whipped itself into a gallop before she remembered that Robbie was gone.

"My family?" Catherine saw a couple of the kitchen girls scoot into the dining gallery with a plate and jugs, and she motioned toward the room. "Come and sit by the fire. Your men, as well."

She left the big chair at the end of the table for the archbishop and waited until two of the men had seated themselves. They'd left the seat to Gardiner's right unoccupied, and Catherine ordered the maids to pour before she slid into it. "Have more wood brought," she said, and the girls curtsied and tiptoed away.

Gardiner reclined and let his head fall back so that he could study the ceiling. Catherine thought he was trying to make out the designs through the soot, and her cheeks went hot at the thought of how many months it had been since she had had it cleaned.

He finally sat up and said, "Your son, Robert Overton."

Of course. Catherine reined in her voice. Steady now. "My son."

"He has been in the company of the Duke of Suffolk lately, or so we hear. And one Peter Carew. Do you know him?"

Catherine shook her head. She could speak the simple truth. "The duke is Jane Grey's father, is he not?"

"He claims to be," said the archbishop. He leaned back again, as a man brought in logs and arranged them over the dying fire. The flames licked upward, and he sighed. "But this Carew. He's an adventurer. Old enough to know better than he acts."

"I do not mingle with adventurers. I am more of a home body."

"Yes." Again he straightened. "Her Majesty tells me that you prefer your kitchens to the court."

"The court is for greater persons than I."

"But you have done well for yourself." He let his head fall back yet again and gazed upward. "This house would hold multitudes."

"It is comfortable for our family," said Catherine, "but it is shallower than it appears. We provide well for our servants, and they reward us with loyalty."

"Loyalty. Now there is the point," said Gardiner. "You have vowed your loyalty to our queen."

"I have done so, many times."

"I hope the promise is not as shallow as your house."

"Indeed not. I have sworn my duty to her many times."

"She remembers this. She has a great deal of affection for you. But this Carew. He's a more unsteady sort of person. He prefers to play. He likes a challenge, and he likes loud companions. And yet, like so many of his character, he is loose of tongue when he drinks. And he likes to drink."

"I would not have him near my daughters," said Catherine.

"Your daughters are not my object," said Gardiner, "nor his. Your son seems drawn to him. Almost a man, isn't he?"

"He will be seventeen this winter."

"Mm. A difficult age. And young men are impressionable, like heated wax. And like wax, they melt. Like moths, drawn to the flames of exploits, real or imagined. Like this." He plucked a loose thread from his sleeve and tossed it into the hearth. It sizzled and was gone.

"What are you telling me?"

"I am telling you a story. A moral story. Some men's mouths work faster than their minds. And their deeds run along with their words, on wind. Such men often blow up trouble, when they cast them to the ears and arms of others. Such a man is this Peter Carew. Ask your son about him. And tell him to steer clear, lest he be shipwrecked. Do you understand me?"

"I think I do," said Catherine.

Gardiner gulped his wine and belched. "Good day to you, Lady Catherine." The men were up before the archbishop had pushed back his chair, and they flanked the door as he went out. They mounted their horses and were gone, the line of attendants slithering after the great Lord Chancellor.

Catherine stood at the open door. The day was stark and frigid. The sun had already begun its retreat into a mass of cloud, and she closed the house against its weak face. Ann, behind her, said, "What was all that? It sounded like nonsense from where I stood."

Catherine said, "It was a warning. It was a threat."

# Chapter Thirteen

Catherine spent the afternoon and evening in her still room, wiping jars that were already clean, refolding linens into the bottoms of baskets. She snapped at the maids, and then asked their forgiveness. She paid the tutors without counting the coins. The girls crept around her, and she finally fell into bed and a fitful sleep. All the next day, she waited, but no one came from the court or the church. Ann walked down into the city with two of the manservants to buy bread, but came back empty of news. The men were safe in the country, Catherine told herself. No one could fault a man hunting on his own land with his own stepson. No one would arrest them for felling a deer or two.

By the morning of the third day, Catherine was blurry-headed with sleeplessness. She wandered into the dining gallery with a handful of rosemary and stood in the empty room, unable to remember what she had been carrying it for. She tore her forefinger open helping the maids pull pin feathers from a couple of hens for dinner and spent an hour stopping the wound's flow with rags.

When she heard the horses clop in, she bit her tongue to prevent herself from running. Halloos sounded from the stable, and her husband's voice called out that they were half-frozen. The kitchen door boomed open and men's feet stomped, as though crushing the cold. She smelt sage, and looked down at her hand, full of mashed and broken leaves.

"Catherine!"

He was already on the stairs, and Catherine held herself back while she counted ten, and then followed, ordering ale to be brought as she went. Ann was already in the dining gallery, holding Reg's sleeve, and he was silent.

Benjamin nuzzled Catherine with a wet beard and said, "We have taken a young buck. Fat as an old bishop and almost half as intelligent. Your son brought him down."

Robbie warmed his hands at the fire. He was grinning. "'Twas a lucky shot."

"Luck. It was a good eye," said Benjamin. He aimed a finger at the boy. "Next, you'll be wrestling wild boar to the ground."

Catherine poured for them and waited as they settled around the table and told their tale. The days had been grey and windy. They had ridden for miles without seeing anything more than a skinny rabbit. Then the deer had shown himself, and Robbie had felled him while the other men's backs were turned. Benjamin clinked his goblet against his stepson's. They were, miraculously, friends.

Ann sat with Reg. The girls dashed in and got the story of their brother's triumph. He let Alice hug his shoulders. Veronica gave him the old familiar gaze of a sister, and he smiled over the younger girl's head at her.

Catherine wanted to weep. Ann, across from her, threw her a dark look. Reg was watching Ann. The inevitable question came from Benjamin.

"And what have you ladies been doing with yourselves all these days? While we have worn ourselves to the bone bringing home your dinner?"

Alice said, "We have been copying passages from S. Mark, while Diana worked at her lute. I finished a handkerchief with roses. My brother should have it."

Robbie ruffled her hair, knocking her coif askew, and she grinned before ducking away from him.

"And you, Wife?"

Catherine looked to Ann, who nodded. She took a breath and said, "I have had a visitor."

"Someone who failed to come for a Twelfth Night gift? I hope you told him we are gutted for loose coins and sent him away."

"It was Gardiner. Girls, let your brother breathe." It was a signal to depart, and Veronica took her sister's hand and dragged her out. Diana had been standing in the doorway, and she turned without a word and went with them.

Benjamin's hand lingered on the stem of his goblet. "Stephen Gardiner?"

"The very one," said Catherine. She put her hand on her chest, afraid she had forgotten to remove the beads. But all she felt was the pounding of her heart. "He has grown very grand."

"Just passing by?" said Benjamin.

"No. He was on a mission."

"Of mercy, no doubt," said Robbie. The words were tipped with acid and they stung his mother's ears.

"He was gathering information," said Catherine. She stood to fill the cups again. Then she walked over and poked at the fire. Retook her seat. "He says that Suffolk has been in London lately." She pushed Benjamin's drink closer to him. She did not look at her son. "He spoke of someone I am unacquainted with. A man called Peter Carew."

"I don't know him," said Benjamin. "What, has he said he wants to marry Diana? Veronica? They're not for sale."

"I know him," murmured Robbie.

"So says the bishop," said Catherine. She reached for her son's hand, but he put it onto his lap. "Who is this man, Robert?"

"He fights for freedom. Freedom of conscience and freedom of belief. That Gardiner is the devil's own ambassador."

"Are not all of our consciences free?" asked Catherine. "Except in what we owe to God?"

A fire smouldered in Robert Overton's face. "Some say not, as long as we have a Roman queen on the throne. She has already thrown a dozen good men into the Tower, Cranmer among them. She will execute them. Then she will marry the Spaniard. She will seize men's lands and take their wives from them. She will force us to bend to statues and worship old bones like savages." He turned to his stepfather. "Carew says that we should do to them all as you and I have done to that deer, and save ourselves."

"Robbie," whispered Catherine. "What you say is treason."

He stood and leaned over the table. "And when you resisted the king in your youth it was called treason, was it not? And yet you did it. And for what? Conscience. The freedom of your mind. Why is it wrong for me to do the same?"

The truth of it pricked her, and her breast went cold. "You? Are we speaking of you?"

Robbie sat again. "I mean Carew. But I am in accord with his mind."

Benjamin said, "Is Suffolk in this with him?"

"Suffolk is an old fool," said Robbie. "He is spineless and white-livered. He talks and talks, but his own men ignore him."

"Fools can be dangerous," said Benjamin. He walked to the hall and looked around, then heaved the big doors shut on them and returned. "Tell us. Tell it all."

A board creaked on the other side of the wall, and Catherine listened. The night was coming down. The house might be cowering and shrinking beneath it, nothing more.

"There is little to tell," said Robert, suddenly bright. His voice was tight and high. "Men are angry and they talk. If this queen does not conform herself to the kingdom, the kingdom will squeeze her into shape. I do not speak treason. I just repeat what I hear said. Walk into any public house and you will hear the like opinion."

"Christ on the Cross," said Reg. "It will be killing all over again. Over God."

"Only if the queen makes it happen," said Robert. "She has a sister, more to the people's tastes, even if she is only a woman. This Roman Mary can give over the crown to Elizabeth and save us all. She can stop this with a snap of her fingers. Or she can remain as she is. And if she does, then, yes, the blood will run."

# Chapter Fourteen

Catherine and Benjamin lay in their bed, side by side, holding hands. Snow was falling through the wan moonlight, like a veil being pulled over the night. "Cover him," Catherine said to the window. "Cover them all."

"He said nothing about action," said Benjamin. "He's right about Suffolk. He couldn't raise an army of pet mice. It's all talk."

"Talk leads to acts. You know it as well as I. Suffolk is not the only voice in this."

Benjamin said, in a softer tone, "I've made a start with Robbie, a good start. Let's not chop off its hands before it takes hold."

The wind shoved a load of snow from the sill and the panes protested. Catherine rolled away from the storm and held her husband. "I know, but it's only been a few days with you. Who knows how long he has run with this pack of friends? He is so violent with his beliefs. I cannot judge him. He is too like me. Who would be a mother in these times?"

"I've told you. I've promised you. I'll be his father, as much as he'll allow."

Catherine twirled a lock of his hair. "Where is Elizabeth? She must know if the people are plotting against Mary."

"Who says they're plotting? They're just angry and scared."

"Suffolk is angry. Jane is bitter. Plots have risen out of less."

"Jane has cause enough." Benjamin raised himself on one elbow and checked the fire. "I would hate to be in the Tower on this night."

"I mean Jane Dudley, not Jane Grey."

"Now, that's a different horse altogether." Benjamin flopped down again and put his face against Catherine's chest. "She has no power, and she has three sons within a stone's throw of the axe. She will have to eat her bitterness and smile while she swallows it."

"I feel the same as she does. Who would have thought I could ever think such a thing? To be afraid of Mary Tudor?"

"But Elizabeth? It will be her own neck on the block if she rises against Mary. She had best learn to kneel and say, 'Your Majesty's will.' And keep away from men, talkers or not."

"Elizabeth is a shrewd one."

"She had better be."

"Are we talking of executions? Of who will live or die on how they say prayers? I thought the world had outgrown it."

"The world will never outgrow it. Sleep, Catherine. We can do nothing about Elizabeth, and definitely nothing about Mary. I will keep watch on Robbie." Benjamin pulled the blankets up to their chins, kissed her, and closed his eyes. Catherine lay awake long after, watching the specter of the storm dancing on the opposite wall.

They woke to the clomp of Reg's boots as he came in to stoke the hearth. "Your son has gone to seek news," he said.

"What news?" asked Catherine. She stayed under the covers while Benjamin rose to dress.

"I don't know." Reg pointed at the window with a stick of kindling. "A man rode in just at first light, and they were off."

The hoof prints were still in the courtyard, and the servants cleared them away with the heavy drifts. But then the snow warmed to rain, and they finally gave up their labour and let God do the cleaning. Benjamin and Reg saddled up to go find out what they could. Catherine found Ann down in the kitchen, heating a bucket of water over an iron grid for a washing. Three maids surrounded her, and when Catherine came in they broke apart, scattering wide-eyed glances among themselves.

"What's happened?" asked Catherine. "Ann, what's the talk?"

Ann shook her head. "They say someone has been arrested. Nobody seems to know who it is."

One of the maids said, "Old Moll says she heard it on the street. She says the heads will roll."

"Where is she?"

"She was here," said the maid. She opened the back door. Closed it again. "I don't know, Madam. She didn't give names. I think she might be mad, Madam."

"Mad as a fox," said Ann.

Catherine stepped out back herself and put her foot into a puddle of slush. She came back inside, cursing herself.

"Robbie didn't take anything," said Ann, stirring a pile of hose into the water, "so he can't have gone far, not in all this snow. And now it's turning to rain and the whole city will be flooded." She hoisted her big ladle and sniffed. Dropped it. "Drink something. Go see to the girls. Their tutor won't come today."

"They'll work with Diana," said Catherine.

"Then go make a potion. Do anything," said Ann. "You'll spoil the soap with your fretting."

But Catherine worried, upstairs and downstairs, standing at the windows and wondering whether she should ride out herself to find him, wondering if she'd gone mad herself. She had no idea where he'd be. She thought, once, that she saw the hat of the bishop over the front wall and her legs went liquid with fear, but it was only a man with a small boy in a red cap, holding a rooster on his shoulders, and they passed by the Davies gate with never a sideways glance. The rain came steadily down, on flesh and fowl alike.

Ann finally came up, rubbing her raw hands together. "Any sign?"

"No," said Catherine, but as the word left her mouth, Robbie turned in, another young man at his side. She flew out the door and skidded on the slick pavers. Fell onto the gravel. Her son sat back and his companion smiled. She looked a fool.

"Mother, you will break your neck," said Robbie.

"The weather is not fit for riding," she said. "I have been praying for you. You will have the fever from this."

He leapt to the ground and waited for a damp stable boy to come running. "Go on around back," he said to his companion. "The kitchen is just inside the rear door."

"You won't come in this way?" said Catherine.

"I'm filthy as an old hog, Madam," the stranger said. "I won't put my feet on your good floor."

Robbie and Catherine went in side by side, stamping the cold out of their feet by the big fire. The boy shook out his hat and held it to the flames. "It's the judgment of God on us, Mother."

"What? The rain? This is England, Robert. God must feel a continual resentment."

"Perhaps He does. I will have to go. I go now."

Catherine grabbed his sleeve. The arm inside it was like a reed; she was afraid she might crush it. "What is it? What is happening?"

Robert twisted his mouth, as though the words in it ached him. "There's a man called Edward Courtenay. Have you heard of him?"

"The queen's Courtenay? The one who wanted to marry her? That one?"

Robert blew his nose on a handkerchief and stuffed it away. He dripped onto the floor and tried to brush the rest of the water from himself. "He's not the queen's suitor any longer. She rejected him, didn't she? In favour of that foreigner. It won't be tolerated."

"He can do nothing but tolerate it. The woman won't have a ring forced onto her finger. She doesn't like the man. That's her right. Women have few enough of those."

"Her rights are married to England. And he is English. She's as much as spat on her subjects."

"She can spit on Courtenay if she wants to."

"She's done more than spit on him. She's had him arrested."

"For what? What's he done?"

Robbie shrugged. A door slammed downstairs and he tilted his head toward the noise. "For being a Protestant, I expect. But it means I must go."

"But why? What do you know of him?"

"Nothing, Mother. I was not here, and you have not seen me." He kissed her on the cheek and ran upstairs. When he came down, he had on dry clothes, his new clothes, and his dagger.

"Son, tell me, I beg you. What is this?" Catherine tried to block the door, but he set her aside.

"It will be everything. Or it will be nothing. And it is better for you not to know."

And then her son was gone, with the stranger riding beside him.

# Chapter Fifteen

Benjamin galloped in, almost skidding into the side of the house. He fell when he dismounted and threw the reins to a panicked groomsman. Then he was running inside. "Catherine!" he called, but she was already in front of him.

"What is it?"

"They've got Edward Courtenay. He's talking. There's been a standard raised in Devon."

"What? Where? Devon? What are they doing?"

"Where's Robbie?" asked Benjamin.

"Gone off with another. He said something about Courtenay. I didn't know the other man. He took his side arm."

Ann and Reg came in from separate doors, and Reg said, "It sounds like an uprising."

"Who? Who is rising?" asked Catherine again, but Benjamin was shaking his head. "Damn it all! Who?"

"That Peter Carew." Benjamin leaned over, hands on knees, and groaned. "Let me breathe. There's one Peter Carew."

"The one the bishop spoke of," said Reg.

Ann rubbed his back. "Slower. We know this."

Benjamin stood and wiped his forehead with the back of his hand. "Carew has gone to Devon and word is that he is raising an army."

"And what does Edward Courtenay have to do with Carew? What does he have to do with Robbie?" asked Catherine. The hinges of the open door behind Benjamin whined, and Catherine's ears filled with wind. A gust whipped a pile of old leaves into a drum-shape, rising upward, and she thought for a moment that her son had appeared, but it was nothing but the weather, trying to get inside. The leaves collapsed into a dead pile on the threshold, and Ann heaved the door closed.

Benjamin pulled off his riding cloak and dropped it. Reg didn't move. Both men stared at the flames.

"Benjamin?" Catherine's ribs had gone icy, and she turned to stand beside him, facing the fire, trying to see something in the flames. "Who is arrested?"

He said, "No one says 'arrest.' They say he has been called to the court."

"Who says all this?" asked Ann. "This sounds like ale-house talk to me."

Reg picked up the cloak and took his own off. "It's more than that. We rode all the way to Hampton Court. There's no one there, but the servants know."

"Where are they?" asked Catherine. "What is happening?"

"Courtenay's at Winchester, with Gardiner," Benjamin said. "They say he undergoes a close examination. They say he means to marry Elizabeth, without the queen's permission."

"She'll kill them if he does," said Catherine. "Mary will kill them." She backed a step and tripped on the edge of the carpet. Sat down like a drunken maid. Her legs would not let her rise. "She'll kill them. No, no. I don't mean that. She will not. She will be merciful. She must. I'm going to be sick." She lay flat on her back, and Ann knelt beside her.

"Courtenay hasn't achieved it," said Benjamin. "They've got him. He won't be marrying anyone."

Catherine watched the rafters, high above her, dance with golden spots. It was like looking at heaven, sparkling through the roof. The tiny flickers burned out, went black, and she was looking at nothing. "Where is Elizabeth?"

"She's at Ashridge."

Catherine closed her eyes and let the image of that house rise into her mind, along with the skinny prince who'd won her son's loyalty. He became a king, but never became a man. Now he was rotting in his grave. And Guildford Dudley, that shining boy, was rotting in the Tower. How they ran together when they were children, like a herd of young colts, through the high, bright rooms. "Robbie," she said.

Benjamin sat beside her and rubbed her hand between his, but his fingers were cold and wet, and she shivered. He said, "What does she need?"

Ann said, "She needs her son."

"He's gone," Catherine said. Her skin resented the clammy touch, prickling all the way to her elbow. But the diversion settled her head, and she sat up. "Put your palms on my face." He did, and the freezing burn drove the muddy heat from her. "Robbie knew about Courtenay. He was furious about it."

"What does he think he'll do, drive the bishop into the street?" asked Benjamin. Catherine was struggling to her feet, and he pulled her up. "They cannot rise against the queen in the city. They won't get as far as London Bridge before they'll be caught."

"It's madness," said Ann.

Reg said, "We should find them. If they've gone that way, we can catch them. We can tie Robbie and bring him home by force if we must."

"Get two new horses," said Benjamin. He hugged Catherine, hard. "We must go."

"Eat first," said Ann. "You'll fall out of the saddle."

"No time," said Benjamin. "God knows who Courtenay'll pull down with him if they rack him. He'll point the finger at the whole lot of them."

Reg had already gone, down the back stairs. Catherine pushed herself to her feet. Her head would not sit straight on her shoulders, but Benjamin didn't notice. He was rubbing his beard, saying "They're fools, all of them. Fools."

Catherine felt Ann's warm hands on her back. Steadying.

"Pack us some meat and bread," Benjamin was saying, "so that we don't need to stop."

Ann gave her a push, and Catherine ran.

# Chapter Sixteen

The men were gone, and again the women waited. Ann forced bread and cups of wine into Catherine's hand as she paced the front rooms, and Catherine wadded the bread and threw it to the dogs and gulped the wine. The day waxed and waned, and Veronica and Diana brought Alice down and sat at the table. The maids served them, and they ate. The older girls took Alice back up and put her to bed, then returned and remained, silent and waiting.

When Catherine could see nothing but her own pale form, restless in the panes as a ghost, she went into the dining gallery and sat.

Veronica said, "What's happening, Mother?"

Catherine sat. "Some men have risen up against the queen. Your brother is gone again."

Diana said, "He is in it with them?"

Catherine gazed at her stepdaughter. Her brown hair was neatly covered, and her wide, dark eyes were steady and intelligent. So sober and solitary, like a nun. She could be a nun now, in fact, if she chose. Today, she could choose. And tomorrow? Would it get her hanged for a heretic? Catherine took the younger woman's hand in her own. The flat fingers were calloused from her lute strings. Hard-labouring hands, pulling music from dead guts. Catherine stroked the tough pads until Diana winced and pulled back.

"I've hurt you. Forgive me."

"Your mind is elsewhere, Mother," said Diana. "You wander to Robert. Do you truly not know where he is?"

"I don't. He came and went like the lightning. He said it was better if I did not know."

"I heard Father earlier. There is an armed uprising?"

"Is that it? Will there be deaths?" asked Veronica. Her red hair would not be tamed by her coif, and her eyes, blue as a spring sky, shifted from her mother to her stepsister. She drummed the fingers of her right hand lightly on the table, and Catherine stilled them with her palm.

"That's what the men say. It may be all talk. Men will talk."

"Is my brother a traitor?" asked Veronica. "Will they kill him?" Her voice had winged upward, and she almost sang out the question. "Will the queen hang my brother?"

"Don't talk of hanging," said Catherine. "He is gone, but he's only a boy. The men won't want him holding them back. He's eager to do something noble, but he's young."

"Boys," said Veronica. "They will always be riding off to show themselves to the world."

"That they will," said Catherine. She looked at Diana. "Your father's gone to find him. Reg as well. They will bring him back to us." She thought that if she made the words form in her mouth, they might have the force of the truth.

Ann appeared at the door with a jug. "And he had better come back in one piece." She set the drink on the table and went out again. She returned with goblets for them all and poured the wine. "You must have yours tempered," she said to Veronica. "Let me get water."

"They will not allow her to be queen in peace," said Diana. "They must make up a war out of their anger. Why is this always the way? Christ teaches us to love one another, and for that love we cut each other's throats. What difference can it make whether the priest holds up the host or throws it to the cats? Whether we pray in Latin or English?"

Catherine regarded the young woman. "I used to ask the same questions. Why the king would not let us live in the convent, as we had always done. Then why we were required to bow and scrape for a living. Even for a morsel of meat."

Ann returned with a second pitcher and they all drank. Veronica hiccupped, and Ann said, "Too strong yet." She threw in an extra splash of the water.

Diana said, "You see? We women take care of each other without drawing swords upon one cross word. What is the need of a battle? She is the queen. Let her be the queen. Her grandmother was a queen. Her own mother was a queen, at least when the king was in another country."

Ann said, "You have been studying in your stepmother's books. But women can go to battle, too. They generally give out tongue-lashings, though, when they've got their enemies cornered."

"That's true enough," said Catherine. "But I think this queen is made of more than words."

"She's a Tudor," said Ann. "They contend if they don't get what they want."

Catherine nodded.

Veronica said, "So she will. She will kill my brother!" Her face was spotted red, and her lips were bleached at the corners.

"Don't overwork your imagination," said Catherine. "We don't know where he is, or who he is with. You must practice patience."

"Patience? When you talk of swords and contentions and treasons? I'm not a child. I know what happens to traitors."

But she was a child, and Ann poured her another drink, this one of water with a splash of wine. "It's my fault, Vere. I spoke too rashly. Put it out of your mind."

The girl chewed her lower lip. "When will Father and Reg be home?"

"When they find Robbie," said Catherine. "Or when they have something to tell us."

Diana stretched and said, "Let's go to the bed, Vere. This cold makes me sleepy."

"But if they come home? I want to be awake."

"Then Mother will wake us. I will tell you a story."

"The stories are all downstairs. And outside. I want to be here."

Diana smiled. "I know a tale about a young girl who was sitting by a fire, late one night, when the fairies came and whisked her away. They left only her skirt and bodice behind. And a single shoe."

Veronica sat forward. "What happened to her?"

"You will have to come up with me to hear the end."

Veronica seemed to struggle against this offer, but could not resist at last. "Don't let Alice hear. It will bring the nightmare to her."

"This story is only for grownups who are not afraid of the dark. It is very frightening."

They were up now, and Veronica followed her stepsister, tugging at her sleeve for more.

Ann said, "Diana has a genius in her." She listened for a moment to the silence in the vast room. A log fell. A beam overhead groaned. "City of ladies. Do you remember? We used to talk of one. You used to read that Christine, the one from Paris."

"Yes, sometimes," said Catherine. "How I used to long for it, Ann. For Mary to get the throne. For England to return to the church. It has been so long that I have forgotten what it feels like, to have nothing but women around me, to have books and arguing." She almost smiled.

"We had some freedom then," said Ann.

"We have some now. More than we have ever had. We have the power to come and go. We have good husbands. Many women have much less."

"But little governance of ourselves. If it weren't for Reg and Benjamin, our lives would be poorer, indeed."

"We have chosen well."

"We have been fortunate," said Ann. "And you would not wish your son unmade, whatever his father was."

"Not for the world." A maid peeped in and asked if they would like the cups removed, and Catherine waved her in. "Bring two clean ones for the men."

"Yes, Madam."

Catherine waited until the girl had gone. "I have vowed my loyalty to Mary Tudor, since we were barely women. I have washed her very hair with these hands." Catherine laid out her open palms on the table. They were stained with streaks of green, and the scar from an old dog bite stretched, a white thread, from her thumb to her forefinger. It still ached on wet nights, her history speaking to her through her flesh. "I have fed her and clothed her. I have sworn to uphold her rights. I swore it before God and meant every word." She closed her right hand and felt a knuckle snap. She was getting old. Creeping up on forty years now.

"And Robbie?"

Catherine closed the left, folding in the cicatrice. "He is my son. A mother vows to protect and love her children when she gives them birth. To punish them when she must. Doesn't she?"

"You look like a woman bent on a fight," said Ann.

Catherine knocked on the table. "I cannot do battle when I am pulled between two armies."

"Perhaps it is not as dire as all that. This may all be the bragging of men in their cups."

A chunk of wood rolled and shattered, spraying sparks into the room. "Let us pray so. But my heart feels as splintered as that log."

# Chapter Seventeen

It was almost morning, the dawn trying to break the dismal, dark air with a few frozen fingers when Benjamin and Reg returned. Catherine was dozing, her head on her arms, when she heard the horses snorting in the courtyard. The stable hands were all in their beds, and the men walked the horses around themselves. Catherine was in the kitchen, lighting a candle from the embers of the hearth, by the time they came in, stamping the mud from their shoes. Robbie was not with them.

Catherine poured two mugs of ale and let them sit while she chocked up the fire at the grate and poured a bucket of water into a small cauldron for their wash. She squatted and blew under the kindling until the strands of loose wood caught the heat. The men drank and waited, silent.

When the fire was hot enough to begin warming the iron pot, she sat and folded her hands in her lap. She bit through her lower lip and tasted her blood.

Benjamin finally spoke. "No word of Robbie. Not a sign, anywhere in the town. We have asked at inns and ale houses. We walked the streets of Southwark until we could stand it no longer. It's a stew down there at night. I'd not thought the bishop kept so many geese at his very door."

"They're poor, and they've no other way to earn their livings," said Catherine. She wondered how many of the prostitutes had once been nuns, and her heart shuddered. "You thought you might find him there?"

Benjamin shrugged. "Many a man has gone astray over the river. And there are plenty of haunts for a band hunting trouble."

"But he was not among them."

"No."

A current of relief rippled through Catherine. But it ebbed, and she said, "Is there any word of him at all?"

"Men are talking of Courtenay: unthought-of yesterday, and the name in every mouth today. So goes fame." He struggled to his feet and walked to the fire. His legs were stiff, and he bent at the waist, holding his face over the pot. "Is this for me?"

"Yes." Catherine tested it with her finger. It was barely lukewarm. "Let it heat, if you can stand yourself."

"I stink of the sewers. Don't get near me."

"Nonsense. Reg, do you want to bathe?"

"I will go upstairs." He nodded and retired. Catherine knew that he would wash alone at his frozen basin in the dark of his chamber while Ann slept and would not complain about it.

"There's rumblings from Devon," said Benjamin, stripping off his shirt and casting it aside. Catherine latched the doors and checked the shutters. He said, "Carew has gone, and somebody's already nailed up a notice, warning the people of London that he's marching on the queen."

"What a fool," said Catherine. "She'll have him in a pie to break her fast."

"No one seems much alarmed." Benjamin took up a clout that lay nearby and began scrubbing the pits of his arms and his chest. Catherine washed his back and he rolled his head.

The bones of his neck cracked, and she rubbed the grease and sweat from him.

"You are tight as a yoked mule," she said.

"And as bad-tempered. I haven't been this weary since the night you had Alice."

"Is it safe to sleep?"

"Safe enough, I wager," he said. He hefted the pot, and Catherine opened the back door for him to throw the water out. The cold dawn blew in over them. His skin pimpled with goose-flesh, and Catherine wrapped her arms around him. He laid his face on her shoulder. "We might as well rest, in case the men of Devon are on our doorstep in the morning."

But it was already morning, showing the outline of a grey day. Catherine shut the door and followed him up to their bed.

The day came on despite them, relentless, dull, and sullen. Benjamin slept until almost the noon hour, Catherine dozing beside him, when the sound of Diana's lute awakened them. The tutor had arrived, and they heard Alice practicing her French as they went down to eat. Veronica was probably at her writing. The household was up, chattering as though nothing in the world were amiss, and the fires were lively. Someone in the kitchen had put on a venison roast, and the meat wafted a holiday scent through the rooms.

But it was the middle of January, with no celebrations in sight. Catherine looked out the front windows. All was still. No bells rang. Nothing moving inside their courtyard walls except one of the dogs, digging in the corner. A winter morning, like any other.

Benjamin's eyes were bagged and heavy, and he slouched over his ale in his long nightshirt and a pair of woolen hose, pulled up over his thighs. Reg had brought clean clothes, but he hadn't put them on yet. Ann came in when she heard them in the dining gallery, and sat across from Catherine.

She looked tired, too. Benjamin pulled on his breeches under the table and thrust the tails of the shirt into them.

"I hear no one besieging us," said Ann. She put her chin on her hands. "Except for the lute strings." She cut her eyes at the stairs beyond the door. "Can you tell her to leave off for one day? It's pulling my brains out of my ears."

"She'll run mad if we tell her to stop," said Catherine. "She needs music to keep her spirits in harmony."

"Very well," sighed Ann. "I suppose I can sleep under a pile of clean sheets downstairs."

Benjamin tried to smile, but the effort was lopsided.

"We might ride down to Winchester," said Catherine. "It will be safe enough by day, I think. We might ask the women if they have seen him."

"I'm going nowhere today," said Ann. "The weather's foul. Have you looked outdoors?"

The rain fell, a dreary curtain for the window, and Catherine nodded. "Benjamin and I might manage."

"Which Benjamin?" said Benjamin. "This one? This one is wrecked. And we were just there. The women who live in Winchester sleep by day and work by night. I think I will lose my stomach if I have to hold conversation with another one of them so soon."

"The bishop," said Catherine. "He seems to have his ear to the ground. He will see me."

"You'll get drenched," concluded Ann. She stood and covered her ears with her hands. "But it'll be quiet."

"The bishop will know, if there is anything to be known. It might do us good to show at his door. He will not think us to be in league with the traitors, if traitors there are."

Benjamin downed his ale and combed his fingers through his hair. "If we're going to go, we might as well go now, while I still have my eyes open. Reg needs sleep."

"Let him sleep," said Catherine. "We will do it, you and I. He knows my face, and it will go better for us if we don't seem to appear with an army of our own."

The groomsmen were huddled in the stable, glaring out at the gloom, and the horses pawed the ground in resentment at being led from their beds of straw, but they rode out into the cold day, heads down. No one was about until they reached the city proper, and there the streets were muddy, and beggars crouched in foul-smelling puddles under leaky eaves. A couple of women hurried past them without a greeting, their baskets covered with woolen blankets. The bulk of S. Paul's shouldered its way into view on their right, and they turned east to avoid the alms-seekers, only to find themselves at the wall of the Tower, where they rested for a few minutes. A man stumbled from an alehouse nearby and cursed the sky. Cursed Devon.

Benjamin shouted a hallo, and the man wove his way over to them. "What d'ye need of me?"

"Devon. I heard you say Devon. What's the word?"

"They're not comin'. All that talk and no fight. What's a man's word worth if he can't raise an army?"

"You want a war?" asked Catherine.

"Eh." The man regarded the grey sky. The rain had let up for the moment and he took off his oily hat. He was white-headed. "It's a sight better than being driven into the grave by a cloud. But there'll be no swords. Nothin' for a man to do but get drunk and wait for spring." He trudged off.

"Can it be true?" asked Catherine.

"We've almost lost our way. Come on."

They crossed a crowded London Bridge, twisting among shopkeepers and wet buyers. A dirty boy raced in front of them, chasing a mangy dog, and Benjamin pulled his horse up short, almost backing over an old woman. She slapped the animal's flank and said, "Get off the bridge. There's decent folks hereabouts."

They hurried on, not looking up at the heads rotting in the rain overhead. The south bank of the Thames was sodden, and the river had risen, bringing brine and muck and the smell of dead fish up to the house fronts. Catherine thought of the prisoners in the nearby cells, up to their ankles or shins in the filthy stuff, or sunk in the oubliette to their necks. Forgotten indeed. She knew the feeling well enough.

The bishop's gate was unmistakable among the broken shutters and unpainted walls of the Southwark lanes. The gatekeeper was swilling from a jug, and he turned the key to let them in without a second look or a request for their names. When Benjamin thanked him and offered a coin, he looked at the silver token for a second before seizing it. "You pay to get in. Some would pay to get out," he snickered.

The bishop already had a roomful of suppliants, and Benjamin and Catherine gave their names to the stiff manservant and prepared to wait, grateful to be out of the weather and the stench. But the palace was cold, and they were wet, and they were inching their way toward the hearth when a man took Benjamin by the shoulder.

"Davies?"

"Yes."

"Come with me." He pulled Benjamin after him, and Catherine followed. The others grumbled as they went in before them.

Stephen Gardiner was at table, thick in his robes and his satisfaction, and he motioned with a duck leg for the two to sit. Then he said, "Stand by the fire. You look like a couple of wet hens." The chair he occupied was glossy, carved wood, throne-like. It creaked when he shifted and settled his bulk, and Catherine's mind skidded for a moment to the pressured joints. She rubbed her knuckles.

They obliged the order to indulge in the fire and stood, dripping over the pavers, near the flames. Gardiner ripped the meat from the bone with his teeth and tossed the remainder to a couple of dogs at his feet.

"You want to know about Courtenay," the bishop said without taking his eyes from his food.

"We hear disquieting stories," said Benjamin. "The men of Devon?"

"Carew's a fop and a weakling," said Gardiner. He chose an apple from a pewter plate, bit into it, and set it aside. "He's likely on a boat by this time."

"So London is safe?" asked Catherine.

"Now that's a condition every mother wants, isn't it?" the bishop said. He beckoned a servant, who brought wine. "Women want peace and quiet."

"We want our land to be at peace, yes," said Catherine. Her skirt was boiling in back, and she turned to give the front a chance at the heat. She felt like a fowl on the spit.

The man brought them each a cup, and Catherine drank. It was good wine, and she tipped back her head to let it warm her insides.

Benjamin moved toward a chair. "And Courtenay?"

Gardiner said, "A popinjay. He's being questioned."

"What does he answer?"

"This and that. Sit, man, if you're going to. You hover like Death himself."

Benjamin sat. The servant pushed a plate of meat toward him, but he waved it away. "Does he mean to marry?"

The bishop laughed. "I expect every man means to marry, those that haven't promised themselves to the church. Those may mean to unmarry, as things stand."

"Courtenay's no cleric. Or so I've heard."

Gardiner scratched the back of his neck with his greasy fingers. "No. God would probably send lightning with the rain if he tried on a collar. But he won't marry; no, not any time soon."

"That's one less fear," said Catherine. She was steaming now, and she joined the table, sitting beside Benjamin.

"What have you to fear from him? Your daughters are all within doors, aren't they?"

"They are," said Catherine. "And I mean to keep them there until these rumours of treason die."

"Treason. Who speaks of treason?" Gardiner set down his cup and gazed at Catherine.

"There is talk of an uprising in Devon, as my husband said."

"Devon is loyal. They stick to the queen." He turned to Benjamin. "You have people in the midlands, don't you?" His lips puckered. "Welshmen."

Benjamin shook his head, but it was not a denial. "My family is in the west. I'm the black sheep, gone English they tell me. My elder brother does his duty in keeping up the line."

Gardiner laughed again. "Well spoken. And a good brother, you. Made your own way, have you?"

"I have." Benjamin showed his hard hands. "By dint of labour, in the manner of old Adam."

"And you have no sons."

"None of my blood. One by marriage." He glanced at Catherine.

"Ah. There's the rub. This son." Gardiner massaged his mouth. "You have come in excellent time." The outer door boomed shut, the servants leaving them alone. Catherine's shift went icy against her skin. The Lord Chancellor said, "I have been meaning to speak to you again about this son."

# Chapter Eighteen

The Lord Chancellor took his time, fiddling with the scraps of meat on his plate. He lifted a bone on his knife and pulled a string of flesh from it. "You are acquainted with the Duke of Suffolk?" he said to the dangling joint.

Benjamin said, "Grey? We have been invited to his London house. Once. I wouldn't call it even an acquaintance. A passing knowledge."

"And you have a passing knowledge of his family?"

"Everyone knows of his daughter," said Benjamin.

"Yes," said Gardiner. "Good Lady Jane. The girl scholar. Our nine-days' queen. She has grown notorious."

Catherine asked, "Is her father in London now?"

Gardiner snorted. "Who would be in London when he has a rebellion in mind? He would raise his men outside of the city, would he not?"

"Suffolk?" said Catherine. "Is he mad? His daughter is in the Tower."

"Yes," said Gardiner. "Mad to think he could make her queen. Mad to think he can set her free. Perhaps he thinks he will take down both sisters and put her back on the throne. Mad indeed."

"Surely the queen will show mercy," said Catherine. "She has seen troubles enough in her own life. I have always known her to be kind. She has no wish to harm a mere girl, even a misguided girl."

"Kind she may be," said Gardiner, "but not foolish. And Jane is no longer a mere girl. Tell me, what do you know of this Wyatt?"

"The poet? I know many of his verses by memory," said Catherine. "I heard he died of a fever. Very quick."

The Lord Chancellor pinioned a wedge of bread with a gnawed wing. "Who does not know that story? I mean the poet's son, and you know it right well. The one in Kent."

"I could not have told you that he had a son," said Catherine. It would have been true, only a matter of weeks ago.

"We know nothing of him," said Benjamin. "Why should we?"

Gardiner's eyebrows rose and he freed the bread, let it fly over the table. One of the dogs snapped it from the air as it came down. "You should not know him at all. Better that you don't. My home is a sanctuary." He smirked at Catherine. "A haven against sin. And treason. You may want to stay here for a short while. To keep safe in all this unquiet."

"We cannot stay," said Benjamin. He scooted his chair back, and Gardiner laid his palm on the air to stay the motion, but Benjamin stood anyway. "We have business. We have our daughters."

"I will have a message sent," said the Lord Chancellor, "to let your household know you are here with me. I can set a watch upon your daughters."

"No," said Catherine. She stood, too, and Gardiner watched her. He did not move.

Benjamin said, "We cannot be detained. We came of our own will to seek your help in finding our son, not to add to your own household. We must go."

"Sit."

Benjamin and Catherine remained standing. Gardiner coughed, and the door opened. Three men entered. One tended the fire and moved behind Catherine. The other two placed themselves on either side of Benjamin.

"Sit," the Lord Chancellor said again. "You are in no danger here." He indicated the men. "You see, we are well protected. Why do you behave like guilty creatures?"

"Would we have shown our faces here if we were guilty of anything?" asked Benjamin.

"God knows what men will do. Or women."

"What do you know of Robbie?" asked Catherine.

Gardiner's face split. It might have been a smile. "Robbie. A sweet name. I know very little of him. I know that he returned lately from Wittenberg. I know that he came through Kent. I know that you," looking now at Benjamin, "have interests in Dover."

"Wool. That's my only interest in Dover," said Benjamin. "I sell there. I sell in Calais, as well. This is no secret. And no treason."

"Eat something," said Gardiner. "The meal will turn cold."

Catherine looked at Benjamin, and he dipped his chin. She sat and flapped a napkin like a finicky lady. "My son has disappeared. We don't know where he is or who he is with."

"That's good," said Gardiner, watching Catherine lift her cup to her lips. "You do know that he keeps company with a group of young men, though. Don't you?"

"He's a boy," said Benjamin. He reclaimed his seat and pulled up to the table. "He has not been part of our household. He was the companion of the young King

Edward. And then he left England after the king died. Boys have companions, and they don't always inform their parents."

"I see." Gardiner cocked his head and the men backed away. "This young Wyatt, now. Wyatt has companions, as well. And he has no parent to tell at all. He has sent a very pointed message to the Duke of Suffolk. Perhaps he is in need of a father. Sadly, he takes as little care with his messengers as he does with his rhetoric."

"My son is no message boy," said Catherine.

"No, he is not. Of course, he is not. A companion of the late king's could never be pushed so low as that. It is a servant's task. But servants cannot always be trusted."

"You know more of Robbie than you say," said Benjamin.

"A sharp perception," said Gardiner, and Benjamin flushed to his ears. "We know what we know. Tell me, what is the date today?"

Benjamin thought. "The twenty-fifth day of January, is it not?"

"I believe that to be correct. The winter has been bitter, and I have counted every day."

"What difference does that make?" asked Catherine.

"What does the twenty-fifth day of January mean to you?"

"It means we have more winter ahead of us. What else might it mean?" The heat of irritation had dried her through, and her skin itched. She wanted to scratch the smug expression off him, tear that doughy skin.

"It might mean cold weather," said Gardiner, "and it might mean trouble, if a man cannot wait for the spring. Have you never seen a root, uncovered to the heat, begin to sprout out of season? Or a shock of hay, brought too near the fire?"

"What are you talking about?" asked Catherine.

"Why don't you stay?" said the Lord Chancellor.

"Is that a question or a command?" asked Benjamin.

"A suggestion, nothing more," said Gardiner. "If you prefer to go home, I will send a pair of men to ride along with you. To be secure in these dangerous streets."

Catherine felt sure they could handle a pair, if it came to nothing more. "What were the contents of this letter, the one that Wyatt sent to the Duke?"

Now the Lord Chancellor smiled fully. "You haven't heard?"

"Why would I have heard? I don't even know the man."

Gardiner sighed, weary of his world. "Well, now. The mighty Grey Duke seems to think that he might engage in conspiracy. Out in the country. In this mud." He gestured to the long windows, darkened by cloud. "He has thought to bring armed men into the city, to grow a rebellion in the springtime, but he has been uncovered. What make you of that?"

"He is a fool," murmured Catherine. "What will the queen do?"

"She will rip out his guts for him," said Gardiner, cracking a breast from the mangled duck. "And she'll hang his scholarly daughter with the intestines."

"She will not," said Catherine. "Jane Grey does not aim to be queen again. She has seen too much of death. Mary Tudor is a woman of God."

"And God has made Mary Tudor a queen. She will not be threatened by a pack of sniveling braggarts and their ragged followers. Or their brats." Gardiner tore the greasy flesh loose with his teeth and dropped the ribs to the dogs. "Stay. Perhaps your son will find you here."

"He will never come here," said Benjamin.

The eyebrows went up again. "Because he is a heretic, is that not it? A bishop's home will strike a flame in his black thoughts and burn his conscience. Will it not?"

Catherine's heart shriveled. "He keeps his own conscience. And his own counsel."

"Spoken like a generous mother. You must not say I didn't offer. I have offered sanctuary, safe haven, and you have most ungraciously refused my hospitality." He fluttered his fingers at them. "Go then. You two, go with them." He nodded at the men beside Benjamin. "See that they get home. And stay with them for a few days. A week." He looked at Benjamin. "You can feed them, can't you, man? With your great hand-gotten wealth?"

"With pleasure," said Benjamin. But he was not smiling.

Catherine said, "You say you have heard news of Suffolk. But what of this young Wyatt? What was in his letter?"

"Nothing to alarm you. Nothing yet. Keep your peace while you may. Spring will not come for everyone. You'll know what I mean, soon enough. And I do hope your son has the sense to come home before you do."

# Chapter Nineteen

The two servants were not pleased at leaving their bishop and their palace, and they rode along behind Catherine and Benjamin at a gloomy pace. The bridge was even more crowded on the way back, as the clouds had begun to leak again, this time with sleet weighing down the rain, and wet Londoners clustered in sullen knots, unwilling to move aside for horses. A man covered in oozing scabs and showing a milky eye muttered, as they passed, "rich bastards." Catherine briefly wondered what his ailment was, then was pushed on past, despairing of a cure for the disease of being human.

The days were still short, and it was full dark by the time they turned into their courtyard. The visitors remained in their saddles until the Davies servants appeared, lifting lanterns into the night, to relieve them of their animals. The hounds gathered round to sniff the strangers' legs and crotches, and one man cuffed a large dog on the muzzle, sending him howling back to the stable.

"Don't strike them," said Benjamin. "They'll bite."

"They run like country curs," said the man. "A dog with breeding knows to mind his master."

"I'm their master and I'll set them on you myself if you touch one of them again," said Benjamin. "The maids will make you up a room. Do not speak to the young woman or the girls of the house."

"They got names?" said the other.

"Not to you, nor do you to me. You sleep. You eat. You stay out of my sight and out of my business."

Catherine walked inside without a word or a look back.

Ann, wrapped in a heavy cloak, stood in the front hall with a taper. Robbie had not been heard from, and Catherine hushed her worried questions as the bishop's men came in, smearing slush and mud over the pavers. At least they took care to avoid the carpets. Reg was waiting nearby to take Benjamin's cloak, and he shot them a hostile eye. "They need a room," said Catherine to one of her maids. She took Ann's arm and pulled her upstairs.

"What's the word?" Ann asked, when they were behind a closed door.

"Devon is not rising. Not yet, anyway. Something has happened up in the midlands involving Jane Grey's father."

"The Duke of Suffolk? Hasn't he had enough of a battle?"

"It's hard to tell truth from tale. Gardiner tried to make us agree to be detained, but we refused. I know Courtenay is there, in the palace. I think he has been tortured."

"And so he has sent his spies along with you?"

"It seems so." Catherine undressed her head and scratched at her scalp. "London is a great sickness, Ann. The people down by Southwark, you would scarcely believe them to be creatures of God." She rubbed her eyes with her fingers, but the image would not fade. "It makes our little villages of Havenston and Mount Grace seem a paradise of good health. Everywhere you look, it's all boils and scars and rotting flesh. They can't see. They can barely walk. Women who look as though they've never seen a basin of wash water. They smell like dead fish. And there are rats in the roads, big as puppies. And someone wants to take this away from the queen?"

"Someone always wants to take something from someone," remarked Ann.

Reg and Benjamin came in and Benjamin collapsed onto a stool to let Reg pull off his boots. The room was cold, but Catherine was too tired to stoke up the fire. She wanted to be left alone.

Reg looked them all over and withdrew. Ann followed him. Catherine let Benjamin unlace her, and she, in turn, pulled off his shirt. He dropped his breeches onto the floor and they crawled into bed. Benjamin said, "I have put our David from the stables on the watch at their chamber door. They won't set a foot outside it without feeling his cudgel."

"That's good," said Catherine. But it did not feel good at all, to have an armed watchman to guard the other watchers, within their very walls.

The sleet fired away at the window, and in the rhythm of its assault, Catherine was alert for a scuffle, blows in the hall. But nothing came, and the striking continued outside.

The morning brought thunder, and Catherine woke. The sound was far off, and she lay on her back, listening. The sky was blue, but she heard it again. She sat up, shaking Benjamin. The sun shone into the window. Another low boom. "What is that?"

"Thunder," he said, rolling away.

"It cannot be. The storm has passed. It's clear." She shook him again, harder, and a knock on her door made her heart jump.

Ann peeked in. "Do you hear that noise? What is it?"

Now Catherine was out of the bed and at the window. A stable boy was in the front courtyard, his hand shading his eyes, gazing southward.

Benjamin was aware of the day now, throwing off the covers and looking out the other window. He yanked it open, and his shirt eddied in the morning breeze. "What's that?" he shouted to the boy below.

"Don't know. Sounds like something fired off, that way. Are we under attack, Master?" The boy pointed and Benjamin leaned out to look.

"What is it?" asked Catherine.

"Get back to the stables, boy." Benjamin pulled himself inside.

Reg came in with clean breeches. "Something's happening, down south," he said.

"I hear," said Benjamin. He stepped into the clothes, leaving the night shirt on. "Get the horses."

"I'm coming with you," said Catherine.

"No. You'll stay here, where it's safe. What if there is fighting?"

"Then I will turn for home. Robbie could be out there. I'm coming or I'm following after."

"You are the most stubborn woman in the world. You will keep behind me, won't you?"

"I will. Ann, stay with the girls?"

"Yes."

Alice and Veronica were in the hall as they came through, and Veronica clutched Catherine's sleeve. "Are they soldiers? Are they attacking us? Who are those men in the dining gallery? Are we prisoners?"

"No, no, no," said Catherine. "Your father and I will find out. Stay here and wait for your tutor. Stay upstairs with Ann."

Alice held onto Catherine's waist. "Don't leave us! Not with them. They're ugly and dirty."

"I am dirty too, Daughter." Catherine eased the girl's hands away. "And those men will likely come along with us."

The sound boomed again, and they all ran downstairs. The Lord Chancellor's men were at the front door, talking to the stable boy. They turned at the footsteps, looking less threatening than they did in the dark. They were young, not any older than Diana, and the one who had hit the dog said, "What is that sound?"

"We aim to find out," said Benjamin. "Can you ride?"

He nodded, as though he were one of their own servants. The boy went for the horses, and Benjamin stepped into the dining gallery to grab a loaf of bread. He broke it and gave half to Catherine. "Have you et?" he asked the men.

They nodded. Catherine bit into the crust, and Ann handed her a cup of ale to wash it down. The melting sleet sparkled under the fresh sun. The thunder sounded again. And now, over the tops of the buildings far beyond them, rose a tendril of black smoke, twisting like a serpent into the open sky.

# Chapter Twenty

They rode all the way to London Bridge without stopping, then turned toward Blackfriars, keeping close to the river. People muttered and cursed them as they went by, but the sound had stopped. No one spoke of a rebellion. No soldiers in sight.

"It's nothing," said Benjamin. "It's vanished, like any dream."

Then the sound came again, far behind them now.

"The Tower," said Catherine, and they returned the way they had come. "What is the noise?" she asked a boy, who stood in their way, holding a small terrier in his arms, but he sniffed and would not speak. "What is it?" she asked again of a woman walking, head down, with a hen dangling by the feet from one hand.

"Ah, it's them cannons in the Tower," the woman answered, and she pointed by flapping the chicken forward. "There's been men all over the city. Aim to hit Spain from here, I reckon. They got so much lead to waste, I got a roof they could mend. A body could use some peace, in this doleful time of the year."

They finally stood outside the massive walls, but they could not see anything but a couple of monkeys in a cage beyond the moat, clinging to each other, and the bulk of the White Tower within. Its four thick spires were decorated with the pointed domes Henry VIII had placed up there to celebrate the coronation of Anne Boleyn, and they now seemed a tribute to folly, to lust, to greed, and to murder.

Catherine hated the Tower. She could feel the hum of death from its very stones. The Lord Chancellor's men wrapped themselves up and stared over the river, toward Southwark. Benjamin said, "Do you know what this noise is about?"

They looked at each other, and one of them finally said, "It's the marriage." Catherine, still gazing at the domes, thought for a moment that they meant old Henry's, and had to shake herself back into the present. The man went on. "The bishop says there's talk all over England. The queen's going to marry the Spanish king. I expect they're celebrating. They could do it with less noise, though."

He remained staring over the Thames and looked so forlorn that Catherine said, "What are your names? If you are condemned to live in our house, we might at least act as householders."

"Stephen, Madam," said the talker. He chuckled. "Like the bishop himself."

"I am Edward," said the other. He stretched a little in his saddle. "My father says it's kingly."

Catherine had to laugh. "And so it is. Tell us, is there danger?"

"I don't know," said Edward. "Nobody knows. There's hugger-mugger and whispering. There's talk of risings and fallings. Men with armies and then men without armies. I can't make sense of it. This is London. We're civilized."

"It's the marriage, I say," said Stephen. "I heard the bishop tell about it. The rebels aim to stop the marriage. They claim the Spanish are savages. She wouldn't marry the

English one and they can't abide her taking on the foreign one."

Another low boom sounded on the other side of the wall, and they watched the smoke etch the blue sky. Benjamin said, "Are they blowing up their own city for it?"

Stephen shook his head. "I'd judge they're practicing."

"A waste of ammunition and time," said Benjamin. No one on the street even looked up now, and they turned their horses' heads north, toward home, to deliver the news that was no news.

The next three days remained quiet, and Edward and Stephen accustomed themselves to the rhythm of Davies House. They were good with the horses, and liked to work with leather, so they spent their days in the stable, repairing harness while the Davies men replaced shingles blown off in the rains. They took their meals in the kitchen, and Catherine, from the door, saw Stephen fix the belt on one of Alice's old dolls. He added an extra hole and a small brass stud to hold it closed. She admired it in the window light, and he said, "Girl ought to have nice things." Catherine withdrew silently to her still room. Old Moll stumbled past the window, which was set high in the wall, holding a dirty bundle against her chest, and knelt at the side of the stable. Edward came out. Catherine stepped onto a stool and saw the man wrench the rag from Moll and open it. Moll howled and cursed. Inside was a dead cat, and Edward flung it down. Moll snatched it up and rolled it again into its rag. Edward knelt beside her and whispered, one hand on her shoulder, and the madwoman seemed comforted. She spoke back to him. Maybe he could calm her if no one else could.

But on the afternoon of January's last day, Catherine saw the two men, together, in the front courtyard, staring southward, talking. Benjamin was behind her at a table, working at the accounts from their Yorkshire properties, and she said, "They expect something."

"What?" Benjamin said. "Who?"

"Edward and Stephen. They're talking out there, just the two of them."

"Men talk. They're good workers. They don't want to be here."

"No, this isn't idle chat. They're watching for something."

Benjamin joined her. He studied the pair, and when he went outside, they stepped apart, and Catherine saw them point at the sky. She strained to see, but the day was cloudy, spitting rain again. No birds, no smoke. Ann came up from the laundry and took Benjamin's place beside her. "Are they leaving?"

Catherine shook her head.

"They're not bargaining for a new set of clothes out there."

She shook her head again.

Benjamin came back in. A line had furrowed itself between his eyebrows. "They say the streets are fuller than they should be. Men running. They seem to be headed south. I think they are telling the truth."

"Should we ride out?"

Ann said, "Have you seen the western sky? You'll be drenched in a moment."

The tutor came downstairs, pulling on his cloak. "I must flee for the day, Madam. It will burst out right over my head."

"You may stay the night, if it's convenient," said Catherine.

He considered it. Looked out the window. "That I shall, if I may," he said, and retreated back upstairs.

Benjamin said, "If he cannot ride, then we shouldn't either. Let's wait until morning."

Catherine was still watching Gardiner's men. "We can trust them?"

"As far as a man can trust another man, I suppose. I haven't caught them going through our desks or cabinets."

Edward and Stephen finally turned back, toward the stables, and Catherine could breathe again. But then, two strangers ran past their front gate. Then another. The sky split open, and in the downpour she could see no more. Benjamin and Ann were right. It was lunatic to start out anywhere in such a storm.

They ate early. Edward and Stephen continued to take their meals downstairs, and Catherine saw them slip past the dining gallery, headed up to their chamber. The girls didn't even notice them now and they worried that the dogs would be cold outside. Benjamin insisted that he would have no wet hounds stinking underfoot, but Alice produced her two favourites from the side room, perfectly dry and panting with wide grins, and he relented, but only if they would take them upstairs. They went, happy to have won the day. Benjamin said, "It won't hurt them to have a couple of watch dogs."

"I thought you trusted Edward and Stephen," said Catherine.

"I have seen no reason not to," said Benjamin. "But something is happening."

They sat up a while with Ann and Reg, watching the dark storm pelt the panes, until they could stay awake no longer. Old Moll came slipping past the doorway, headed downstairs. Edward and Stephen stayed in their chamber. The house was silent. No one knew what to say. No one said the name Robbie.

# Chapter Twenty-One

The morning rose with shouting from beyond their front wall, and Benjamin and Catherine were up and dressed by the time Gardiner's men were bringing horses around from the stable to the courtyard. "We should go and see," said Edward, standing at the front door. "The word is that they're down at the bridge."

"Who?" asked Benjamin.

"Don't know," came the answer.

"Who says it?"

"Nobody. Man in the road. Man passing by. Your woman says so."

Catherine looked outside. Old Moll was at the gate, begging from a passerby. "She's not our woman. What did she tell you?"

"That there's men at the bridge. I have said so already," said Edward.

"What else does she have to say?"

But before he could answer, Diana came down with Ann, and Catherine said, "There is news from the city. Men. It's Old Moll's word, and I can't say what that's worth, but we need to go. Stay with the girls. Be ready to remove. Ann, can you help? Pack some bags."

Ann handed Catherine a thick cloak, and she went out with Benjamin.

The streets flowed with scum: melting snow and icy puddles, mud over the horses' hooves, dead rats and sparrows, one young pig, trampled over and left to rot. Men and women shoved and ran. A boy fell face-first into the roadway before them, and Catherine started to dismount, but Benjamin grabbed her elbow and Stephen jumped down to haul him to his feet. The child bit into his saviour's wrist and stumbled away. His hat lay where he'd lain, and a woman used it for a stepping-stone to cross over. Her skirts dragged through the muck but she kept going.

New pamphlets had been nailed to the walls and posts, and Benjamin tore one loose. They sidled to a quieter spot, under a broad eave, and he scanned the paper.

"It's treason," he said. Londoners shoved past, almost knocking him to the ground. Another rumble from the south. Another spiral of dark smoke. A scrawny dog hobbled by, and Catherine saw that it was missing a hind foot. Someone would throw it to the lions at the Tower for sport if it couldn't move faster than that. Benjamin muttered something in the tone of a curse.

"Who is it?" said Catherine. "Who's written it?"

"It's a speech," he said, "or part of one. Listen. 'Forasmuch as it is now spread abroad and certainly pronounced of the Queen's determinate pleasure to marry with a stranger, we therefore write unto you, because you be our neighbors, because you be our friends, and because you be Englishmen, that you will join with us, as we will with you unto death in this behalf. We seek no harm to the queen, but better counsel and counselors. For herein lieth the health and wealth of us all. Lo now, even at hand, Spaniards already are arrived at Dover. We shall require you therefore to repair to such places as the bearers hereof shall pronounce to you, there to assemble and determine what may be best for the advancement of liberty.'"

"Who has signed such a thing?" said Catherine. "Are there Spanish at Dover for sure?"

"It's that Wyatt," said Stephen. "They've failed in Devon. They've failed in the West. The man can't see that he's doomed. This is the first I've heard of the Spanish being anywhere but in the queen's court."

"And what will they do with the queen, once they have her?" said Catherine. "Put her to work shining their buckles? Lock her up in a cage and parade her through the streets?"

"They haven't thought farther ahead than the noses on their faces," said Benjamin. Stephen and Edward were listening, sober-faced, but with eyes like a couple of spaniels.

Under the pamphlet was another, older but still clinging to the wall. The paper was sodden and torn. It was Gardiner's address to the people from the coronation day. Catherine could still see "Mary, rightful and undoubted inheritrix by the Laws of God," but the rest was blotted and faded. The new nail had left a great hole in the center of "England."

"We must get the girls out of London," she said.

But they could not turn their horses. The mob had grown thick as fleas, and they were heaved along. Someone said, "The queen is come in to speak," and the crowd surged westward, driving Benjamin and Catherine along. The earth seemed to melt and roll beneath them, and they could barely keep their footing. They were separated from Gardiner's men, and Catherine hoped they would find them again, a couple of familiar faces at least. Spies, perhaps, but spies they recognized in this storm of human bodies.

Mary was already speaking when they were flung into view of the Guildhall, and they hung back. Catherine pulled so hard on her reins that her little mare nearly sat on her haunches. But the mass of people would not part, even far enough for the animal to fall. The palfrey began to snort and paw, flinging up clods of filth, until a woman carrying an infant strapped to her chest stopped to stroke the lathered neck. She reached under the mare's damp mane and said, "Whoa there, lady. You want to hear the queen, don't ya, old gal?" The animal quieted and the woman walked on.

They could not hear the words, or see the woman herself, but Mary's voice thundered over the heads of her people, who cheered and waved their handkerchiefs. Applause rippled through, and a man shouted, "Kill the traitors! Quarter them!"

The crowd had stilled now, absorbed with the queen's speech, and Benjamin tugged on Catherine's elbow. He was backing his gelding inch by inch, and she followed his backward lead. They achieved the edge of the throng and turned. People were still coming, but less urgently now, and there were Edward and Stephen, waiting, crowded up against a house.

"I never thought I would say I was glad to see them," Catherine said. "But four through this crowd is better than two."

Benjamin said nothing.

"What does she say?" Edward asked. "Has she got them? Will they die?"

Benjamin said, "I could not hear."

"Nor I," said Catherine. "We must go home."

"The queen is alive and she's in command here. That much we know. We should go and see what the noise is," said Benjamin. "Then we can decide a course of action."

The pamphlets calling the city to rise against the queen were everywhere they looked, some hacked, some ripped. Someone had scrawled "NO TRATORS" on one, and beside it someone else had written over another "NO SPAINISH."

They rode down lanes and narrow alleys, avoiding the hordes, but here the way was even worse, the horses over their hooves in garbage and foul water. They turned a corner and almost walked onto a boy, who'd dropped his breeches and was defecating against a wall. His shoes were sunk into the mud, and he clasped the tails of his shirt in one greasy hand.

"Down to the water," said Catherine. "I cannot breathe here."

They turned south, but the stench of the Thames was little better. They were almost back at the Tower. Then something exploded ahead, and Catherine's mare shied and bucked. She almost slid off backward and clambered at the saddle to right herself. Wood and shingles splattered into the river and a woman was screaming. Smoke wafted heavenward. Benjamin had her reins, and was shouting at the palfrey.

"I'm still on," said Catherine, pushing her skirt over her ankles.

Another eruption went off, and the mare plowed up the mud, slinging clods left and right. Catherine turned her in a circle. Men rushed onto the bridge, and an entire wall fell, splintering, into the water. The windows floated away, like loose sheets of ice. The sun sparkled on them, and a man on a small barge retrieved an unbroken pane from the surface.

People charged around them, waving hoes and hammers. Catherine and Benjamin were wedged between them, and they tried to stop a couple, joined arm in arm as they marched forward. "What are they doing?" Benjamin asked, but the man shook off his hand and moved on.

They followed, Edward and Stephen behind them. A great hole gaped at the center of London Bridge, and astonished heads showed among the loose beams and broken siding, then withdrew. Someone was herding the people off. A small, spike-haired dog leapt into Thames and swam for the south bank. Their horses nipped at passing shoulders and got slaps in return, but on they went, until they saw a man near the river, standing on a makeshift platform, directing the crowd away. "There is reward for traitors who will turn again to England," he yelled, "and pardon for any who submit to the mercy of the queen."

"This is a suicide, clear as day. Who would put himself at that mercy?" muttered Benjamin, and this time he got an answer from a woman, leaning on a cane.

"My man says he knows of three who joined the rebellion down in Kent. They've run off from the rebel army down there. Say they can't bide with 'em no more."

"What army?" asked Catherine. Her feet itched to feel solid ground, but there was none. The woman, now at her side, seemed to float, the hem of her skirts swirling in the mud.

The woman shrugged and patted the mare's flank. "Some villain down there rounded them up. Have ye seen the speech?"

"We saw it," said Benjamin.

She nodded. "We all heard it. It was read out down at the ale house." She pointed a thumb over her shoulder. "The three who went off to rebel, they were there. And the host there said there's been an offer of pardon. And away go they, back to be loyal again. Say there's no profit in fighting the anointed queen, even if she does mean to marry with that Spanish."

"And is it true that they've landed at Dover?" asked Catherine. "The Spanish?"

"I heard it was the French." Another lifting of shoulders. "Haven't seen it. Wouldn't a body think they'd be here on our doorsteps by this time?"

The man on the platform still commanded, and a few had ventured close enough to tug at his jacket. Catherine wondered whether they meant to claim some reward for being there. A chunk of the bridge collapsed into the water.

"What do they mean by blowing up the bridge?" asked Benjamin.

"Make the opening wider. Keep the rebels down there with the punks, I'd wager," said the woman. "Work out their bad spirits that way."

"But who? It looks calm," said Catherine. The south bank was clotted with onlookers, but they seemed peaceful enough. The severed heads rotting on their spikes rocked gently, their empty eye sockets staring down, as if looking for their bodies. All seemed normal.

"The upstart army," said the woman. She seemed to be explaining the facts to an idiot. "They're coming. Thousands of 'em. They just don't know what they're going to find when they get here." She chuckled and limped on. Her feet found a long plank, almost buried in the liquid muck, but her weight sank it. She walked on, stepping onto another board as she went, tottering along the floating walkway. She halloed into the distance, and a man waved at her. Soon, she was lost in the mass.

"We must go home," said Catherine. "Take the girls away. We must think of our daughters' safety before anything else." But as she spoke, she was searching across the river. She was looking for the face of her son.

# Chapter Twenty-Two

Going home was as difficult as moving into the city had been. Londoners wanted to watch their bridge falling down, and the horses resented the stream of human obstacles. Benjamin and Catherine let Edward and Stephen go before them, shouldering a narrow passage through which they could nose ahead without trampling anyone.

The sky had given up its light when they finally made their own road and could step up their pace to Davies House. The courtyard was alive with servants, and Ann came running when she saw Catherine's mare. "I thought you'd been shot down," she said, as Catherine dismounted.

"They're shooting down the bridge, not the people. They've blown it in half. There are whole shops drifting in the water."

"Where is this army of rebels?" asked Reg, coming out behind her. He took Benjamin's reins, then handed them to one of the stable boys.

"Old Moll has been saying that we're overrun with traitors," said Ann. "The girls are hiding under their beds."

"We saw no one," said Catherine, "but the word is out. Mary's offered a pardon to any who will surrender."

"So they are here?" asked Ann.

"Not that we noticed," said Benjamin. The sky rumbled and they all looked southward. But it was only the grumbling heavens. "Let's get inside."

Ann went up to drag the girls out, and Benjamin said, "Edward and Stephen. Into the gallery." He went first, and sent a girl for food and wine. Reg waited at the doorway until Benjamin ordered him in.

"We can eat in the kitchen," said Stephen.

"Not until you tell us what you know."

The men sat. Edward blew his nose; Stephen examined the stubble on his jaw with one hand. "We only know what we hear," said Edward. "We're not in the bishop's circle."

"Servants have ears," said Benjamin.

"We've got no secrets but we spread no tales," countered Edward. "I've heard that a pardon was being offered. That was days back, before we came here. Didn't hear anything more of that. It was down in Kent somewhere. There was a scuffle down in Devon. One or two over in the west. That Courtenay, the one the bishop's got, he told it all. But the battle never came to anything. A little speech-making. A standard raised. No one else was supposed to be coming, that we'd heard of. I thought it was all over, truth be told. This rebellion business."

"I heard the same," said Stephen.

"And you were sent here because it was all over?" asked Benjamin.

The two men let their eyes meet for an instant. "We were sent here because of your son," Edward said. "I thought you knew that. The queen doesn't want any more trouble."

Rage badgered Catherine's mind, and she beat it back. "And where is he?"

"You are supposed to be the one who knows that," said Stephen. "We are just here to note him if he arrives, or to see if he is hiding here."

Cold meat and wine were brought in, with a platter of bread, and they fell to it. The anger still nosed Catherine, but her stomach craved the food and she tore into a heel of the closest loaf.

"Do you?" asked Stephen. "Do you know where he is? Is he with those Kentish men?"

Catherine forced down the wad and swallowed wine. "If I did, would I tell you?"

Benjamin said, "No. She does not know. Say you do not, Catherine."

"What? Or they will turn me over for a traitor? Very well, I do not know. We went to Winchester to ask for him. You heard us ask. Tell me, do you know where he is? Are you here to trap him if he comes home?"

"We have no orders for that," said Edward. "We were told to listen and to watch."

"Watch. We all know what that means," said Catherine. The fury nipped her, hard, again. "You have et our meat and slept in our beds and you have been nothing more than spies the whole time."

"You knew that when we arrived," said Stephen, a spark of offense in his voice. "We have been just what you see. You know where we came from." A little more heat flickered from his words. "Did you think we were sent here for a holiday?"

It was true, and Catherine's face burned at it. They might be spies, but they were honest spies.

"Stop," said Benjamin. "We are all watching for the boy."

"If he is coming from Kent, you can sleep sound enough," said Edward. His voice was matter-of-fact. He snagged a chunk of bread and shoved it into his mouth. "He won't get here. Nobody's coming over that bridge now, from anywhere. Leastways, not alive."

# Chapter Twenty-Three

They spent the night packing up the girls' clothing. Ann brought clean things up from the laundry, and Reg went out to make sure the palfreys were sound and ready for an early morning ride. Catherine felt the seams of her heart splitting as she threw skirts and hose and warm cloaks into chests downstairs. The servants would all hear what they were doing, but what did it matter? Edward and Stephen knew everything anyway.

She should go with them, she thought, holding up one of Diana's stockings. No, she should stay and wait for a sign of Robbie. The storm pounded the roof and Benjamin threw a few more logs onto the fire.

Catherine said, "They'll need at least three men with them. The weather will be rough."

Benjamin sat by the hearth and warmed his hands. "We should send them to Wales. If anything should happen, Overton House will be the first place Mary will have searched."

Catherine stopped in the middle of folding a shift. "Wales? They know nothing of Wales. It's wild, isn't it?"

Benjamin smiled. "Wild if you don't know it. No wilder than Yorkshire, in my experience. And I have seen both. Diana knows it, well enough. My brother will keep them."

"Lewis? You say he's a lecher."

"He is. Confirmed. But these are his nieces."

Catherine bristled. "Veronica is not his blood kin. Her home is Overton House."

"And when has she seen it last? Two years? This is her home, the only home she knows now. She's being sent away for her safety, and she is old enough to know that. Lewis is a dog, but he is not a fool. He has maids and village girls enough to keep him occupied. The house is isolated and well-fortified. They will know if anyone approaches before they are even crossed over from England."

Catherine laid the shift onto the skirts and closed the chest. She sat on it. "Should I go with them?"

Benjamin shook his head. "The girls' absence will be less conspicuous if you remain."

"The whole house will know they are gone by the middle of tomorrow."

Benjamin thought. "If Robbie is among those Kentish, you need to be here."

"To beg at the queen's feet for him, you mean."

"Exactly." Benjamin rose and began handing Catherine things from the pile on the floor. She rose and opened the chest again. Ann brought another handful of clean stockings and dumped them on top. Benjamin's fingers fumbled in the delicate cloth, and he ended up wadding the neatly rolled hose and throwing them in.

Catherine said, "She will show mercy. I know she will. She's followed God all of her life. She's risked her own life to do God's will."

"As she sees it. But you know what a crown does to a person's wits."

"Listen to Benjamin," said Ann. She looked from one to the other. "If you speak of Robbie, he's right. She's been waiting for her revenge against the reforms a long time."

Catherine nodded. She took a skirt from Benjamin's hands and shook it out, folded it and put it on top. "I have vowed my service to her. More than once. She did not condemn us when we married. Not as others did."

Ann threw up her hands and went out.

"Nor did she call you to her side," said Benjamin. "She let you toil away under the eyes of Jane Dudley and that woman of Cleves. If it hadn't been for Alice, you'd be there still. She let you work like a whipped cur for them. And what thanks did you get, good Protestant women that they were? They treated you like you'd whored yourself to one of your servants. Don't tell me you didn't earn Mary's forgiveness."

"But she gave it, I think, in the end. No one has tried to end our marriage. And there's been no talk of retribution against the sisters who haven't returned to the convents."

"What convents? The lands are gone. I haven't seen her opening her palaces to give sanctuary to the old nuns. And the priests? They have nothing now. Wives and children and no livings to support them. Is that mercy? Is that her God?"

Catherine went to the window and peered out, into the blackness. The rain had frozen into snow, and the icy pellets popped against the glass. The roads would be treacherous. Yorkshire would be worse. And no one there would be expecting the girls.

"I thought when Mary became queen, time would run backward and the women would all be free," murmured Catherine to the night. "I thought the houses would spring up again and they would run into them. But we are old and changed. And most of us are gone." She wiped her breath from the pane and wondered where they all were. The nuns from Mount Grace were mostly underground. And her own sister-in-law, her first husband's sister, disappeared into a shameful marriage. And that one, yes, to a servant. Catherine had not heard her name since the news had come that she'd given birth to a still-born son, except from the mouth of Mary Tudor. The child would have been Alice's age. Her own cousin. "I wonder what has become of Margaret."

"Who?" asked Benjamin.

"Margaret. Overton."

"That's a name that hasn't crossed your lips in almost a decade."

"I wonder if she is still in England. The queen spoke of her. She has not been forgiven."

Benjamin shook his head. "This is not the time to send anyone to look for her."

"No. I didn't mean that. But think how far she has fallen. I wonder where she could be. It could have been me, you know."

"Only if I had been your servant," said Benjamin. "She chose it."

"No one chooses a life of misery and poverty and degradation. She wagered and lost. I wagered and won." Catherine turned. "Is there God in that? I thought Mary would bring all of us women back together."

"You and Margaret? You remember the past differently than I do." He stood and pulled her into his arms. "You two were always at each other's throats. Come, tell me. Were you happy with her in your house?"

"No," Catherine admitted, "but I thought I was happy as a girl. I had Mount Grace and the convent and the other sisters. Even Margaret was a sister to me then, though a sharp-tongued one. I thought that was enough."

"And you would remember away your children and me?"

"I would not." Catherine let him kiss her mouth. Her blood still warmed at his scent, and she put her face on his chest. "Time runs only one way for us, and we must follow it."

"And so I will bow to her priests and say amen to their prayers," said Benjamin. He leaned back and touched Catherine's breastbone. "But I know that God lives here." He tapped her temple. "And here."

"She cannot mean to kill her subjects for their consciences. She hated her father for doing it, even as she knelt at his feet."

"Perhaps you are right. I hope that you are. But I will not have my daughters in the way, if the axe begins to swing. You have vowed your loyalty to the queen, and perhaps that will protect us all, but I have vowed to you, and I will keep all of our children from her if I can—even your son."

"All right. They will go to Wales. Let's finish this packing," said Catherine. She did not want to talk about whose vow might be the wiser, if Robbie returned.

# Chapter Twenty-Four

They sent a lone man ahead, riding fast with the message that the Davies daughters would come to the Lewis Davies House in Wales. Benjamin, unwilling to write out directions, chose four men who knew the way to accompany them.

Alice wailed and clung to her mother, but Diana gently unpeeled her fingers and squatted before her. "There is a field of ponies and you will dine on the finest lamb every night. They let the dogs sleep in the beds, and the mattresses are all feathers."

Alice sniffed and said, "Do they? Can I bring Fluff and Sniffles?"

"Yes. And you can almost walk to the sea with them."

"Mother, do you hear?"

"I am green with envy," said Catherine. Alice ran upstairs to tell Veronica, who was packing her combs and shoes into a special bag. "Where do you learn such things, Diana?"

Diana said, "I know that anticipation is half of joy. By the time we arrive, she'll be happy just to have her mangy old mutts with her, if they're all sitting by a friendly fire. My uncle will be good to us. He loves his family well enough. And he does love dogs."

Catherine could see in her eyes that she knew the man's nature. "Vices are best kept in the dark."

"If one must keep them at all."

Diana had an air that the queen would have loved, if the queen had ever stooped to know her. Catherine embraced her, and Diana said, "Be careful, Mother. I'll pray for you."

"And I for you," Catherine said.

Veronica held in her tears and Alice waved as they rode out, the two dogs trotting contentedly alongside her. Diana went behind the younger girls, and Catherine could hear her chattering in an unnatural, cheerful tone. Ann had wavered between wanting to go and to stay, but Benjamin finally asked her outright to remain, and she was decided. They all turned mournfully back to the house, but just then another group of riders clattered in and they were forced to attend to their visitors. Edward and Stephen were standing at the front windows. Before nightfall, Gardiner would know that the girls had left.

The visitors were two men, with a woman between. Catherine almost left them to Benjamin, but the woman pushed back her hood. It was Jane Dudley. She let herself be helped to the ground, but found her feet fast enough and came running to Catherine.

"You must go to the queen." Jane's face was red and chapped. She looked as though she'd been standing out in the cold wind.

"The queen has enough business on her mind," said Benjamin.

"That is exactly why you must go," Jane said. She took one of Benjamin's hands, and Catherine thought she might kiss it. But she wrung it until he withdrew a few steps. "My sons. That woman will murder all of my sons."

"Wherefore should she kill them?" asked Catherine. "They cannot be among these rebels. She has your sons where she wants them. You might ask God's blessing just now that they're safe."

"Safe? In the Tower? Who was ever safe in there? No, mark me, she will have their heads on platters for this. You must go and beg, before your own son is found and you are as ruint as I."

"For what?" asked Ann. "I have not heard their names mentioned at all. Jane Grey is the one I fear for, and if you hadn't married your son to her, he and his brothers would be home with you now."

"That girl." Jane Dudley spat into the slushy piles left by the Davies horses. "She is the cause of all our troubles."

"I did not hear you say so when your husband married her off to Guildford." Ann stepped up to Jane Dudley. The sky tore open above them and let a spear of light through.

"I was not in their conversation," said Jane. She turned again to Catherine. "I wasn't! They made that marriage against my will. It was my husband's doing, and he's paid dearly for it. Now she will want to kill my sons, and I have done nothing. They have done nothing. I will have no one."

"Jane," said Catherine. She hoped the words were not audible through the windows. "You know as well as I do that this is not the truth. You were almost on your knees begging him to take her."

"No! I was not!" She took Catherine's hand now. "Then you will not help me?" Jane cast her gaze about, searching for a sympathetic face. "I am almost desperate."

"If the queen summons me," said Catherine, "I will go. I will speak of your sons if she asks me about them, but I have a son of my own who is more in my thoughts just now. And he is not in the Tower. I don't know where he is."

Now Jane wrung her own hands, but half of her mouth smiled. "You think he is among the rebels. Oh, it will go badly for him if he is, and for you. You will see what it is to be a mother of unruly boys." A notion lit her up. "We could go side by side, you and I. Plead, two mothers for their sons. Mary Tudor wants a child. She will listen to unhappy mothers."

"Or she will have all of our heads along with theirs," said Benjamin. Catherine gasped, and he added, "I am only speaking in the extreme. We must not go like penitents before the sin is committed, bringing tales of treason to her ears. For all we know, she has forgotten Dudley and Overton boys alike. Catherine has always been a great friend to her, but you, Jane, you have always plagued her. And you have done it as though the disease would spread. Your very face at her throne might be the instrument that cuts off your sons' heads. I will not have Robbie's go the same way."

The light was absorbed in cloud again, and they moved toward the door. The curtain at the front window dropped, and Gardiner's men were out of sight as they entered. Benjamin said, "We aim to ride down and see what the news is today. You should go home, Jane, and keep yourself low. The less said of a Dudley right now, the better."

"Might I stay here? My house is lonely."

"No," blurted Ann. Her face flushed, and Catherine strangely wondered that she had seldom seen Ann with red cheeks. "I mean, the house is full."

Full of men, she might have said, but did not. Catherine put her arm around Jane's bony shoulders. "We are under observation," she murmured. "It isn't wise."

Jane looked up in horror, and her mouth opened, but Catherine shook her head and she remained silent. Catherine cocked her head toward the door to indicate the men inside, and Jane turned aside with her as the others returned to the house. The courtyard was empty except for Jane's men, and Catherine walked her to her horse. "My son may be a greater thorn in the queen's side than your own. Trust me, I will speak well of yours if I am called on to do it. I will not speak ill of them, not a word. But you must not speak of them at all, and you must not be seen riding in here as though you have messages to carry."

"Catherine, I am sick night and day. I ache all over. What should I do?"

Catherine foraged in her mind for some pity, but all she found was the familiar rage. "You want me to play the physician while my son is missing? Go home, Jane. Take a cup of wine and go to bed. Read your Bible and pray that the queen knows her God. That is the best receipt I can give you."

"You have always been kind to me." Jane mounted up.

"How have you heard this news of my son?" asked Catherine.

"The walls have ears," said Jane, "and eyes." She rode out without a word of farewell.

'I have been kinder than you have been to me,' thought Catherine. And yet she knew that Guildford had been a sweet boy. She sighed. Benjamin came out, ready to go, and she turned a brave face to him. "I will ride the mare," she said.

Catherine's mind was nagged with images of boys as they rode. Boys who knew no better than to follow the ambitions put into their heads by their fathers, their companions, their kings. But King Edward had been a boy himself, led by John Dudley. John Dudley, who had been good to Catherine, had paid for her freedom when she was in a prison, accused of a sin she would never have committed. Theft. The word still made her spine shiver. Those days in that cell, with Ann at her side, not knowing where their next scrap of food might come from: John had paid their way out. And then he had put his own son in the Tower by putting him on a throne.

Ambition. Catherine's imagination was tugging at its worth when Benjamin said, "God in Heaven, the whole of London is down here."

She looked up from the pit of her melancholy. People lined both banks of the Thames, hanging from windows, shouting and waving. On the south bank, the colours of hoods and hats made a bouquet of the queen's citizens, reflected by another, muddier version of themselves in the water. "He has been here!" a woman shouted when Benjamin inquired. "He has taken down the gatekeeper's house and found himself nose to nose with Queen Mary's cannon."

"Who? Who has been here?" asked Catherine, but the woman was gone. They made their way to the open bridge. Cannons were, in fact, posted, facing across the space, and the people had scrambled onto them to yell at their compatriots on the other side. Soldiers shoved at them, but as one group fell, another climbed up, and it was all they could do to keep the entire mass from falling into the river. The queen's standard flew from either end of the bridge, and passersby kissed it as they went.

"They are captured?" Benjamin asked a weary soldier. He was trying to protect the flag, but it was already streaked with mud.

"Who?" the man asked.

"The rebels. Who else?"

"Who can tell, in all this? I'd throw the whole mob in the Clink if it'd hold 'em," the man replied. "Every mother's son is down here."

"They want to show that they love their queen," offered Catherine.

"Then let 'em go to the church and kiss the new priests," the soldier said. "They want this sort of love more than I do." A woman had taken hold of a corner of the standard and pressed it to her lips, and he yanked the fabric free. "Off with ye!"

She smirked and fled, crying, "The queen has won! She has beaten the traitors!"

"Beaten," muttered the soldier, lifting the battered standard to tie it higher. "She hasn't even seen 'em, hardly."

"Is there a boy with them?" asked Catherine. "A black-haired boy, tall as me, thin?"

"A boy? Christ, woman, there's a thousand boys with 'em."

"Where?" asked Benjamin. He was scanning the triumphant crowd.

"Gone to the west, I think," said the soldier. Another man grabbed at the standard and he shouted, "Off!" Then he said, "They won't get far. She's got the whole city out to hang 'em." And then he took the beloved banner down, rolled it up, and walked away.

# Chapter Twenty-Five

They rode west, leaving the Tower with its batteries aimed over the river and the swarms of London Bridge behind. The day was a drudge, dragging dark clouds along over their heads, and snow fell half-heartedly, only to be smothered in mud.

"How does Wyatt's army aim to make headway in this?" said Benjamin.

Edward and Stephen cast longing looks over the water as they trudged past Southwark. "You may go home if you can find a way across," remarked Catherine, and the men jerked their heads toward her. "You can see that we do not have the boy."

"We will stay, if you will have us," said Edward. "We were not raised to be spies, and the job doesn't suit me."

"Nor me," added Stephen.

"Very well," said Catherine. "You had better stick close then." But she was not convinced that their loyalty would last any longer than the sunshine that poked feebly through the clouds. "Have you met Jane Dudley?" she asked.

"The mother of that boy who married Jane Grey?" Edward smiled, an evil slit across his face. "I know of her.

Going to get all her sons killed, that woman. Never laid eyes on her."

Catherine gnawed the inside of her cheek, studying him. He seemed to be telling the truth.

The word came down the bank that the bridges were all being opened or broken down, and even from where they stood, Benjamin and Catherine could see the smoke roiling down the river. A cry went up and was echoed along that the queen was calling for men to join with her forces to find the traitor Wyatt, to round up his rebels. Men shouted and ran, this way and that, and Benjamin stopped one as he slipped alongside the horse.

"What is it?" he asked. "Are the queen's forces coming?"

"And all of London with them," the man said. "The Wyatt is declared a traitor. We're goin' to sign up for the queen's troops. There's money in it; be sure of that." The man ran off, into the wave of men like him, surging vaguely westward. A few ragged flags fluttered above them.

Catherine was surrounded and her mare's hooves were mired. She sat back and crossed her hands, gazing at the chaos. She scanned the river, a mess of small boats, boards, a few discarded hose, and one dead dog, spinning unnoticed down the middle of the stream. On the other side, a wagon, its wheel snapped and broken, lay on its side. A small cannon of some kind she did not recognize had capsized into the mud, and a couple of women picked at it, as though they might draw something useful for their kitchens from it. A mule, still attached by a rope to the tongue of the wagon, sat and brayed tunelessly.

"Look there," Catherine said to Benjamin. "Why would they leave their weapons behind?"

"I can't see how something that small will win the city," Benjamin said. "If they have a devil's chance with S. Peter, they had better have bigger wagons than that."

They were not even in sight of Blackfriars by the time night was falling, and they finally gave up. Catherine was almost dead in her saddle, and the sky was too dark to see even the people pushing past her feet. If Robbie had been at her side, she might not have known him. The alehouses overflowed with drunkards clamouring for Wyatt's head, and they passed on by, though Catherine's mouth ached for a cup of something. They located a side road that was nearly deserted and plodded through the dung and water holes until they found their way back to the main road to Davies House. It would be nearing midnight before their feet were on their own floor.

Catherine's head swam with exhaustion by the time they made it home. She kept dropping off in the saddle, almost dreaming, until she began to fall forward and jerked awake. When she saw the familiar gate, her head cleared for a moment, but even with the horses put to stable and their muddy clothes removed, no one's mood was the brighter. A yawning manservant stoked the fireplace in the dining gallery, and Ann and Reg, still awake and worrying over a jug of ale, sat with them at table to listen as they ate, but the story of it was no more uplifting than the experience of it had been.

"Mud and more mud," Benjamin repeated. "They're mad to attack London in this weather. The Tower is all guns and men. The bridges are impassable. What do they think they will do, take her prisoner in her own palace?"

Ann waited until Catherine had finished her plate and drunk down three glasses of ale. Then she asked, "Is there any sign of Robbie?"

Catherine shook her head. "No sign and not likely to be. It's like the hell of your worst dreams. No one seems to know what is happening or who is on which side. I don't like to think how many Londoners have trampled their neighbors underfoot in the name of peace. And at this time of the year. They should be on their knees, repenting, not running through the streets. They should sit by their fires and wait for the spring."

Edward and Stephen excused themselves for the night, and Ann watched them go. "What of those two?"

"They are hired eyes," said Catherine, "and they know it. I cannot find it in my heart to hate them."

"That doesn't mean you should trust them," said Ann.

"Nor take them along with you," said Reg. "I would not want them in my company if I happened upon the boy."

"No," said Benjamin. "Tomorrow, they stay here."

"Tomorrow?" said Ann. "You're going back out?"

"We've no choice," said Benjamin. "The rebels are said to be moving west. Their numbers will shrink as they go, I know they will. And when Robbie falls off from them, I will be there to catch him."

"If he falls off," said Ann.

"That is what I meant to say," said Benjamin. "I think he is caught up against his better judgment and he will see more clearly as the day grows darker for them."

Catherine went to the window. "Can it grow darker than this?"

No one answered. But in her mind, Catherine saw that soaked, forgotten dog, spinning in the Thames, and knew what they all were thinking.

# Chapter Twenty-Six

Someone was slapping against their front wall the next morning, and Catherine awoke to the feeling that her face was being struck with a wet clout. Then the stable boys ran into the courtyard, and from the window she saw them, shouting at the strangers to move on. She opened the latch and called down, "Who is it?"

They all looked up, as though God had spoken to them through the clouds. Catherine never called out from the upper windows, hardly raised her voice to them at all, and they froze beneath the uncovered head of their mistress. Her hair was down, and she realized it had tumbled over her shoulders and hung outside. She twisted it in one hand and held it back and said again, more softly, "Who is it?"

"It's, ah, it's a man plastering our walls with pamphlets," said one of the boys. The others still stood, their mouths gaped, unable to utter a word.

"Bring them inside," Catherine said, and shut the window.

Benjamin leaned on the pillows, his hands crossed behind his head. "So I have married a fishwife after all." He grinned, for the first time in weeks, and Catherine climbed in beside him.

"The whole city's come undone. I'm not going to stand about picking at my hood while they burn us out." Then she pictured herself as the servants had seen her. "I am turning common indeed. Who can ride through the mud every day and not feel herself drawn downward?" She put her face against Benjamin's chest and breathed in his scent. Her eyes ached. "I miss the girls. Will they be safe? The way is so long."

"They are in good company," said Benjamin. He stroked her back with his forefinger. "The house is quiet. But we will send for them as soon as all this nonsense is past. It won't be long. It cannot be."

Catherine's muscles unwound under his touch, and the pressure of tears receded. She let her breathing fall into the rhythm of his heartbeat. "And I will become a fishwife, shouting at the servants from the windows."

"Shout from the chimney-tops if it pleases you," Benjamin said. "If we can have a woman for our king, I can have Boudicca for a wife. I will have a suit of armour made for you."

"Don't tease." Catherine's face burned, but he ruffled her hair and then she smiled. "A skirt of iron might do me nicely, but all of this sleet and mud will rust it."

"A body can scarcely move through the streets in our everyday woolens."

They rose together, and stood for a moment, both listening to the silence. "The girls will be far out in the country by now." She made herself add, "I'm glad for it," thinking to hear it might make it true.

"But I miss their voices," said Benjamin, and Catherine was almost crushed under the weight of her sorrow again.

Ann knocked and peeked in. "The men have a fresh pair of rides ready for you. Your spies are already breaking their fast downstairs. Please let me be the one to order them back to their rooms."

Benjamin handed her his little side dagger. "Do you want arms?"

Ann showed her fists. "I have arms given to me at birth. These will do me."

"When you are a crone, you will beat the children with your cane," said Benjamin.

"Only the ones who spy," said Ann, withdrawing.

Reg was down by the front fire, breaking the dried mud from Benjamin's heavy boots onto a rug, and he set them out for assessment. "The best I can do," he concluded. The leather was stiff and discoloured, but the chunks had all been knocked off. He began rubbing the surface with lard.

"They will only get ruint again," said Benjamin.

Gardiner's men were still at table, arguing with Ann. She had taken up their plates, and Edward clung to his cup as she tried to take it from him. "We're needed," he was saying when Catherine and Benjamin entered. "Aren't we needed?" he said to Benjamin. "The ways are crowded. There is danger."

"The more reason for you to stay. You will stay. Reg will come with us today."

Ann lifted one brow in triumph, and Edward released the cup. He and Stephen muttered something about being prisoners wherever they went and slunk off. A kitchen maid came in and Ann ordered her to remove the men's remainders.

"We will fail again," said Catherine. The day was dark already. A sheaf of papers lay on the table—the pamphlets from the front wall—and she held one to the window. "She is offering land."

"The queen?" asked Ann.

Catherine nodded. Benjamin had taken up another of the papers. They were all alike. He whistled. "For the person of Wyatt. A hundred pounds per year to anyone who brings him in."

"What?" asked Reg. He was at the door with the boots dangling from one hand.

"A parcel of land, worth a hundred pounds per year," said Catherine. "For anyone who brings in Wyatt."

"Half of London will sign on to that task," said Reg.

"They have done so already," said Benjamin. "Catholics and Protestants at each other's throats over pieces of land. Do we need more of that?"

Catherine said nothing. They would chop her son in half to get at Wyatt. And he would stand bravely, condemning Pope and queen as they did it, as her mother had stood and let a man stick a blade in her gut to protect the convent and the nuns. People had called her a tyrant. A fool. And they would call her son a traitor and a heretic.

And Catherine? She had knelt for Henry VIII. And for the boy king, Edward. For Mary Tudor. And for the girl Elizabeth. She had been rewarded with her life. But what good was it to have a living heart, beating her to a slow death with its refrain of coward, coward, coward? It hurt her even now, battering her chest.

"We should ride," she said.

"I will come," said Ann. "Reg and I can divide from you and Benjamin and we can search the faster."

"Who will watch the bishop's men?" asked Benjamin.

"Let them watch themselves," said Ann. "If they follow, we will spy them out as fast as they spy on us. Let them go home if they are weary of us."

"They cannot go home," said Catherine. "The bridges are gone."

But if Gardiner's men were behind them that morning, they kept themselves out of sight. Catherine saw nothing but hordes of Londoners, armed with kitchen knives and pokers from their hearths. We look like savages, she thought, until they approached the river and she saw the cannon and mounted men. The poorer folk, on foot, dragged themselves westward through mud. They clutched the pamphlets, and they stopped now and then to peer at the words they probably couldn't read and compare them to the sheets in their neighbors' hands. Men on horses cursed and drove them on.

The entire tide of people surged toward Blackfriars, and there was no breaking off from the crowd. Ann said they should turn north and try Fleet Street, but the crowd was too dense and she almost fell as she leaned to shout at Catherine and Benjamin. Broken wagon wheels and pieces of doors littered the way, and the board walkways were all sunken beyond sight. Catherine's mare shied when her hoof stuck in a cleft between the shattered staves of a discarded slop bucket, and Catherine was forced to wait while she worked it out herself, for there was nowhere to dismount.

A cheer rumbled toward them, and Benjamin stretched in his stirrups to find its source. "Have they got him?" asked Reg, but Benjamin shook his head.

"I cannot see. Whatever it is, they're triumphing."

"Move on," said Catherine, nudging Benjamin's gelding with her toe. "We must."

But the noise was coming their way, and Benjamin motioned them back with his arm as the people came headlong toward them. Eggs flew and splattered. Rotten apples. A window opened, and a woman dumped a chamber pot onto the heads below. A few groans went up, but the applause was louder. A man on horseback beat at the people with his whip. And still they came on.

One man threw a handful of muck from the ground and ran toward them, passing close enough for Reg to grab his shoulder. "What is the uproar?" Benjamin asked.

"Deserters from the rebel army. They've caught a mess of them, sick as dogs and loose-tongued as your lady's maid. They'll tell the queen where that traitor is." He whooped and ran on, flinging more mud as he went.

"Don't move," said Ann, putting out her hand. "We will see them as they come by."

The captured men were fewer than a dozen, shivering and whey-faced. They had lost their coats, or had had them taken away. Their heads were down, and the horseman with the whip kept the people from hauling them bodily off. Other armed men walked behind the wretches, elbowing the Londoners back.

"Where do you take them?" Benjamin shouted.

The horseman nodded at Benjamin. "To the Tower." He grinned. "For their safe-keeping."

They shuffled on. But the last of them lifted his eyes as he went, and Ann took hold of Catherine's arm. "I know that one," she said.

# Chapter Twenty-Seven

The deserters had already been herded by before Catherine could make Benjamin understand. People shoved and shouted, and Benjamin kept saying "No, he's not among them" to Catherine's frantic dragging at his arm. She finally withdrew into a side lane and he was forced to follow. Ann waited until they were gathered together under a dripping overhang and repeated herself.

"I know one of them. He was with Robbie when he came from Kent. That first day before Christmas. I swear he was."

But it was too late. The captives were gone, and there was no catching up to them. The day was waning fast, the west a dark spillage gathering over the gloom of the dirty river and the furious faces of the Londoners. It was deep midwinter, outside and in, and Catherine's breastbone, tightened by the cold, made her shiver. "We would have seen him. It means he is still with Wyatt."

Ann said, "We know where some of the deserters are, but are they all together?"

"I don't know," wailed Catherine. "He's not with them. That's all I know." She saw her son in every lanky boy who rushed by, and then she saw him in her mind's eye, swinging from a rope. She saw the child he had been, had always seen the child inside the young man, even when he spat and cursed her, had seen the youth, the babe behind the face of the angry boy, as though the fierceness of his expressions had been burned onto him like a scar from the outside. But the infant's face, the face he'd worn as she held him in her arms, remained beneath it. And she had been forced to let him go, wearing that anger for anyone to see.

"I know who can get you inside to find out," said Ann. Her hand was cool on Catherine's hot skin. "Listen to me. Those men. Edward and Stephen. They can invoke Gardiner. That'll get you in to speak to the traitors. You can do it in the name of the queen."

"If they are still at the house," said Reg.

Catherine turned her mare around. "Home," she said. "Now."

They worked their way up narrow lanes, ducking the swill slopped from upper windows. The rain fell, thickened with snow, and Catherine's vision warped in her hunger and fatigue until she could barely distinguish Ann from Reg. She imagined that Benjamin was Robbie, then, weirdly, he became her first husband William for a moment, and she saw the ghost of her young self, riding through a summer night toward a convent that the king had already seized. She shook herself alert and plodded on.

The Lord Chancellor's men were lounging at their ease by the fire when they all fell through the front door of Davies House, soaked to the bone and too tired even to ask the maid for a cup of wine. But drink was brought anyway, and they stumbled into the dining gallery, where one of their men squatted with an armful of split logs, building up the fire.

"Have you won the day?" asked Edward. He did not rise but shifted in the chair, Benjamin's chair, and set his clean-shod heels on the hearth.

Benjamin took another seat without a word of complaint and Reg sat beside him. The serving man at the fire came to remove their sodden boots, and Stephen stood to offer Benjamin his place, closer to the flames.

"Sit, man. I cannot move," said Benjamin.

Stephen said, "The ladies will have their deaths from the cold." He went, like a member of the household, and Catherine heard him call for the maids.

Three girls scampered in, and Stephen directed them. "Take your mistress and her lady upstairs. They are well-nigh exhausted from the snow."

Catherine felt herself lifted, and she leaned on the arm of the big old laundress, but she couldn't remember her name. "Agnes?" she said, but it wasn't Agnes. Agnes was dead and gone to her tomb, how many years now was it, and the woman said, "Come with me, Lady Catherine."

She was stripped and laid in her bed, and Ann crawled in beside her, wearing a dry shift. The linen was clean and smelt like clouds and sunlight, and Catherine rolled over and put her head on Ann's shoulder. She wept, and Ann stroked her hair.

"We will find him," Ann murmured. "Sleep now."

But in her dreams the Tower walls had somehow grown around her own house, and she was walking out, into a spring day, to find that she was imprisoned, that her front courtyard held a scaffold, and on it stood a line of boys she did not know. The hangman appraised her with beady eyes, and the boys began to call to her, "Mother, Mother," but she did not recognize their faces and could not say who they were. The nooses were fitted over their heads and they continued to cry out. She reached for them and reached for them.

She woke in the cold room. Ann was deep under the heavy covers, and Catherine listened to her steady breath.

She could almost foretell, after all the years, when Ann would sigh or grumble in her sleep and turn over, taking the warm blanket with her. She touched her own face in the dark, searching for the furrows that would remind her of her age, but her skin felt smooth as a girl's in the night, and they were young again, just beginning to try themselves against the world. She could have gotten nowhere at all without Ann, who had held the children when they cried, who had corrected their manners, who had corrected Catherine herself.

Ann grunted and shifted, and Catherine almost laughed. The covers went, and she hauled them back. She closed her eyes and slept again, until dawn.

# Chapter Twenty-Eight

Benjamin was sitting on the edge of the bed when Catherine opened her eyes again. He said, "My place has been usurped," and Ann woke at the words and stretched.

"My bed is softer than yours, anyway," Ann said. "And my room is warmer."

"That I grant you," said Benjamin. Ann and Reg had the room over the bigger of the kitchen hearths, and they almost never needed a fire. "But your husband is a louder sleeping partner than my wife."

Ann laughed. "I have thought I might fashion a night-muzzle for him, but I can't find a piece of leather big enough for his nose."

"My ears are plenty big enough, as well," said Reg. He was standing in the doorway. He looked pasty and tired. He rubbed his face as though his head ached. But he smiled.

Catherine knew the play was for her, and she lay in the pleasure of it as long as she could. But the sun shone into the window, and she said, "Have you spoken to Stephen and Edward about the prisoners?"

"Not yet," said Benjamin. "I could barely keep my thoughts straight last night. Get dressed and we'll break our fast with them."

That was enough to raise them up and into the dry clothing the maids had brought, and they met the men downstairs. The two spies were already at table, and they both looked up, sparks of alarm in their eyes, as the four came in together.

Catherine sat across from Stephen. "We saw deserters yesterday, a dozen of them."

The men glanced at each other. "Was your son with them?"

"No. But Ann recognized one of them. The queen's men had them in hand. They've taken them to the Tower."

Stephen nodded. Edward did not move.

"He was here, before Christmas," said Ann. "With Robbie. I don't know his name."

"And they are taken," said Edward. "So that's an end to them."

"They may know where my son is. They may know where Wyatt is," said Catherine.

Edward said, "If they know, the queen's men will squeeze it from them."

"But I want to know about Robbie. And you want to know. You are Gardiner's men; they will allow you in."

Edward's face screwed in on itself. "Oh, I see how it is. Now you want us along with you. Now we are your dear friends."

Catherine said, "I have been harsh. And you have done your duty to the bishop. We all see the lay of the land plainly enough. Let us call a truce between us and go as allies."

Stephen said, "The lady talks sense. There's gain for us all in this, if we work as one."

"He is my son," said Catherine. "You cannot ask me to hate him. You cannot think a mother would turn her own son over to the law willingly."

Edward said, "I know mothers who would sell their sons into service with barely a look back."

"I am not such a mother," said Catherine. She wondered what sort of house Edward had come from.

Edward rotated his cup, seeming to study the engravings upon it. It left a smear on the table, and he smudged the wood dry with his forefinger. "I see that you are not."

Stephen said, "I will go with you. Perhaps we can gain a traitor and win some favour for your boy. It would be well for us all."

A maid brought in a platter of bread and set it between them. Edward said, "I will go."

They dispatched the food and rode out at a fast trot under a cold-eyed sun. The fury had blown westward, and though men still walked up and down the city, they arrived at the bridge before midday, unharried. The bridge was manned, but the watchmen were watching no one, and the Tower was almost deserted, save for the gatekeepers and a couple of drunkards who sat in the mud and sang a song about King Arthur. Edward and Stephen wore the Lord Chancellor's livery and sounded a note of authority as they demanded entrance, but the keeper hesitated, trying to judge the others, who carried food and clothing for a prisoner whose name they didn't know. The song, now swelling into its verses on Guinevere and Launcelot, overwhelmed him and he let them inside.

The last time Catherine had been inside these walls had been the execution day of the Howard queen. It had been cold that day, as well, and she had been carrying Alice, barely a sprouted seed inside her. She'd been sick with it, and she could still smell the blood that tainted the air that day. Her stomach turned over at the memory, and she leaned against Benjamin. "No more killing," she murmured.

"They won't be killed," said the guard leading them across the green, which was in fact dun-coloured. The crispy grass crackled under their feet, and when they walked into the shadow of the White Tower, keeping watch at the dead center of the field, the ground was frozen hard as any stone.

"What will become of the deserters?" asked Catherine.

"Depends on what they have to say." The guard led them into another of the buildings that lined the perimeter and up a narrow set of slick steps. The air was frosty and damp. Catherine breathed through her mouth to strain out the scent of rotten flesh and excrement. He stopped in a hallway and raised his arms at the doors. "Which one do you want?"

"The tall one," said Ann. "He has brown hair, hanging to here." She chopped at her neck.

"Don't talk of hanging inside these walls," said the guard. "Makes 'em howl."

"He's thin," said Ann. "A man of twenty-five years or thereabouts."

"Well. That's about all of 'em," the guard said. "Have yourself a look and pick out the one you like. Can't take him home with you though."

Ann's hand shook as she placed it on the barred window of the first cell and peered in. She shook her head and backed away, wiping her fingers on her skirt. Catherine knew she was recalling their days in the city gaol, accused of that theft that had never occurred. But that was long ago, in the days of King Henry, Catherine reminded herself. The days of tyranny and of heresy. The world was restored now to its order, to its first God. It would be well, she told herself. All would be well. She let her eyes, now adjusted to the gloom, scan the stained stones, the filthy buckets and manacles tossed into corners. It looked sadly like the same world they had always known.

Ann looked into another cell and said, "No."

Reg moved to her side. He tottered a little as he walked, and his hair, when he pulled off his hat, was sweat-soaked. He put his arm around Ann's shoulders and they moved to the third cell.

"You," said Ann. "You there. I know you." She looked over her shoulder. "This is the one."

"I will have to be right here while you talk to him," said the guard. "That's the rule."

"Very well," said Catherine.

The cell was low but broad, and the man sat on a stool in the corner, watching them. His lips were blue with the cold, and Catherine offered a blanket. The man wrapped himself, and Benjamin set down a bundle of bread and cheese. He eyed it for a few seconds, then fell to, ripping the loaf with his teeth and shoving the cheese in before he'd chewed the first bite. They poured ale for him, and he washed it down. He sat, rocking, for a few seconds, then turned and vomited the whole mass in the corner.

Ann had a clout in her pocket, and she knelt beside him to wipe his mouth. The man gazed up at her and said, "Christ, I'm cold. I've never been so cold. I'm cold clear through my guts."

Catherine walked closer. He had a fever in him, that was clear, but no pustules or dark swellings. "How long have you been thus?"

"It started when we tried to cross at Southwark. We were out in the snow all night." He slopped down a swallow of ale and mopped his chin with his hand. "He made us take down a whole wall, right by the gatehouse. Took us most of the night to get it done." The man had begun to tremble violently, and Catherine took the other blanket from Benjamin and said, "Wrap your legs and feet. The stones are like ice."

He obeyed, and when he was swaddled, he began again. "Almost until dawn it took us. We went in through a window into the gatehouse. And what do we find? The gatekeeper himself and his whole family. It's his lodge we're in, and our man Wyatt says for them to stay quiet if they mean to stay alive."

"Did you kill them?" whispered Catherine.

"No, no. No murder. Not there." The man laughed, and his foul breath almost staggered Catherine. He coughed and spat a bloody wad onto the floor. "But the bridge was open and there was no crossing. All through the dark in the snow, and me already feeling the winter in my bones before we made Southwark, and we find a hole where the bridge ought to be." He chuckled again, then wept a little and reached for the cup. "All night and the bridge is gone. And what does the man say? 'Move on, men.' And our wagons up to the beds in the mire and the guns wetter than Satan's arse and pits full of water everywhere I step, and the snow turning to rain. And then we hear that there's pardons for those that turn themselves in, and us headed to Kingston. I say to myself it's enough, and me and some others, we ran. There was a barge still going, thank God, and we took it in the early morning, before anyone could see. But I'm gone already, I feel it in my belly. Too long out there. There's sickness everywhere among them."

"Your innards are frozen," said Catherine. "You need sleep and a warm bed."

"The only bed for me is the coldest one a man knows." He looked into Catherine's face. "These blankets feel good."

"We will bring more if we're allowed," said Benjamin, and the man nodded his gratitude.

"Do you know aught of a Robbie Overton? Robert Overton?" said Catherine.

"Robert? Overton? Yes, Robert." Now recognition cleared the man's eyes. He reached out and put one finger on Catherine's cheek. "You. You're his mother. I have slept in your very house."

"That you have. But we have no word of Robbie."

The man shook his head. "Nor do I. He was with Wyatt, down in Kent. Whipped up and shouting about the foreign marriage. He's wild in his hatred of the Roman church. But I lost sight of him when we moved. The last I saw him was Dartford. But the men are here and there, and I was sick. Sick when we made Southwark already. All night in the snow and no bridge to cross. It makes a man wonder whose side God is on. Not on ours, I'll bet my right arm."

The guard entered. "That's time enough." He gazed on the prisoner with something like pity, but he closed the door behind them anyway, leaving the wretch shivering in his borrowed blanket.

Back in the hallway, the guard said, "They'll be let free in a fortnight or so. Long enough for the queen to get a noose on Wyatt's neck. These ones are the wise ones."

"That man won't live long enough to be freed," said Catherine. "He ought to be let go now."

The guard shrugged off his part in it all. "Not for me to say. He might recover. Some do. Them that're still out there are in the worser shape. They ought to follow the example of these ones and save themselves. Did you hear what you wanted to hear?"

"No," said Catherine. She turned to Edward and Stephen, who were watching the prisoner through the cell window.

Edward said, "I heard nothing that would interest our master."

"Nor I," said Stephen. "But, Lady, if your son is still with Wyatt, he has a greater enemy than any bishop in England."

# Chapter Twenty-Nine

The guard led them back down the grim stairs, and Catherine wondered how many feet had slid along these worn stones, slipping downward toward the scaffold or the block. As they stepped out and cringed under the bright eye of the sun, someone scratched at a pane above them. Catherine shielded her eyes and gazed upward, but the glare claimed the window. "Guildford," she said.

"It's just one of the deserters," said the guard, "wanting a cushion for his skinny arse, I expect. Better off here than they were with the Wyatt. Ought to count themselves lucky."

"But Guildford Dudley," said Catherine, "and the Lady Jane. Where are they?"

The guard heaved a player's sigh and flopped his arm on the air. "That way. She's over there. You can't see either one of 'em. But it's a wonder you can't hear him crying."

"He weeps?"

"Like a babe in arms," said the guard. "The lady's got more steel in her, young as she is."

"Might we not see him?" asked Catherine. Benjamin shook his head, but she persisted. "For just a mere moment?"

"Oh, no, Lady. Those two cannot be disturbed. Must not be disturbed at all. No. They have all the business they can manage, getting their souls prepared."

"But they will be released, won't they? With the deserters? They must be just as penitent. They could perhaps use a word of comfort."

The guard stretched his neck and harrowed the skin beneath his beard with four fingers. "Why are you so keen to speak with them?"

Again Benjamin shook his head, and Catherine said, "I knew him once, for a while. When he was just a little boy. I knew his mother. We served the Lady Anne of Cleves together. That is all."

"Mm. The mother. She's been here. The woman acts as though there's something inside her, trying to eat its way out. The boy could use a friendly face, but not hers. I expect he's praying, crying and praying. That's better for him than trying to be King of England."

"But they are children," said Catherine, "almost."

"Children or not, makes no difference here. They're the pups of traitors. His father, and now hers. They'll catch the old man, sure as you stand on two feet. There's the loyal and the disloyal in here, and that's all. And then, at the end, there's the weepers and the no-weepers. He's a weeper."

"He does not want to go, not at his age," said Catherine.

The guard settled his beard over his breast as neatly as he could and looked at Catherine. "None of us wants to go." He finger-combed the tattered strands of hair and patted himself on the chest.

"Catherine, come," said Benjamin, taking her arm. They turned toward the western gate, Catherine pulling Ann, whose eyes had been fixed, all the while, on the spot where the Howard queen had lost her head. But before they took three steps, Reg's legs buckled.

Benjamin bent beside him. "What is it, Reg?"

"Forgive me, sir," said Reg. "I am sick."

The guard backed off, covering his face and pointing toward the gate, and Stephen caught up Reg's left arm while Benjamin took the right. They hauled him to the horses, and the three men, Edward at Reg's legs, managed to throw him onto his horse. Ann took the reins, asking, "Where do you hurt?" but Reg gave no reply.

They could not ride as quickly as they wanted to. The sun was giving off a little heat, and the way was now pocked with water-holes and sloughs of mud. Reg groaned and bent his head to his gelding's mane. Catherine wished she had not given away the second blanket. He was dry-white as old linen, his cheekbone resting on the heavy mane, and trembling. Ann kept her right hand on his shoulder and murmured to him, but he did not look at her. Before they had gone half a mile, he began to cough, but nothing came of it. He hacked, then he wheezed, a parched sound that clearly pained him. Catherine rode up on his right and helped Ann to keep him in the saddle as they made their way through the pitted, twisted city.

Benjamin himself carried Reg over one shoulder, into the house and up to his chamber, while Catherine and Ann ran to the still room. The maids were at their dinner of soup and bread, and Catherine stirred a draught of hot wine and cinnamon with her own shaking hands. She scarcely ever used the spice, but she had read that Hildegard of Bingen had praised its properties. She had nothing else to hand. She cursed the winter as she broke the bark apart.

"What is it?" said Ann. "What ails him?"

"He looked unwell this morning," said Catherine, "but I thought it was weariness. The cold may have gotten into his lungs. This stinking, filthy city is bad for anyone's health. It may be just a common fever. He's strong, Ann. He brings up no phlegm or dark matter. Did you hear how dry his cough is?"

"Is that good or bad?" Ann wound a handful of rushes that the girls had left for making mats, into a skein around her hands, and they cracked. She crushed them and scattered them at her feet.

"I don't know. We need to warm him up and make him drink." The city had few markets for fresh herbs and spices. Here, at the center of England, she thought, a woman had to make do with the musty wares of the merchants. She missed her great Yorkshire gardens, but the girls always wanted to be here, among the crowds and the shops. She wondered, for a moment, how they were faring in Wales.

She lugged the pot to the table to cool, and Ann fetched a pitcher and cup. The maids sniffed at the concoction, and Catherine told them to put a spoon through it now and then. Upstairs, Reg lay under a pile of blankets, but still he trembled. Benjamin and a servant were working at the fire in the hearth, and the man was sent for another load of wood. Catherine put her palm on the sick man's cheek. Moist and cold. She said, "Bring me a taper," and Benjamin lit one in the hearth flames and held it out. Reg's skin was smooth, and Ann pulled down the coverings to expose his chest. No pustules or swellings or blisters here, either, but Catherine said, "By your leave, Ann," and put her ear to Reg's breast. The heart pulsed, but the beat was shallow and rapid, and she could hear a sound like paper being torn when he breathed inward. She said, "Reg? Do you hear my voice?"

He said nothing.

"You speak to him, Ann."

"Husband, look at me," ordered Ann, and he drooped his head to one side and opened his eyes.

"Ann, I burn," he said. "No, methinks I'm cold."

"I know," she said, pushing back his hair. She lifted her hand to Catherine to show the sweat-sheen left on her palm. "Can you drink?"

"No," he said, but Ann put the cup to his lips anyway and dribbled the wine in. He licked at it and shook his head.

"It's medicine," said Ann. "Catherine has made it. You must drink."

He opened his mouth and she let the liquid trickle in again. He swallowed, and Catherine listened at his chest as he did so. No change. He said, "No more, please, Ann. Not now. Let me sleep."

"I will stay with him," said Benjamin. "It is my doing that he was out in the rain and snow. Ann, you bed with Catherine. I will call you if he wakes."

"I'm his wife," said Ann. "It's fitter than I tend him."

"We can sleep in the next room, Benjamin," said Catherine. "I will have the door unbolted between."

Benjamin looked at his man. "Very well. But I will not forgive myself if he does not heal."

Catherine did not remind him that it was her son who had been the object of their search.

# CHAPTER THIRTY

Catherine woke the next morning to a day that seemed darker than any Yuletide evening. The sky refused to brighten, and the clouds seemed to claw at the very stones of their courtyard wall. She could hear Ann, already awake in the next room, talking to Reg, and she dressed in the gloom and left Benjamin sleeping, to join her friends.

A boy came in, carrying wood, and said, "There's word that the rebels mean to cross over west of the city, at Kingston." He let the logs fall onto the hearth, and Ann shushed him. But Reg was awake, too, and he struggled to sit up.

"We must ride," he said, but a cough capsized him, and he fell back onto the pillows.

"You will go nowhere today," said Ann. "I don't care if they are at S. Paul's."

Catherine agreed. "You should not even try to stand." She showed the boy how to arrange the kindling beneath the larger pieces. "You must let the fire breathe. It needs air, like your body." She stood and brushed her hands clean. "The day is damp and it will sink that cough right into your belly. You must stay down."

Benjamin opened the connecting door. He was still wearing his nightshirt. "I will go," he said. "Listen to the women, Reg. I can find another right hand for today."

"I can do it, sir," said the boy. He barely came to Catherine's shoulder, but he was sturdy and clear-eyed. "I can ride with you. Take me."

Benjamin looked the boy up and down. "What's your name?"

"Arthur Huff, sir. I'm Jack Huff's kinsman, from your country house. I'm his cousin."

Benjamin laughed. "Well, then. You've a great pedigree. Any kinsman of old Jack can ride by my side. He won't take your place, Reg, but he'll be company for me." He trained a serious eye on the boy. "We've got two shadows riding with us, Arthur. You're not to be too friendly with them."

"I've seen 'em," said Arthur, screwing his face into a sober match to his master's. "They're rat-eyed, if you ask me. They'll be no friends of mine."

"Then we're a party," said Benjamin. He bent over the bed and peered at Reg. "You say your prayers, man, and drink whatever foul thing my wife puts to you, do you hear?"

Reg closed his eyes. "As you command. Ride with care, sir."

Catherine followed her husband back to their chamber to help him dress. "The storm sits almost on our heads," she said. "The boy said that Wyatt is heading for Kingston. You cannot go that far."

"I won't. I mean to scour the jails for deserters," said Benjamin. "If Robbie has the sense of a wren, he'll leave that pack. They can't put them all in the Tower." He filled a purse with coins and stuffed it into his pocket. "If I find him, I'll buy his freedom."

Catherine walked him down and stood at the front door as Arthur brought around the horses. The boy was fairly dancing at the prospect of a prisoner hunt, and in the lowering fog, he looked like some sprite, come to cast a spell on their house. Edward and Stephen dragged their feet at the threatening weather, but they went at Benjamin's word. They all disappeared into the ghostly air before they were fully out the gate, and the clouds closed around the courtyard once more.

The house was cold, dark, and quiet. Catherine sat by the front window watching the fog swirl and thin, drawing itself back into the sky, and imagining what her daughters were doing, and whether they rode in rain or sunshine. Benjamin's brother would be their family for a while. Her heart skidded a little. Her daughters were intelligent and well-tutored, but they had never been sent from their home before, not without one of their parents. She set her palm against the pane and let the heat of her blood steam a print onto the glass. Ann came in and sat beside her. Catherine said, "Should we have gone with them to Wales?"

"I don't know," said Ann. She wiped the window clean of Catherine's sweat. "You'll not summon him that way." She took up Catherine's hand in her own. "You could not go without knowing where Robbie is. You have made the best choice there was to be made." She sat silent for a minute. "He has had a hard time of it, by my troth. I recall when he was just a little thing. He was the sweetest boy I have ever known. All he wanted was to be loved as other boys are loved."

Catherine's eyes ached and she could not stop the tears. "Did I not love him enough?"

"You loved him as well as you could," said Ann. Her grip tightened. "But the world judged him, and it is a large place. You were outnumbered in the battle. I am sorry for it, Catherine. You are not to blame, either for loving your son or for the man your son is becoming."

Catherine put her head on her friend's shoulder and they watched the window. The day did not brighten.

By afternoon, Reg wanted to come downstairs to the big fire, and Ann helped him from the bed. He took a bowl of beef broth and a chunk of bread but he complained of his head. "It whirrs between my ears like there's bees in my brain." Catherine opened the curtain enough to examine his skin, but he was clean, though pale enough to show the map of his veins across his chest, rivers of blood under the chalky surface. He should have a better colour, she thought.

"I feel stronger," he said.

"It may be a passing fever," said Catherine. "Too much cold inside you."

"It has passed already," said Reg, but when he stood by himself, he staggered and fell again, into the chair.

"Not so fast," said Ann, and he obeyed the hand on his arm that kept him down.

The sun never showed its face, and so they barely noticed it had left them when a maid came in to light candles. "Shall I bring the dinner, Madam?" she asked. They had sat in silence for so long that her voice cut through Catherine's ribs and made her ache again for Alice and Veronica, for Diana's gentle voice.

"I have no appetite. Ann, will you eat?"

"I am not hungry, either," said Ann.

"You must eat," said Reg. "I would like another bowl of soup. If I must do it, then so must you."

Catherine nodded. "Bring us light fare. Bread and some white cheese and some of the French wine. Broth for Master Reg. Bring him the cinnamon wine. It's in the small pot in the still room."

The girl went, and as her steps faded, the sound of hooves came into the courtyard, and Catherine ran to the door. She heard Ann behind her, flying down the back stairs to call for the full dinner. Arthur and Stephen had taken the horses around to the stables, and Benjamin came in the front door with Edward, bringing clouds of cold swirling into the rooms. They were mud-splattered to their hats, and Benjamin threw off his cloak and kicked away his boots, walking in stockinged feet to the dining gallery.

"You're up," he said to Reg. "How is the hacking?"

"Much improved," said Reg. He was in Benjamin's chair, but Benjamin pushed him back when he started to rise. "Stay where you are." He put a couple more logs on the fire. "Have they fed you?"

"Just bringing it now," said Reg.

They were too worn out for decorum, and Edward had left his wet outer garments in a pile beside the front door with Benjamin's. When the food came, Stephen came with it, and he too stripped off his muddy outer layers and tossed them with the others. The girl made a sour face as she laid the table, but she went out of her way to gather the mess and take it all away as she departed.

Benjamin took a stool farthest from the fire to let Stephen and Edward warm themselves and said, "It's almost over. There are so many deserters on the streets that a man can't tell the rebels from the Londoners. Every householder has a boy guarding his doors, and the women have their maids waiting at the upper windows with the slop buckets, to defend the queen's honour." He laughed. "We got doused a couple of times ourselves. We must look like villains. It looks like hundreds have fled Wyatt, and a raggedier set of boys you've never seen."

"Where are they putting them?" asked Catherine.

"They've let some go free. The jails are filled, so they say," said Benjamin. "They're putting them in the churches. They will have to be nose to nose with the priests. They will probably be made to hear the Mass night and day until their wits give out and they convert back to the old religion for a little peace and quiet."

"Then they will be freed, as well? All of them?" Catherine could not believe the good fortune of it. Then she checked herself. This was not the whimsy of fortune. It was the queen's mercy. Mary would do it. She would let them all go for a bow and a word of contrition.

"There are so many," said Benjamin. "They're threadbare and sicker than dogs. I spoke to one of the Royal Force, and he said that the queen means to let the ones go without penalty, who show contrition."

It was the very thing Catherine had prophesied, but she did not say it. Triumph was an invitation to a fall. "But you did not find Robbie?"

Now Benjamin sobered. "That I did not. But there are many of them, Catherine. Many."

"And what is to become of the ones who stay with Wyatt?"

The fire popped, and Benjamin went to tend it. He poked and flipped the logs, sending sparks spraying into the dark room.

"Benjamin?" said Catherine.

"They are to be punished hard," said Edward. He did not seem to enjoy saying it, and Benjamin said, "We don't know that."

"Tell me the truth," said Catherine.

Benjamin gave the fire a last shove. "They say that ones who dare to come into London armed will be hanged."

# Chapter Thirty-One

They all slept, all but Catherine, who lay listening for the cough from the next room and hearing nothing but the wind picking at the shutters. She tried to form a picture, behind her eyelids, of Robbie huddled in a church, frightened but fed and warm and away from Wyatt. He would be with other young men, men that he knew, rebels no more but subjects again of their queen, however reluctant. And that queen would accept their penance and their promises of loyalty, and he would come home, chastened but whole. She opened her eyes and the darkness showed her absence. She didn't know where he was. If he had deserted Wyatt, he would have sent word to her, wouldn't he?

She finally fell into a dream of Yorkshire. It was warm there, the sheep fat and clean and her women all busy at their books and their spinning wheels. But she woke again, her eyes gritty and swollen, to the cold, whisking under the windows. Her nose was numb, and she burrowed under the covers, pushing her face against Benjamin's shoulder.

"Agh!" He pushed her away. "You are a chunk of ice!"

Catherine felt, for a moment, like a bride again. The sun was showing its face, and she took it for a sign. They would find her son. "Reg must be improved. I heard no coughing in the night."

Benjamin padded into the other room, scratching his arms. Catherine heard him say, "How are you this morning, man?"

Ann grunted, and something hit the wall. Ann's waking hand, no doubt. Catherine wrapped herself in a thick robe and followed Benjamin. Ann was stretching, and Reg was awake, rubbing his eyes. "Better. Ay, my chest can breathe." He sucked in air and blew out a stream, visible in the cold.

Benjamin called into the hall for a boy to lay the fire, and then turned back to Reg. "You'll stay in there until the room is warm."

"I'm strong enough to ride," said Reg.

"Not today. Give yourself time."

Ann said, "At least one more day."

Reg sighed. "I will stay if I may drink good English ale rather than that stuff you choked down me yesterday."

"Very well," said Ann. She put out her hand and he shook it. "We're agreed."

"I will go with you," said Catherine. "We will search the churches. And if Robbie should come home, Ann and Reg will be here to greet him."

Downstairs, they found Edward and Stephen huddled by the hearth. Edward had the cough now, and Stephen was disinclined to leave his side. So it was left to Benjamin and Catherine, with a happy Arthur Huff alongside, and they rode out under a sun that seemed friendly enough, though it melted the ice into a slippery mush. The churches were mostly empty along the way, the priests opening the doors and shaking their heads at the question of prisoners. They spoke of poor, misguided sinners and traitors against God's anointed queen. They all prayed together for peace and forgiveness, though Catherine could feel the impatience coming from Benjamin like a heat as they spoke.

They rode on, and Catherine watched the reflected suns in the puddles shatter as they stepped into them and wondered whether God had any use for either side. The light shone on the good and the wicked alike, on Catholic and Protestant. How many of the priests had left wives and children behind, no one would say, and whether they had been called again by God or by the queen was a question that no one raised.

Catherine's own father had left off wearing his clerical robes at the end of his life, and had taken to going about in a farmer's brown breeches and undyed hose. He began speaking of God as having many faces, women's as well as men's, and of hell as a place where sinners would be condemned to gaze into mirrors and see their true souls. When Catherine had gone to tend him at the last, she found the village of Mount Grace divided, some calling him mad and others divine. They said he was a mystic, a seer, a lunatic, and a heretic. He called himself a sinner and a fool, and died with a smile, saying that at least he could speak the truth.

Her stepdaughter, Diana, had lived, like Catherine, through the changes, and now attended Mass with the same quiet diligence that she had shown in attending the reformed church. She bowed her head and said the required words, then retired to the hermitage of her chamber, calling prayer from the strings of her lute. Was that hypocrisy? Or a greater devotion than the ferocious beliefs that fired Mary on the side of Rome and Robbie on the side of Wittenberg? Catherine had once felt that fire in her own breast, first for the Church, but just as hot for her children, all born under the Reform. And now that fury melted like the crust beneath her mare's hooves, and she felt a great sorrow for them all, drowning her spirit.

"Why so melancholy?" said Benjamin. "We have only barely begun to search."

"I was just remembering Father," said Catherine.

"That old pagan," said Benjamin. "I loved the man."

"As did I," said Catherine.

"If we had more priests like him, we would have fewer troubles all around. He should have been our king."

Catherine had to smile at this. "He would have given the crown to the first passing child for a toy."

They were in the city proper now, and, on either side, doors and windows had been barricaded with old boards and bent nails. A few churches here held deserters, and Catherine walked among the wretches, who lay on the cold stones and squatted around the altars. Women were feeding them bread from large baskets, and sending around jugs of ale. They were ragged indeed, and many shared blankets. They were not chained or guarded, but sat of their own will, watched over, and prayed over, by the attendant priest, whether they wanted him or not.

They cringed from her as she bent to look in their faces, like beaten dogs, and Catherine wished she had brought something to give, though she was unsure what good money would do them. They could not have carried blankets enough. She saw one young man with an open wound on his arm, oozing blood, and she cursed herself for leaving clean linen behind. When she asked to look at the injury, the deserter wrapped the damaged arm around himself and eyed her with suspicion. An air of resigned hopelessness hung over the whole room. Her son was not there.

At the next church, Catherine smelt the tang of disease as they pushed open the door. A clot of men had been squashed into a corner, and they coughed, spitting phlegm onto the floor. The stones around them were slick with blood and pus, and two women were absorbed in wiping the floors. Benjamin caught her elbow as Catherine moved forward. He called "Robbie! Robert Overton!" and when no one even lifted a head, he pulled her backward. "I will not have you fall sick for their sake," he said, "no matter how pitiful they are. We have illness in the house enough as it is. You have nothing for them."

The priest was going around with a pitcher to give them drink, and an old woman brought a bucket and clout closer to the sick men and got on her knees to slosh the floor around them a bit cleaner. But even she turned away her face as she worked, and she held the dirty water far away from her body as she carried it off. Catherine's thick skirt and heavy cloak suddenly felt sinfully luxurious. Benjamin dragged her outside, where the air was sweet, and she felt tears, hot behind her eyes. She would cry herself dry at this rate, and she bit her lip to stop the flood.

"They are almost dead already," Catherine said. "They must have walked through the storms and the mud with nothing on their feet or heads."

"They can thank their saviour for it," said Benjamin. "I mean Wyatt, not Christ."

Catherine could hear the coughing, even through the fat walls of the church. At least her son was not among those. But he was not found, either, and she trudged through the muck to her mare, and they rode on.

# Chapter Thirty-Two

The next church harboured only a small clutch of deserters, and the priest led them in, relieved to pass his charges to someone else's attentions for a while. These were cleaner, and they had heavy clothes. Their shoes had been scraped. Catherine could see at a glance that her son was not among them, but she called, "Does anyone here know of a Robert Overton?"

"I know him," said one. He was a tall man, maybe ten years older than Robbie. He smiled, showing crooked, dingy teeth. "He walks with Wyatt, almost as though he thinks he's his right hand."

Catherine caught at this. "He's not?"

The man shrugged. "Wyatt takes all comers. That Robert, he wants to show himself. He's a boy. He ought to be home with his mother." Again the unfortunate, unwashed smile. "Would that be you?"

"Yes," said Catherine. "He wouldn't stay with us."

The man nodded and sniffed, wiping his nose with his forefinger. "Forward boy like that ought to be rapped on the knuckles and sent on his way. But Wyatt's all on fire, and he burns anyone who comes in his path. He's going to bring down some good men, boys, too."

Benjamin said, "Where are they now?"

"We left them when the call went out for Kingston. I've had enough. The queen is the queen, and England wants her. Be done with it all, I say. Your Robert, though. He knows the queen's sister, doesn't he? He brags on it some."

"He knows her from their childhood," said Catherine. "I wouldn't say he has ever been in her books since they grew up."

"Better stay out of those books," the man said. "Word has gone round that Elizabeth's in the Tower. Those Boleyns. They won't stay away from the Wyatts, will they?"

"Shh," said one of the others from between his hands.

"I can speak my mind as well as the next man," said the first, "prisoner or not. It's true. Wyatt means to marry her to that Courtenay. The English suitor. Wyatt says if Mary won't have him, Elizabeth will."

"Shut your mouth," said the second. He'd raised his face now, and he glared at his companion.

"I will say it to the queen's face, if I ever see her. But I wonder if they've told Courtenay or Elizabeth."

Catherine's breast had gone cold, and her ribs shook. She looked up at Benjamin. "Have you heard any of this?"

"Not before this moment," he said. "You say Elizabeth is in the Tower?"

"That was the rumour. Wyatt said it, just before we made our, um, departure from his company. I expect they'll all be quartered together and shoveled into the same box. Nice marriage that would be."

Catherine backed off. "And Robbie is with him?"

"As near as he can stand without landing in the man's very arms."

Catherine stumbled from the church without even a blessing from the priest. She slid in the mud and skinned her knees on the wet gravel, and she could not rise. She groped and groveled until Benjamin caught her arm and raised her. "She cannot. She will not." Catherine heard the words spill from her lips, but her mouth could not make them sound true. "She will show mercy. She has always valued mercy above all. She is no butcher."

Benjamin was watching the sun, torching the western sky. "She values mercy more than truth? More than power? More than her crown?"

Catherine could not say yes. "We must ride farther."

Benjamin said, "You bleed." He squatted and ran his hands under her skirt and withdrew bloody fingers. "You've hurt yourself. You've torn your skirt. It's growing dark."

The pain sang from her legs, and Catherine looked down. The fabric was ruint, ripped and mangled with mud and her blood. Her shoe felt wet, and when she lifted her foot, the leather was stained already. Her hose looked black. Her head twirled and she thought she would faint.

Benjamin said, "You cannot ride. Get on with me." He lifted her onto his gelding and handed the reins of her mare to Arthur Huff. "We must go home."

The words of the young man with the yellow smile rattled in Catherine's head all the way, and by the time they turned into their courtyard, her mind was filled with its sediment. If she would imprison Elizabeth, Mary would surely imprison her son. But execute them? A girl? A boy? Like Jane Grey and Guildford Dudley. But they were still alive. All of London would know if they were not.

Ann met her at the door and helped her inside and down to the kitchen, where a maid washed her legs and bandaged the wounds. Ann stood by, her arms crossed, frowning silently until Catherine could stand again.

"How is Reg?" Catherine asked.

"Better," said Ann. "And you are worse. What has happened?"

"Robbie is with Wyatt. Wyatt means to marry Elizabeth to Courtenay. Elizabeth is in the Tower."

Ann sat on a stool and rubbed her face. "All of this today?"

"From the mouth of a man who seems to know. He is very sure of himself. Ann, what will become of them? They cannot win this. The deserters are everywhere."

"They will not win," agreed Ann. "I think you can do little but pray that Robbie sees sense before Mary sees him." She lifted Catherine's foot and ran her fingers over the bandage. "You will be stiff as a Maypole in the morning."

Catherine winced and pulled her leg back. It was already growing inflexible. She was clumsy. Worse, she was a fool. "I don't know what else we can do."

"You can eat your dinner and sleep. Sleep mends much. It clears the mind."

They went up, and Catherine ate as instructed. Edward still suffered with his clogged head, but he had no fever. The Lord Chancellor's spies listened to the stories of the day without crossed glances or raised eyebrows, and when everyone decided to go to bed, they went without complaint or comment.

But sleep would not visit Catherine, and she lay in bed next to Benjamin, listening to his breath. She dozed and started awake again, sure she heard pounding at the front door. But it was only her busy heart. She'd almost fallen into dream when the clanging began. A thumping, deep beneath it. Catherine listened. Touched her breast. But, no, it came from without, and she rose at the same time that Benjamin sat up, saying "What is that?"

Catherine opened the curtain. "What is the time?"

Benjamin was beside her, shaking his head. "Wee hours." The adjoining door opened and Reg and Ann came in, saying, "Do you hear? What is it?"

They all stood at the window, watching. Then Catherine pushed open the pane to the bitter night. Bells were ringing, somewhere far off. The beating was louder now and defined itself as it shaped the night. It was the sound of far-off drums.

# Chapter Thirty-Three

Catherine and Benjamin were dressed and waiting in the dining gallery by the time the boy they had sent out returned with the news. "The Royal Force is out," he called, panting at the front door. They hauled him inside, and he said, "There's men out. Everywhere. They're called to arms. The streets are filled with men."

"In the middle of the night?" said Benjamin.

"They say that Wyatt's in London with his rebels," the boy went on. "Coming to Charing Cross. Going to take the queen by force."

"Then there I will go," said Benjamin.

"I will go with you," said Reg, from the stairs. Ann was behind him, and he raised a hand at her squawk of protest. "Don't begin with me. Not now. I'm well enough."

Edward and Stephen had also been raised by the noise and had come to the top of the stairs, behind Reg and Ann. They insisted that they would also ride, at Benjamin's side or on their own. Catherine could see the negotiations working in her husband. He finally said, "Come with us."

The stable men were nearly half an hour getting the horses awake and dragged from their stalls. The maids brought clothing enough to keep off the black cold, but still the February morning blew in like a shrew's tongue, all insult.

"Bring him home," said Catherine as the men went out, knowing it was a silly thing to say. She followed into the courtyard far enough to see them mount up and to hear Benjamin promise that he would find Robbie. Then they were gone and she was left alone with Ann and the servants.

The day came up, suddenly bright but frigid, and Catherine thanked God for the freezing of the mud. The women went outside and listened for the sounds of battle but heard nothing, even standing at their gate, but the puddles cracking under their feet as they hardened. The sky was clear of birds, and the shriveled, distant sun hung in it like a saint's heart in a painted reliquary. Catherine tried to petition God but did not know what to ask for. There might still be time for a pardon, for her son to break from the rebel and kneel to the queen, but it would cleave him to do it, and she did not crave a child fractured in spirit. She thought of a prayer for his escape, but where would he go as a confirmed traitor? It was no use. She had no answer and muttered a resentful "Thy will be done" under her breath.

"You're shivering. Come inside," said Ann.

Catherine turned and the soft scabs on her knees split open. Her hose would stick to them again, and she would have ruint another pair. The housekeeper in her cursed, but she wanted to rip every stitch from her body and throw it in the fire, let the winter course through her until it quenched the heat of misery in her guts.

"I cannot stand here like a wooden post and do nothing while our husbands put themselves in danger for my son," she said.

"What do you want to do?" said Ann.

"Find him."

"Don't talk like a simpleton, Catherine. It'll be a hell down there. You won't be allowed close enough to see. It's treacherous, even for men. You're injured."

"And so I will wait here while my son walks into his death?"

Ann shook her head. "Catherine, what if he seeks it? You cannot save him from his own desires."

The words stabbed, and her heart opened up at last and seemed to bleed, along with her skin. "Oh, Christ, don't say it. You speak my worst fear. I haven't wanted even to think it. What have I done to drive him to a suicide? I cannot bear it." She felt herself fainting and grabbed at the iron gate, but it was so cold it burned her and she jerked away. At least she could still feel.

"This is not you," said Ann. "This is Robbie. He has his own soul, and it's been hardened against you for a long time. You cannot run him back to being a child again."

Catherine began to weep. "I have failed him. He was born under an evil star and I have not protected him from it. He was a gentle child. He could not harm even a kitten. What have I done to drive him from me?" And now the hot tears came, and Ann held her and let her cry. When the storm in her was spent, she raised her face. The sun had not moved, nor had the day gone dark. It was shining and cold all around her and she felt that she was in another world, bitter and bleak and scorched, looking out onto a false and golden image.

"We could ride down a way," said Ann. "If we are forced back, we will return. We can take Arthur Huff with us. He's been out with Benjamin and knows the direction to go."

Catherine looked at Ann and felt a little of the light enter her. "I must wrap my knees fresh," she said.

"Let me do it for you," said Ann, turning her by an elbow.

Arthur was willing enough, bounding off to order the horses while Ann knelt before Catherine and rewound the linen coverings for her knees. Their maids wrapped them for the journey in layers of woolen capes and fur collars, until Catherine was not sure she could even walk, let alone ride her palfrey.

But Arthur was already outside, bouncing in his saddle, eager to get moving. The women waddled out and let the stable men bundle them onto their horses. Arthur was already moving before Catherine was completely settled in her saddle, and he led them out at a trot and down into the city. Catherine expected fighting men, cannon and drawn swords, but the streets were quiet as the aisles of a church. Windows and doors closed. Men wandered about, but none of them was armed. None of them waved flags or pamphlets. Catherine caught up to a group on horseback to ask what they knew of invasion, but they shook their heads as though she'd gone lunatic and hurried on ahead, westward.

"Where are the fighting men?" wailed Arthur. "They said this morning that the rebels were in the very town. They should be crushing them into the gutters."

"Hush," said Catherine. They stepped along, peering down side lanes and into alleyways, but nothing seemed out of order. Then she said, "Where are the women?"

They stopped and looked around them. Men walked here and there. Some were on horseback, speaking to one another, as though business were being done. But not a maid or a mother was in sight. Not a nun or a punk.

"We are as out of place here as nipples on a boar hog," said Ann.

And then Catherine saw the men's eyes upon them. Just a glance, perhaps a brief glare. Maybe the slightest shake of the head. "What is it?" she yelled. "Where are the women?"

Several men backed away quickly. Two turned and ran from them. Catherine shouted again, and a tall horseman rode toward her shaking his hand before his face.

He said, "Are you mad? Be quiet."

"I have my wits fully about me," said Catherine. "We're seeking our husbands and my son."

"You are on a battlefield," said the man softly. "Go home like the others and bar your doors."

"How is this a battlefield?" Arthur Huff said. He cast his arms around. It was London, with its stench of fish and dirt, sweet smoke and bread. "There's nobody about."

The man on the horse took the boy by one arm and shook him until he rattled in his saddle. "You may ride with the men if you have a sword about you, or you may ride home with your mistress, but you will shut your mouth this instant. Do you hear?"

Arthur regathered himself and murmured, "Yes, sir."

The other man flung out an arm and knocked Arthur back with a blow to his chest. "Which is it? Decide now."

Arthur situated himself again with some difficulty. "I have nothing but my dagger." He removed it from the leather strap and brandished it.

"That's a child's weapon," said the man. "Get you home, and see that these women are safe." He nodded to Catherine. "And you. Go mind your children and your maids. Say your prayers for your husband. That's the only thing for you." He rejoined the other men, waiting for him a few yards down. They kicked their horses into motion and did not look back.

"Should we give up?" said Ann.

"To what?" said Catherine. Her mood smouldered. "A few men on horseback?"

"The air feels wrong," said Ann. "I'm cold."

They stood at a crossroads for a few minutes, looking one way, then the other. A troop of men came past, a street beyond them, carrying bows and arrows. Their bucklers, hanging from the hilts of their swords, glittered. But their weapons were sheathed, and they talked among themselves as though they were a party of simple hunters. The sun rolled up the sky and sat looking down at them but refusing to share its heat.

"Let's walk on for a bit," said Arthur. He was clearly stung by the encounter with the horsemen and wished to prove his bravery. Catherine nodded and they went on.

Soon, they heard the tramp of feet, many feet. But they saw nothing, and Catherine turned right at the next lane and took them north. They peered to the west and saw more men.

"What are they doing?" asked Ann.

They all seemed to be walking, a great mass of men, on foot and mounted, strolling along like a great silent parade of soldiers. But no one spoke, and no one drew. The men on the ground were rain-drenched and watching their feet as they moved. The men on the horses pushed up against the buildings to let the walkers have the center of the street, into which they sank to their ankles. The horsemen moved west, as the walkers came eastward.

"What is this? A dumb show?" whispered Catherine.

"It is the strangest sight I have ever seen," said Arthur.

On came the weary walkers, like a mass of ghosts set loose from a purgatory and unsure what their mission was, back among the living. Catherine thought she saw Benjamin's hat, and called out, but Ann pulled on her elbow.

"Don't," she said. "You cannot get past those archers."

The men with the bows had lingered on a side street and sat observing the troops of walkers. But they offered no violence and let them go by. The mob approached the two women now, the leaders so close that Catherine was struck by the odour of old sweat and urine. Their faces were drawn and fatigued. A couple glanced sideways, suspicious, and Ann said, "Get back."

Catherine and Arthur followed her lead and retreated. A trio of men on horses came around the corner and, seeing the women, charged at them.

"What are you doing on the streets?" the lead man demanded. "Do you want to get your throats cut?"

"We're lost," said Catherine. "I'm looking for my husband."

"If your husband is here, he must either work or be captured," said the man. "This is no place for a woman." He glanced at Arthur. "Or a boy either, though there's plenty out there who will not live to see manhood. Now get away. Go home."

"Yes, yes, we will go," said Catherine, pulling back on her reins. But they turned westward when they moved to the next street instead of fleeing to the east. "I must see," she said. "I thought I spied Benjamin."

Ann called, "Catherine!"

But Catherine moved on, and at each intersection, she saw men laying boards across the entries to the side streets. They acted like carpenters, whistling as they worked, but they all had horses, and they all had swords. She heard her name again, but it came from in front, not behind, and she raised her hand to shelter her eyes from the bright, false sun, and saw two men riding breakneck toward her. By the time Ann and Arthur had caught up, she could make out their faces. Stephen and Edward.

"What do you here? You must flee, Madam," said Stephen. He could not catch his breath, and he tried to yank her around to the east, but Catherine held her ground against him.

"Wherefore?" she said.

"The fight is about to begin," Stephen said.

"To begin and to end," echoed Edward.

"Where is Benjamin?" asked Catherine.

"And Reg? Where is Reg?" said Ann. Her voice jangled with fear, and she planted her mare in front of the men.

"Gone, both of 'em," said Stephen. "They parted ways down near Hyde Park, and we went with the man, your Reg. I can't say where the master went, but the servant man, he's sick. Can hardly keep his horse. We had a skirmish, nothing you'd call a battle, and we lost him in it. We were in with the rebels, cheek by jowl. No staying there, not now. Haven't you seen them? The whole Royal Force is out, and the queen's archers with 'em. They'll cut 'em down, sure as my hand."

Ann covered her mouth with her knuckles. Then she made a fist and beat at her chin. "You left him? Too sick to ride? And you left him? Where? Where is he?"

"Come on," said Edward. "We must go."

"You go," said Ann. "Go where you will. I don't care. But I will find him."

And she was off, riding west. Edward and Stephen looked after her but they did not move. "Our time here is done. Yours should be too, Madam. Whatever you have searched for, that boy or your husband? It's too late. It's all over."

The two spies headed east, as fast as the syrupy road would let their horses go. Arthur looked to Catherine. Catherine looked at Ann, riding away. She slapped her mare's rump and went after her friend, Arthur at her side.

# Chapter Thirty-Four

"Is this wise, Madam?" panted Arthur as they caught up to Ann. "Would it not be better to go home? Those men—they carry weapons. And they are so many."

"You may go if you choose," said Catherine. "You know the way. No one will stop you if you put on a savage face and look as though you're about your business. Or the queen's."

Arthur hesitated, looked over his shoulder. Catherine and Ann were beyond him already, but he soon came trotting up beside them. "You women need a man at your side," he said.

Ann heard nothing. She was searching down the side streets, and whenever they passed a man down, she stopped to look at his face. There were more of them as they went, deserters and worn-out rebels who'd given up the assault and lay in the alleyways, waiting for a sign of mercy. One man leaned against a wall, wiping his face, and Ann said to him, "Reg Goodall. A tall, lanky fellow with a long nose. Have you seen him? He's sick unto his death."

"We're all sick to death," said the man. "And we've all grown lanky these last few days."

At the next road, a pair of soldiers was tying a group of boys and men like ducks for a market, and Catherine's heart twisted. But Robbie was not one of the captured, and no one as old as Reg was among them. She asked, "Have you seen a sick man? He is lost among the rebels and cannot find his way home. He is loyal to the queen."

"He has chosen a rotten day for sickness, then," said one of the soldiers. He gave the rope a pull and one of the boys cried out. "But if he's with this lot, he'll be found before day's end."

They passed a church and Arthur jumped down to look inside, but he found it empty. Even the priest seemed to have hidden himself away. They could see as they went past lanes and side streets that Fleet Street was being shut off with wooden barricades. Men were assembling, and they no longer wore the cheerful expressions of men bent on killing animals. These had the grim faces of killers of men. Catherine and Ann hurried on, Arthur falling behind, then hurrying to catch up, and as they neared a dark alley, Catherine felt a groan cut through her. She opened her mouth, touched her own lip, but the noise had not come from her. It came like a shudder through the air from the east and a softer, deeper reverberation from the ground before her. It was Ann, but it was not Ann. It erupted from the muck beneath her feet. It rained down from the cold sun, plastered against the bright sky. The whole world was shaking. And then the noise was centered in Ann again, who was crying louder, then it was Arthur shouting, "It's begun! It's begun!" and pointing to the east and then it was Ann sliding from her horse and plowing through the dank mud, crying "Reg, Reg! What have they done to you?"

Catherine covered her ears, and as she shook her head to clean her mind she saw him. Ann crouched over him. Reg lay before them, alone and sunk in the filth, and the Royal Force was just beyond, propping old barrows and boards into a makeshift barrier, though no one was beyond them in the street, the rebel cry going up somewhere east of them all and

Reg murmuring "Ann" and laying his head in her lap as she slumped into the mud beside him. His front was bloody-dark and the shout was going up and the soldiers were then leaping their own fence to charge away, leaving them without men's arms to assist them. Ann ripped away the cloth from Reg's chest to show the narrow mouth of the wound. Catherine had seen such a gap in human skin before, in the gut of her own mother—how many years had it been?—but that had been deeper, lower, and this was just under the ribs, where a dagger might not pierce a lung or the heart or the entrails. A man might survive such a stabbing, but not here, not in the cold mud with an unfriendly sun glaring down, and the cry from the east rose again and she said to the boy Arthur, "Fetch one of those barrows and bring it here."

The ground still seemed to lift and fall, as though an angry river ran under the mud. It took all three of them to heave Reg up and tumble him into the wobbly little cart, and Catherine stole leather straps from the barricade to tether it to her mare, who rolled her eyes and shied at the strange contraption at her heels. She was no working mare and she stamped and splattered them, but Catherine finally wooed her into compliance and swung herself into the saddle. "Ride behind him," she said to Arthur, and Ann went beside, commanding Catherine to slow her pace or move on, as the barrow would have it. Beyond them, the roar of men in conflict rumbled on, and here and there a few came running toward them, daggers in their hands or terror in their faces, then on past, not shifting their eyes even for a moment to the sight of two women dragging a man in a barrow through the muddy streets.

And Catherine bit her lip, not to say to each one, as he splattered on by, though the words burned on her tongue, "Have you seen my husband?" and "Have you seen my son?"

# Chapter Thirty-Five

The battle had commenced only a street or two north of them, but Catherine and Ann rode along without looking that way, dragging the barrow, with Arthur bringing up the rear. The noise might have been a great masque or the mystery plays of the old days, Herod bellowing out his orders for the deaths of the first-born sons, or the devil seducing Eve. Reg moaned when Catherine's mare hit a pit of water, and it was a lovely sound, because it meant he was alive. From far away came the cry of "A Wyatt!" and Catherine hoped for a moment that it meant someone had put a blade into him, until she imagined Robbie at his side and cursed him back among the living, but only long enough to return her son to her.

But she knew it was not Wyatt who had won Robbie from her. It was the church of Henry VIII and his prince Edward. A church of murder and destruction, of rape and defacement, but also the church that had allowed her to have a son at all, and then Veronica and Alice. Confusion clamped her heart. Swords clanged on their left, and Catherine turned her head without thinking, only to see, as they passed by a side street, a battery of arrows fly. And on they walked, unmolested, unnoticed, until Ann said, "He is thirsty," and they stopped.

They had carried no ale or wine, and Catherine urged her palfrey on ahead until she saw a sign, a phoenix and a dragon, and she dismounted onto a sunken board and picked her way over the mud to pound on the locked door. She called, "Drink for one of the queen's men!"

A window opened and a woman gazed out. "Are you mad? What do you do, on the open street? The rebels are in London. Can you not hear them?"

"Yes, I can hear. And I am taking one of the fallen soldiers to his home," said Catherine. "He is loyal to the queen, as I have said." She put on the most pitiful expression she could muster, and the woman shook her head and handed out a jug of ale. Catherine found a coin in her pocket, and the woman said, "No need," but she took it anyway and shut up the building again.

Reg allowed Ann to pour the liquid into his mouth and swallowed well enough. Then Arthur drank, then the women. Ann tucked the jug into the barrow beside the man, and they rode on.

They seemed now to skirt the very center of the contest, and Catherine's head went numb with the shouting. The air smelt of iron and ice, and more men came toward them now, but no longer running. These were stumbling from the north into their path and swiping at the horses, but unable to gather the strength to take them down. None of them was Robbie and none of them was Benjamin. When she saw a dead man, face-down in the mud, Catherine could do nothing but note that he was a stranger, step around him, to keep the wheels of the barrow from crunching over his spine, and move on.

Before they reached London Bridge, the city had fallen quiet. The downcast sun had withdrawn its light, and windows began to open. Women and men stuck out their heads and asked, "Is it over?" as Catherine rode by, but then they spied the bloody man behind her and banged their shutters closed again. A doleful bell began to sound, and Catherine turned north, toward its tolling, toward home. No one fought in the streets here, and no one stopped their passage.

They denied themselves food and drink and pushed through the gloom and then the falling curtain of the night. The bell ceased. No one spoke, and Reg had gone silent, and when finally they turned into the courtyard of Davies House and servants came running and halloing, the din stabbed at Catherine's ears and she felt it go through her, a clamour under her ribs. The ground was still again, but as Catherine's foot touched the gravel, she felt those waves and thought that someone was surely firing cannon somewhere nearby.

The stable boys lifted Reg and carried him down to the kitchen, where Ann made up a pallet beside the fire. The maids were ordered out, and Catherine and Ann undressed him down to his shirt. Catherine then left Ann to wash her husband and went on through to her still room.

She lit a taper from a stick she'd lifted from the hearth and watched the flame, a bright bud in the darkness. When the room bloomed with light, she took down her knapweed and let her hands do the work. It felt good, familiar, to watch her fingers move as they should, crushing the herbs and releasing their scent. Her mind was still filled with fierce men running this way and that, all of them determined, all of them strangers to her eyes. She heard a soft booming and laid her hand to her bosom to convince herself that it was only the thumping of her own heart.

She returned to the kitchen to find Ann laying a thick blanket over Reg, leaving his chest exposed. Catherine knelt and pried open the wound. It was not as deep as she'd feared, but it was frilled and pink at the edges, like a gruesome flower. She saw no blood erupt from it now. "Can you hear my voice, Reg?"

"I hear you, Madam," he said. So formal. Like a man at prayer.

"It's Catherine," she said. "I'm here with Ann."

"Ann," he repeated.

Ann smoothed the hair from his forehead, and Catherine staunched the hole with the poultice and wrapped him up with clean linen. "Can you drink?" she said.

Reg nodded, and Ann scooted under him to prop his head on her lap while Catherine fetched a cup of ale and held it to his lips. His eyes were closed, but Ann's were open and on her, asking the question she did not want to say aloud. Catherine set down the cup and put her palms together and Ann nodded.

Catherine could not think of a suitable prayer, though, so she just thought 'God, God, God' until the word had skidded free of its meaning and she stopped. "He will be better in bed," she said and called for the boys to come carry him. Now Reg looked alert and alarmed. "Do you feel pain?" Catherine asked.

"Mm," he said. "Hot."

"Deep down or in your skin?"

"The skin. Feels like I've had a coal set on me." He grinned a little but it faltered on the pain.

"But you can feel and that's a promising sign," said Catherine. "Can you move your feet?"

His face twisted up and Catherine set her hands on his toes. They wriggled, and she said, "Very good." The boys hoisted him and he cried out, but they took him on as gently as they could, Ann and Catherine following. The maids had already set the fire to blazing, but the bed was cold, and he gasped as they slid him onto it.

"Come here, beside me, Ann," he whispered, and she did, on the left, unhurt side. He said, "I never thought to see your face again."

Ann chewed her bottom lip, and Catherine knew she was trying not to cry. Then Ann said, "If you had let me find you dead, I would have kicked your body down the street."

He laughed, and then grimaced, and Ann laid her head on his shoulder. And Catherine could finally say, "Tell us what you saw."

Ann wanted Reg to sleep, but he said no, that he wanted to tell it, tell it all while it was fresh in his memory. "What if I should die in the night?" he said.

Ann hushed him, but they all knew that men had been felled by lesser wounds and that the body sometimes answered, without warning, the call of death.

"You were with them?" asked Catherine.

"I was with Benjamin," said Reg. "And it was dark as any tomb, and we could barely see the horses' heads before us. The drums were going all around, but the streets were empty."

He flinched and Ann looked at Catherine, who said, "You should rest," and rose to go.

"No." Reg adjusted himself in the bed. "I want to tell it. The sun rose and it looked to be a rainy day and I thought to myself that there would be no rebellion in a storm. Our own horses could barely keep their feet and they were not worn out with walking. But the sun burned through and here they came, right into London, and I didn't know where we were, but Benjamin said we should go on, and then we were among them. But I didn't know who they were."

"Wyatt's men," said Catherine.

"Yea, as it turned out," said Reg. "But they were just a band of raggedy men, coming up the street, and I thought it was a party of travellers arriving home at a sorry time of the day and then your man says, 'There he is.'"

"Who?" asked Catherine. "Who was it?"

"Robbie. I should have known him first, but it was Benjamin who saw him."

Catherine's throat gripped her voice, and she put her warm hand to her own neck until she could speak. "And how was he?"

"Hale enough. Wet through, like all the others, from the days of rain and the night. They must have been marching since the day before. A sorry batch of human flesh if ever I saw one. And Benjamin called out to him, to Robbie, and he turned and saw us."

"Did he come? Does Benjamin have him?" Catherine moved forward and stopped herself before she sat on the bed next to the wounded man.

"I didn't see." Reg shook his head, but the movement hurt him, and Ann pulled the covers higher, as though to protect him from his own motion. "I knew then who we were among, and I hailed the boy along with Benjamin, but he wouldn't come. He saw us, sure as I lie here, but he would not come."

"Did you see Wyatt?"

"I saw men. I saw one in a velvet hat, all ruint by the rain, and a velvet cassock with yellow lace. He looked high and mighty and angry enough. I guessed that was the man. And your son, not right by his side, but close enough. But he would not come."

"And so you fought to get at him?"

"I wish I could say so. No, it was Benjamin who went for him. I tried to hold him back. I told him that it was no use, that he must not join them, not right in London town with the queen's men surely out with the drums and all. I told him no."

Ann said, "And he did not heed you, did he?"

"He did not," said Reg. "I called and called. And he turned to me then, right in the street, and said he would get the boy or he would ride with him, but he would not leave him alone to walk into his doom."

Catherine could almost see it, the gloomy, sunken street, the proud boy and her husband, who had vowed he would win Robbie back. And she had accepted that vow. She wanted to hammer the bed with her fists. She wanted to weep. But she could not release her muscles, and she stood like a woman of stone.

"And how came you to be stabbed?" asked Ann.

"The Royal Force. They had come walking along the street against the rebels, calm as you please, like men out for a stroll, some of them on horses, up against the buildings like they were the most courteous riders in the world. You wouldn't know if you hadn't heard the drums. A man might not know even then. I didn't rightly know what the business was, who they were. I tried to cross over, after Benjamin, but the queen's men were in my way, and I pushed one aside. I should have considered what I did, but I thought them just any London men, and my mind was on Benjamin and he was disappearing with the others, and I pushed the man aside, and he took some offense at it."

"He gutted you for a push?" said Ann. She gave Catherine a fierce look. "These are Mary's men of God?"

Reg put his hand on Ann's arm. "They are trained to fight. I pushed and he took it as an insult to his honour. He might have thought me a rebel. I moved too slowly, and he was very quick with his weapon." Reg moved the hand to his side. "And precise."

"Not too precise, thank Christ," said Catherine.

"Christ," said Ann. "What has Christ to do with any of this? Men cutting one another down in the name of God. It is just like the old days. It makes me sick. They would cut old women in half if they got in their way or said their prayers wrongly."

"Ann," said Catherine. But she knew it was true. And what had she thought? That men would set down their weapons and train their eyes on the heavens, now that the priests were back in the churches? She said, "What has become of them?"

"They went on, and I went down," said Reg. "I crawled to where you found me. I thought when I heard your voices that I was hearing the call of the angels."

Catherine went to the window and opened it far enough to listen. Bells pealed all over London. "We heard it all," she said. "The battle. As we were searching."

Reg was falling asleep. "I thought you were angels, then I thought I was being turned by Satan, like an old cock on the spit," he said. And then, "Are those bells?"

"Yes. I think the queen has won the day," said Catherine. "I think the rebels have been put to rout. They were running. We saw them run. They may have escaped at the last."

Ann said nothing, but Catherine knew what she was thinking. Or they are all in the Tower now, waiting for their heads to come off.

# Chapter Thirty-Six

The next morning, Catherine and Ann stumbled downstairs to an empty house. Ann had slept fitfully next to Reg, believing each hard-drawn breath to be his last, and twice she had wakened Catherine to check the wound for festering. Twice, Catherine had unwound the linen and held a taper to Reg's chest. The hole was hot to the touch, but the edges had already begun to pucker in on themselves. His fever was upon him again. He should not have been out with Benjamin at all. It was no wonder he had moved slowly. Her knees twinged as she bent over Reg, and she felt shame at the complaint her body made. The third time, Catherine had insisted that Ann return with her and let Reg have the bed to himself. "We will all die of exhaustion," she said, and Ann had reluctantly climbed in with her.

Reg was still sleeping as they dressed and wandered through the silent rooms. One of the maids had set bread and cheese and jugs of ale on the table, but they were untouched.

"Where are Edward and Stephen?" Catherine asked.

Ann went back up to look into their chamber, and Catherine called into the well of the kitchen stairs for a maid.

The girl from below arrived just as Ann returned, and they both said, "They're gone."

Catherine sent for Arthur Huff and anyone who had seen the men. An old iron-worker, who kept the hinges and shoes and harness buckles in working order, said that Gardiner's men had come back to Davies House, had gathered their few belongings, and had gone again. "Home," said one of the stable men, "if they could find a barge. Or so they told me. I took them to the river myself and brought the horses back. They took that old wretch with them."

"What old wretch?" asked Catherine.

"That lunatic one, that beggar, the one who sits and digs in the dirt with her fingers."

"Old Moll?"

"That's the one. Glad to see the back of her. All filth and gossip."

"Why would they want her?" asked Ann.

"She thinks she has stories to tell," said Catherine. "They'll find her clawing through their chamber pots before they get a sentence of reason from her, but at least we are free of them. Go tell Reg, and Arthur, take one of the other men and go find out the news." Her heart lifted and she thought she might sing a few notes, but she clasped her hands together and let herself rock back and forth on the balls of her toes. They were fled. It might mean that Robbie was no longer under suspicion. Maybe he had left the rebels at last and was receiving his pardon even now. Or that they had ceased to care about him. He was only a child, if in a man's body. And children were easily swayed in their opinions. The queen was merciful. She would not punish boys for the lies men told them. She would not punish Catherine's only son. She dismissed the men and walked to the window.

Where were they? Her chest grew tight. Benjamin was clever and he cared little for pope or king, saying God was above them all and he would render unto Caesar as he was required, whether Caesar was English or Romish. But his conscience, he maintained, in the privacy of their bed, would always be his own. He would use his wits to get himself and Robbie pardoned. Yes, he would be standing before one of the guards this minute, pleading their innocence. He would win.

Ann returned to say that Reg was awake and asking to come down for food, and before Catherine could say "no," he was dragging himself down the stairs behind her, leaning on the railing, and Catherine said, "You will tear yourself open."

He'd achieved the bottom step and stood triumphant on the pavers. "My guts will tear their way out in search of victuals if I stay up in that bed another moment. Where is the bread?"

Catherine laughed despite herself. He had probably gone most of the previous day without a meal, and she took one of his arms, Ann on the other, and helped him to Benjamin's big chair. She called for a man to stoke up the fire and served Reg with her own hands. "I've sent Arthur to see which way the wind blows this morning," she said, and looked up to see a bright, still day. Nothing seemed to move at all, and she took it for a sign that the chaos was over and they would all settle under the new queen and the old church once more.

They ate in good spirits, Catherine's mind still worming with worry over Benjamin and Robbie, but her mouth saying that the worst was past and the men would come back laughing and bragging of battles. Reg took it for knowledge and filled himself until he had to sit back and let his stomach have more room.

"Ale and bread, that's what a man needs," he said. "And if I encounter that villain again, I will show him what I am made of, when I am not distracted."

"That you will," said Catherine.

Ann said little. Her eyes were on Catherine, and when Catherine raised her cup, as though in celebration, she lifted her own. But she took only the merest sip.

The morning passed, and Reg feigned strength, but his face grew pale and he finally admitted that he was tired and would like to lie down. Ann helped him out, and Catherine descended to her still room to make a fresh poultice. Men's boots went past the high window, and their voices carried from the stable. Two maids walked by, a bucket of milk swinging between them. A striped cat sauntered along behind them, and one of the Davies dogs routed her with its wet snout. The maids yelled for it to be gone, or they would take off its ears.

A winter day. The work getting done while the light held. Someone came into the kitchen, complaining of the cold, and logs tumbled heavily onto a hearth. Catherine's hands crumbled some hogs-fennel into a lump of warm butter and she mashed the herbs into a paste. She spread it on some bread and set it aside to make the knapsweed paste. She piled the physic onto a plate and took it upstairs. Reg was already asleep but allowed himself to be roused just long enough to pack the wound and wrap it with clean bandaging. Catherine required him to eat the bread. He refused, but Ann sat in a chair by the window, darning some raveled hose, and when she frowned at him, he put it into his mouth.

"I will just walk out a little, just down the lane," said Catherine. Ann set the hose aside, but Catherine held up her hand. "No, you should stay by his side. I won't go far."

"See that you don't," said Ann.

Catherine threw on a cloak, but it was not warm enough. The sun reigned still, but the air was icy, and her nose was bitten with cold before she had travelled a hundred yards. There was nothing to see, anyway. Or hear. The London bells had all fallen silent, and she imagined their tongues hanging, frozen, and then her mind saw dead men's mouths, and she stopped. The few houses nearby were shuttered, and no one lingered outside. She listened for horses, for men's feet, but all was quiet, and she turned for home.

She had taken up a seat by the downstairs fire and was almost dozing when Arthur returned. He came right in the front door, like a son of the house, and Catherine said, "What is it?"

"Good news." He looked like a sentry, standing as straight and tall as he could. He doffed his hat and bowed. Catherine clenched her teeth to keep from smiling. He said, "There's pardons being issued, Madam, or so they say. To anyone who has turned himself over to the mercy of the queen. The rumor is that Wyatt himself has been promised a pardon. They say he gave up his sword at Ludgate and let himself be taken."

Catherine jumped up and almost hugged the young man. "Thank God! I knew she would. I knew it."

"But there's many who haven't surrendered," continued Arthur. "And Wyatt seems to be waiting his turn for the queen's mercy in an odd place indeed."

"Where is he?" asked Catherine.

"I heard it at least three times. They're saying that Wyatt's in the Tower."

# Chapter Thirty-Seven

Catherine spent the evening wavering between elation and despair. If Wyatt himself was to be pardoned, then surely the lesser rebels would be freed. Perhaps a few would be whipped. A few might be pilloried to set an example. But a boy? And a man out searching to bring him home? They would be scolded and sent home. They would. Others had come out of the Tower alive. Wyatt's own father had done so. He would be freed, and Jane Grey and Guildford Dudley with him. And Robbie would have to admit that the queen was just and good.

But where was Robbie? And where was Benjamin?

Reg was hot with the fever after dark, and Catherine spent the night walking back and forth from the still room to the chamber upstairs, while Ann, refusing to allow a maid to touch him, changed the soiled sheets and washed him with her own hands. He finally fell into a fitful sleep, sweating and fighting off his nightmares, and the two women sat on either side of the bed, touching his arm when he flailed or putting a soothing palm on his forehead, until he sank into a quiet, unmoving slumber. They set a maid to watch and took their rest down in the kitchen with a jug of wine and the last loaf from the baker. "We can send them out again tomorrow for more," said Catherine. "If Arthur has heard the truth, we should all be safe again now."

It felt almost like the old days, sitting together in the dark over their cups. But the old days had not always been pleasant ones, and Ann, as she had always done, finally spoke her mind for them both. "Where can they be?"

Catherine waited until the kitchen maid had come in for her last cleaning-up, curtsied, and disappeared to her bed. Then she said, "Maybe word has not gotten round. They could be hiding somewhere, afraid to show their faces. If the danger has passed, they will know soon enough. Benjamin may be protecting Robbie."

Ann nodded. The room grew cold, and Catherine sniffed. Something stank, and she smelt her way around the room and stopped to lift one of the rush mats. Its underside was damp and mould was sprouting on the underside. "When were these last changed?"

"September?" said Ann.

Catherine groaned and dropped the mat. She had spent too much of the autumn watching the queen and waiting for the return of a country she knew. She had spent too much time upstairs, forgetting where her real pleasure lay—in the still room and among her books. In her garden. Her journey to Yorkshire had been brief, and she had thought only to pack a few herbs, believing she would return in the spring. In truth, she had been in high spirits, eager to be in London for the coronation and to watch the churches revert to the sanctuaries she recognized. To let the prayers and rituals of her childhood rise through her again, as though they would renew her from the inside out, rejuvenate her body as well as her soul.

In town, she could only keep a small garden. She bought most of her herbs now from the merchants, and they were musty and old. Now, even the floor mats were moulding under her feet.

"We could move back to Yorkshire," she blurted, "or to the country house."

Ann laughed. "Benjamin's country house? It's dark as a tomb and almost as smelly. You think you won't find mould there? It's growing out of the very walls. I don't think the north side has seen the sun since the old king went to his grave."

"I miss the open fields," said Catherine. "I miss the feel of earth in my fingers." She sniffed her hands. "Clean earth."

"I know," said Ann. "But Benjamin likes to be close to the markets. It would wear him, all the riding. He will never hire a man to do the bargaining for him. And Eleanor would think you no longer trusted her to manage Overton House."

As was usual, Ann had hit every point. Overton House's flocks produced masses of wool, and the women of the village respected Eleanor Adwolfe as their mistress. Eleanor was honest as a June day was long, and her sons worked like day-labourers. Catherine herself was always welcome, but she was underfoot in her own house much of the time when she visited and knew that everyone breathed relief at her departure. And still the idea of her home in the moors lured her, with its isolation and its sturdiness.

"I'm a jester," said Catherine. "Don't listen to me. My mind is tired and it wanders. Let's go up."

Before they went, Ann rolled the offending mat and threw it out the back door as a sign to the maids. They found Reg sprawled across the entire bed, snoring. He looked comfortable. Catherine didn't relish sleeping alone, anyway, so she and Ann crawled in together and hoped for a brighter morning.

A pink dawn woke them. It felt almost spring-like in its sweetness and soft colour, and Catherine went downstairs at a tiptoe to send one of the older men into the city to find out what he could about Wyatt. When she returned to get Ann, she found her in the chamber with Reg, who was already up, trying to dress himself.

"No heat in me today," he announced. "And look at this." He raised his shirt to show the wound. The edges had roughened a little into pale ridges, and when Catherine poked at them, he only winced a little. "Doesn't hurt at all," he said.

The wound did look less inflamed, but it was young in healing. Catherine said, "You are not ready to ride yet." She placed her hand on his cheeks and wrists. He felt cool enough and his eyes were clear. Good signs. "Do you have an appetite?"

"I could eat a whole pig," Reg said, rubbing his belly.

Ann said, "I could perhaps locate a squirrel for you."

"There's no bread in the house," said Catherine. "Let me send the maids." And she left them alone to quarrel happily together.

The maids were afraid to go without men, thinking that bands of rebels roamed the streets, and Catherine brought in one of the keepers from the kennels to ride with them. "Take a couple of the dogs," she said. That satisfied everyone, including the dogs, and they all went off into the mild morning, in search of a baker. The house felt suddenly empty, no daughters, no husband, and no son. Catherine needed a task. She checked the wine cellar, but it was full. The stables were clean, and the rush mat in the back had already been burned and replaced with a fresh one, from where she did not know. The floor had been washed, and the new covering was sweet-smelling. The other mats had all been turned and scrubbed, too, and though they were damp, they were unspotted. Catherine stood in her still room and looked at her empty hands. Her fingers had lost their callouses and her nails were soft. When she turned her palms down, she saw small dark patches in the skin and the blue rivers of blood bulged a little above the bones. They looked like her mother's hands, but it did not displease her. She flexed and watched the skin grow taut and shiny. She could still work with them if she needed to.

The maids returned, burdened with loaves and a jug of vinegar and gossip. Catherine heard them enter the kitchen door and went through, to let their mood flood her. The kennel man was with them, setting a basket of tawny apples and a small package full of soap cakes onto the table. The girls chattered and laughed, stopping to curtsey and say, "The markets are alive, Madam, and bursting with goods!"

"So the city is back to itself again?" Catherine asked.

"People are about," the kennel man said, lifting the apples from the basket and laying them out for inspection on the broad table. "There's talk of the taverns hiding rebels, but the queen has issued an order saying that the keepers'll be arrested if they harbour fugitives from the law. That'll turn 'em out, I will wager."

"Fugitives?" said Catherine. "I thought there were to be pardons."

He shrugged, then bowed and backed toward the door. "People are talking," he said. "It's just rumour, Madam. People like to repeat it."

He went out, and the day blew in, bright enough, but on the back side of the house still bitter cold.

# Chapter Thirty-Eight

Ann called down to Catherine as she was unwrapping the soap to let the scents fill her head. Two men had ridden into the courtyard, and she was to come and greet them. Catherine relinquished a ball studded with violets to one of the maids and dragged herself upstairs. The men had dismounted and stood on either side of another palfrey, on which a woman sat. She allowed them to help her to the ground, although her ride was low enough for her to have stepped down by herself, and then she ran forward, while the men lingered by the horses. She came forward with her head down and dropped to her knees on the threshold.

"You must come," said the woman. "They're in the Tower."

Catherine's heart lodged in her throat and she froze all over. She stared at the men, trying to recognize them, but they remained unknown to her. The courtyard seemed suddenly unfamiliar, and the stable men, now coming around to see to the animals, mere strangers. She said, "What? Who are you? The Tower?"

The woman rose and almost pushed Catherine backward into the house with the force of her need. Ann, who had waited inside, was beside her now, saying also "Who are you?" The wind made Ann's voice whirl away and Catherine said, "Do you hear? Answer."

"Pardon me, Madam," said the woman. She was younger than she had at first appeared, and within doors she faltered in her confidence. "I am Maud, one of Mistress Dudley's maids. She asks for you."

"Dudley? Who? Jane Dudley?" Catherine's breath would not come free from the lump in her breast and she gasped in the cold. Ann threw a cloak over her and shut the door.

"You have put her into a faint," said Ann. "Can you not give your message with less hysteria in it? Yours is not the only family caught up in this matter."

Catherine fell onto a stool and put her hand on her breast. She tried to swallow, but her throat would not loosen. Her ears heard Tower but her mind saw the gaol, the cell where she and Ann had been thrust, against all common law, to sit alone in the cold, waiting for judgment, and perhaps death.

But death had not come. Benjamin had come. And they had been freed. She slowly worked herself out of the tangle of memory and fear and found herself looking at a skinny, worn woman, really little more than a girl, wringing her hands in Catherine's front hall. "Jane is in the Tower?"

"And Suffolk with her. Lady Elizabeth is there, as well." The woman now rushed over to Catherine and threw herself down again. "The queen is going to kill them all. Every last one. Lady Dudley says that you can intervene. Plead for their lives. Please, Madam, we have no one else."

"No," said Catherine. "You are mistaken. They will be pardoned. Wyatt has given himself up, and the queen is bound, under God, to show mercy."

"Mercy? To Wyatt? They are racking the little Wyatt as I speak. They mean to make him reveal the Lady Elizabeth's part in the rebellion."

"What little Wyatt?"

"The rebel's bastard brother. He is only a boy, a child. And the Lord Chancellor's going to rack him until every bone in his body cracks unless he gives up the Lady Elizabeth's part in the plot." The woman was back on her feet, leaning into Catherine, examining her face as though she thought she had lost her wits.

"No. It cannot be. The Lord Chancellor? Gardiner?"

"The very one. The papist. He had led us all to this, with his priests and his pope."

Now the anger flared in Catherine and the lump in her breast dissolved. "Mind your mouth. I have heard nothing of these tortures."

The woman groveled again, but twitched in the indignity of her submission and stood once more. "I speak the truth. I have been among them, in the very walls of the Tower, and I have heard the guards talking of it. And Lady Dudley is there. And the other one, the queen Lady Jane. And her father. And Lady Dudley's sons. And they are all going to be killed as soon as they have got the story of the queen's sister out of them. It was done most treacherously."

Ann was gazing up the stairs, and Catherine followed the line of her sight to see Reg at the top, leaning on the rail. Ann shook her head, and he remained where he was.

"I don't understand," Catherine said. "What am I to do?"

"See the queen," said Maud, clutching Catherine's hands. The woman was scrawny as a cheap rope and her ragged nails dug into Catherine's skin. The pain made Catherine's scabbed knees itch and for a moment she could not keep her mind on the woman's words. She was saying "You must plead for their release, both the Lady Jane Grey and Jane

Dudley. The men must suffer the fate of their actions, I suppose, but the women? Tell her to set the women free."

"And women are not to feel the effects of what they do?" said Catherine.

The woman pulled back. "My mistress has done nothing in all this. She is innocent. She has had the bad fortune of strong relations, and servants with loose tongues. That is all."

And a beautiful son, thought Catherine. Is that also a misfortune? But she said, "The queen is occupied. She may turn me away. I will do what can be done."

The woman laid her face on Catherine's hands and said, "I thank you," as though anything at all had been accomplished. Then she backed away, ducking and smiling. "I must go. The Tower is very cold at night." She turned and almost ran flat into the closed door, and Ann stepped forward to let her out. The men had not left their rides, and when the woman had mounted up they all flew through the gate.

Ann shut the door again, and Catherine said, "Can it be true? That women are to be hanged for what their husbands and children do?"

"Anything can be true," said Ann, "but the woman is almost lunatic with fear."

Catherine said, "Where would I find the queen? Where do I begin to search her out?"

"S. James's Palace," said Reg, now making his way down. "She was there when the latest battle began. I heard a man say so. It is close enough."

Catherine rose and looked out the window. The day was on the wane already. "Send Arthur to find out. Have him leave a request for an audience if she is there."

Reg favoured his side as he turned, and Catherine said, "You are still stiff. I will find Arthur myself."

"No." He straightened and stretched. "I am man enough at least to walk down a set of stairs to deliver a command." And he was gone.

Catherine was left at the window with Ann. "And where are our messengers?" she said. She leaned down and rubbed at the scabs through her skirts. She wondered if they would rip open when she knelt before the queen.

"If they are not returned, then they have not found our men." Ann laid her hand on Catherine's shoulder and the touch weakened her heart. She bit her lip, hard, and Ann said, "If they were taken to the Tower, we would know. As long as we have no information, we have no need for grief."

The messengers returned before dark, without Benjamin or Robbie. They had looked into a dozen churches and taverns. They had ridden streets, lanes, and alleyways. They stood, caps in hands, dejected and weary. Catherine sent them down to the kitchen for a meal, but as they turned away, she said, "Wait."

Reg was leaning against the hearth, scratching his side, and Catherine said, "Have we got a map of the city?"

"An old one," Reg said. "I keep it in the bottom of a chest in our chamber."

Ann ran to fetch it, and when she returned, already unrolling it, Catherine had her lay it on the floor. The lines in the parchment were faded, and the creases where it had lain folded could not be smoothed away, but Catherine traced her finger along the river until she could see the city appear. The palaces were marked. Here was S. Paul's. Here, the bridges. The Tower. Southwark Cathedral, near the bottom. She motioned the men over and moved out of the way gently, so that her knees would not tear and bleed. "Show me where you went."

The men squatted and studied the map. Swiveled it into the light from the hearth and looked some more. They stepped out of the path of the firelight. Catherine called for a taper, and Reg came. He'd already lit one below, and he was holding it over them before Catherine's order had faded into the cold air. One of the men pointed. "There. We started there." North of the Tower. "We made a circuit, this way." He ran his finger around, almost to S. Paul's. They couldn't have gone that far, but Catherine let him talk. "We asked and we begged, but all the innkeepers say that they've emptied their rooms and turned the rebels out, them that didn't go on their own. They're empty, every one."

"Did you stop at the Green Key?" asked Reg. "Here?" He laid his finger on the map, well inside the path they had marked.

The men looked at each other. "Did we?" said one.

"Don't recall a key," said the other. He stared again at the map and Reg's finger upon it. "Didn't ride that far, don't think." He looked blankly at the map beneath him. He glanced up at Catherine, wanting to tell her what she wanted to hear.

"It's a meeting place for wool merchants," said Reg. "It's just here." He tapped the parchment, but the place would not make itself known to the messengers.

Catherine said, "Wool merchants? Are they Dover men?" She should have sent him to do the searching. He could ride straight to the places Benjamin would go. "The queen's men will search the places where men from Dover go, surely. They will look there first."

"Wool merchants from all over use it. Benjamin knows it." Reg pushed himself crookedly upward, holding his side. "Not just Dover men. It's not large. The queen's men might not even know of it."

Catherine sent the messengers off to their food. "Do not speak of it any more to anyone," she said softly. She rolled the map and tucked it against the wall beside the hearth. "Can you find it? The Green Key?"

"I can," said Reg. "But you mustn't punish the men for overlooking it. The sign is not fresh-painted."

"I'll punish no one. I'm glad of it. Can you ride if we go slowly?"

"I can." Reg tested his side with his palm and nodded.

"Then we're gone at first light," said Catherine. "We will get there before her men do."

"She is our adversary now, is that it?" asked Ann. She gazed at Catherine, something like a smile imping her mouth upward.

"Ah. No," said Catherine. Her knees began to ache, and she bent to rub them. Her face grew hot, and she was forced to stand upright again. "I only meant—well, I mean to say that only we know the hearts of Benjamin and Robbie."

"Very well," said Ann. "But Reg rides nowhere without me. Even slow."

"Of course not," said Catherine, glad to escape the discussion. "Come, let's all to bed, and wake with the sun. Do you need a fresh bandage, Reg?"

"I do," he said, "but if you'll beg my pardon, I will have my wife wrap me tonight."

Ann and Reg occupied the room next to hers, while Catherine slept alone in her big marriage bed, watching the stars through the window. The glass wavered, and she seemed to be looking through water. As her eyes grew heavy, she recalled a summer night when her mother, the prioress, had taken her to the low, slow-moving river and shown her the heavens reflected in the water. She had thought it a miracle, she a girl who had never owned a vanity like a mirror, that God would make two identical worlds, one above and one below. But then her mother had thrust her hand into the surface and broken up the stars, saying that it was no miracle but a lesson in duplicity. "Your eyes can deceive as well as illuminate," her mother had said. "You must put your hand to the world."

When Catherine woke, she thought her mother was calling her name. But her mother was long dead, and Ann appeared in the doorway between the rooms, calling "Catherine! The sun is almost at his zenith."

She rubbed her eyes, horrified at her own sloth, and, throwing off the bedclothes, looked out. The sun, in fact, was barely showing the top of its head. But she dressed quickly, stopping the maid who had come to lay her fire and ordering her to fix her hair in the back. The girl, startled, pushed her hands down her skirt and examined her palms, but Catherine said, "You are clean enough to fasten me up this morning." The girl obeyed, carefully placing the pins where Catherine directed with shaking fingers. "There, you see? You'll make a lady's maid before long," said Catherine and the girl curtseyed and beamed her way from the room.

Reg and Ann were already at the front door, and the horses were saddled in the courtyard. The bread and cheese on the table turned Catherine's stomach sideways, and she said she would fast until midday. 'Until we have found the Green Key,' she thought.

"You will starve yourself?" said Ann. "Benjamin will not be happy to see his wife all bones."

Bones. The word clutched at her gut, and Catherine said, "I have no appetite. It's too cold."

Ann patted her back, nodding, and they went out to the two little palfreys. Reg would have one of the big geldings, the fattest one, who rode with the gentlest gait. He grimaced as he swung himself into the saddle, but he sat straight enough and led them out into the dawn.

The air was smoking, all the morning fires twisting into the tendrils of fog that were left over from the night.

Catherine's stomach grumbled now, but she pressed it to silence with her fist and pushed on, following Reg through winding lanes. The doors of London were still closed against the weather, though the people were out, gossiping and arguing. Dogs roamed freely, and rats nosed down the alleys. Merchants had their stalls open, and from somewhere, Catherine could smell bread baking and her guts rumbled again for it. Ann was right. She should have eaten. But then she saw the pamphlets, warning of the rebellion, and more pamphlets, proclaiming its end. All had begun to tatter, and their sodden corners flapped in any passing breeze. She thought she would be sick, and was glad that her stomach was empty.

They rode and rode, until Catherine began to fear that Reg had lost his way, when he turned a corner and said, "There." He pointed down the lane at the little wooden sign, swinging, crooked, from a beam by two old chains. It hadn't seen paint in a long time, and the green key at its center looked more like a discarded anchor covered in moss. Catherine wondered if their messengers hadn't been here unawares. But Reg slid from the gelding, and Catherine followed suit. Ann seemed wary in the deserted, narrow lane, but Reg was certain, and she dismounted, frowning at the muck underfoot.

There was no one to keep the animals. Reg said, "I will stay with them, right here." Catherine looked at Ann, who said, "What choice do we have?"

The public room was low and soot-stained, with a large round table at the center and an innkeeper before it, laying a fire. He turned at the light from the door and said, "What do you do here? Where's your husbands?"

Catherine could not see for the darkness and stood for a few moments until her sight opened up and she spied two men watching her from a far table. She said, "Have you two travellers here, a man with a grizzled beard and a boy about this high?" She lifted her hand above her head.

One of the sitting men said, "Men? Is that what you are searching? We have men here, sure, for women alone. It's early in the day for it." His companion snickered nastily and started to rise, tucking in his shirt.

"No," said Catherine, backing away. "We are not alone and we are not looking for you. I seek my husband."

"I'll make you a husband for a night or two. A good one," said the man, and now the first one snorted and said, "And I'll take the other one, old as she is."

Ann stepped forward and said, "You'll take this if you take anything." She shook her fist at him and the standing man retreated a step. "There's been a war on, if you have lifted your snouts from your tankards long enough to see it, and there's men gone missing. This lady has lost her husband and her son and we have been told that they come here for business." The fist was still aimed at the two men. "I see that you're not fit for arms, but if you want to try one, you may come on and greet this one. I have a man outside who will match it."

The innkeeper laughed out loud. "A lady warrior. She has put you down, gentlemen, and I will lay my money on her cause." He came forward and said, "But I fear I do not have your husband, Lady. I have no one here but these two villains, and they cannot be bothered to move more than a foot or so, come rebels or redemption."

"His name is Benjamin Davies," said Catherine. "He trades in wool. He has hair with curls, dark with streaks of white. He wears a long beard."

"I know Benjamin Davies," said the innkeeper. "He trades here. And he has been here. He is not with those rebels, is he? I never knew Benjamin to be a man of politics."

"When? When did you see him?"

The innkeeper pondered the air. "Hmm. Three days ago? Two? It was just after the scuffle with that Wyatt, and men were to and fro in here. And he had a young man with him, indeed he did. Spent a night. He asked for a letter to be sent and paid a man to take it. Spent one more night, methinks. Then he paid his reckoning and went. No more or less than that."

"Where did he go?"

"I don't ask a man his business. It's not wise. And in these days, I don't ask a man much at all. If he doesn't draw arms in the public room and he pays for his drink, I say let him be."

Catherine said, "I thank you." Ann glared at the other men once more, but they had already returned their attention to the mugs in front of them. The women turned and went out to begin their search anew.

# CHAPTER THIRTY-NINE

Reg knew of two other alehouses that Benjamin frequented, but no one in either place had seen him. The tavern keepers eyed Catherine and Ann, up and down, with open suspicion. Two women without their men. It could clearly come to no good. One followed them out to the lane, and when he saw Reg, holding the horses, he shook his head and turned away, as though a man who would wait upon a woman already bore a deeper injury than any street scuffle could have inflicted.

They asked at churches nearby, but the priests had either already turned their charges loose or had become gaol-keepers and would only allow Catherine and Ann to peer into the makeshift cells that their naves had become.

"You cannot take any of them," said one, folding the black wings of his arms over the crucifix that lay against his breast. "They belong to the queen until the guilty are sorted from the innocent."

But Benjamin and Robbie were not among any of the dejected, dirty prisoners, anyway, and the women rejoined Reg and mounted the horses. They kicked them into motion, and the animals began trudging resentfully homeward.

Catherine finally said, "If they were killed, we would have been told. If they are prisoners, we would have been told."

Ann nodded without seeming fully to agree, and they rode on in silence. The sun had dropped away, leaving a slit of bloody sky along the west. Londoners hurried to their homes and public houses, cursing at the slop the horses slung from their hooves. It grew cold, and Catherine's knees ached and itched. She said, "How do you, Reg?"

"I am ready to sit beside a fire," he answered.

They turned onto the lane to Davies House just as Arthur came riding from the opposite direction. He waved, and they slowed to let him catch up. "I have your message!" he said. "The queen will see you!"

"At S. James?" asked Catherine.

"The very one! Oh, Madam, it was grand indeed, with all of the fine folk in their clothes." He had not noticed that they'd arrived without Benjamin.

Ann coughed out a little, cold laugh. "Well, I would hope they were not out of their clothes," she said, and the boy ducked his head. She rubbed his cap around on his hair and set him grinning again. No need to punish him for being full of spirit. When they turned into the courtyard, he whooped and jumped to the ground, calling for his fellows to tell them what he had witnessed among the palace-dwellers.

Catherine waited for an older, more sober, stable man to come for their horses. He took the reins and said, "That young rascal claims we've got a queen in England, why, in the very town of London." He was watching Arthur, who was chattering away to a pair of his mates. He said, "It's a wonder and a sign."

Catherine smiled, despite her weariness, and let him help her to the ground. "He's a boy and boys must have excitement."

"There's been too much excitement for these old bones, Madam," said the stable man. "I am content to let the queen be the queen, as long as we have some peace on this island. Let them go to France if they want excitement." He gathered the other reins and headed around to the back.

"He says rightly," said Ann.

"Catherine." The name was almost a streak of wind in the air, and Catherine thought it was Reg. She turned to where he'd been standing, saying "Are you sick?" But Reg was already at the front door. There was no one behind her.

"Catherine," the voice said again. It was a wisp from nowhere.

"Who's there?" Catherine called into the darkness. "Who says my name?"

"Shh. Over here."

The bushes by the front wall whispered, and Catherine stepped backward. "Show yourselves. Reg, don't go in. Stay here."

He was at her side, trying to see through the gloom. His dagger was out and he said, "Come out. Be men and show yourselves or I will cut you to pieces where you lie."

"Mother."

"Robbie?" said Catherine, creeping forward. "Benjamin, is that you?" Her voice came out shrill and high, and a man burst from the brush and grabbed her. Her heart lurched, and a smelly hand went over her mouth. She was held fast by the waist. But under the unwashed skin and muddy clothing was the scent of her husband.

"Quiet," he said, into her ear. "Is anyone in the front hall?"

Catherine shook her head and he released her. Ann and Reg stood mute and unmoving. Robbie had crawled forward and now crouched near the wall, still half-hidden in the branches.

Catherine said, "I don't know. We have only just arrived from searching for you." She squeezed his arms. His ribs. His head. "Is it you in the flesh? You are not a ghost?" A laugh erupted from inside her and she could not force it down. "No, ghosts do not stink."

"Shh," said Ann. She shook Catherine a little, and the fit passed. "Reg, go see that the house is clear."

He went, and Catherine followed him as far as the door and waited. Reg called, "All clear," and she beckoned. The two men ran, heads low and backs bent, for the house.

The front hall and the dining gallery were deserted, but tapers had been lit and Catherine could smell roasted meat. The servants were still awake. She could only see a few feet down the upstairs hall.

"Madam!" came a call from downstairs. It was Arthur, eager to share his conversation with the queen's ladies and gentlemen. Perhaps it had been the queen herself. He was coming up, his boots heavy on the stone steps.

In the corner of the front hall was a small closet that Benjamin sometimes used for an accounts room, and Ann herded him and Robbie into it. "Stay there. Don't make a sound," she hissed, just as Arthur came bounding into the front hall to greet them again.

He bowed with a flourish and said, "Shall I tell you all? I think I have served you right well, Madam, and showed that Davies House is a place of repute."

"Yes, but what sort of repute?" asked Ann. She seemed no longer in a buoyant mood.

Catherine rested her hand on Ann's arm. "Tell us, by all means," she said, "as soon as we have taken off our shoes and had something to eat. Go tell the kitchen girls to bring food and wine and you can have your meal with us." She resisted an urge to giggle like a green girl. Her husband was found. Her son was alive.

After he had gone, Ann said, "I will pretend that I am going to my chamber and take Benjamin and Robbie a portion. That boy's happiness is insufferable just now."

"Wherefore should he not be happy?" said Catherine. She was grinning like a child, and she bit her lip to kill the smile. She must look like a simpleton.

"Who knows who has followed them here?" said Ann. Her voice was a blade in the air. "They have slunk in like guilty men. We could all be hauled in as traitors."

Catherine said, "But they are here. I'm glad enough of it."

Ann sighed and sagged. "I know. I am glad, as well." But she looked tired and frightened. "You have some cause. Arthur is behaving like a clown."

"He's just young," said Catherine. "But go on, if he winds you up too tight." She removed her cloak and brushed off her sleeves, then glided into the dining gallery to wait for the servants, trying to look the lady, as though she knew nothing at all of her own men. As though her husband and son were not cowering like a couple of outlaws under their own roof.

# Chapter Forty

Arthur Huff didn't look twice at Ann, as she gathered up bread and slabs of lamb and tucked the loaf under one arm. She swept past him, letting her skirt dust him as she went by. Unaware, he perched on the bench that sat along the west wall and almost bounced as he held his cup, swigging great draughts of wine as he talked.

"I saw her with my very eyes, the very queen. And regal she is, though thicker at the waist than I would've thought for a queen. Her father was a thick one, too, though, wasn't he, Madam? A right big one there at the end, so they say, could crush a horse." A large drink and a loud swallow. "Or a woman, so they say. Not to speak ill of the queen's own father, of course, and not to say a word against the dead." He crossed himself and threw a splash across his own breast, then swiped at it with his wrist and landed another spill on his crotch. "She looks every inch a queen, though, and made me come forward herself, said my very name. It was 'Arthur Huff, I hear you come from Catherine Davies,' and I went a-scuttlin' across the floor, though I thought I'd slip, the palace is so clean and bright. And she just sends off the light like it comes from her very eyes."

Catherine dug her fingernails into her thighs and waited. She drank off a half glass herself to keep from interrupting the boy. Ann had surely gotten Benjamin and Robbie fed, at least, by now. From where she sat, at the head of the table in Benjamin's chair, she could see that Ann had gone in and come out again, but then she'd returned, backing a few steps to look this way and that over her shoulder, before she creaked the door open and went in a second time. She was still with them. Reg was nowhere in sight. The candle before her guttered, and Catherine wondered if someone had opened the front door. But it seemed only to be Arthur's unstopping breath as he rushed through the tale of his encounter with Mary Tudor.

"And you are to attend her tomorrow," he went on. "I could ride with you, since she knows my face now. I could be of service to you there, Madam, if you'll have me."

"Yes, Arthur, of course you may go, if you're not fatigued from your exertions today."

Now Ann appeared again, and Reg, clearly coming up from the lower stairs, met her. Together, they checked in all directions, then ushered Benjamin and Robbie out of the small room and up the stairs. Catherine's could hear the boot soles on the steps, and her heart beat along with the rhythm, but then they were out of sight, and she could only pray that they would meet none of the other servants upstairs.

"—not at all," Arthur was saying. "I feel like I've just leapt from my morning bed. Yes, it gives a man strength to serve a great lady. I'll have the horses brushed and fed and ready to ride before first light for you." He upended his cup, but it was empty and he lowered it again without seeming to notice.

"Very good," said Catherine. "Then you had better get yourself down to bed so that you'll be fresh enough to show me the way."

"I know it like the back of my hand," said Arthur. "I will have you there and home again before you know you have left our front gate." He rose, set the cup on the table, and bowed. "And now I am off to my slumber."

"Sleep well and deeply," said Catherine. She almost ached to be free of him, but his farewells included multiple bows and promises of duty and speed. Finally, he managed to get himself to the door, and when he found himself on the other side of the threshold, gave a final flourish of a wave, and was gone.

"Thank the Lord," said Catherine to her plate. But her meat had congealed into a grey mass, and she pushed it away. She took up the wine jug and three cups and, pleading the headache to the maid who came to the door, went up in search of her husband and son.

Benjamin would be in their own marriage chamber, and Catherine knocked on that door with the rim of one of the cups.

"It's only me," she said to the sound of skirts swishing on the other side, and the door opened a crack. Ann's eye and a sliver of her face. "I'm alone," whispered Catherine, and the door swung open just far enough to let her slip inside.

Benjamin and Robbie were both there, on stools, bent over the fire, and Reg leaned against the far wall, close enough to absorb some of the heat.

"Who brought the wood?" asked Catherine, setting the drinks on a chest.

"It was already here," said Ann. She bolted the door and put her ear against it for a few seconds. Satisfied, she poured two cups and joined Reg, putting herself on his far side to give him the benefit of the flames. Benjamin got the third cup for himself, and handed it over to Robbie after he drank.

Catherine sat on the edge of the bed, almost afraid to approach the men. "Where have you been? We have looked in every tavern and church between here and Blackfriars. Are you hurt anywhere?"

"No," said Benjamin. "I have been telling it, so I will have to make myself dull with repeating our adventure."

"It's no matter," said Ann.

Benjamin gathered a breath, took the cup from Robbie and drained it. The boy refilled it and sat again, beside his stepfather. Benjamin said, "Well, Wyatt is a dead man, that's flat."

"What?" said Catherine. "People say he will be pardoned. That he gave himself up and he'll be shown mercy."

Benjamin spat into the flames. "He gave himself up, that's true, but he gave himself up to a herald. He's the one who promised the pardon."

"And so the word has been said and the queen will honour it, will she not?" said Catherine.

"Why should she?" said Robbie. "Wyatt is a fool and a liar. He said we would walk into the town and the people would come over to us. He said we'd be greeted as heroes. And that Courtenay, he never showed his face, not at all. They are all weaklings. They are popinjays, every one." He sounded a bit like Gardiner, though Catherine would not say it.

Benjamin said, "The herald had no authority to promise anything. Only the queen can pardon him. And if she has a drop of Tudor blood in her, she will not. Robbie knows what he says. Wyatt's put his own head in the noose. He gave up his sword, and then they were all taken. We saw it all."

"And why were you not taken with them?" asked Catherine.

Benjamin laughed from his throat, a bitter sound. "You won't believe this, but it's true. We simply turned and walked the other way. It was pandemonium, everywhere you looked. Men running, screaming like stuck pigs. A few of them tried to get to the gate. They thought they would break it down, but it was fast as a castle." He laughed again and shook his head. "Simpletons, every mother's son of them, not just Wyatt. And we set our weapons into their sheaths and walked away. We stepped into the first tavern we came to and asked for ale. The tavern keeper was busy at the window and told us to draw it ourselves. And so we did, and enjoyed his drink while he told us the tale of a battle going on, right outside his window. And we listened like any strangers."

"And you stayed there three days?"

"No. The rebels started pouring in, asking for shelter, and he drove them out again. We said the company was not to our liking, paid our reckoning, and moved on, like a couple of gentlemen out for a stroll. The next one had a bed, but we found out the following morning that the man of the house was keeping rebels hidden. He was feeding them at the public table. We got our most prideful faces on and shook his dust from our boot soles. By the time we made the third, we were halfway home, and the rebels had been turned out to the queen's men. We wondered at it, out loud in the street, like a couple of innocents, and made our way back here after a couple of days. Saw many a narrow alleyway and the underside of more than one hedge of bushes as we came."

"And no one took you for Wyatt's men?" said Catherine.

"Not a soul that we met. We acted the part of London gentlemen, and we were assumed to be London gentlemen. But Wyatt will be racked. He is probably having his joints stretched as we sit here speaking. And he knows young Robert here, by face and by name. He saw me, as well, and he will learn soon enough who I am. When the blood begins to run, someone is going to say our names."

# Chapter Forty-One

They all slept in the marriage chamber that night, Benjamin and Catherine in the bed, Robbie on a pallet made of blankets in front of the adjoining door, and Reg and Ann bundled against the door to the hallway. Anyone trying to break in upon them would have to force his way past both locks and limbs.

Well before dawn, Catherine and Ann slipped out to gather the servants in the kitchen and inform them that Reg had suffered a worsening of his wound and could not be disturbed. They were to move quietly in the upstairs rooms and were not to enter the master's chamber, where they had placed him for comfort. Ann would see to the fire and to his meals. He seemed to have been taken down with a fever, as well, they said, and the servants were to stay as far as possible from the door. There was no telling how dire the disease might be. Perhaps it was the plague.

The kitchen girls trembled and the men put on such brave faces that Catherine felt a worm of guilt wriggle through her at telling such a lie. But no one would go near the room. That was certain. If Ann carried in enough food for three men, who was to say that a sick man couldn't have a hearty appetite?

Catherine dressed in Ann's chamber and then sat with Benjamin and Robbie. Her son paced the length of the room, then back again, stopping every time at the curtain. Catherine said, "Don't look out of the windows, Robbie, no matter the noise."

Her son cast her a withering glance and said, "I am not stupid, Mother. I don't love your queen, but I will not put the axe in the executioner's hand to spite her, neither."

"No talk of executions," said Catherine. "They are nothing to speak lightly of." She kissed his head and kissed Benjamin on the mouth. "And, you, no sneaking down for wine. Ann will bring it when you require it."

Ann came in through the adjoining door, locking it behind her. She had wine. "What do you say I will bring?"

"You come like the angel from heaven," said Catherine, "upon my prayer. Give these men some drink to calm them."

Benjamin was lying on the bed, fully clothed, with his hands behind his head. "I am so calm that I think I will fall asleep if I must stay here any longer."

"At least you are in your home," said Catherine.

"Home. Yes. Well, I will lie here patiently then and force Robert here to read some Lutheran philosophy to me," he said. "Solid Protestant thoughts on grace and the best way to pray ourselves into heaven. Every man his own priest, isn't that it?"

"Don't mock me," muttered Robbie.

"Mock you? I've walked into hell for you and then walked you back out of it, all the way home. The least you might do is comfort me on our way to the scaffold." Benjamin's tone was bold but his eyes showed fear. "I cannot even go down to my own wine cellar. I've never wished for secret passages in Davies House before this day."

"Stop," said Catherine. "There will be no scaffold. You may have to do some penance on your knees, however."

Robbie stopped his circuit. "I will not go on my knees before that woman. She's a popish bastard."

Ann gave Robbie a thump on the side of the head with her finger. "You speak mighty big when you have a warm fire at your feet and a dish of meat at your elbow. But you are just a boy, and you would do well to remember it."

He glared into the flames.

"One of Jane Dudley's women was here," said Catherine. "She says that Jane is in the Tower. She spoke of some treachery in the household. A servant, I think." She thought it better not to speak of Elizabeth or Jane Grey's father.

"Everyone acts the spy these days," said Benjamin. "They all want the queen's blessing."

"Yes. And I must go to her now," said Catherine. "If you will not kneel, then I will do it for you."

Ann walked into the empty hallway with her. "They are all murmuring below about contagion and sickness."

"You might drop a word about the sweat into your conversations," said Catherine, "if anyone shows any curiosity."

"Plague and the sweat? We will have an army of doctors here before nightfall. And no servants."

They went down to find Arthur in the entryway, boots on and ready to ride. He showed not a shadow of fear, of plagues or queens. He'd brushed his best breeches and coat and flung open the door when he saw Catherine. "The horses are waiting, Madam."

"We had best get upon them, then," said Catherine.

They rode through a quiet city. A few people were about, but moving along with their heads down and their voices low. When they were far enough south, Catherine could hear the sound of hammers. The bridges were being repaired, and soon the river would look itself again, and the merchants would renew their trade. They rode past S. Paul's, and Catherine stopped to gaze up at the enormous red length of it, like a rusty beast that had settled its haunches down there, among the lesser, drab buildings. She tried to remember the first time she'd seen it, what she had felt. Had she been awed at the grandeur of its size? She must have been. All she had felt for years now was a hollow feeling that she was looking at a giant's tomb, the place where the church had died. It was the sentiment of a silly girl, as inflamed as her son's hatred of the queen.

She tilted her chin up to stare now at the walls. Her church had returned, but the great cathedral did not seem to breathe with a resurrected spirit. It remained dark and gloomy, cold and bloody-looking. She had read too much of the corruptions of the priests and bishops, of the sales of indulgences and pigs' bones palmed off as saints' relics. And yet, to make husbands into their wives' priests, as the Protestants did, was intolerable. An insult to their souls. Man and wife were one flesh, not spirit and flesh. Her own father and mother had shown her the truth of this. Everyone needed a priest or no one did. How many of these reformed sinners would stand before the face of God and wish for some good soul to intervene before the wrath struck them? And how many of those good souls would be revealed as rotten at the core?

The building now disgusted Catherine, doing nothing but crushing the clean dirt below and blocking the view of heaven above. A tomb indeed.

"Madam?" said Arthur.

Catherine tore her eyes from the dim sight. The boy was turning his gelding in circles, and her palfrey had turned back her ears to listen. "Show the way," she said, and they rode on.

S. James's was a small palace but no less heavily guarded for its size. Catherine made herself known, and Arthur almost skipped alongside her as they made their way to the receiving room to wait. It was already late, and the halls were packed with petitioners and courtiers, ladies-in-waiting and ladies who would wait all day without being invited to see the queen. The air smelt sweet and a little fetid, something fragrant burning near unwashed bodies. Arthur bobbed and bowed, turning this way and that to be sure he snubbed no one. Catherine could smell her own scent, almost acrid, and wondered if her monthlies would come early. She had used the chamber pot before they left, but she squeezed her arms against her sides and kept her knees close together. She mustn't stink of weakness or terror.

They waited for more than an hour. The day was waning. Perhaps they had been called simply to wait and would be turned away at the end. Catherine wondered if all was well at home. She might go. She would not be missed. But as her foot turned, someone called her name and she was thrust by one arm inside the receiving room. Arthur had stuck to her and was told to remain at the back of the room. The lady at her side drew her forward. The river of people parted, and Cathcrine once again found herself standing before Mary Tudor.

# Chapter Forty-Two

Catherine had seen Mary Tudor dozens of times. Too many to count. She knew the planes of her cheekbones, the curve of the eyebrows over those eyes. Blue eyes that looked unaccountably black when she was angry, as though a storm, or a demon, had risen behind them. She knew the feel of her royal hair, both dirty and clean, and the fineness of her skin. It looked coarse now. Catherine walked up to the throne and curtseyed, and the weight of the room seemed to sit upon her shoulders. The woman seated above her was no longer the woman she had known, no longer the woman, still unsteady under a new crown, with whom she had walked through a garden, just weeks before. Mary Tudor had put on the bearing of a queen, distant as a star. Catherine looked at her feet until she heard her name. She glanced up. Mary was raising her palm, and Catherine rose as though she were on strings. This woman was a stranger, carrying death on her face, and she gazed down at Catherine without a flicker of recognition.

"Well. Catherine Davies."

"Your Majesty."

"You look well."

"I thank you. We all look our best under Your Majesty's rule." She wondered if it sounded too servile. Insincere. A clear lie.

But the queen smiled. "You have always had a clever tongue, Catherine." The courtiers tittered and Catherine felt the heat rush into her face. The room was cold, but sweat ran down her sides and she hoped it would not bleed through her bodice and expose her. The queen said, "Come closer. I want to speak with you more privately."

The surrounding men and women lowered themselves and backed away, like a retreating sea. Catherine wondered how the women managed not to have their skirts trampled as they went, in a wave of silk and wool, across the floor. Sunlight streamed through the windows, and Catherine felt nauseous. She swallowed and took a gulp of air.

She waited until the swishing of fabric and feet had subsided and then moved toward the throne. Up close, Mary Tudor was still Mary Tudor, though her face had fallen somewhat, even since Catherine had seen her, before Christmas. Her eyelids held up pleats of skin, and they shifted when she blinked. She was jowly, and her colour was uneven. Catherine almost expected her to leave her high seat, to descend and walk her outside, as she had done before. But she remained sitting, though near enough. She held out her fingers, and Catherine offered her hand. The queen's was damp and hot, and the rings she wore were slick. When she leaned forward, Catherine could smell her breath. Like old metal, or crushed stones from a mossy river. Vinegar, left too long in the jug. "How is your family, Catherine?"

"Gone," Catherine blurted. "They are all gone."

"They've run away from you? You, who have always been so kind to them?"

"We sent the girls to the country."

"Ah. Home. It is very far away."

The queen thought Catherine meant Yorkshire. She did not correct her. "When the news of the rebellion came, we thought it safer for them. Particularly Diana. She is not much in company. She prefers her solitude for contemplation and prayer. She requires peace and quiet."

"Diana?"

"Our eldest. Benjamin's elder daughter. I think of her as my own."

"Of course you do." The queen nodded. She ran her thumb down Catherine's knuckles and let the hand drop. "And your son?"

Catherine wiped her palms against her skirt and felt the smear of sweat. "I fear that I am not in my son's good books these days, Your Majesty. He is grown into a willful young man and will not listen to his mother. It is the complaint of many mothers of sons. They grow minds of their own."

"And does he not mind his father?"

"I have lost Benjamin in the chaos," said Catherine. "He went out in search of Robbie and has not returned home." The deceit fell from her lips without pain. It inspired a memory, and she added, "The Lord Chancellor's men were with him. They went off and I have not seen them since."

"Winchester's men are safely with their master," said the queen.

"I am glad to hear of it." That was true enough, and it allowed another truth come up her throat. "Benjamin's man, Reginald Goodall, has been stabbed almost through, and we found him and carried him home. But he says that he lost my husband among your own men and could not move to seek him out."

"Among my men?"

"So he says." Catherine's tongue worked on. Her mind could not fully form the words before they were out, and she listened to herself construct the tale. It sounded like a history, like fact, but her ears could not be sure. "He was with Benjamin, seeking Robbie, and they came upon your men, your archers and the soldiers who fought with them. I believe it was a brawl in a moment of misunderstanding. Reg will heal. There was no lasting harm done."

"How blessed for him," Mary Tudor said. Her voice was even. "But not to know what has become of his master?"

"That wounds him more than any blade could have done," said Catherine. "We have asked and looked. We have searched among the wounded, but Benjamin is nowhere to be found."

"Have you not searched among the arrested?" Now the left side of the queen's mouth turned up, and the folds at her eye bunched and bulged. "I have had word of him. And of your son."

"Oh, thank God! Is he hurt? He is not dead?" Her voice filled the space, with what sounded like genuine fear. Catherine's ears were filled with a pounding like the beat of those drums. Those drums that had sent her husband and Reg out, into the night. The fear was real. She could feel it in her bones. That Benjamin was in danger. That Robbie might be killed.

Mary was watching her. "Whether they are alive or dead, I cannot say." The mouth came down again and freed the eye-skin to ooze back into a curtain over the royal gaze. "I have heard from the mouth of the rebel that your husband and son walked with him. And I have heard that the rebels have been much in your house."

"He would not say so!" Catherine arranged her face into what she hoped was an expression of rage and resentment. Now she held up her hand, as the queen had done. "I will cut off my own finger if you find them among the prisoners."

"Calm yourself, Catherine. Those hands may have healing in them yet. Your husband and son have not been found. But there are many men, still uncounted and unnamed, among the prisoners. We may find them yet."

"Pardon my boldness, Your Majesty, but I swear that you will not." Catherine crossed her breast and looked directly into Mary Tudor's eyes.

"You are very certain," said the queen, "for a woman who cannot tell me where they are."

"Where they are, God knows, but I will wager my soul that they are not among your prisoners." Catherine had gotten her wits together enough not to say, "the followers of Wyatt."

Mary Tudor folded her hands, and Catherine saw how knotted the knuckles had become. She wondered if the rings could ever be removed.

"Soon I will have a husband by my side, and then I will be like you, Catherine, worrying about where he has gone of a night." The queen smiled, and for a moment she looked like herself again.

Catherine's knees relaxed, and she was afraid she would fall. "Any man who wins the heart of Your Majesty will never leave your side. And when the child comes, he will be the proudest father of them all."

"Yes. A child."

Mary's face looked less of the cat now and more of the mouse. Catherine pressed on. "We will have the old England again, and God will smile on us. We will be a merciful and peaceful land, the envy of the world."

"Peace." The storm came up and clouded the blue eyes. "Mercy does not always bring peace, Catherine. Sometimes the sword of justice must cut out corruption. You have seen such things yourself, a boil that will not heal until it is lanced, a limb that must be lopped for the body to live on."

"Your Majesty?"

"It does not please me to wield the knife."

"It is a queen's duty to see that her subjects receive trials when they have stood against her and find themselves in the wrong. You will be fair, as every prince in Christendom is bound to be fair." Catherine did not have to mention Mary's mother by name. They both knew how desperately she had pleaded her innocence before the king, and how efficiently she had been dispatched when Anne Boleyn was found to be with child, despite those pleas. "You have seen trials in your own life and you know what harm they do when they are unjustly conducted."

"Some have already been tried and convicted," said the queen, "of crimes against the throne and against God. Do you know that Suffolk meant to raise an army against me? Think of it. Suffolk!" Mary leaned forward. Her face was very close to Catherine's, and her eyes were red-rimmed with rage. "With his daughter in the Tower, under lock and key, already proven a traitor. Is that not reckless? Does that not require justice?"

"Jane Grey is just a girl," said Catherine. She was choking and she wanted to draw back. But the queen was in command again, and the stare held Catherine where she was. "We women should not contend over this. It was Suffolk who put the crown on her head, and Dudley. He wanted his son on the throne."

"And Dudley is dead by a just law, is he not?" said Mary.

"Your laws must be just. You are the queen," said Catherine softly. "God's anointed."

"Suffolk may have set my crown on that girl's head, but she is the one who wore it. And as long as she has that head, my own is not secure." Mary's hand went to her temple, as though she expected to find a wound there. "Those who would depose a rightful monarch have already condemned themselves. I need not do it for them. It is God's law. And I am His servant and His right hand."

Catherine's arms and legs shivered but her belly was hot. She ached to run but she bowed her head and said, "Yes, Your Majesty. You must have peace." She looked up. "Jane Dudley has done me a good turn or two, despite her harsh ways and the behaviour of her men."

Mary regarded Catherine. Her lower eyelids twitched. "She has done you a bad one or two, as well. Perhaps more than you realize."

"I think the death of her husband has put a penitent spirit into her."

"Perhaps it has. It shows a Christian spirit for you to believe it. But her household is full of mouths." Mary thought a moment. "Be sure that your family is pure. And loyal. We will have peace in England, and we will not tolerate those who disrupt it. If you must go to the Tower, I will not prevent it. You must ask for Lord Chandos. He is lieutenant there and will know if your family is inside its walls."

"Yes, Your Majesty. I am sure they are not."

"I hope you are in the right." The storm had passed, but Mary's eyes still scrutinized Catherine. "Find your husband. And find that son of yours. I want to see them, kneeling before me. I want to hear them swear that they are my true subjects with my own ears. As you say, we women need not contend. But the men must submit. Do you hear me?"

"Yes, Your Majesty. I will do whatever is in my power," Catherine said. It sounded squeaky, the vow of a cornered rodent.

"And I must do what is in mine." Mary Tudor sat back on her cushion. Her eyes lifted to a spot beyond Catherine. "You have leave to go. In peace."

"I thank you, Your Majesty." Catherine retreated, her knees knocking, until she saw Arthur beside her, then turned and scurried out.

# Chapter Forty-Three

In the hallway, Catherine told Arthur to wait where he was. She saw a maid leaning against the wall, looking as though she belonged to the palace. "Girl," Catherine called. She could feel the heat trickling down her leg. Her knees ached. The maid glanced up and Catherine caught her arm. "I will pay you a wage to guide me to a private room, this minute. I have woman's needs."

The girl looked at Catherine's feet, then into her face. "Follow me, Madam." They shoved through the crowds and up a set of narrow, winding stairs to another hall. The girl rapped on a narrow door tucked into the corner and pushed it open. The room was cold and empty, except for a hole in the far wall and a stone bench under an open window. The wind blew through.

Catherine lifted her skirt. Her left leg was damp and dark. "I have ruint my hose. I need some napkins, any old clouts. I will pay."

The maid said, "Latch it from the inside and I will knock twice when I return. Strip off those wet things. No one will bother you."

Catherine locked the door after the maid and stepped out of her shoes. She'd torn her knees open and had not even noticed. And her monthly had come. The hose could not be saved, and the blood came fast, spotting the floor between her feet. She knelt and scrubbed with her handkerchief, but she only smeared the stones, and when the double knock came, she left the mess gratefully and unlocked the door.

"Oh, Lord, Madam, are you unwell?" The maid had a basin of water and clean clouts over one arm. Catherine had never been so glad to see coarsely-woven linen and a pair of old hose.

"No." It had only been two weeks since she'd last had her flowers, but Catherine knew the effects of grief and fear on a woman's rhythm. Not even the moon could keep her right when the world beneath it was out of tune. She turned her back and lifted her skirt to wash herself, and the girl slipped out again. Catherine stepped over and fixed the latch, holding the fabric between her legs. She cleaned herself as well as she could, folded the pad and tied it around her hips. Then she dried her legs, wound fresh linen around the split knees, and pulled on the fresh hose. They felt dry and warm and as luxurious as anything she had ever had against her skin. The two knocks came again, and the girl entered with another basin of water and got down to wash the floor. Catherine stooped to help, but the girl waved her off with one hand.

"Don't mind it, Madam," she said. "It's a woman's burden. We must all share that."

"Let me clean the floor. You have other work."

"It's not fit work for you, Madam." The maid slapped the water around, then gathered all of the dirty things into a pile, emptied both basins down the hole in the bench. She dumped the filthy hose and washrags into the smaller basin and set it into the larger. "You see? Clean as ever. I may not have a grand bearing, but I can clean a stone until it shines like my lady's gems." She grinned, and Catherine almost laughed.

"If you find yourself wanting a new position, you must seek me out. My name is Catherine Davies, of Davies House." She found some coins in her pocket and dropped them into the girl's apron pocket. "You are worth your weight in gold."

"I thank you," said the girl. She managed a slight curtsey, even weighed down with the washing basins, and led Catherine back out, nodding in the direction they'd come, by way of good-bye.

Arthur stood where she had told him to stay, though he looked frightened and lost, and when he saw her, his face broke into a beaming smile. "I thought you had left me behind!" he said, running toward Catherine. "I thought you had forgotten me."

Catherine said, "I could ride nowhere without you to lead me, Arthur. And I am ready for you to take me home. I'm afraid we'll be riding in the dark."

He ran to find their horses, and now Catherine waited, staring up at the sky. The sun was losing its battle with a heap of clouds. A headache began to gnaw at her right eyebrow, and her mind travelled through the rooms of Davies House, trying to locate a corner, a chest, anywhere she might hide a man and a big boy from the queen's men if they came to search. If? No, when. They would come. If Wyatt had told all, they would come soon. Catherine wondered how many prisoners had been taken, whether the guards would ask questions of them all before they sought out fugitives. And how long might that take. And how long could she conceal them, if a place were found?

Time might bring forgiveness. She had herself been forgiven for her marriage to Benjamin. Benjamin had made himself well-loved by the merchants and wool-dealers and, if not beloved, at least tolerated by the queen. Alice was everyone's delight. Her husband could win back Mary's approval, if he was proven not to be a follower of Wyatt. And in time, the memories would fade. He could appear, here and there, doing his business as he always had. In time, the queen's fury at the rebels would fade. It might. 'It must,' thought Catherine. Mary would have other concerns to fill her mind. A husband of her own. Perhaps a son.

Catherine tried to imagine Robbie doing as Benjamin would do, staying low, staying quiet. He was a hot-headed boy, but in time, in time, he might settle down, adjust his opinions to the new queen. But would he ever denounce Wyatt? He had already called the man a fool. Perhaps, in time, he would come to see how senseless the whole scheme had been. In time. But how much time? And how much time would it take to cool that Protestant fervor?

"Time to go, Madam!"

Catherine's stomach turned over and the headache bit through her face. She whirled to see Arthur holding the horses. She laughed, but it sounded like a madwoman's screech, and Arthur's brows furrowed.

"Are you well, Lady Catherine?"

'As well as any woman who lies to her queen and then steps in her own blood,' thought Catherine. She tried out a dignified smile. "I am fit and ready to ride, Arthur," she said.

But the palfrey's back was no comfort to her, and Catherine's head was a clutter of worry and pain by the time they achieved their courtyard. It was the middle of the night, but she had hardly noticed the sinking of the sun. She had almost nodded off in the saddle, and she heard Arthur call, "My mistress is sick," as they rode in. Ann was beside her, helping her to the ground, and her vision swam.

"What is it?" Ann said into her ear.

"Just my monthlies," whispered Catherine.

"So soon?"

"My skull wants to split itself open. Get me inside."

There was a fire and Catherine blessed it, placing the soles of her cold feet to the heat. Ann said, "This is the result of all that riding about London. It has worried you sick."

"That it has," said Catherine. She put her head back and let Ann knead her forehead. "Ah, that helps me." She closed her eyes and saw the face of Mary Tudor behind her lids. "But the danger is not done. There will be no redemption, not for Wyatt. And not for Lady Jane or Guildford Dudley. They will not survive this. The rebellion has made the queen murderous."

Ann's strong hands moved to Catherine's hair and pushed the headache down. She bent and whispered into Catherine's ear, "Let her feed on them and maybe she will be too full of blood to attend to Benjamin and Robbie. They have been quiet as a couple of mice all day. We will keep our secret."

The face of Mary Tudor turned cat-like again in her mind, and Catherine opened her eyes. She nodded. "And perhaps if we do, we will be able to keep our heads. And now, upstairs. We will have to prepare the chambers ourselves."

Catherine and Ann emptied the chamber pots with their own hands and carried up the firewood, dark as it was. Reg wanted to come down with them, and he put out his arms to show that he could handle a load, but Ann pushed him back.

"You will split yourself open, and then where will we be? You are supposed to be sick unto death. Now stay here and be sick."

But he opened the door for them when they returned, and Benjamin, seeing the women labour with the wood, took the armload from Catherine. "They are my own servants. Surely they can know that I am here. Arthur can do this work. Wake up a few of them."

"No," insisted Catherine. "No one is to know. Arthur is a good boy, but he loves to tell tales. I'm afraid of all the servants. Jane Dudley may be in the Tower because of a servant."

Robbie sulked in a corner, accepting wine but nothing else. He did not approach the hearth when Benjamin laid on the new logs, and he did not offer to help Ann. Benjamin finally sat back on his heels and said to the boy, "Do you think you might hand me that poker? It's not very heavy."

Robbie met his stepfather's eyes and shame swept over his face. He went at the fire with a fury, stirring it so hard that he almost smothered the small flames.

Her head was still thumping with pain, and Catherine said, "We will sleep next door. I need a woman's company this night. Reg, will you lie next to the hallway door? I don't think any of the servants will pass you."

"That I will," he said, "if I can persuade you, Robbie, to drag the bed?"

And the boy did as he was asked, with hardly a look of resentment, and so Catherine was sure she would be able to sleep.

# Chapter Forty-Four

Ann fell asleep within minutes, but Catherine slept badly, tired though she was, the pain in her head turning to heat and then to cold. Her legs ached, and then her back, and she wondered if the change of life was coming upon her. The image of Mary Tudor would not leave her, and the more she turned over the meeting in her memory, the worse she felt. 'I am infected with a plague of the mind,' she thought. 'Blood between my legs, and blood between my ears.'

At dawn, Catherine was out of the bed, despite her lack of sleep, fetching food and drink before the maids noticed, but the smell of the day-old bread sent her stomach skidding. She woke Ann and left it to her to deliver the breakfast to the men. She was sick herself, in earnest, but her malady could not be put right by rest. She went down to her still room and heated a pot of water, throwing in the rose petals she loved. She locked the door and peeled off her clothing. So little time to herself these days.

The scent, as she wiped the water over her skin, cleansed her thoughts, and Catherine lingered at the bath, washing and rinsing out the rag until the water had gone cold. The throbbing in her head ceased, and she could think again. Her knees had scabbed over, and she wrapped herself with a clean pad and dressed herself, then tied up her hair and went out, calling for a maid to dispose of the wash. She could sit at the dining table now, and she went up like a lady, unafraid.

Ann was already at her meal. "How is your head this morning?"

"Better. The court is a dirty place, and I think it had gotten all over me."

"Mmm," said Ann. "And it will worm its way inside, will it not?"

Sitting beside her, Catherine nodded. The bread smelt good again, like summer, and she bit into a chunk of it without the rope of pain tying itself around her head. "A crown must sit heavy indeed," she said. "How does anyone endure it?"

Ann started to speak, but one of the maids came running in. "There's news, Madam. The boy who comes with the woodmen has just been here. He says the trials are beginning." The girl was twisting her hands into her apron, not knowing whether to be excited or scared.

"Who says this?" said Ann.

"The men that bring the hearth logs and their boy. This very morning, he says."

"Go on with your tasks," said Catherine, and after the maid had curtseyed and gone, she whispered, "We must go down to the Tower. I should see Jane Dudley if I am allowed."

"That woman has given you nothing but the sharp edge of her tongue," said Ann. "You owe her nothing. You will give yourself the headache again. She doesn't deserve it."

"Perhaps. But I want to know what she knows. And she has also shown me kindnesses. As did her husband. You can't deny it."

"And see what good it did him. He is just as dead for all his kindness."

"You can stay if you want."

"I will go," said Ann, throwing down her handkerchief. "Let me tell the men and get Arthur."

They were on the road within the hour, carrying blankets and baskets of food and ale. London was bright with gossiping merchants and fishwives, the talk all on rebellion and execution. Catherine tried to close her ears to it, but she couldn't ignore the drunken men stumbling out of taverns, laughing and wagering on who would lose his head first. "Hang them all," one shouted to his neighbor as their horses went by. "Let them rule London from the point of a pike."

Arthur turned in his saddle, almost grinning, but fear had gutted Catherine like a fisherman's hook, and when he saw her face, he looked forward again.

The Tower was a crowd of spectators and hangers-on, men and women, pulling at the guards and shouting over each other's heads. They were on foot, though, and Catherine forced her way through them. A guard looked up at her, and she said, "I am here at the queen's request to see Jane Dudley. I seek news of my husband. I am to speak to Lord Chandos."

The guard looked perplexed and unsure and turned to his companion, who shrugged and said, "Let them in. Chandos is in there somewhere."

The two fought back the crowd as they squeezed through the west gate. Catherine expected to find the buildings cold and quiet, the swathes between them empty and silent, but guards swarmed in and out of doors. She stopped one and said, "I am sent to find Lord Chandos."

"Well, good luck to you, Madam. He is somewhere hereabouts." The guard started to walk on, and Catherine called, "Where is Jane Dudley?"

"Dudley." The guard stopped and grabbed his chin, musing. "The Dudley boys are up there." He indicated a small section of the row of buildings with the free hand. "I reckon they might have put the bitch with the pups." He walked on.

They dismounted and left the horses with Arthur, who was gazing around with wide eyes, as though he feared he might be the next one locked up. "Take this," said Catherine, sliding off her ring with the initials on it. "Show this to anyone who requires a sign." Arthur nodded and dazedly fisted his hand around the token. Catherine and Ann walked inside, unmolested and unnoticed.

They met a riot of wailing and shouting. Men's faces at cell doors, boys' faces. The cold chambers were all full, and the women pushed past pleas for pardon. For release. Pleas of innocence and mistaken identities. Cries for food, for ale, for blankets. 'The clamour of purgatory could not be worse,' Catherine thought. A hand clutched her shoulder and she jerked away. "Madam, help us," said a young voice. She turned to see a man, no, a boy, no older than Robbie, at a grate. "I've been taken up with the rebels, and I've done nothing. Tell them. Tell them to let me go. Tell them that I am your son."

Ann pulled Catherine away and she stumbled on up the steps, a stone in her stomach.

They searched as they had searched before. Some doors were solid and did not admit a look, and some showed men, who asked for the baskets and blankets. Catherine soon could look at nothing but the people behind the bars, and then at her feet, as they moved on. And at the last, in a far corner, they found her, huddled in a low, damp compartment with two of her women. Catherine peered in and said, "Jane, is that you?"

Jane Dudley looked up. Her face, never full, had grown hollow, and it looked longer, witch-like, and when she recognized Catherine she scrambled to the door and shook the grate. She looked like a madwoman, a wraith, a deserted, hopeless soul. "Get me out before they kill me," she begged. "They will chop off my head and throw me in the river."

"They will not," said Catherine, but Jane would not be stopped.

"They will cut up my sons and make me watch while they do it," she said. "They will boil them up and throw the meat to their dogs."

"Jane, stop this. Your fancy runs wild," said Catherine, but her legs were shaking and her healing knees thumped with pain. Ann was right. She should not have come. She put her hand against the front of her skirt to be sure that the pad was in place. She took a breath. "The queen must have peace, but this is no land of savages. This is England."

"Your queen." Jane spat onto the floor. "You think all women will be friends. I tell you, she will kill us all."

"Here," said Ann. "We have brought you food and warm coverings." But nothing would fit through the bars, and they had to go in search of a guard with a key. By the time they returned, Jane had retreated to the corner and sat muttering to herself.

"Jane," said Catherine. "Your woman said you were here by treachery. She spoke of a servant. Who is this servant? What has he said?"

Jane chuckled. "Not a he, a she, a she-devil, and one whose name you don't want to hear." She covered herself with a blanket and turned away.

The guard shook his head. "That one's already in hell." He pushed them out and locked up again without a word more.

Jane did not look back, and Catherine and Ann made their own way toward the west gate. The sound of hammering in the distance, beyond the walls, was unmistakable, and Catherine wondered that she didn't hear it when they entered. She knew that sound, a scar deep in her memory. They were building a scaffold. Ann gripped her arm and towed her toward Arthur, who was chatting with one of the younger guards. "Have you heard, Madam?" said Arthur, as they approached. "It's already begun."

"What has begun?" said Catherine.

"The hangings," said the guard. He lifted an arm toward the west wall. "Didn't you see the people? They're all wanting to see for themselves." He chuckled. "There's going to be plenty for everybody. If you hurry, you might see them die."

# Chapter Forty-Five

The executions had begun, and London was alive with them. People shouted. They hooted and called. All the way into the city, Catherine and Ann wound through clots of men and women who were unable to arrive soon enough at the scaffolds. A few were gambling, right in the streets, on the amount of time it would take this one or that one to die. They met a few already returning from the city gate, boasting to the newcomers about how close they had been when the men dropped. These stopped long enough to point, guiding their fellows to the best places to see what was left to be seen.

Catherine and Ann let Arthur lead them. The boy wanted to rush forward and kept turning in his saddle, trying to hurry the women. But Ann lagged, and Catherine stayed with her. She wasn't sure she wanted to see. No, she was sure she did not want to see, but Catherine was also drawn toward the spectacle, to know for herself what her queen had ordered, and what would await Benjamin and Robbie if they were arrested and found guilty. She hunched and let her eyes slide over the crowd who surged with them. A great wave of bodies, she thought. All of us herding ourselves toward death.

But so much death. She hadn't imagined it until they arrived. The sky was darkened with the hanging bodies. Some men hung slack, already gone. Some kicked and twitched. Some swung loose, neither surely alive nor dead, their feet slapped at by the taller spectators on foot, who seemed to resent the fact that the prisoners had already passed beyond their insults. Men twirled in what must have been the wind, though Catherine could not feel any breeze. So many bodies. The air stank of urine and loosened bowels, the last humiliation.

The faces below were shadowed with the multitude of the dead, strung out along the gate. It was a curtain of corpses, so many that some hung with their heads uncovered, and some stared out at the jeering Londoners. Some had shut their eyes and choked in their private darkness. Many had lost their boots, and their spoilt hose showed soles scabbed and filthy, blue with the cold. Catherine counted thirty, then lost her number and began again. She lost count a second time and began to feel that she was losing her wits. "How many?" she said to Ann. She needed to put a number to the sight. Something exact. Something cool and precise.

Ann scanned the line. "Fifty? More?"

A couple of the hanging men still lifted their feet, as though they were walking on the air, but they didn't respond to the tugs on their toes. Catherine sat and watched, unable to move forward or back. A woman set her hand upon Catherine's own foot and she jerked it away.

The woman said, "Did you see them fall?"

"No," said Catherine.

"Eh. Too bad, that. We're the less fortunate, left with the leavings. Still, it's good to see that they're dead. Isn't it? Makes us all the safer, that." The woman looked up, seeking agreement, hooding her eyes with her hand. She was old, her face creased like a map. She should be sitting by her fire with a couple of dogs at her feet.

"Yes. How safe we all are," said Catherine. The woman took that for approval and moved on, waving at someone else among the onlookers. Catherine swung her palfrey around and said, "I have seen all that I can bear." But the way before her was eclipsed by dead men, like ghosts above the ground, and the thought passed through her that she would never see light again. The bones in her arms and legs were cold, and she felt that her fingers might break off if she squeezed her reins. Ann sat without moving, her gaze on the twisting forms. Then she too yanked her horse around, and Catherine pulled on Arthur's arm. She had paid him no mind, but when she looked at him, she saw that the boy was weeping silently in the shadow of the slaughtered men. Catherine said, "We need you to lead us home," and her voice jolted him loose. He nodded and swiped a hand under his nose.

The crush of merrymakers would not allow them to ride straight north, and they went west, toward the cathedral. The whole city was a gallows. At every crossroad hung a body, or two. Sometimes three. And at every spot the people had gathered, in celebration. But of what? That the rebels had been halted? Or that men had been strung up like pigs? Men and women, who spent their days building and growing food and making children, now raised their cups to the stretched and bloating forms of their countrymen.

Catherine studied the ears of her palfrey as they went. How delicate they were, how sweetly shaped, the fine hairs seeming to guide each ear to turn toward any small sound or sudden movement. Catherine had seen a shell from the sea once, that Benjamin had brought, and she imagined that her little mare's ears were that fragile, that they would break if touched. The mare's head bobbed forward as she moved along, but the ears went left and right, and the soft fur that lined their edges caught the stray sunlight and shone almost red.

Neither Ann nor Catherine spoke. Arthur could do nothing but wipe his face with his sleeve as they rode along.

The cathedral loomed ahead, and Catherine raised her eyes to it. "Deliver us," she said to herself, or to the building's rooftop. She knew not which. She aimed her palfrey westward, riding ahead of Arthur, who moved as though possessed by some heavy demon. Ann came behind her, more quickly now, and Catherine could hear her, telling the boy to come along. Catherine thought that if she could make the churchyard, she could rest a while. A small yew grew in one corner, and she could sit there, if only for a few minutes. Her belly ached. She was likely bleeding. But she could sit there.

They rode in and Catherine searched for her tree, but it was obscured by three dangling bodies, and she cried out, pulling back. Her palfrey startled and skidded, and Catherine slid off and let herself lie on the cold earth. Ann had the reins and was calling her name. Arthur was on his feet, and then he was beside her, holding her elbow, saying "Madam? Madam? Are you injured?"

"Even here?" said Catherine. "Must they do their murders even here, beside God's house?" She sat up. "Don't mind me. I am not the damaged one." She looked up at the dark hulk of the cathedral. No one moved through the doors. They were all outside, snickering and making mouths at the dead. It was not God's house anymore. Perhaps it never had been God's house. It was the pope's. And the queen's.

# Chapter Forty-Six

The ride home was a pageant of Death. Every crossroad seemed to have its swinging corpse, and finally, Catherine no longer looked up. Nor did she weep. She rode beside Ann, and Arthur came behind. They wound through narrow lanes and alleys, avoiding the greater ways and their hideous trees. It was well into a cloudy night by the time they arrived at Davies House, and she was glad for the forgiving blackness, and for the cold that would clean her nostrils of the stench of rot.

Inside, she found Benjamin, pacing their chamber. He grabbed her when she slipped through the door. "Where have you been? I thought you'd been locked up, down there with that damned Dudley woman."

Catherine clung to him. Her tongue stuck on her words. Her teeth chattered and he rubbed her arms.

"You are frozen half to death," he said.

"Don't say that word," said Ann. She was checking Reg's wound. "We have seen enough of it today."

Catherine could smell blood still, in the air, on her clothing, the blood of her own body, and she shook, even beside the fire. She said, "You must go. Get out. Out of London. They will come for you and you must not be found."

Benjamin said, "But I have done no wrong. We can conceal Robbie until this business blows over. By spring it will be forgotten."

"It will not be forgotten. You have been with them, and you have been seen," said Catherine. "That may be enough to get you hanged. You would not believe how many there are."

"I should have stayed with Wyatt," said Robbie. He regarded his mother. "At least he will die like a man. The streets are not a place for a woman. Your sex is weak and cannot confront death. You should be with your children. Let the men mind the business of England."

Catherine's hand shot out in a slap. It caught him low on the jaw but he flinched. She said, "Weak? How dare you speak to me in such a way? You are my child and here I am, with you. Or have you forgotten that?" The rage blazed up in her and she wanted to strike him with her fist. "I have seen men die before my very face. I have watched your own blood father die. You are not a man, you are a boy, and Benjamin has risked his head to bring you home. Reg has been run through because of you. If you had stayed, you'd be strung up like the rest of them. Let me tell you, they do not look brave now."

Robbie's face had gone scarlet and hard. "I should go. I will give myself into the hands of the Tower guards. I should die next to Wyatt."

"You don't know anything of death. You want death?" She held out her hands. "Smell it, then. It's blood and dirt and a body befouling itself. It's ravens pecking out your eyes when they stick your head on a pike at the end of London Bridge. That could be Benjamin out there. It could be Reg. You think that hanging is a glorious death? I will tell you. It is choking on your own bile while ragged men tear the boots from your feet. It is shitting yourself while you struggle for air, for all to see. It is ignominy and shame. There is no glory in it. If it would not mean seeing your head in one of those nooses, I would take you myself and show you."

Catherine turned away from her son, and she heard him kick at the hearth, but she could not look back. She could not take him in her arms. Benjamin said, "Listen to your mother, boy," but he gave no response.

Ann said, "Catherine speaks right. You two must flee London."

Now Robbie spoke again. "I will not run away. I am no coward. And I am no boy."

"You ran fast enough when the soldiers were at our heels," said Benjamin. "That is easy talk when you're safe by a fire."

"I only followed your lead. You gave me to think there was hope for our cause."

Benjamin snorted. "Your cause. Your cause was a fop with pretensions to the throne. I'll wager Courtenay won't find himself on a scaffold. He'll kiss the queen's backside if he must. And he'll do it with a smile on his face. And what did you think you would do with her when you had her? Make her Elizabeth's lady-in-waiting? Chop off her head?" Benjamin spat into the fire. "Your Wyatt didn't even have sense enough to bring wagons heavy enough to haul your guns. You're a pack of madmen and idiots, the whole lot of you. You want to die? Go, then, and die. But do not speak to your mother of it. Look at her. She knows what you're consigning yourself to. You don't."

"Someone is in the courtyard," said Ann. She was standing beside the window, and she could just see through the crack of the shutter. "Douse the light."

They had only lit the one taper, and Reg blew it out.

"Who is it?" asked Catherine. She moved to the other window. A couple of men had come, yawning and pulling on cloaks, from the stable. But there was no light, and the visitors wore hooded cloaks. Then one of them spoke, in a tone that was familiar to Catherine's ear, even through the window. "It's Edward. Gardiner's man." Her belly froze over and she whispered, "There is a panel behind the shelves in the still room. Two boards loose. There is a space behind it. Ann, take them down the back stairs. Reg, get in the bed. The nails must be driven back in to make the boards stay. Go. Go now."

They ran out, all three, and Reg kicked off his boots and got into bed in his breeches and shirt. Catherine prayed that the kitchen maids were already asleep, and that Benjamin and Robbie would both fit behind the wall. The pounding on the door began. Was there a stone or a hammer in the still room for Ann to put the nails back in place? She walked down as slowly as she could, taking one of the cups from the chamber. Reg could be thought to have ordered the other. She had not changed the pad between her legs and she could feel the sodden cloth as she stepped down, but there was no time. She could not be thought to be hesitating. The pounding continued. She was calling and then she was down and at the door. Opening it.

Edward and Stephen stood in the dark, and she said, "I must have some light." She turned to find a maid behind her, bringing a taper from somewhere.

"Madam?" the girl said.

"Go upstairs and ask if Reg needs anything else," said Catherine, taking the candle. "He seems better. The fever has gone away." She turned back. The men were now inside Davies House, shoving her aside. "What do you do, breaking in upon me in the middle of the night? I am a woman alone, as you see. I am sick with woman's sickness and you come like a couple of thieves upon me?"

Stephen said, "I'm sorry, Madam."

Edward said, "We are sent by the Lord Chancellor."

Catherine looked from one to the other. "Of course you are. You seem unable to move on your own power. But what does he want with me?"

"It is not you in particular that he seeks," said Edward. His teeth showed like little fangs in the yellow light. "We are ordered to make a search of your house."

And before Catherine could speak, they were at it, tearing into cabinets, peering into the dining hall, then going straight for the little closet where Benjamin and Robbie had hidden themselves when they arrived home.

"I must find my woman," said Catherine. She had no need to feign distress. She could feel the blood running down her leg. She stepped backward and left a stain on the floor. The men averted their faces, and she said, "You see? I am not in a condition to entertain you." She fled to the lower stairs, where she shouted, "Ann! I need you here!"

The knocking below echoed upward, and Catherine banged her hand against the wall and shrieked—a hysterical mistress demanding attention. Edward and Stephen remained by the door. They would believe all the noise was from her, a woman, of course they would. And she was bleeding freely now. She bent and held back her skirt, still slapping the wall, so that they would witness her lonely distress. The noise ceased and Catherine wailed until Ann appeared.

Ann took one look at Gardiner's men and almost yelled at Catherine, "Have they stabbed you?"

"I'm having my monthlies!" Catherine shouted back. She battered her fists a little on Ann's chest, and Ann said, "There, there, Madam. It's nothing."

"Nothing? I bleed upon the floor and you will say it's nothing?"

"All is well," said Ann, and Catherine took the hint and collapsed, like a woman unable to look upon her own body's functions. Ann said to the men, "Will you stare at a woman in this shape like a couple of apes or will you give her some privacy and air?"

"We're sent—" began Edward, but Stephen cuffed him on the arm and dragged him into the dining gallery. Ann and Catherine ran downstairs. She needed fresh linen in truth, and they dawdled over the warming water, listening for footsteps above.

"Is it secure?" whispered Catherine.

Ann nodded. "But small."

Someone was moving in the stairwell, and Edward soon appeared at the kitchen door. He was looking at his feet. "Is the lady patched up?"

"I will mend quickly enough," said Catherine. "If you don't mind looking at women's blood, you may search and I will tell you when you must leave me. You won't find them in the oven. We have a fire going."

Edward made a cursory round of the room, scrutinizing the spaces under tables that could be seen from yards away and opening pantry doors. He did not lift his eyes to Catherine and made a wide circuit around her. "I will search elsewhere," he said, slinking out.

He went next into Catherine's accounts room beside the kitchens, and they could hear him sliding drawers open and unlatching the small cabinets. "How small does he think they are?" muttered Ann. She went to the laundry to fetch the clean linen, and Edward returned to dog her heels. Catherine followed closely enough to watch. Ann offered up the tubs of dirty towels and hose. They were big enough to conceal a man, and she grinned while he sifted through the stinking cloth. He'd smell like filthy clothes. The washtubs were open-topped, and a glance told him they were empty. He bent to look underneath them, though they sat on a table that could hide nothing the size of a man.

They had to pass the still room on the way back, and Edward said, "In here."

"This is Lady Catherine's room," said Ann, but she unlatched the door and led him in. She helped him open the lower doors, and she removed all of the crocks from their shelves, setting them with care on the table that she had pushed in front of the panel she'd removed. The table itself was made of flat boards, so dry that they'd separated. Still, Edward looked it over, knocking on its surface. He pushed back the hanging bunches of rosemary and garlic and onions, as though Benjamin and Robbie might be hanging upside down from the ceiling behind them like a couple of bats. Ann opened the small oven in the corner so that he could see the sooty insides, cold from standing unused for several days.

"You may stay, but Lady Catherine needs these linens to use in private," said Ann. She went to the door, where Catherine lingered, and he followed them back to the kitchen, turning off to the second, smaller kitchen as the women went back into the larger one.

By the time Catherine was cleaned up and padded afresh, Edward had searched the entire lower floor. They went together up the back stairs and began again with the dining gallery, this time opening the wall cabinets and the smaller doors, where the kindling was stored next to the big hearth. Stephen was already there, and he walked around, knocking on the paneling. Catherine dared not look at Ann.

The two men went floor to floor, looking in every cabinet, chest, closet, and chamber. They searched under beds and chairs. Stephen tilted back a couple of Davies portraits and looked behind them, then blushed to discover Catherine watching him. Upstairs, the maid sat on the hall floor outside the master chamber, and Catherine sent her away to bed. They took their time in the room, rolling Reg from one side of the bed to the other, while he groaned and complained, turning back all of the covers and shaking them.

"Is this not Master Benjamin's bedroom?" asked Edward.

"It is," said Catherine, "but Reg is wounded, and he needs comfort to heal. And, as you can see for yourself, his master is absent."

"If his wound breaks open, you will be to blame," said Ann.

"You have your lady here to sew him back up," said Edward. He set his fists on his hips and examined the room. He and Stephen had been everywhere. "We will check the attics, and then the outbuildings."

Stephen said, "In the night, Edward? It's cold as the devil's arse out there. Can we not wait until daylight?"

"A man can ride away by night," said Edward. Still, a look of relief crossed his face. He'd been given an excuse to quit for a few hours.

"The courtyard is gravel. We will hear horses on the stones if anyone tries to leave," said Stephen. "There are plenty of empty chambers here."

Edward gnawed the inside of his cheek. "I would be fresher in the light. A few hours' sleep would do us good. We may use the chambers we used before?"

Catherine wanted them gone. "Would you not rather be in your own beds?"

"You want us gone, is that it?" asked Edward.

"That is not what I said. I was thinking of your comfort."

"The room here is clean and the beds are already made," countered Edward. "It's empty."

"As you have seen with your own eyes," said Catherine.

Edward blinked slowly, as though anticipating a soft mattress. He sighed. "Very well. We will stay," he said, as though Catherine had been urging it.

Stephen's face broke into a smile and he said, "Thank you, Lady Catherine. You were always a thoughtful hostess."

"You must forgive my outburst earlier."

Edward dismissed it with a wave. "It is the weakness of women. It is to be expected."

Catherine bit her lip and counted ten. "Of course. It is gracious of you. Tell me, why has the Lord Chancellor sent you to us again? Has someone spoken evil of Benjamin?"

Edward almost smiled, but his face wouldn't show joy. His mouth was crooked, and the best he could manage was a malicious smirk. "Oh, he's been spoken of. They say Wyatt himself knows your son." He leaned toward Catherine, but not close enough to touch her. "But there is someone closer. Someone who claims you have been keeping them all this while. And rebels with them. Under your very roof."

Catherine could feel her face going cold and was glad for the warmth of the fire to keep her from turning pale. "Our son brought men, before Christmas. I have said this myself, to the queen's face. It is no secret, and no reason to badger a couple of women and a wounded man."

"We hear that they have been here right through the Yuletide. That the plans were made under this roof."

"Who would say such a thing?" said Ann. "Only a lunatic would believe that. Why, you were here with us, night and day."

Edward scratched the side of his face. The smile must have hurt him. "You have a maid, one called Moll. She tells tales. Many tales. Of plans and secret rooms. Of men in the cupboards, right beneath our noses."

"Old Moll is melancholy and mad," said Catherine. "She sees demons living inside the loaves of bread she eats. She thinks the chamber pots are full of treasure."

"Does she? She has much information for a madwoman. And she gives it freely enough when she's put to a bit of interrogation."

Catherine felt herself hover between fear and relief. Moll carried an anger in her that would flame into an accusation at anyone if she felt a little pain. Catherine's own resentment flared out at her. But an interrogation. It would mean torture of some ingenious variety. Even for Moll, she could not feel anything but pity.

The men stepped into the hall. Ann said, "I will rack her myself with a couple of old ropes when I get hold of that old bitch."

But Catherine was thinking of her husband and son, stuck behind the wall downstairs. She made a show of tucking Reg in and murmured to Ann, "I do hope we have stocked blankets enough."

Ann nodded, understanding Catherine's meaning. "We have. It is a cold night coming indeed."

# Chapter Forty-Seven

Catherine dared not move toward the still room during the night. Edward and Stephen might be prowling the halls, even through the frozen wee hours. Stephen she might trust, if he were alone. But Edward? Never. And Stephen was bound to Edward, and to Gardiner. She lay alone in the room adjoining her own, with Ann in the master's bed, next to her husband. No noise from that direction. She imagined Ann and Reg in close conference, whispering under the sheets. And Benjamin and Robbie, straining to move inside the wall downstairs. It would be frigid by now, even with blankets. She listened for the creak of stockinged feet on the floorboards outside her door, and once even rose to put her ear on the threshold, but nothing moved. She wondered if Ann had thought to stuff in a basket of food before she nailed the wall back together. She shivered under her covers and felt her bowels shift inside her. She wondered if Ann had remembered to give them a chamber pot. Even an empty jug. There would barely be room to squat in there. She thanked God for the construction of the house, its ample space between the weather and the plastered inside walls. But still, it would be tight, and they would have no hope of lying down to sleep.

The night ticked by. Stars winked through her window, and Catherine heard something scratching behind her head, likely a mouse, scrabbling toward its secret nest. If she were back there, it might scramble right over her feet. She shuddered, and snuggled down into her thick covers. She prayed for the moon to hurry along its path and give the sun leave to take its place. She wanted to curse Old Moll and her tales that had led the Lord Chancellor through a maze of madness and landed on the truth. But she saw the pitiful shape of a crone with her bones broken or sunk into suffering cold water and the words would not come.

She must have slept, because the first bright fingers of dawn beckoned her from a dream of Yorkshire. Her father still alive. He was giving her a book, a book he said was for her, her alone, but she could not read the print, and as she tilted the pages to the light, her eyes opened to the morning. She leapt out into a bitter winter day. The air was brittle, and she wrapped a heavy cloak around her shoulders and tapped on the private door between her chamber and Ann's.

"Join us," called Ann, and Catherine pushed her way in. Reg lay in the bed. "He is still 'very ill,' if anyone asks," said Ann. "And it seems to suit him to lie about all hours of the day, ordering food and stretching his arms."

"I am deeply injured," said Reg. Then he whispered, "Can you get them out now?"

"Let me see," said Catherine. She ran back to fling on a garment and went in search of Edward and Stephen.

The Lord Chancellor's men were already in the stables, turning over harness and opening the barrels of grain. Stephen half-heartedly dug through the pile of fire wood. "They aren't here," he said, examining his palms for splinters.

Edward coughed and spat. "Look in the lofts." One of the servants from the house came out for kindling and he shouldered Stephen aside as though he were a dog. Stephen slunk off to obey Edward, but when he saw the narrow ladder, he said, "Must I?"

"Yes," said Edward. "I will go through the kitchens again, and when you've finished, we will look in the attics."

'The warm kitchens,' thought Catherine. She followed him. The spit-turner had put a pig's hindquarter on to roast, and the girls stood around him, sniffing the fragrance as the skin crackled. Edward hesitated, inhaling, and Catherine said, "That is our supper. It won't be ready for hours yet."

"Well," said Edward, a note of disappointment in his voice, "perhaps you will be returned by that time."

"Returned?" asked Catherine. "From where?"

"The Tower." Edward made a quick glance through the cupboards again and waited for Stephen to come in, rubbing his hands and blowing on them. "Did you find anything?"

"Not a hair," said Stephen.

"Then we go up," said Edward. "You may order your horses and your riding companion while we finish."

"Wherefore do I need to go to the Tower? I have been there of late. It's not a sight to see twice in a week."

"There's a sight today that you cannot miss," said Edward. "Order a man to come with you."

Catherine thought of Arthur Huff, but, not knowing what was in store, she stood, unable to decide. The spit-turner said, "My brother will go with you, Lady. The horses are in good order, and the stables are all clean."

"Thomas, isn't it?" asked Catherine.

"He's the one," said the spit-turner, and Catherine sent a girl to fetch him. Edward and Stephen went on their search of the attics, and Thomas entered with a question on his face. The house was not his usual province, and he stepped from one foot to the other, afraid to touch the pavers with his boots.

Catherine said, "I need a man to ride with me. We are going to the Tower to see I know not what. Those two men will accompany us down, at least. I will need you to ride home with me."

Thomas glanced at his brother, who nodded. He said, "I can ride, Lady. I will bring the horses around," and bowed out.

Catherine ran up to tell Ann and Reg. Reg was still abed, and Catherine breathed a prayer of thanks. Ann was sitting by the window, mending a glove. Catherine had left the door open behind her, and when Ann looked up and looked down again, Catherine turned to see Edward behind her. He said, "We have found nothing. We will go."

"Did I not tell you that Old Moll has lost her wits?" Catherine turned back to Ann. "I am riding out with these men. They say there are doings at the Tower today. Not to be missed."

"Everything I have ever seen in that place was better unseen," said Ann. "Reg is too weak to ride."

"I am taking Thomas from the stables."

"He's a good man," offered Reg. Then he gave a great cough. Catherine wondered if it hurt his chest to produce it.

"I will return tonight."

Ann nodded. She let her eyes meet Catherine's for a long moment, as Edward departed. She nodded, ever so slightly. They met Stephen in the hall, who was dusty, clearly having done all of the digging into old musty chests. He shook his head, a little resentfully, at Edward, but followed along as they went down. Thomas, true to his calling, had brought out the Davies horses in fine form, brushed and saddled. Edward's and Stephen's horses were held by another of the stable hands and looked frowsy and dull next to the little palfrey that Catherine favoured.

The four rode quietly, Thomas in the rear, whistling tunelessly, Edward and Stephen in front, unspeaking. Catherine mused to herself, hoping that Ann had opened the panel as soon as they were out of view. Benjamin and Robbie would be stiff and sore, but they would be unharmed. She could hide them in the still room until the kitchen girls went out to collect eggs or milk. The spit-turner was not a nosy man. He kept his eyes on his work. She could slip them past him and upstairs. If Robbie would be quiet. If he would submit to her.

The bulk of the Tower finally appeared over the housetops to the south, and Catherine called, "What is this business? Why have you dragged me out of my warm house?"

Edward idled, and Stephen side-stepped to let her come between them. Catherine looked at Stephen, but he busied himself, buffing the edge of his saddle with this thumb. She could feel Edward's ugly grin, and made herself turn to him. He was triumphant, in possession of information she could not guess. "Have you ever witnessed a killing, Lady?"

Catherine almost laughed out loud. She might have been talking to her son. How many had she seen die, even before the dozens, now hanging all over the city? The sweet rot, like something sour and fermenting, was in their noses even as he spoke.

"I have seen a husband die on a sword. My mother, run through with a dagger. I have seen a man shot in my own house and felt his blood run into my shoe. And look," she waved above her head. "Are these dead in my fancies? And have they climbed into the nooses on their own?" Her lip curled at the smell and she almost slapped the man. "I have seen a queen's head struck from her body and rolling in the dust. Is that killing enough for one woman's viewing?"

Edward watched her. He was gnawing the inside of his cheek again, and the action twisted his mouth. He would say something crooked with that mouth. Catherine put her hands over her ears. "Do not tell me. I don't want to know who dies next."

Edward pried her fingers off and held them in his glove. The leather was greasy and pliant. "You have never seen anything like this. The young queen-who-would-be and her upstart boy will have their day. You have never seen a pair of traitors die, have you?"

"Lady Jane?" said Catherine. He must not have heard her. She had seen Catherine Howard die. She had no desire to see another girl queen beheaded.

But Edward continued. "The very one. It will do you good, to see what becomes of traitors. And the families of traitors." He let go of her hand, and she was left grasping at nothing but the unforgiving air.

# CHAPTER FORTY-EIGHT

The crowd was already gathered at Tower Hill, but Edward pushed through, showing something that must have been a sign or a seal from Gardiner, and settled himself near the wall. Stephen was less eager, but he followed, and Catherine could do nothing against the crush of the mob but try to keep her palfrey from biting nearby shoulders. Thomas said nothing. The sun gleamed overhead, casting down a cold, unfriendly light.

And suddenly, there he was. The golden boy Catherine had once known. He'd been an angel, perhaps the most beautiful child she had ever seen. Guildford Dudley was led out before the hour of twelve, the hour of no shadow, and it seemed to Catherine that he was already a specter himself, with no mark on the earth to show him he existed. Men shook his hand as he progressed to the scaffold, as though he were going to be crowned again. He had no priest, no one to pray for him, so he fell to his knees and prayed alone. She could smell the bloodlust from the men beside her, like the sweat of illness, rank and acrid. Guildford's yellow hair lifted and curled. It had not been washed recently. He looked thin, the bones of his cheeks making hollows of his eyes. He petitioned his God fervently, his lips moving without producing any sound.

The last time Catherine had witnessed an execution like this, she had been ill with early pregnancy, and her stomach remembered, clutching and turning over. She breathed in the winter through her mouth, trying to cool her insides. But her guts churned against the prospect of death, and she leaned against the cold stone of the nearby wall to shock her body out of the desire to vomit.

Guildford raised his hands into the air. He now prayed aloud for the people and for England. He drew them back to his chest, as though to warm his fingers, and prayed silently once more. Then he cast them aloft again, in useless entreaty, and, finally, he seemed to have spent himself. He resigned his head to the block. He was nineteen years old. Older than Robbie, but not by much. He looked like a skinny child, bent for some routine punishment.

The axe came down and the people cheered. Tears came up in Catherine's eyes. She'd hardly known Guildford. He'd done a stupid thing. Others had died for lesser ambitions. Maye he'd wanted to be king. Maybe the marriage had been half his idea. But she could not let go of the image of the child he'd been, the easy smile he'd always worn. A thing of beauty, whatever else he had grown into being.

Edward, beside Catherine, said, "There's one. Shall we visit the other?" and clucked to his horse to nose through, as though a man's head had not just been chopped from his shoulders. Catherine sat, stunned, until Stephen, on her other side, said, "We must go, Lady Catherine. Go on," and let his horse nudge her palfrey forward. Thomas was still staring at the bloody platform. A dozen people had filled the space between them before he realized that Catherine had been ushered off, and he started forward with a dazed and tight expression.

The name Gardiner opened the Tower gates to them. Tower Green was also flooded with Londoners, and Edward, led by a guard, took them along the edge of the crowd. They did not go far. Catherine's eyes and ears were dulled, and the high sun blurred her sight. She did not want to see any more, but the girl was already being led to her stage, and the viewers surged up to the edge of the boards to get a closer view. Jane Grey was pitifully small, and when she began to address her audience, the words seemed larger than the body from which they came. Catherine couldn't make sense of it. She thought it was one of the psalms, but if it was the word of God, she could not hear it, though the people had fallen silent in the face of the girl who had been their queen for a few days.

Catherine watched a couple of the Tower ravens yap sullenly at the intrusion on their realm from a low piece of wall across the Green. Two women nudged each other and whispered. What did they do here? This was no entertainment. Catherine could tell them, if they would listen. It was all blood and seeping bodies, heads, first shining and smooth on top of well-formed bodies, then grisly, just gaping meat and bones and gore.

Jane Grey wrapped the big blindfold around her own eyes, trapping tendrils of her hair under the binding. Now she knelt, and from her saddle Catherine could see that she was feeling for the block. But it had been placed too far out, or she had gotten to her knees too soon. She could not find it, and the delicate, white hand grasped at the open air before it. Her lips moved, in a plea or a prayer. The crowd stood, unmoving and open-mouthed. The girl's hand was still out. A man stepped forward and guided her forward, still on her knees, inching through the straw like an animal. She laid her young head on the chunk of wood. The axe came down. Catherine covered her face.

"And that finishes it," pronounced Edward. "You see the work of my master, lady. You will not forget it."

"The Lord Chancellor has done this?" said Catherine. "And not the queen?"

"Indeed he did," said Edward. "Those young vipers would have poisoned the whole of England, he told her." The body would be quickly boxed up, and a hum of satisfied, soft chatter rippled among the people. A man near the front dipped his handkerchief in the blood. These loyal citizens sounded like townsfolk at the end of one of the old Moral Plays, their souls settled after an imagined struggle with the devil. Goodness had prevailed again, as it always did in the interludes.

Catherine said, "Told who? What are you talking about?"

"The queen," said Edward. He was trying to maneuver his horse backward, and the animal resisted, flailing the ground with one hoof and chomping at the bit. "Make me some room there, Stephen." Stephen obliged, having more room to turn, and as Catherine's palfrey gave way, Edward turned to face her. The departing people were too thick for them to ride out and so they hugged the wall together. "You know that it was the Lord Chancellor who convinced her. It was his sermon, a great work of rhetoric. He will be remembered for it." Edward smiled, as though he was somehow responsible for the persuasive skill of his master.

"Do you say that the queen did not assent to these deaths?" asked Catherine. "She did not order them? Tell me!"

"Oh, she assented at the last, but she was made to see the need." He leaned forward in the saddle. "She is a queen, but even a queen is a woman. And a woman needs a head to guide her."

Catherine bolted backward and her stirrup collided with Stephen's. They were locked together for a few moments, and she almost overthrew her palfrey getting unhooked from him. "Get away from me, both of you. Thomas, take me home. I have seen what these men have brought me to see."

"Not so fast, lady," said Edward. "You will injure yourself in your haste." He edged along the wall, forcing her back, forcing Stephen in turn, and finally Thomas. They found themselves at the gate, with barely enough room to flank the walkers and file in reverse to the street outside. Catherine thought she was free, but Edward took hold of her rein.

"We leave you here, Lady Catherine, and we will return to Winchester. But remember this day. The Lord Chancellor does not suffer traitors or those who harbour them. And the queen does as the Lord Chancellor commands. You are not a stupid woman. Do not do anything foolish." With that, he let go, and the palfrey sprang away. Catherine had not known how hard she was pulling against the force of Edward's hold. He called, "Farewell, Lady Catherine," as she found a gap in the people and let the mare have her head.

"Home," said Catherine. "We must go home." She hoped Thomas was behind her as she threaded her palfrey between houses and people, stray dogs and other horses. She did not look at the signs swinging above doors. She did not look back. She let the sky take her north. The sun had begun its relentless flight westward, dragging the light with it, but Catherine did not stop. Wherever she might have let her eyes land, she might see another corpse, rotting where it had dropped. Rotting where it hung. Gardiner had done this, the Lord Chancellor. Another so-called man of God. He had led her queen astray, and the people of England were paying the price for it.

The padding between her thighs loosened and slipped a little. But she rode on, until Thomas called "Madam!" and she was forced to rein in and turn.

"Slower, if you please," the man said. He caught up to her, his horse blowing through its nose and foaming about the mouth. "He's old and this pace will break him."

Catherine felt the sides of her own mare heaving against her shins and she stroked the lathered neck. "Forgive me, girl," she murmured. She looked up at Thomas. "Forgive me. My fears carried me away."

"It was the most horrible thing I have ever seen," said Thomas. "I won't sleep this night. The people cheered at it, Madam. They took pleasure in it. It sickens me to have been in the same place with them."

"You will be dreaming of this when you're an old man, Thomas. Such things don't leave the mind's eye. But you're innocent. You've nothing to do with any of it," said Catherine. It was only a half-lie. If she could get Benjamin and Robbie out of Davies House, all of them would be safe from inquiry. If they were still concealed. She clucked her palfrey to a walk and the animal obeyed with a lowered head. She hauled her hooves along as though they were made of lead.

"It mars us all," remarked Thomas, "to kill men in such numbers, and women, too. That girl was a child. She was our queen once. I cannot make an entertainment of death. Do all kingdoms do such? Or only ours?"

Catherine was surprised at how similar his thoughts were to her own and felt shame at her amazement. Thomas was a creature of God, after all, as well as she, and had the power of reason despite his station. Station. When had she grown aware of stations?

They strolled along now, side by side, like old friends. Catherine said, "I cannot speak of all kingdoms. I've heard of such things in other places. I've seen too much of it among the English."

"I wonder that God does not sink us beneath the waves," Thomas said. His face closed up then, and Catherine felt that he wanted to be alone with his thoughts.

The streets emptied as they went. It might have been any London day when they were out of sight of the Tower and its bloody Green. People spoke to each other in low voices, no one shouting or flinging pamphlets, no one calling for arms. No one crying out for the girl who had worn their crown for nine days, less than a year ago. Catherine wondered where she was now. Tidied under boards and nails. Ready to slide into darkness, into a tomb with the other unwanted queens.

Ann walked out to meet them, as at last, they rode in. Thomas took the horses with a wordless bow and returned to his duties in the stable. Catherine looked up at the house.

"All is well here," said Ann. "We thought they might take you to Winchester. I was ready to send a party of men to rescue you."

Catherine shook her head and they went inside. The warmth and the sweetness of the candle scent almost cut through her. "Jane Grey is dead. Guildford Dudley as well. I wonder if his mother will be able to live without him in the world."

"What?" said Ann. "Have they killed them?"

Catherine nodded. "Cut their heads off. Gardiner persuaded Mary to it. Like any traitors. As though they were just like the rebels."

Ann stared at the flames in the big central hearth for a few seconds. "How do you know she didn't order it herself? She's the one on the throne."

"Edward said it was Gardiner's sermon. He persuaded her."

"And what else would Edward say? He wants to be the servant of a great man."

"You've seen him. Heard him. Gardiner senses a threat in every shadow. I believe Edward. Gardiner wanted them dead. He was the one."

"Perhaps. But the queen signs the death order."

Catherine checked the dining gallery and the lower stairs. Then she pulled Ann closer to the fire and whispered in her ear. "It was a warning, taking me there. Edward and Stephen will come back here. I know they will. We are under suspicion and we must move them."

"Where? Gardiner's men are probably already on their way to Yorkshire to tear your houses apart searching for Robbie."

"Where is he?"

Ann pointed above their heads. "With Benjamin."

Catherine said, "Let me clean myself and I will join you there."

Every month, Catherine wondered that she still had what seemed to be a working woman's body, though it would bear her no more children. In her still room, she used the basin to wash. The flow was heavy, and she took down some ivy and laid it into a heating pot of water. She had no time to cook it through, but by the time she had cleaned the blood from her legs and folded a clean pad of linen, the leaves had wilted, and she peeled them apart and laid them against her belly and thighs and covered them with the cloth. She still seemed to stink of iron, though, and she hoped the smell would not penetrate her clothing.

Upstairs, Ann had already told the tale, and Benjamin was thoughtful, stroking his beard and studying his feet. Robbie sat with his face to the wall. Catherine came in and locked the door behind her. "Have you survived your imprisonment?"

"We could barely move our legs," said Benjamin. "I didn't know a wall could be so cold. And so hard."

"We are cowards and villains, not fit to be called men," said Robbie. He turned. "Is it true? Have they killed Guildford?"

"As true as the sun shines," said Catherine. "They cut off his head with an axe. And you cannot remain here. The danger is not past. Gardiner has an army of spies, and they are still on the hunt. You have to go." Robbie's face went hard, and Catherine added, "This is not cowardice. This is prudence. If you die, you will not see another day for battle."

"The continent," said Robbie. His face suddenly kindled with a plan. "We will hire ourselves onto a boat. We can find good company in Wittenberg. I have friends there, and companions we can trust. We will be free and we may practice the true religion."

Benjamin said, "No."

Catherine agreed. "Every boat will be watched. The sailors will turn you over to the law for a new pair of shoes. And you cannot go to Yorkshire."

"Nor would we," said Robbie. "They are likely rebuilding houses for the monks up there."

"Where does that leave?" said Ann.

"Wales," said Benjamin. "No one knows my family. They have never been people of the court. They are farmers and sheepmen. They keep to themselves. I'm known as a London man."

"But everyone knows where you're from," said Ann. "It's printed in your very name."

"And who has seen my name printed? Almost no one. The queen herself has Welsh blood in her, and nobody says a word about it."

"But the girls are there," said Catherine. "I won't bring them to any harm. We could lead Gardiner's men directly to them."

"My brother has more than one house. He has dozens of tenants. The place is wild, and wooded, and there are plenty of places to hide."

"Places you know?" asked Catherine.

"I wandered those hills all my boyhood," said Benjamin. "I know of places that no soldier would ever find." He put a hand on Robbie's shoulder. "The people there are no lovers of English kings. A man can have possession of his own conscience there."

"Truly?" said Robbie.

"Truly," said Benjamin, and Catherine wondered how much of what he said was a lie.

# Chapter Forty-Nine

Catherine could not go to Wales. That was decided almost at once. Her absence would be conspicuous, and she would be sought, on the roads and in the towns. The Lord Chancellor would likely know, within days, that she was not in Yorkshire, and that might point his men in the direction of the West.

She told the stable men the next morning that she had sold two of the big geldings. Hay was always dear at this time of the winter, and the news was received with indifference. It meant less work, after all. Thomas trained a steady look on Catherine, but she simply nodded him toward the stalls.

"Brush them and get them ready, Thomas," she said. "We will have men coming to take them away. We have no need of so many animals to feed. Make sure they have an extra ration this morning." Thomas gazed at her for a few seconds more, and then turned away.

Ann was in the kitchen, and Catherine sent the maids upstairs to clean the room that Edward and Stephen had occupied. Ann set about packing bread and wine, sniffing loudly about mouldy smells and dishonest merchants. One of the kitchen girls came in with a pail of milk, but she barely noticed Ann's presence. Catherine told the girl to begin polishing the silver spoons, though she knew they were already spotless.

Chests upstairs held plenty of unused clothing, but much of it belonged to Alice and Veronica, and Catherine sifted through to find things warm enough for a winter journey. At the bottom of one, she found some old men's things, and Catherine held them to the window to check for moth holes. A few here and there, but that was what she wanted.

"You must dress as a labourer or a travelling merchant," she said to Benjamin when she took an armload of brown and grey things into the master chamber. "You cannot look like a gentleman. You'll be noticed."

"And what am I to be?" said Robbie, holding a grubby pair of Reg's old breeches at arm's length. "A servant?"

"There is little here that's narrow enough for you," said Catherine. "You cannot go dressed as you were when you were with them, in that red coat. Anyone will know it."

Ann came into the chamber then, bringing their noonday meal. She set down the tray and cocked her head to one side. "They'll be looking for a man and a tall boy. You should go as his wife."

"A woman?" said Robbie. "I will never dress in women's weeds. It is against God's law."

"Ann, you are the wisest person I know," said Catherine. "That's it. You will wear Diana's things. She is near your size, and she will want more of her clothing. You will be this sorry merchant's wife." She put her hand on her son's cheek and he turned it away. "You have barely any beard at all. You'll make a fine young mistress."

"It is a heresy," Robbie said. "I will not do it."

"It is a suicide to put yourself under the axe when you might stay alive," said Catherine. "This is what we will do, and you will do it or take your chance with the Lord

Chancellor. He may put you next to one of your mates on the rack, and you can trade war stories."

This sobered the boy, but he did not agree to the plan.

"You will like a skirt better than you liked the inside of a wall," said Benjamin. "If they cut your head off, you will be inside four walls for the rest of eternity, and they'll be tighter than the ones downstairs. Colder, as well."

Catherine could see the night of hiding pass through his mind, and Robbie sagged. He coveted glory and he was in love with the idea of danger. Clearly, the reality of discomfort had fewer attractions.

"You will leave this night," Catherine pressed on, "after the servants are abed. I have already told them that the horses are to be sold. I will walk them out of the gate at dusk and tie them nearby. You will eat your fill and take more for your ride. Do not stop until you must."

"How will I deliver you a message?" said Benjamin.

"You will not," said Catherine. "You will go, and when you can safely return, I will come and lead you home."

He said, "Very well. It's decided then." And said no more.

Catherine ached to spend the rest of the daylight in their marriage bed with him, but there was no time, and no space for private love. The servants were up and down the stairs, as was their duty, and the story of the horses had to be carried through. Food was needed, more food, and the pretending that it needed to be discarded and the packing of it into bags, then the carrying of it stealthily out the front gate, took up the hours before dinner. Every odd sound sent her dashing to the window, in fear that Edward was riding in with a company of Gardiner's men, and by the time the sun began to set, her whole body was alive with twitches and jumps, as though a tiny army of rats had set up camp beneath her skin.

The stable men seemed willing enough to believe that the "gentleman" who had purchased their horses was waiting "in the road," with so large a train of servants that they would not fit into the courtyard. Catherine walked the geldings out herself, happy that she had chosen tractable ones, who would plod along on either side of her and wait patiently while she tied them to a sturdy bush up the road. Some dead grass still tufted nearby, and they were content to be left on their own, to tear at the bristly clumps and keep each other company.

The sun would not go all the way down, lingering on the horizon with its bloody eye directed at the Davies House. Catherine watched it from a back room upstairs while the men dressed, willing it to drop and then praying for it never to move again. The eye finally drowsed, then closed, and soon the sky had pulled a black lid over itself.

A couple of tapers still shone in the stables. The men were playing at cards or dicing. She could hear a chord of laughter now and then. A loud curse. One of the maids came out of the kennel, straightening her apron, and after Catherine heard the kitchen door thud shut, she saw the master of the kennel emerge from the same door, adjusting the front of his breeches and heading for the stable. Well. Let them occupy themselves. Who knew how little time anyone had with breath in the body?

The games went on, but no one else stirred, and Catherine slid over to Reg's chamber, where Benjamin and Robbie were waiting for her signal to go. She almost didn't recognize her son. He might have been a merchant's wife indeed. Ann had packed his bodice with flat pillows, and he was practicing walking in the skirt. Twice he stepped upon his hem and almost sent himself tumbling into the hearth.

"I will have to claim you as a drunkard," said Benjamin, helping him stand. "The men will all pity me for having a dissolute bedmate."

"Do not jest or I will stay here," said Robbie.

"And a shrewish one, to top all," said Benjamin. "Come, what will we call you?"

"Rosamund," said Catherine. Robbie protested, but she said, "It is close enough that if you misspeak, it will go unnoticed as a pet name."

"And I will take Lewis."

"No. Not your brother's name. Nothing to tie you to that place. You will be, let me think. Matthew? Matthew what?" She looked at Ann. "Smith. Matthew Smith."

"Excellent, forgettable name," said Ann. "I have taken a bundle of embroidered linens down to the horses, and you may say they are for sale. They are not much, but you may say that you are headed home to get more."

"And where is home?" Benjamin was adjusting Robbie's hood, and Robbie was fighting his hands. He almost slapped like a girl.

"Home may be wherever you like. Wherever is west of where you are."

"That will do. I know plenty of villages that no one has heard of." Benjamin set his dagger into its sheath. "We are ready then."

"No long goodbyes," said Catherine. She could not bear even the thought.

"No. And no long separation." Benjamin took her in his arms, kissed her on the mouth, and set her away from him. Robbie came forward, keeping his toes free of the skirt, and kissed her cheek.

Reg led them out, and Catherine and Ann watched from the window. They moved quickly out the front door, and after Reg had checked both corners of the house and beckoned, they ran across the courtyard. Then they were gone, and Reg closed and latched the gate after them.

## CHAPTER FIFTY

The Davies House was searched three times in the following weeks, by Edward and Stephen. The first two times they went through the house cursorily, opening the cupboards and peeking into the smaller closets. Catherine said nothing. She waited by the front door, her hands crossed over her breast, while Ann followed the men, complaining about their dirty boots.

The third time, Stephen did not come, but Edward brought a band of unspeaking ruffians with him, and they surged through the front door and fanned across the rooms. They'd brought hand tools, and as Catherine took up her usual position at the front, she could hear them, breaking chests into splinters with axes and knocking holes in the walls. Cups and bowls were smashed in the kitchen. She could stand it no more and ran downstairs to find the floor strewn with the broken crockery and the kitchen maids weeping over the mess.

Edward and his men had gone out back and left the door open, and before Catherine could close it, here came the dogs, loosed from their kennels. She ran out to find two stout servants of the Lord Chancellor stabbing at the straw bedding. One of the bitches had whelped, and Catherine grabbed one man before he stuck his sword into the pups.

"Are you a beast?" she cried. "There is no one hidden here. These are little ones, you see?" She set back the straw to show the whimpering muzzles.

The man turned a red face on her. "I have orders," he said. "The old woman says they're here."

"In a dog's bed?" said Catherine. She lifted one of the quivering pups from its nest and held it out. She was glad that Alice was not at home to witness the cruelty. "We will be fortunate if the mother doesn't eat them after this."

The ruddy stain in the man's cheeks deepened from rage to shame, and he slunk out. The others had already gone through the stables, and Catherine thanked God that Edward had never made a count of the horses.

Inside, the maids had swept the floor and now cowered under the tables, clutching their pet cats and each other. But the men didn't notice them. They followed Edward upstairs, where the destruction continued. They upended the beds and smashed them. They emptied the chests. Edward himself shredded several of Catherine's bodices with an enthusiasm that bordered on glee. He used his own dagger and flung the heap on the floor in the upstairs hall. Then he put his hands on his knees, panting over the mess.

"Where are they?" he said to the scraps of clothing.

Catherine was flat against the wall. She'd never seen such a show of fury over nothing. "You have seen for yourself. They're not here. Nor is anything else, since you've destroyed half of what we own."

Edward waded through the pool of ripped fabric, his dagger raised, and Catherine thought he might cut the clothing from her body. He said, "She swore they were here, and her daughter along with her. She said you would admit to it if pushed to a confession." He pointed the tip of the blade at Catherine and let it ease toward her throat. "Confess, then. Tell me where they are."

The steel was cold, and Catherine said, "Remove your weapon first." The muscles in her thighs shook, and she was afraid she would faint. Or wet herself. Ann appeared at the end of the hall and stopped with a gasp.

Edward's eyelid twitched and he stepped back. He lowered the dagger. "Tell me."

"They are not here," whispered Catherine, and Ann came shouting down the hall, knocking Edward backward onto the pile of bodices.

"Has he cut you?" she said.

Catherine touched her throat and checked her fingers. "No." Edward was struggling to his feet, and she said, "Get out of my house."

He managed to get upright, and, as he dusted himself, Ann let a kick fly and caught him on the backside, sending him into the wall beside Catherine. "You ought to be whipped all the way to London Bridge."

His men had gathered at the head of the stairs and someone snickered as Edward righted himself once more. He tucked in his shirt and began to walk away, but Catherine hooked his arm.

"Wait. You said 'swore.'"

"Swore what?" Edward said.

"You said 'she swore they were here.' Wherefore not 'swears'?"

Now Edward laughed. "They don't last long in the gaol. Not when they're old and bent at the beginning."

"You killed Old Moll?" asked Catherine.

"Not I," said Edward. "I might have done it well enough, but it's not my task."

"But your Gardiner might take it as his. And who is this daughter you spoke of?"

He shrugged. "Some woman. I don't know. I am not the master. Why do you care? She'd've had you there beside her, if she'd had the power to order it. She probably figured on a reward. She got her reward, for certain." He gave Ann one more glare, then turned and ordered his men out.

Catherine and Ann did not have them ushered downstairs, and they heard the door slam shut below. Ann said, "That woman had a demon in her. Why do you care?"

Catherine kicked the pile of clothes. "Who is the daughter?"

Reg opened the door of the master chamber. He had his dagger in his hand.

"A bit late with that," said Ann. "They've gone."

Reg looked crestfallen. "I was told to keep up the appearance of a sickness," he said. "What would he have done if I'd come charging out like Saint George?"

"He's right," said Catherine. "What good would it have done us to have Reg hauled off with them? They know he was down there with Benjamin when the fighting broke out."

"Ah, well," said Ann. She kissed Reg on the cheek as he sheathed the weapon. "You know what you're about, after all."

"If I'd heard fighting, I would not have cared for my life," he said.

"I know," said Ann. "Shall we follow them and see that they've gone?"

"Reg must not go," said Catherine. "Get back into bed. We can take Thomas. And set the girls to cleaning up whatever can be saved."

Edward and his men were long gone by the time they walked out, Thomas beside them with a blank face, as though the stables had not just been ransacked. The streets, even this far north, stank of rot, and Catherine could not endure it. "The bodies will have to be taken down soon, won't they?"

she said, but Ann wasn't listening. She was pulling a pamphlet from a nearby wall.

"What is this?" she said, handing it to Catherine. "What does it say?"

Catherine read a few lines. "It is not possible," she said. "We cannot have sunk so low."

Ann said, "Read it to me. Read it all." Catherine folded the pamphlet, but Ann insisted. "I want to hear."

"We are an island of monsters."

"Read it."

Catherine skimmed the writing again. She did not know where to begin. At the beginning? But it had begun months ago. It had begun when the queen rejected the English suitor. When Jane Grey allowed herself to be crowned. When she married Guildford Dudley. When Edward VI had died.

Ann was waiting. Thomas watched a sparrow pack loose straw into a nest in a nearby eave.

"It is worse than it was, if it can be worse," said Catherine. She did not want to give sound to the letters on the page. "The bodies are being taken down."

"That's good," said Ann. "Give them a burial, rebels or not."

Catherine shook her head. Her voice lodged in her throat and her tongue thickened. She thought if she said more, that she would surely cry. "They are being taken to Newgate."

"The prison?" said Thomas. "What can they do to them there?"

Catherine turned away. She held her breath, trying to slow her heart. Ann came around to face her. "Can you not tell it?"

Catherine shook her head. Her body began to shake. The trembling washed through her and out. She whispered, "They're boiling them."

Ann stepped backward. "What do you say?"

Catherine held out the pamphlet, but she was the only one of the three who could read. "They will be boiled and quartered. The remains will be hung out for all of London to see."

Thomas leaned against the building, laying his hand where the pamphlet had been. "Ah, Christ," he said. "Christ in heaven, this is not England."

Ann snatched the pamphlet and stared at it, as though the words would conjure themselves into meaning for her. Then she crumpled it in her fist. "And when was England ever anything but a dirty island in a cold sea?"

Catherine said, "I recall my childhood as a kind of paradise. There was dirt, yea, and cold. But there was fire in the winter and bread enough. There was nothing like this."

"Because you were in the convent," said Ann, "snug in thick walls and safe from the secret of your own birth. It was different for others."

And that was true. It was Henry VIII and Thomas Cromwell who had taken that sanctuary from her.

"And do not blame Henry for it," Ann went on. "I see it on your face. I hated him as much as you did, but do not pretend that you did not have a place that others envied."

And that was true, too. Ann had come later, after a life of hunger and an evil marriage. Catherine had grown up inside, with the nuns, and was petted and protected. If it had not been for Henry and his greed for an heir, she might be there still. She might be a prioress herself.

Ann said, more softly, "Forgive me. This news overwhelms my spirit." She touched Catherine's arm, then scratched at her wrist with the edge of the crushed pamphlet. "I don't mean to blame you for any of this."

"But the queen?" said Catherine. "You mean to blame Mary."

Ann shook her head. "I don't know. She must know what is happening. She cannot pretend she doesn't, after all of this death."

"It is not over yet," Catherine said. "The killing will go on." She uncurled Ann's hand and removed the paper. "They have dechartered the town of Maidstone and will hang twenty more there." She did not look down. She knew what it said. "Jane Grey's father will be executed."

"What is Maidstone to the queen?" asked Thomas.

"Wyatt's town," said Ann. "The rebels began their march there."

"And Edward Wyatt is to be sentenced," said Catherine. She looked at Thomas. "The rebel's brother."

"He is a little boy," said Ann. "Will nothing satisfy Gardiner's hunger for blood?"

Catherine nodded. "I want to go back home." They walked inside without speaking. Catherine was sure she could smell blood on the air now, but it was her own body, stinking of its mortality.

They sat beside Reg, upstairs, all that afternoon and evening. The next morning, Catherine could not raise herself to leave the house, and she spent the day trying to balance the account books downstairs. But the furniture had been destroyed, and the numbers swam as she sat on the floor, and after she had made the third error, she leaned back and shut her eyes. Reg ventured downstairs with Ann, and together they ordered the disposal of the broken chairs and crockery and doled out the torn clothing to the servants who were clever with their needles. The house was clouded with dust, but Catherine was almost glad to see the goods going out the door and into the fires. Every time a servant approached with a twisted hinge or a torn sleeve, she said, "You keep it," or "Give it away," and as the day went on, her heart lightened. Empty the house. Clean it.

Ann came up from the kitchen with a jug of wine and two intact cups and pulled up a stool beside her. Catherine said, "Our Lord rode into Jerusalem on a borrowed ass. He had nothing but the cloak upon his back."

Ann offered a cup. "And they killed Him just the same."

Catherine drank. A girl carrying an armload of shredded linens whisked down the stairs and around the corner, headed to the lower stairs. She wore a heavy dress, made out of an old one of Veronica's. "So they did," Catherine said.

"You cannot stop it by hiding," said Ann.

"Nor do I have to watch them do it," said Catherine. Ann lifted her cup at that, and Catherine touched it with her own.

# Chapter Fifty-One

Edward Wyatt was to be hanged, and Catherine could almost not believe her ears when the maid came up to the master chamber with the whole story. She'd gotten it straight from the others when they came back from the baker. "And they will draw and quarter him after," the girl continued. "Will they do that, Madam, to a little boy? Because he followed his older brother?"

"They will probably slaughter his horse, too, if he had one," said Ann. The maid's face showed horror, and she added, "But he was likely too young to own a horse of his own."

Reg was sitting up, and he said, "We could ride away. We could do it today." The girl left and he said, "No one suspects any one of us."

Catherine considered it. "But if we go, will it not look as though we are admitting to guilt?"

"The decision is yours," said Ann.

Catherine said, "The time is wrong. We cannot call any more attention to our family. Not now. This killing must stop. Soon."

But as the days went on, the revenge against the rebels grew warmer with the air. The boy was hanged indeed, and his lanky child's body cut down, drawn, and quartered. Someone drew pictures of the maimed corpse and plastered them all over London. Ann found one as she and Catherine walked back from a Mass, and though she could not read words, Ann could read a drawing well enough, and she handed the paper to Catherine without a comment.

And then it was that the tortures of Wyatt himself began. The news was whispered in the church doors, in the taverns, in the streets and under the awnings of the merchants. Elizabeth Tudor was said to be the cause. Elizabeth Tudor had planned the war against her sister and had promised money to the men who would set her on the throne. Wyatt was being beaten, racked, starved and left naked in a cold Tower cell. He would confess. He would implicate her. They would die together.

The sun grew fatter and shone with a brighter light, and the wind along the river brought a green smell into the city. Catherine awakened one morning in her lone bed to the sound of larks and sparrows, calling to their mates to begin the spring nesting. One of the mares foaled, and Catherine almost cried when she was led into the stall to greet the new addition. She sat in the dirty straw and pulled the hard body onto her lap, letting the knobby legs flail in the air. The mare snuffed in mild alarm at her baby's hooves, and the stable men cried out, "Madam, the straw is all muck!" but Catherine put her face down, breathed in the scent of hay and sweat in the soft fur, and cried.

In the end, Wyatt was condemned to die, as all knew by now he would be. As his life grew shorter, the days grew longer. Edward and his men invaded them no more, and Catherine wondered whose house they were destroying next. Catherine no longer left Davies House, because she no longer had a place to go that was free of the stench of death. And on the afternoon of a day in early April, when one of her maids crept up to her, she knew what the message would be.

"Madam? The men are returned from the wine merchant," the maid ventured.

Catherine was sitting beside her window upstairs. Ann was beside her, stitching the hem of a doublet that Benjamin had left behind.

Catherine turned to look at the girl's wide face. She was no bigger than Alice. Unless Alice had grown. She would have grown. Catherine's heart felt barbed all over. "And there is news?"

"The Wyatt has been killed," said the girl. She did not move to go.

"And is that all?" Catherine said. "After these weeks of butchery, they have done him in so neatly?"

The girl's cheeks flushed. "They say that he has sworn the Lady Elizabeth is innocent. That he said it on the scaffold, so it must be true. They claim that the priest tried to say him nay, but he put on the blindfold himself and told them to kill him right then and there."

"And what is the news of the Lady Elizabeth?"

"No news. People say that the queen will release her. She's her sister, after all, isn't she?"

"Yes. And the queen must be merciful at last. They are both women, after all, and they are kindred."

The girl brightened. "And they say the axe man held up the head after he cut it off the Wyatt and took off the cloth so that they'd all see it was truly him. He's to be quartered, they say."

"Enough," said Catherine, holding up her hand against the torrent of information. "I can hear no more."

The girl curtseyed. "Forgive my loose tongue, Madam."

"It is not your tongue that's at fault, child," said Catherine. "You speak the truth. The truth is sometimes simply too much to bear. Go on down and have a rest, if you can pull together enough cloths to make a pallet."

"Thank you, Madam." The girl rose and backed out.

When the door had closed behind her, Catherine said, "How much of this butchery has the queen ordered, do you think?"

Ann stuck the needle into the fabric and looked up. "Do you want my opinion or do you want me to soothe you?"

Catherine shook her head. "It's too much. There's nothing left here except the walls and the food we've bought. We must go from this place. We must go now."

"Well, at least we are in agreement about that," said Ann.

## Chapter Fifty-Two

Reg would not let them go without him. He spread the word among the servants that the mistress would travel into Yorkshire, now that the days were longer and the rains had let up. She would go to see about the new lambs, the shearing, and spinning and weaving. He ordered in boards for making new kitchen furniture, and Ann ordered food and drink to be bought for the journey. The horses were made fit for travel.

Arthur Huff asked to be allowed to ride along, and Catherine gave him permission gladly. He would be a safe enough companion. Reg said, "We must take Thomas."

"Is he not needed to help the carpenters?" asked Catherine.

"He must come along with us," said Reg.

Thomas had earned her trust, and Catherine agreed without further argument. Reg seemed set upon it, and five would be enough. Large enough not to raise the attention of the Lord Chancellor but small enough to evade particular notice along the road.

The morning of their departure, Catherine woke agitated, her skin alive and itching. What if they lost their way? What if they were caught? What if they were followed?

But who would catch them? And what could be said? That a woman travelled to her own family, with her woman and her servants? There was no treason in it, not a thing upon which to hang a person. Unless it was known that she had told her household she was going north and then went into Wales. But who would arrest a woman for changing her mind?

No one. Or so she hoped, as she rose and called for a maid to help her dress. She needed warm clothing, subdued in colour and spacious in cut. Forgettable clothing. A matron's weeds. The girl dawdled over her hood, worried that it did not sit correctly, and Catherine, impatient, finally said, "Go on and break your fast. I will finish this."

The girl ran off happily, to her chores or to her play. Let her play. Catherine didn't care. She wanted to be as far from London as she could go.

She left the old master of the stables in charge of the house. He was a sober widower in his middle sixties, too old to handle the horse work, but still a capable jack-of-all-trades, not given to drink and uninterested in women. He nodded gravely and promised to look after the young ones, as she handed over the keys. He had five grandchildren of his own, and three of them were right here under the roof, working in the kitchen and the stables. He would put things into what order he could.

Thomas brought around the horses, and Reg helped him load them. Catherine didn't bother to check the supplies. She pulled herself into her palfrey's saddle and turned to the gate without a qualm, and as she passed through, the road north, out of London and its stink of rotting bodies, lay before her like a promise.

But they did not ride north for long. They turned westward once they were clear of the city, Reg and Thomas in the lead, and Arthur, riding at the back, called, "Madam? Have we turned the wrong way?"

Catherine slowed her mare to allow the boy catch up. "We are not riding to Yorkshire," she said. "We will hold that for another day."

Arthur said, "Where then?"

"Wales," said Catherine.

Arthur said, "To Master Benjamin's people?"

"The same. Keep your voice down." A couple was coming down the road toward them, their horses trotting. They must be eager to get to the town. Go back, Catherine wanted to say. Turn around. But she held her tongue and drew Arthur toward her by the reins. "No talk of our destination, not between yourselves or to others. We are on our way to Yorkshire, if anyone asks."

Arthur gazed at her hand upon the leather strap that he held. "To Yorkshire."

"We have properties there, sheep and business to tend. We're going to Yorkshire."

Thomas said, "When do we give up that story?"

Catherine looked toward the west. The sun was already before them. They couldn't go much farther before dark. The journey stretched out in her mind. "When we see the big mountain. What's it called? The mountain of snow."

"Snowdon," said Reg.

"Yes," said Catherine. "We must ride toward the great mountain, and then we will be within calling distance of our destination."

"A snow mountain," echoed Arthur.

Reg said, "That is a long way westward for people who are supposed to be going to Yorkshire."

Catherine thought. "Once we get into the west of England, we will say we are going to Yorkshire after we buy some sheep. The sheep are in the west of Wales. After that, we will say nothing, but that we are headed to our family home. Let's hope we are not asked at all."

"A snow mountain," said Arthur. "I will see that."

"Yes," said Catherine, "but not if we sit here upon the road."

Thomas and Reg led on again, and Arthur trotted up to ride beside them. Catherine rode behind, with Ann. She allowed herself a smile. She had brought the best companions with her. They would be safe enough.

In the country, England seemed a different land altogether. Sheep and cows grazed in the open fields, carelessly chomping at whatever young grasses and old stems they could find. The villages were quiet, and smelt clean, of pig dung and chicken feathers, of life. They passed no great houses and no great men. The inn where they stopped the first night was empty, and they lodged in the best rooms. Catherine was presented with a long, narrow chamber that contained a table at one end and a feather bed at the other, next to the hearth. She sniffed the sheets for mildew, and, finding them fresh, threw herself backward onto the covers, sighing at the softness. She breathed in the scent of firewood and lavender flowers. They must have been strewn beneath the bed, but she was too tired and stiff to get up and look. Wherever they were, they weren't the stench of dead men and fear.

She almost missed supper, waking only when Ann came in to shake her shoulder. "Have you sworn off our company now?"

Catherine opened her eyes and laughed out loud. "I'm coming," she said. She stretched and jumped up. "We have done it, Ann. We are out of that stew."

"Indeed we are," said Ann, "and now I would like to eat one."

Catherine wrapped her arm around her friend's waist and walked with her, out to the big table, where the innkeeper and his wife were laying platters of meat and carrots with leeks and bread. Three big jugs had already been placed, and Thomas sat at a low spot, watching the metal sweat.

"Drink, Thomas," said Catherine as she sat. "You have led us well today."

He poured for himself, gratefully, and for Arthur Huff, who had taken the seat on his left. Reg had been out back, washing himself, and came in rolling down his sleeves. He sat next to Ann. Catherine looked around the table and almost wept at the beauty of it. Men and women together, without rancor or mistrust. No one vying for the high place. "Will you not sit with us?" she said to the innkeeper's wife.

"That we will, Mistress," said the woman, "if you want the company." They sat, introducing themselves as Maud and Simon. Maud only stood as high as her husband's shoulder and while he was narrow as a quill, she was amply padded from shoulder to hip. Together, they put Catherine in mind of a tidy shrub growing beside a gatepost. But they fitted each other well, saying their graces in turn, Simon asking that the country be not overrun with strangers and Maud petitioning God to protect the queen. Catherine found herself able to say amen to it. Then Simon cut the slabs of pork and handed them around, and Maud sent the bread toward Reg, who was clearly hungry. "Where do you ride, then?"

"To Yorkshire," said Catherine quickly. "We have been visiting family and must make our way north as the roads clear."

"We must buy some sheep as we go, west of here," put in Reg.

Catherine had forgotten her own story. "Yes. We own sheep, and we sell the wool."

"Ah," said Maud. "Cold in those parts. In Yorkshire. And where do you come from?"

"We have a winter house in London," said Catherine easily. "And the traders come there when we bring the wool."

"London!" repeated Simon. "So you have seen the great rebellion? You must tell us all the news. They say that armies of the Spanish have been quartered and thrown into the sea and that we are now safe from them. Do tell us. Tell us all."

Catherine did not relish the tale, but she told it, and from a distance it took on the sound of something she had only heard at many removes. The destruction of the bridges. The ragged men, thrusting their way into the city. The captures and the spilling of hunted men from the London taverns. But she choked on the killings. The scent of blood and rotting bodies rose into her nostrils again. She said, "They were not Spanish. They were English, to a man, or so I saw it. I wonder if the Spanish king will set a foot on English soil after this."

"Our queen ordered this?" asked Maud. Her black eyes stabbed into Catherine. She looked ready to turn rebel herself.

Catherine looked at her hands. Her fingers were mashing a wad of bread and she shook the crumbs to the table. "I heard that it was the Lord Chancellor who ordered it, the man who was Bishop of Winchester. A man named Stephen Gardiner."

"This sounds not like a man of God," suggested Simon. He rose to refill the ale jugs. When he returned, he said, "Perhaps these were heretics. I hear that they burn heretics in other kingdoms."

"Perhaps," mused Catherine. Ann was watching her, and she could feel the warning in the look: take care with your words. "Heretics might be punished under the rule of the Church. I'm a simple woman, unskilled in the law. I have never been outside of England."

"Well, we are happier in the country, away from the great ones," said Maud. "We see battles only among the roosters in the hen yard." She lifted her cup and Catherine raised hers to it and said again, "Amen."

But the meal suddenly seemed slick on her tongue, and tasteless. Catherine ate enough for politeness' sake and said, "I feel a great weariness on me. We have ridden a long way. I think I will retire."

"Bad memories," said Maud, patting her hand. "Off with you, Lady. And sleep in peace."

A few minutes later, Catherine could hear Ann and Reg in the next-door room, murmuring, chuckling. Catherine lay alone in the roomy bed, stretching her limbs to the four corners, listening to the familiar rise and fall of her friend's voice. She was safe here. She was comfortable. She, too, would have her husband with her soon. But the face of Jane Grey appeared behind her closed lids, blindfolded and groping the air. She felt herself falling into a drowse and the face became Robbie's, angry and demanding to know where they'd put the block. Catherine startled awake but opened her eyes onto blackness and quiet. Someone moved, whispering, past her door, the innkeeper or his wife, trying not to wake their guests. She wondered whose God they prayed to, when they knelt together in private at night.

The morning rose clear and fine, and Catherine paid the reckoning with a smile and good wishes. Then she asked for directions north and led them out along the road that Maud pointed to. But as soon as they were clear of the village, they turned westward.

They rode five more days to their last shreds of sun before they saw the vague, vast bulk of the great mountain before them. But the daylight was with them longer now, and they had fine weather and solid roads. They met few travellers, and none who paid them any attention. The innkeepers along the way were diligent and the food well-cooked. Catherine gave her name as Eleanor Adwolfe, her Yorkshire manager, one night and, on the other, Christina Bridle. It would have been her mother's name, if her mother had married her father, and Catherine felt it a bit of a joke, until she said the name. When it came out of her mouth, her guts shivered and went cold, as though she might have summoned a malicious spirit in speaking it.

But no ghost haunted her dreams, and she slept soundly. The scent of new grass and the tang of fresh lambs' wool washed the dead smell of London from her head, and she imagined the blue air filling her like clean water.

And there, before them, the mountain grew, bigger and more solid. What had been a shadow in the distance, or a low storm cloud, a gentle smudge on the bright west, rose and became a solid thing, stark and demanding. Catherine had seen hillsides all of her girlhood in Yorkshire, but this mass of stone, capped with snow, made her stop her mare in a sort of reverence.

"The cathedral of S. Paul would fit inside it like a child's toy," said Ann, pulling her pony to a stop beside Catherine. "It looks as though it wants to fall on top of us, devour us."

Reg laughed. "You are all fairy stories. You'll be telling us you see trolls now."

Ann slapped his arm. "I just might. And I suppose you will conquer them with your dagger."

"No," said Reg. He shaded his eyes and stared. "I wonder, though, that a man could grow up under the brows of such a thing and leave it behind for London."

"It frightens me, a little," said Catherine. "I am with Ann. It moves when you look at its summit. See there?" She pointed up. "I cannot hold it still with my eye. Is it alive, do you think?"

"Alive with what?" said Arthur Huff. "Are there demons in it?"

Now Reg fidgeted in his saddle. "We lose the time." He looked over his shoulder. "The sun is chasing us."

For hours it lay before them, seeming to move away as they approached, and Catherine felt the gaze of the great promontory on her. No one spoke much, and Reg whistled a nervous tune. He, too, must have been feeling the strangeness of the land they had entered. Catherine was thinking of sprites and knew herself to be thinking like a silly girl. And yet, they were the strangers, and who knew what sort of beings might inhabit such a place?

"Lady Catherine, has Master Benjamin never brought you to his home, in all your years of marriage?" said Thomas. He'd been silent most of the day, and Catherine startled at the sound of his voice.

Ann glanced at the man, as though she thought the question impertinent, but they had been together for so many days that Catherine had gotten easy in her talk. And with the great mountain there, she craved some normal converse to make the land familiar. She said, "He cast off Wales before I met him, Thomas. He did come back here twice, but Alice fell ill on the eve of the journey, and she was just little then, and so I stayed at home. On the other occasion, the rain was heavy and we determined that it was not fit weather for any of the children."

"Do you know the way, then?" Thomas asked.

Catherine laughed. "I know that Wales has a great mountain and that the Davies properties are not far from it." She looked up. The mountain had gone filmy in the late air, as though she could almost see through it. "Tomorrow morning, perhaps."

Thomas looked at Reg. Reg nodded. "Perhaps," Thomas said. "I must make a confession to you, Lady Catherine. We have ridden past the Davies lands and will circle back tomorrow."

"What? How do you know this?" said Catherine. She backed away, but Thomas raised his hands.

"I came from here," he said. "My brother was with your Benjamin from the time he was a boy, but I come from Lewis. I know these hills from many years back." He glanced up the darkening road. "He bade me, before he left, to lead you here if there was danger, but not to tell you, in the case of your being taken prisoner. Better for you not to know, until we were here."

Catherine looked at Reg. "And you know this, I suppose, already?"

Reg flushed. "The secret was kept to protect you." He caught Ann's eye. "And you. Thomas and I have been watching for followers. We have seen none. We judge that it's safe enough to turn now and find our destination."

"I never knew you for such a keeper of information," said Ann. The two men sat, awaiting the lash of her tongue, but she said, "Well, the world has turned us all the wrong way out. Lead on, and bring us to a bed, if you know where one is."

They followed Thomas now, against the setting sun and under the slivers of crimson and gold that it scattered in its wake. At the very last light, they came upon an inn, and Reg went in to ask for rooms. The innkeeper came out with him, clucking about the darkness and the danger of thieves, though they had seen nothing for hours but old men herding sheep along the road and a couple of women with chickens under their arms. The man squinted up at Catherine and she almost laughed at the froth of white hair below her. He looked like a mushroom with a dollop of cream on its head. "Noswaith dda," he said.

Catherine, perplexed, said nothing.

"English?" he said.

"Yes," said Catherine.

"Esgusodwch fi," he replied, more to himself than to her. "I don't speak the English too many. Come in, come in."

His wife, who was his match in height and width, with her white hair neatly twisted onto her head, spoke no English at all, but she could see well enough what was wanted and went about directing them all to rooms and snapping her fingers for her maids. They must have been her daughters, as the three were images of their parents. Lamb and carrots and brown bread were laid on the table, and jugs of ale with them. The family stood watch as they ate, and Catherine finally turned to the husband and said "Do you know of the Davies family?"

"Davies, yes. Much Davies here."

"Lewis Davies? Son of David Davies? Brother to one Benjamin?"

The wife laughed out loud and said "Davith Davies?"

Catherine nodded, unsure if she understood.

The woman pointed to her feet and Catherine looked to the husband. He said, "This land sits almost against Davies land. Much near."

"And Davies House? The house of Lewis Davies?" said Catherine.

"The push of a stone. That way." The husband pointed east. Thomas smiled at his plate. Their journey was done.

# CHAPTER FIFTY-THREE

The morning rose wet and cold, but Catherine could wait no longer. The innkeeper offered a map, but Thomas assured them that he had one between his ears, and they flew east, through wind and slapping rain. Mud-splattered and soaked, they turned into the lane before the sun was at its zenith. The trees were thick, so thick that the earth was leaf-strewn and matted, and Catherine had some misgivings about Thomas's memory. This place did in fact look like a land of trolls.

She slowed her palfrey to a walk and said to Reg, "Does this look like a road to a house?" Thomas laughed and rode off, away from them, and around a few of the trees.

"I see no one," Reg said. "This lane is nothing but dirt." But here came Thomas back again, waving them forward.

"On we go, then," said Catherine. "I remember when the lanes of a couple of villages in Yorkshire looked no cleaner than this." She took it at a walk, though, letting Reg ride ahead, one hand on the hilt of his dagger.

The trees thinned, and they spied a trio of sheep. When the ewes saw them, they came ambling over, their speckled faces open with expectation. "Those animals think we have food," said Arthur.

"That's a good sign," said Catherine, just as they turned a corner.

The house was before them, a massive presence, four stories high, at least, but dark, as though it had been rubbed all over with soot. Fat stone towers jutted from the top, and Catherine wondered if they sheltered guards. The place was grand but forbidding, a murky palace, and Catherine did not know whether to gasp at its size or to shudder at its mood. Thomas had circled around and sat behind her. "Is this it?" she said, but he had no time to answer, as a band of men was already riding toward them. One of them raised his hand. He was calling out a greeting, or a warning, or an oath. It was impossible to tell, and Catherine reined her mare. The men came on, spreading out so that two were on either side of the party while the speaking man remained in front. Thomas moved in front of Catherine and Ann, and the lead man rode up to him and spoke. But none of them could understand his words. The stranger clapped Thomas on the shoulder, and they made out "Thomas Jones" in the middle of the exchange.

Reg called, "Benjamin Davies." He pointed at Catherine. "Catherine. Catherine Davies."

The man scrutinized Reg for a few seconds, then turned his eyes to Catherine. She touched her own breast. "Catherine Davies."

The man grinned at Thomas and beckoned. He said something to his fellows, and they all turned and rode back again at a gallop, kicking up clods of dirt as they went. Reg said, "I believe that may be a welcome."

Ann said, "We may as well say so."

They followed, across a clipped lawn. The grass was tawny and stiff with the recent cold, but Catherine could see some green showing beneath her mare's hooves as they went. The shrubs near the house were also trimmed, and the bushes, nearer the woods they had come through, she saw as she looked back, were all at least rough-hewn into shape. The wilderness rose again at a distance beyond the grim structure, and Catherine now saw stables and sheds and other structures for animals. A river ran off to the left, and beside it, more sheep, careless and unbound by fences. Reg took a leisurely pace, keeping some distance between themselves and the Davies men. He was watching for danger, a sudden attack, and by the time they reached the house, a tall man stood at the front door, watching them come ahead. His belly, slung low and protruding like a boulder, had already come outside, but the rest of him remained on the threshold. He was mostly bald but for a white fringe, like a monk gone slovenly in his personal habits, and he wore a short beard that had once been dark but was turning ashy. A wide smile of crooked, stained teeth. Catherine thought he was shouting, but, no, he was laughing out loud, and he called, "You have ridden all this way to seek a husband, Lady, have you not?"

He stepped all the way outside, and in the space he left, appeared Benjamin. Alice held his hand, and Veronica whooped and flew out, running with her skirts in one hand to greet her mother. Catherine slid to the ground and ran to clasp her daughter in her arms. "You are taller by a head!" Catherine said.

Veronica twirled on one foot. Her hair fell loose, and she caught it in her hand. "The countryside does me good, Mother. You see how I have filled out!"

She looked fine indeed, a little pale, but fuller in the breasts and hips. She looked like a woman. Her blue eyes matched the spring sky, and Catherine's heart knocked painfully at her ribs for a moment. The young men would want her for their own soon, and then she would be Catherine's girl no longer.

Then Benjamin was beside her, and Alice wrapped her arms around Catherine's waist. She knelt and held her younger daughter. Alice was brown as a nut, and while her sister spun, Alice stood her ground, gazing out at the world with a sober eye. "How do you, my daughter?" said Catherine in her ear.

"No, you say 'Sut ydych chi?' or 'Sut mae?'" said Alice, and a shy grin spread over her face.

"What does it mean?"

"It means 'How are you?'" said Benjamin.

Catherine stood and embraced her husband. "I'm very happy to see you."

He put his nose to her cheek. "I miss the smell of your hair. Have you come to free us from our exile?"

Catherine nestled under his arm and looked out over the lawn. The house sat in a valley, she could see now, and the narrow river wound through it, right up to the back of the house. The kitchen would likely open almost directly out onto fresh water. And with the sun overhead, the flat land in the distance was showing its first golden greens, with tiny daisies and violets blowing among the young grasses. In the distance, a few sheep grazed in a bored, spoilt way, as though cropping the lawn were their only task in the world. Their fleeces were fat and greasy, and for a brief moment Catherine was tempted to break away and sink her fingers into their wool to see how fine it really was.

"Why would you call such a place an exile?" she said.

"It is too familiar to me," said Benjamin. "Ah, here's Diana."

Catherine's stepdaughter was walking out, dressed in her usual grey skirt and bodice. A nun without a convent, thought Catherine.

"Forgive my slowness, Mother," said the younger woman. She kissed Catherine and the scent of lavender came from her like the breath of summer. "I was teaching the younger maids to play and I had to put the instruments away."

"It lifts my soul to see your face," said Catherine. "And are you well?"

Diana nodded. "I am well enough. The air here is full of health."

"Am I to stand all day like a servant and be ignored?" said the big man with the great guts.

"My apologies," said Benjamin. He bowed, almost ironically. "Catherine, this is my brother, Lewis Davies."

Diana stepped back and folded her hands before her. Veronica stopped dancing. Lewis grabbed Catherine and she felt his belly press against her, just a bit too hard. The stiff beard scraped her cheek as he planted a wet kiss on her cheek, almost catching the corner of her mouth. His hand grazed the back of her skirt, a few inches too low. But then he released her, and except for a damp blotch at her lip, Catherine re-emerged unscathed into the sunlight.

"And here's our Reg and Ann, come to torment me," said Benjamin. He embraced Reg and shook hands with Ann, who turned away to hug Veronica. Benjamin thumped Reg's side and said, "Are you healed through?" and when he had the assurance that everyone was whole, he turned to the serving men. "And you have brought me my very own Arthur. You look more like a Huff every day, boy." He dashed his hand over Arthur's hair, and Arthur endured it, though he was too old for such play, and bowed to Benjamin with a smile that seemed sincere. "And Thomas Jones, good as your word. Thanks for bringing my lady to me."

"Your servant," said Thomas, inclining his head. Catherine had never heard him speak so formally. She had never even asked for his second name and shame scorched her face.

"What is the news from the city?" asked Benjamin. "Are we to ride in triumph through the streets and be served our dinners by the queen?"

Catherine felt the laugh melt out of her. London was far, far away. Queen and court had become even less than a story in their days on the road. They'd turned into a dream she'd had, Gardiner a fragment of nightmare. "I wish it were true. London is become a tomb, and it stinks of death."

The girls all went quiet, staring at her. Even Lewis dropped his unctuous smile and waited. But Catherine did not want to tell about hangings and quarterings of men here in the bright valley, with the river singing over the stones and the heavens wide open above her. She could hear men somewhere behind the house, and someone was calling in a tongue she could not understand, but she knew the tone. They were working together, and they were content. She knew, though she could not see them. She looked around. The door still stood open, but it was vacant.

"By my soul," she said. "Where is my son?"

## CHAPTER FIFTY-FOUR

They found Robbie Overton in the house, in his chamber on the third floor, reading from his Book of Common Prayer. When Benjamin opened the door, the young man glanced up, leaving one long forefinger upon the page and said simply, "Hallo, Mother."

He looked at her as though he had only been away for a few days, as though nothing had come between them but an ordinary journey to see some long-lost family. "Come and greet me with a proper kiss," said Catherine, though it was she who moved across the room and bent to him. He replied with a dutiful pressing of dry lips on her cheek, then withdrew again into the chair. The finger remained on the words.

"Always stuck inside a book, that one," said Lewis from the doorway. "He'll shrivel like an old apple. Doesn't like the fresh air or the horses. What are you going to find in those pages that you can't find out there on the mountain?"

"Your mother has ridden from London to be at your side, Robert," said Benjamin, squeezing past his brother to enter the room. "You might at least lift yourself to your feet."

"I have been thinking upon my soul," said Robbie to the air. He did not look directly at any of the three adults. "All of our souls. I think perhaps we should have stayed in the city and faced our adversary like men. It would have been nobler."

"Well, I am no man, but I have seen enough of what happens to them when they battle," said Catherine. She was less happy to see her son than she had expected to be. That old twinge at the heart, as though a string had been snapped against it, when she saw any of her children, did not strike her now, though the sight of her daughters had been as painfully sweet as ever. Everyone who met Robbie commented eventually on their resemblance—the black, wavy hair, the pale complexion and bright eyes—but Catherine couldn't see it. He looked as far from her as any stranger. She said, "They have killed Jane Grey and Guildford Dudley. They have killed your Wyatt and his small kinsman, in most horrible ways. They will kill Jane Grey's father next, if it's not been done already."

Robbie's finger drummed upon the page. Benjamin said, "All of them?"

"Every one," said Catherine.

"God in Heaven, who are we become?" said Benjamin.

Catherine said, "Enough of this for now. There's plenty of time to speak of it. Let's go down. Ann and Reg and Thomas are likely half-dead from hunger and unwilling to say so."

"Ann? Unwilling to speak? She must be near death indeed," said Benjamin, and he tried out a laugh, but the sound was hollow. Robbie remained impassive and lowered his eyes again. Benjamin shook his head and steered Catherine out. In the hallway, he whispered, "He frets on his cowardice and believes it has endangered his soul."

"Being gutted and strewn about the streets like a calf would endanger him more," said Catherine.

"The boy needs to get outside. He needs to get on a horse and hunt with the other boys," said Lewis, shutting the door after them. He spoke loudly enough to be heard, even through the heavy wood. "We ought to burn his books."

Benjamin said, "Have they truly done so? Killed so many?"

"Killed and gutted," said Catherine. "And worse. I did not see it all with my own eyes. But pamphlets have been nailed up all over the city. And they say that the bodies of the hanged were parboiled and stuck on the gates like chunks of meat. I have seen the heads on London Bridge. The whole place stinks like a shambles. And then some were quartered. I did not witness it. But every fool and his father have made drawings and plastered them on every bare wall." She stopped. If she opened her mouth she would repeat it all yet again. She was afraid she was beginning to sound like Old Moll.

"The city is a dirty place," said Lewis, "and the court is a stew. Me, I like to be where I'm king of the castle, master of my own land. Who needs London when a man has land?"

Benjamin said nothing to his brother, but Catherine saw a shadow slip across his face. She'd heard him express such sentiments himself, though he'd always claimed to love London.

They walked down and found Ann and Reg in the kitchen, already busy with a loaf and a jug of ale, a hunk of yellow cheese. Diana, Veronica, and Alice had the lower places and sat watching them eat. They'd clearly been telling stories, because Alice had her chin propped on her hands. Ann looked up and said, "I cannot understand a word anyone here says."

Benjamin took a stool and let Reg pour him a cup. "Never mind that. We won't stay for long. Will we?" He looked at Catherine, who was settling in front of a plate that Ann had heaped up.

"You are still sought. We came away and told the household that we were going north. Edward and Stephen have returned, more than once, and upended the house. They broke nearly all of the furniture and tore half of my clothes to ribbons. Edward in particular seems set upon warning us. It was he who dragged me out to witness the deaths of Guildford and Jane." She drank from a cup of ale, but her throat had closed. She had to stop and breathe and remember how far away London was. "It was the most hellish thing I have ever seen. The poor girl couldn't find the block. I expect they didn't realize how tiny she was."

"Like the Howard queen," mused Ann. Her eyes were drifting into the past. "You recall that day."

"Yes. I still smell it. But Jane was smaller." Catherine set down her cup. "I have forgotten Jane Dudley."

"I certainly have," said Ann.

"She was in the Tower. Very wretched, a cell barely high enough to stand in," said Catherine. "Jane has a shrewish tongue, but she doesn't deserve to die for it."

"Did any of them deserve to die?" asked Benjamin.

"Edward claims it's Gardiner's doing, all of it," said Catherine. "He has felt himself cast down and avenges himself with slaughtering the rebels."

"Cast down?" said Benjamin. "He's Lord Chancellor. If that's cast down, the then world has turned the wrong side up."

"He feels in danger, then, of being cast down," Catherine corrected herself.

"And your good Queen Mary? She has had no hand in it?" asked Benjamin.

"I have not seen her," admitted Catherine, "but, Benjamin, I remember her back at Hatfield, all those years ago. Had any woman suffered as she had? And still she was kind to Elizabeth, every bit a sister, when she had reason to hate the girl."

"And what choice did she have but to be kind, back then?" said Ann. "And where is Elizabeth now? She signed the death warrants, Catherine."

The room was silent, and Alice scraped back her little stool and came to sit beside her mother. She placed her hand on Catherine's leg.

The cheese stuck to Catherine's teeth and she thought she would gag. Even a swallow of ale would not wash it down. Her mouth felt vile, bad-flavoured. She said, "Elizabeth will go free. Wyatt claimed on the block that she was innocent. She may still be locked up for now. For her safety, I expect."

"Is that Gardiner's doing, too?" said Benjamin.

Catherine took up Alice's hand in her own. "I cannot say."

"Are you all in here planning an uprising?" Lewis Davies was at the door, and he laughed his oily laugh. He slapped Reg on the back, and Benjamin winced. "Have the newcomers brought the reinforcements?" He laughed again, and Catherine felt his hand on her shoulder, squeezing a little. She looked at her husband, who rose and drew his brother away.

"They've come to bring us news of how the rebels died."

Lewis sat and grabbed a cup. "Die to replace one queen with another? That's a fool's errand. I say let 'em do what they will, as long as they stay off my property. Scratch their beads or scratch their heads, it's all one to me."

"But one of my properties is in London," said Benjamin, "if I am allowed to go back to it. My wife says that the times are still unsteady. I'm afraid we'll be trouble to you for a short while yet."

"No trouble at all!" said Lewis. "But where are your wife's lady's maids?"

"I travel with no maids," said Catherine. "Ann and I have long been each other's companions."

"The women will stick upon each other, won't they?" said Lewis, and laughed as though he'd said something witty. Catherine caught Diana's eye for a moment, and seemed to read a caution there. Veronica was watching Diana.

"We must hold each other up, so that the men do not put us down," said Catherine, and Lewis threw back his bald head and bellowed until his face went red beneath the short beard. His teeth were all crooked, and they needed cleaning.

He threw his arm around Catherine and said, "I like her, Ben. She's fair as May and sharp as December."

Catherine shrank from the embrace and ducked under Benjamin's arm instead. "And so you see I give myself the lie," she said. "My husband seems to hold me up as well as any."

Lewis was left empty-handed and rubbed his palms against each other. "I can't say a lady nay. You have a chamber, Ben, big enough for you both. I'll put your man and woman in the one that opens from your own. The girls are at the end of the hall."

"Should we stay here? Is there another house, more hidden than this one?" asked Catherine.

"I have three houses, but none as fine as this. No one will disturb you here, not without finding an arrow in his eye, whether he comes from country or court. And now, I will leave you to your victuals." He grinned, pushed back his seat, and stood, offering a little courtly bow. He withdrew without another word. But he winked at Catherine as he went, and she felt a worm of disgust slither down her back.

# Chapter Fifty-Five

"What is wrong with your brother?" asked Catherine. "Has he never touched a woman before?" She had let Ann take down her hair and unfasten her dress, and Benjamin was watching from the bed. He'd managed to kick off his boots but was otherwise still in his clothing.

Ann said, "I'll wager he's touched every woman on his land."

Benjamin poured himself a cup of wine from the jug on the table at his elbow and drank. "He's had the itch since we were boys. I told you years ago."

Catherine finger-combed her hair. "Yes, you did. I hadn't thought how brazen he would be. I thought he would undo my very bodice."

Benjamin drank again. "He likely would have made the attempt if I hadn't been standing in front of him."

Catherine's mind sparked with an image and she gasped. "The girls. Would he touch the girls?"

"Not if he means to live past forty. He knows better than to touch any of my daughters. Now, Catherine, you have seen the man in the flesh. Our father was the same. I can't begin to count how many of the younger servants are Lewis's natural children, or how many of the older ones are our half-brothers and sisters. Honestly, can we not leave this place?"

"Diana knows his character, doesn't she?" said Catherine.

"I've never spoken directly of it to her, but she has eyes in her head," said Benjamin. "She has kept watch on the other girls, you can be sure. They are innocent of him as they can be. They call him 'uncle' and laugh at his jests. They're too young to know anything else."

"He had better stay clear of them," said Ann. She brandished a brush at Benjamin.

"He has and he will," said Benjamin. "He asked Alice to sit upon his lap one evening, and Diana whisked her away for a music lesson. He knows what's what. I haven't seen him ask again."

"His poor wife," said Ann.

"She died from grief of him," said Benjamin. "She gave him three sons, and still he would not leave the kitchen girls alone. I can bear none of them, Lewis or the boys."

"Don't tell me any more, or I will leave this house tonight. I am off to the bed," said Ann. "Catherine, listen to Benjamin. We should ride north."

Benjamin got undressed without Reg's help and stretched out, as Catherine climbed under the covers. She rolled over into his arms and said, "Wales is beautiful, though, isn't it?"

"As beautiful as anywhere God has made. If it weren't for the men in my family, I would live here."

"It's a shame."

"It is. It has always been thus, though. I can't say I will ever love London as I love the land here." He pushed her away enough to look into her face. "Yorkshire is almost as good. Ann is right. We should go there."

"No," said Catherine. "They will be searching for you in Yorkshire. You will be found. They will lie in wait."

He stroked her hair. "Why? Haven't they already searched there? Isn't that the next place they would go after London and my country house?"

"Yes. They've been. But they will return."

"Why should they? What use am I to the queen?"

"It's Gardiner. Old Moll went with Edward and Stephen, and I think Edward's been shamed by not finding Robbie. They will be looking. They will take you to Gardiner." She could smell the grass in his sweat, the clear sky. She put her face up and he kissed her mouth. "Edward mentioned a daughter of Moll. I have never seen a daughter."

Benjamin raised his eyebrows. "Nor have I. She's probably as filthy as the mother." He stroked her hair. "And where will they think you have gone, when they discover you missing?"

"To Yorkshire, as I say. I told everyone we would go north."

"And you won't be there. If they're lying in wait, they will expect you."

Catherine had thought of this. "They may think I've been detained. They have nothing to lay to my charge. They'll believe what I said—that we are going to see about the wool."

"Perhaps. But think, Catherine. If you were Gardiner, with the fancies of a serpent, what would your reason tell you?"

"Go North? Wait there?"

"Ah, and how long do you think they will wait? Their lives are at the court. They will tire of the wilderness and the loneliness. They're serpents, and they'll need the heat of a palace."

"But how long?"

"Indeed." He kissed her again and let his hand drift over her ribs toward her hip. "We can live in Yorkshire a long time if we must. I would guess a week, a fortnight at the most, will tire them. It has already been longer than that. We should go."

"We have just been gone a week and a couple of days." Catherine gazed up into the darkness.

"And any woman could be lost on the roads for a month or more, taking a wrong turn, becoming ill along the way. We can take our time, linger here and there. Wait them out. We will see all of England, like a band of old pilgrims. Perhaps I will find some new draperies, and study their works. We will be away from Lewis. We know the roads along the way. We can send spies of our own to spy upon their spies."

Catherine's guts froze. "Spies of our own?"

"When they are one's own, they are called servants and friends." Benjamin nuzzled the warm spot between her breasts. "I can hear your heart jumping."

Catherine held his head to her and said, "I am well-nigh sick unto death of riding."

"You can rest here for a while. We're safe enough. When you are well again, we will go. We might just go home to London, if we take our time about it."

Catherine caught his mood. "I might be well in a day or so."

"We can tell the others tomorrow." He raised himself on one elbow and looked into her eyes. "But tonight, we will be husband and wife again. And no queen will come between us."

After making love, Catherine had slept without dreaming, but as the first grey streaks of dawn parted the darkness beyond the curtains, she woke and flung herself out of bed. "Ann!" she called, already breaking the skim of ice on the basin water and splashing her face.

Ann opened the joining door, yawning. "You will wake the entire house."

"You and Benjamin have won me over. We'll leave this place when we've had a rest."

Ann's eyebrows rose. "I see your husband has driven some reason into you. A weighty argument, no doubt."

Catherine threw a clout at her, but Ann laughed. Benjamin opened the bed curtains and said, "I can hear you, Ann Smith."

"You have put on a little girth, Benjamin," she said, "but I'm glad you have used it in the service of our departure. I will shake Reg from the mattress and tell him the news." She withdrew, chuckling.

A soft knock came at the door, and Veronica peeped around the door from the hall. "Mother? Are you awake?"

"Awake and dressing, Vere. Tell your sisters that we need to speak to them."

"Why? What has happened?" Veronica came fully into the room then, and Benjamin pulled the curtain closed again.

"We must go soon," said Catherine. She took her daughter into her arms. "Your father and I have decided between us. Go get your sisters."

"What of my brother?"

"Your father will speak to him. Will you not, Husband?"

"I am upon the task at this moment," said Benjamin from inside the bed curtains.

"Very well," said Veronica. She was backing out the door, a question still on her lips, but she did not ask it.

"Is she out?" said Benjamin.

"Yes," said Catherine.

He leapt from the bed and Catherine helped him dress in the cold. "So where have we decided upon, for our first pilgrims' shrine?" she asked as she held out his boots.

"Why not Dover? I know men there, men with houses. We can turn south and skirt the coastline. If we are stopped, we can say that we have business. It's not a lie, not completely. I do know men there. If they have already caught the rebels, no one will be searching there anymore by the time we arrive. We can circle London and travel north if it doesn't feel safe, through the fens."

"And if we cannot travel all together?"

"You mean Robert."

Catherine nodded.

"Then we will be near the boats, and we can find out a quiet captain who will take him back to Wittenberg until he gets older and wiser. That's where he wants to be, anyway."

It seemed a good plan. Benjamin tied up Catherine's dress and did his best to fix her hair. His fingers were not suited to the job, and when he turned his back, she made a few adjustments. Then they were out, he headed for Robbie's chamber and Catherine downstairs to see to their food.

Two long-limbed young men lounged in the dining gallery, their feet upon the table. They were throwing scraps of bread to a couple of wiry-haired dogs. Catherine entered the room, and one of them said, "Bring us more food, will you? We've gone through this whole loaf." His face shone red, even in the early light, and as Catherine approached she saw that he was covered in angry eruptions. His entire countenance was fiery and enflamed, with bloody scabs scattered among the pustules. Catherine's stomach fluttered at the sight of him. She could imagine him leaning into a glass, squeezing and poking at his skin.

"I am not your servant," she said. "I'm Catherine, your uncle's wife."

The other one turned then. He was the image of the first, narrow-faced and dark-haired, with the same spotted complexion, but this one smiled in an insinuating way and said, "We beg your pardon, Lady." He stood and bowed. "Do you seek our father?"

"Sought and found," came a voice behind her. Catherine stiffened for the fingers upon her back, and then they were there, warm and lingering just below her waist. "This lady is our guest, boys. A great lady. Married to my brother."

"So we have heard," said the first one, with a nasty twist of a sneer.

Catherine stepped away from the hand. "Good morrow to you, Brother Lewis. Be these your sons?"

The boys were now both on their feet, bowing and grinning, bobbing their heads like a couple of sycophants at court. Catherine's stomach had settled back into place, and her heart sank upon it. Her daughters had been in the company of these two. She hoped they were as afraid of Benjamin's wrath as their father was.

"I've sent one of the girls to fetch us up some more victuals," said Lewis. He winked at Catherine. "I trust your night has worked you into an appetite."

She was likely expected to blush, but Catherine was too old for such embarrassment. The faces of the boys bloomed alarmingly, however, and she almost felt sorry for them. She simply smiled and sat at the low end of the table, closest to the door. Ann and Reg came in then, and she was grateful for the distraction. "Have your sons names?" she said.

Lewis laughed and said, "Davies," but when he received no retort, he continued. "That one there, the taller, is my Daniel." The first one bowed, but his foot slipped on the paw of a dog that had flopped beneath his chair, and he almost smacked his face on the table. "And that one is Mark." The second, having observed his brother's indignity, checked the floor before he bent. "I have a third called David, but he is already on his horse at this hour."

"They are the image of their father," said Ann, standing behind Catherine.

Reg sat at Catherine's left and said nothing, but he flicked a look at his wife.

Fish and ale and more bread were brought in and laid upon the table, and the boys fell to their second breakfasts while their father slapped the dogs to drive them out and took his seat at the head, opposite Catherine. Benjamin clopped in beyond the door, and Catherine breathed again. He could tell his brother that they were leaving.

But when he came in, Benjamin said flatly, "Your son says he will not budge."

"What is that?" said Catherine. "Is he ill?"

"Not sick and not hungry. He will not come down and he will not dress. He says that he must attend to his soul."

"What's this business?" said Lewis. "Tell the boy that Daniel and Mark are up and about. Tell him to leave off the books for once and go hunting."

Benjamin threw one leg over the bench and sat astraddle it. "Brother, I fear we will bring the queen's men onto your house. We should ride out of here. We should go tomorrow."

"The queen? Here?" said Daniel. His livid face blazed with excitement. The pustules whitened, and Catherine had to look away.

"Not the queen," said Benjamin. "Her men. She wouldn't ride a mile for the likes of us."

"Oh." The lad shoved a wad of bread into his mouth and Catherine was afraid the pimples might burst from the effort of his chewing.

"Your lady has just arrived," said Lewis. "You cannot drag her onto a horse before she's got her own legs again. You'll wear her out, and no man gets past my gate without my leave."

"I can ride," said Catherine. "Benjamin says right. We must trouble you no longer. Let me speak to Robbie."

She went, relieved, and met Diana, Veronica, and Alice on the stairs. "Is it true that we are leaving?" said Alice, and Veronica added, "It is such a paradise here, Mother. Can we not stay on?"

Catherine said, "Yes, I'm afraid we must, Vere." The girl cast down her eyes, and she said, "We will ride to the sea. Wouldn't you like to see that?"

"Since I was a girl I've longed to see it!" she said. "Will we? It's not far."

Catherine almost laughed. "Not that way, Daughter. We will ride to the east." Diana was holding her upper lip between her teeth to prevent laughing at the girl, and Catherine could have kissed her for her kindness. "But your brother is being stubborn."

"Then let him remain behind," said Veronica. She stood up straight, almost as tall as her mother. "He can stay here and sniff his prayer books."

"Vere!"

"He's the one who's got us into this trouble, isn't he? We don't need him."

"Go on down and break your fast," said Catherine. She hurried on up, away from her daughter's sharp blue eyes.

Robbie was indeed sitting with his face almost against the pages of his book, though the morning light fell full into the room. No one else in the family was short-sighted, and she wondered at the effect of his constant study. He did not look up as his mother entered, but languidly turned a leaf and continued to stare down.

"Robert." She sat on the bed, next to him. "Robert, look at me."

"You may go if you choose," he said. "I have done hiding. It puts my soul in peril. Your husband has forced me to don women's weeds and to run like a whipped cur. If that woman will come and hang me, let her come. I am a man, and I bow to no Roman."

"You are a fool," said Catherine. The words fell from her tongue before she could bite them back. Robbie blinked but did not respond. "Forgive me, Son. Wyatt was the fool, and I will not have you throw your life away on him."

"How can you be sure he is dead?"

"Let me give you the news as it is told all over London. Your Wyatt has been quartered and strung up for the daws to peck. Every maidservant laughs at him, or what is left of him. He will be forgotten in a fortnight, and the queen will still be the queen. She is already crowned, anointed, chosen by God for England."

"By God?" Now he did look up. "When do you begin to believe that God chooses who sits on the throne of England? How many times have I heard you curse the king?"

"I have never cursed the king."

"Not with words, perhaps. But you have cursed him with your tone and with your cold eyes. You did not believe that our good King Edward had God's grace, nor his father before him. Would you have told me to bow to King Henry?"

"I bowed to him myself, more than once," said Catherine. But she knew she was losing the argument. Her son's words were true. She had spoken ill of the king, out loud and without restraint. "You need not approve of the Church," she said, more mildly. "You need not bend your conscience. But you need not call yourself a traitor and walk like a calf into the noose, either. I did not like the ways of King Henry, nor those of his son. But I am still alive. Come with us. Let the time go on. Then behave like a citizen of the realm or leave the realm, and all will be well."

"All will not be well as long as she rules. She is a woman."

"She is that, as am I."

"But you do not sit on a throne like a king. Your husband is your head. He is bad enough, but at least you are constrained to obey him."

"Your father is not like other men," said Catherine. "We love without orders. I do as I please, and I please him. As he pleases me."

"Then he is the fool. And he is not my father." Robbie slammed the book shut. Dust puffed from the pages and clouded the air between them. "I will not go with you."

# Chapter Fifty-Six

Catherine believed that her son would, at last, come along, but even as they packed the girls' clothing to be sent along, even as they gathered the belongings that they needed for the long journey, he remained firm. He came downstairs and watched the bags swing by in the maids' hands, and when Catherine and Veronica brought the small cases of combs and lace, he laid his hand on his sister's arm, but she shied from him.

"Leave off. We must be upon the road, Brother," she said.

"Vere. Tell me where I can find you." He almost touched her again, but his hand stopped in the air.

Catherine said, "We will decide that after we are out of Wales."

Veronica added, "You have shown yourself a traitor both to your queen and your family. Why would you care where we go?"

"Vere—" said Catherine.

"It is nothing more than the plain truth," Veronica said. "He must needs be a martyr to his Luther and will not be content until he has seen us all hang beside him. I know what

I know, Mother." She trained a judgmental look on her brother.

Robbie's face blanched and flushed, and Catherine could see through the young man's expression to the features of the boy he'd been, shy and devoted to a father who had never quite loved him. Her heart swelled with anger and anguish, and she said, "Come with us. Robert. Your conscience will be free. You may believe as you see fit. You may worship as you please. Your sister will be happy if you come with us. If we make Dover and you feel the same way that you do now, you can board a boat for the continent and be done with us."

Robbie struggled with his mouth and nose, and when he'd fitted a look of pride back onto his face, he said, "I will never worship as I please while that woman sits on the throne of England. We will be overrun with strangers, and we will have our wills bent to that Spaniard. That woman will never allow me to go back to Wittenberg."

Veronica clicked her tongue against her teeth. "I have a parrot for a brother. The only word he needs is 'Wyatt.' Or perhaps it's now 'that woman,' as though a woman could not head him. She is every bit the soldier that you are, Robbie." She went out without a look back at him.

Benjamin came down with Reg and Ann. Diana and Alice were behind them. "We have everything," Benjamin said. "Robert, have you decided to come with us? We would be glad for your company."

Robbie was still watching his sister, as though she might turn back to him, but she was counting her cases by the front door, looking inside of each one to see that all of her things were in order. He said, "I am the one they want."

"We want you with us," said Catherine. She touched his arm, and when he did not shrink from her, she put her arms around him. He was thinner, and even through the thick doublet she could feel the cage of his ribs, the heart knocking behind it. "Come, Robert. Your mother begs you."

"I am barely dressed," he said. "And you are upon the road already."

"We don't go until tomorrow. Gather what you need for your person, and we will see to a horse for you. We can buy one of Lewis's. You can choose the one you want. We are not in that great of a hurry."

Diana and Alice squeezed behind her and ran to Veronica, who threw Alice in the air to make her squeal. Robbie said into Catherine's shoulder, "Will you wait?"

"All the day and the one after that if I must."

He nodded, and Benjamin said, "Which horse do you want?"

"The big roan, if I might. I like his spirit."

"He's yours." Benjamin went out, yelling for the men to bring the animal around.

"May I help you, Sir?" said Reg. His tone was honey, and Robbie nodded again. He followed the path Benjamin had taken as far as the front door, and Reg stayed at his side.

Ann grinned after them and Catherine said quietly, "Your man has a genius."

"He does, at that. Come," she said under her breath, "let's get that horse out here and show him off before Robbie changes his mind."

The roan was led out. Benjamin had left the door open, and he stood with Lewis out front, both of the men running hands down the animal's flanks and speaking in quiet tones. A deal was reached, and they shook hands.

Benjamin came back, and, seeing Robbie watching, said, "I have bought you a ride, Son." He called to Catherine. "We could go tonight. The dark would give us some protection."

"Robbie must pack his books," said Catherine.

"Yes," the boy said, but he was already headed toward his new horse.

"At first light, then," said Benjamin.

And so the afternoon and evening were spent in packing and saying their long good-byes. The pimply sons would not postpone their hunting, and would not return before they were gone, so Catherine had to hold a bit of her lip in her teeth and kiss their cheeks in the broad daylight. The third son had not come home. Every time she encountered Lewis, on the stairs or in a room, he said, "We are family, Catherine. Don't be a stand-off," and dragged her into his sweaty embrace. She managed every time to disengage before his hands could move very far, and once, Benjamin appeared around a corner, just in time to step in and clap his brother, hard, on the back.

"We owe you a debt, Lewis. And, remember: you have never seen us here."

"No reckonings between us, Ben. This house is always yours."

At last the day fell toward dusk and Catherine could escape to her bed. The men shook hands yet again, and Benjamin walked up with her. The night was clear, and, down the hall behind her, Veronica was teasing Robbie about the weight of his books. Catherine went a little giddy with the sound. Her family was together, and they were content with one another. Soon, they would be riding away, to a place of safety. England could become quiet, and the queen could be the queen of them all. It would be well. It would be well indeed.

# Chapter Fifty-Seven

Catherine dreamed of light. They rode into the sun, Catherine sometimes shading her eyes against the glare, searching for the shadows of men in the distance, and sometimes drowsing in her saddle to the music of her daughters' chatter. Her son and her daughters were all the same age, not quite children but not yet adults. She woke briefly, remembering a story that her mother had told her once, of a magical goat that came down from the hills at night to try and get the maidens to kiss his snout. How the one softhearted milkmaid who agreed to do it found her lips pressed against the lips of a prince. As she had ended the tale, a great ram from their flock had appeared at the convent window, and Catherine had cried out in such fright that she had not stepped outside for a week. She had enjoyed her dread then, as children will do, and she rolled over in the night, wondering if Wyatt had been such a story-teller to her son. But Robbie had only ever loved stories of battle and conquest. He would not be moved by a fairy tale. He would think it an idle fancy, the delight of a woman.

The darkness lay deep over the house. It was too early to rise. Catherine listened to the timbers, groaning against the cold, and closed her eyes again. The mountain came back into her dreams, but she was only half-asleep. She thought she dreamt that Ann was saying that the mountain was evil, that it wanted to crush them. Or was she remembering?

She must have slept again, because she awoke to the sound of a mouse stripping the wood inside the wall behind the bed. She had been dreaming again, this time of an empty road. She was walking, and she could see a house in the distance that somehow seemed to be her home, but as she approached it, the vision faded and the house appeared, again, far beyond her.

The mouse began to gnaw in earnest, and she knocked against the wall. Benjamin grumbled, "Who is it?"

"A visitor," said Catherine, rolling into his arms. "She should take her teeth to the kitchen if she is hungry."

And then it was morning, the early spring dawn suddenly giving way to a warm day. Catherine woke again to see Benjamin opening the window, and the heat hung so close about Catherine's head that the air itself seemed a bright bowl, scented with violets, pressing the sun into their room. The light was still slant and golden, but the warmth pulled her from the bed, and she stepped through Benjamin's shadow to put her face to the brightness.

"A fine day for riding," said Benjamin. He kissed her and called for Reg. Ann came in and they dressed together, stopping now and then to smell the spring wind. Catherine's heart knocked at her ribs, and she couldn't determine whether she was excited or frightened. Her daughters came out below her, calling for their horses, and the maids came behind them with the cases and bags. The stable boys had done the saddling already, and the packing was overseen by a crooked, white-haired old man who stooped to correct the boys' buckling of the stirrups.

Veronica pointed into the distance and Alice squealed, clapping her hands. Catherine said, "Vere is telling Alice tales about the sea, no doubt. We had better hurry."

"Just let me pin this up," said Ann. She was worrying over Catherine's hood. "You can't be on the road looking like a sloven."

"It might suit our purpose better than looking like a lady," said Catherine. Ann huffed a little, and she sat still. Diana had come out below now and was nodding to the younger girls. Lewis was behind her, and she allowed a brief hug.

"There," said Ann. "You look decent."

"Now let me do yours," said Catherine, but Ann had already fixed her own hair and was ready to go.

The entire household was up, and dishes clattered down in the kitchen. The sound was so homely that Catherine almost wished she could stay for another hour, but Benjamin was already outside with the others, lifting the horses' hooves and running his hands up their legs.

Catherine's clothes already smelt sour to her, but it was too late to change. She could not still her misgiving heart, and held her breath to slow the pounding in her chest. Reg had drawn a map with the help of one of the serving men, and he was leaning over it with Thomas in the dining gallery. Diana had come back in and was with the men, watching them trace a line eastward, then south to the coast. Alice came tripping inside and sat long enough for Ann to braid her hair. Veronica stood in the doorway and said, "When do we ride?"

Catherine looked around the room. Around the entry hall. "Has anyone wakened Robbie?" she asked.

Benjamin headed up the stairs and everyone could hear him, pounding on the door of Robbie's chamber. He pounded again. The house fell silent. Lewis came inside and said, "Well, the horses look fit and ready as any horses I have ever laid eyes on." He crossed his arms and smiled as though he had done the feeding and saddling himself. But behind him, down the stairs, came Benjamin, and Lewis turned, saw his face, and said, "Whatever's the matter with you, Brother?"

"Catherine," said Benjamin, pushing past the grinning Lewis. "Robbie is gone."

It was true. Robbie Overton was nowhere in the house. His roan gelding was gone, and one of the stable men came inside to say, "I heard something in the wee hours. I thought it was a dog come in from the cold. I saw that the horse was gone, but I thought the boy had gone for a dawn ride."

Catherine stood at the front door, looking eastward and feeling the waste of effort but unable to stop herself. There was nothing to see but more Davies land. He had been gone for hours and she knew which way he had taken. He was not headed into the hills to watch the sun rise. He was headed toward London. If she had sat up in the night, if she had gone to the window in her wakefulness, she might have spied him out. She might have stopped him. Benjamin brought out a cloak, and, when he covered her, she realized that she'd been shivering, despite the heat of the morning air.

"What has he done?" she said. "Why?"

"He wants to prove himself a man," said Benjamin. He drew her back inside, and she let him guide her.

"He will prove himself a traitor, and Gardiner will hang him as quickly as he hanged the Wyatt boy. He will bring you down. We must get you away."

"I will be found if I must," said Benjamin. "Catherine, I have tried to be a father to him."

Reg stood, unmoving, in the dining gallery, his finger stuck to the map. They had probably already found the most direct route to the sea. "Robbie wants no father," Catherine said, "and he will take no direction."

The girls sat quietly at the big table, and Ann came up from the kitchen. "They don't know anything about when Robbie left. One of the girls said Daniel and Mark came home late, but those are the only boys they saw."

Catherine shook her head. Lewis shuffled around them, peeking into empty jugs and wringing his hands. He finally called for a servant to take the food and drink away. Then he looked at Benjamin. "Has his bed been slept in? Maybe he has just gone out early to see the sun. You might catch up to him."

But Benjamin shook his head. "He has no interest in sunrises."

"We must go now," said Catherine.

They gathered Arthur Huff from the servants' rooms downstairs, where he had taken up a pleasant residence, and kept their leave-taking short. Even Lewis wore the sober expression of a man who knew that the day had turned serious. He clasped Benjamin's hand and said, "I'm sure you will find him safe and sound."

Catherine turned toward the empty lane and put her heels to her mare. She did not look back, but set her eyes ahead, fixing her gaze on the backs of her daughters, who were silent. Storm clouds rolled in behind them and fastened the sky closed, and by midday the rain was pelting down. Alice was shifted onto Reg's saddle so that he could wrap her into the hollow of his stomach, and they pushed on, stopping only to eat and to shelter in a barn during the heaviest downpour. They did not catch up to Robbie, as Catherine knew they would not.

By dusk, they were soggy in limb and spirit, but the rain had given up. As the sun broke through in the west and streaked the sky red behind them, a swarm of starlings gathered, dipping and swirling, over their heads. It looked as though one of the great clouds had grown a soul and writhed with the burden, and Catherine's own breast twisted with unease. The only inn they could find was musty and cold. But it was dry enough, and Catherine stripped with Diana and the girls in the washroom, while the innkeeper's wife hung their dripping garments from wooden racks and clucked at the condition of Alice's hair.

They choked down their bowls of lamb stew in silence and trudged off to their beds. Diana hugged Catherine. "Courage, Mother," she said, and turned away.

Catherine would not weep. Lying in the narrow bed, her shoulder propped on Benjamin's, she studied the knots and cracks in the beams above. She felt herself floating toward them, light and empty. An image came to her mind of the summer when Robbie was first walking, and Ann had blown some soap spray into the air for him. He had stumbled after it, grasping and clutching as the colours floated and danced away. He'd giggled so hard that he'd fallen to the ground. Catherine had been carrying Veronica then, and now she laid her hand across her flat middle. But her arm felt leaden, and she turned to hold Benjamin.

"Catherine?" he said.

"I need you to tether me," she said. "We are riding into a whirlwind and I'm afraid I will fly away."

He put his arm over hers and said nothing more.

The morning was grey again, but their clothes were dry, and they slung themselves onto the saddles once more. Diana and Ann rode ahead and fell into quiet conversation, Veronica staying nearby to overhear and Arthur Huff sidling up beside them, unnoticed by the girls. The hills and valleys rolled away from them, but no one thought to remark any more upon the vast glory of Wales. Alice asked again to ride with Reg and she fell asleep before they had gone another mile. Benjamin stayed by Catherine's side and let her alone in her brooding. Budding branches and bare ones. Fields and sheep. Cows. Villages, with their pigpens and sooty cottages. Women, waving as they went by. Boys. Dogs. A black cat that shadowed them until Benjamin began to feel haunted and turned his horse to scare it off.

Two days more under a glowering, grey sky. The warmth was overcome by the return of the cold. Rain, then sleet. A brief respite of sunlight that coaxed an unusual whoop of joy from Diana. Hard, dirty beds and clean ones, good ale and bad wine: it all became the colour of mud to Catherine. Sky and soil. The streaked trunks of trees. The old grasses and weeds, bent along the verge.

Her head was so dull with the thud of her mare's hooves that her eyes would barely stay open. The mare herself hung her head and plodded. They would soon need to turn south, away from the court, away from her son. He was too far ahead of them. The clouds split open above them and a ray of sun slipped through. It made Catherine's head ache, and she pulled her hood lower, but as she did so, Veronica cried out and she pushed it up again. There were riders coming toward them. They were coming fast.

# CHAPTER FIFTY-EIGHT

Robbie Overton was not with the riders. They were at least a dozen, and as they approached, they fanned out, blocking the road. Catherine jerked her palfrey back, but the mare skittered and wheeled. By the time she had the mare under control, the others had stopped. The newcomers surrounded them, and a woman appeared from the back, pointing her finger at Benjamin.

"That's him," she said. "That is the one."

Ann spat at the figure, and Catherine nudged her palfrey forward. The woman wore a hood, low over her brows, but she raised her face as Catherine came near. "And her. She is his wife."

The red hair was completely covered, and the face was thicker. A second chin pouched over the covering she wore around her neck, and the eyes were lined, but the face was unmistakable.

"I know you of old," said Catherine. "What do you here, Connie?" She should have known that her sister-in-law's maid was not gone from England, that she would appear like a nightmare from the past. And here she sat, a smug satisfaction riding in her eyes. And if Connie was here, her mistress, Margaret, could not be far away.

One of the men said, "Are you certain?" and Constance Overton nodded. "He had the rebel in his house. And she—she is his mother. She has been his right hand through it all."

Veronica and Diana had pulled their mares together. Ann glared at Constance and finally said, "What witch has conjured you out of the grave, Connie?"

Constance laughed. "Who has ever put me into a grave? I have lived a right nice life, with my mistress. She is almost a mother to me."

"Margaret?" said Ann. "She is here with you?"

Now the laugh was choked by a sneer. "She is at home, where she belongs." Constance leaned forward, toward Ann. "And if you and Catherine here had not kept a rebel under your roof, my true mother might be there with her. But Margaret is more mother than aunt to me these days, so I am well."

"Your true mother?" said Catherine. She knew that Constance's mother had been an Overton serving maid, but she had thought the woman long dead.

"Enough," said one of the men. Alice, riding with Reg, had wakened, and he was whispering into her ear. "Keep that child quiet," the man said. Then he walked his horse up, so that it nosed Benjamin's big gelding. He said, "Are you Benjamin Davies?"

"I am," said Benjamin. "The very one."

"We have taken your son as a rebel to Her Majesty. He is on the road to London as we speak here."

"I am very sorry for it," said Benjamin. "And what would you do with me?"

"You have been named as his companion in the war against Queen Mary. You must have your trial with the others."

"No!" said Catherine, but Benjamin put out a hand to stop her.

"Has Robert given himself into your hands?" Benjamin asked the man.

The other one shrugged. "He did not resist us. We met him upon our way, as it happens. Guilt will make itself known."

"As will innocence, if it is given a chance," said Catherine. "He's a boy. His head was turned. Benjamin has done nothing but try to win him back to reason. To the queen."

The man said, "And you are Catherine Davies. Sometime Overton. Sometime Havens. Once in the convent. Much married. Much vowed. This lady says that you use your powers to seduce men and take away their gold."

"Who says so?" said Catherine. "This one? She is the bastard daughter of my first husband's brother. She is the natural cousin to the boy you have seized upon. She is eaten up with jealousy and will say anything to anyone, so long as it brings down my family and me."

Constance was smirking again under her modest hood, and Catherine could have bitten the nose from her face. "Grin, will you? Smile? I have not laid eyes upon you in ten years, and now you come like the plague that you are to ruin me and mine. What have I ever done to you, Connie, that you are such a bitter thing? Have you taken on Margaret's character along with her cast-off clothing and must soil everyone you come near?" The name of her first husband's sister felt like rancid grease on her tongue, and she wiped her mouth on her sleeve. "Who is this mother you speak of? I have never heard a word of your mother, except that she was a serving woman. Have you made her up out of your fancy?"

Constance Overton laid her hand upon her breast and gazed into the sky, as though she were trying to overcome her great sorrow. She said, "You see, gentlemen? What attacks I must endure?" But when her eyes came down on Catherine, they were mean and hard. "Margaret Overton has suffered enough for you. You stole away her betrothed husband and the grief of it nearly killed her, and you have killed my own mother now, as well." She glanced around. "Such a woman will say any lie to protect her pup, even to her anointed queen."

The men closed in around Catherine now. "Your mother?" she said, over their heads, to Constance. "Who is your mother?" And then, "Where is Margaret?"

"Who is it?" echoed Ann, but Constance ignored her and plowed through the men to bring her mare up against Catherine's palfrey. Her skin was rough and patchy, an old woman's hide, though she couldn't have been much past thirty. And Catherine saw it then. The angry, deranged eyes. The sneer always ready to curl the lip. The fingers, scrabbling at the reins.

"You're Old Moll's daughter," said Catherine. "They said your mother had died giving you birth."

The lip went up, and Connie leaned forward. Bent, she looked as though she might bray or snarl. She said, "She didn't die, she was sent away. And she went, because you were coming to Overton House. You and your bastard son." She flung her head around to look at Benjamin, and the hood almost came off. "And you. You sent my mistress away, after you as much as made love to her, and she fell into ruin because of it. You might have saved her."

Benjamin gazed at Connie as though she had gone mad. Perhaps she had. He said, "Margaret Overton was never anything to me. If she went away, it was by her own decision, and if she fell, she fell with the weight of her own choices."

Catherine was in a daze, and she barely felt the hand on her arm. She looked over at Ann, who had set herself in front of the girls. Reg was beside her, holding Alice. The man squeezed Catherine's arm.

"Enough of this woman's talk," he said. "You will all have to come with us."

The men would not allow a separation. They were all turned toward London, the children, Ann and Reg, Thomas Jones and Arthur Huff, rigid with fear and riding white-faced beside Benjamin. Men before them and men behind, and the long road scrolling ahead. Connie rode with the men in front, and Catherine studied her back, the thick-waisted figure still familiar after all these years. Benjamin had once said, "You know Margaret never meant a thing to me," and Catherine answered, "I believe it."

She was silent a moment, then said, "I thought she had disappeared for shame." For years, she had wondered where Margaret had gone. There had been a marriage, or so the rumour had gone, to a servant. There had been a child. Or perhaps there had not. Maybe the child had died. Catherine couldn't recall how many hours she had spent honing her anger in preparation for Margaret's reappearance, perhaps with a new husband. How she would triumph and call Catherine "sister." Where did she call home these days? It must be Jane Dudley's house.

It put her in mind of the days they had once called each other sister in spirit, those days in the convent when, however bitter their minds and their tongues, they had been bidden to forgive. And the days when Catherine had been married to Margaret's brother William, with Robbie just a little thing and Veronica barely born, Connie had been a sour girl back then, and why not? A bastard, though cousin in blood to her own children. How many times had she heard the tale of Connie's mother, dying after giving birth to her master's child and leaving the baby girl to be raised as a servant in the household? Catherine wondered if William had known the truth all along, if Margaret had known, and Catherine had been the only one in the family without knowledge. It was all long ago, but Catherine had cast her imagination to the day when Margaret would appear again to torment her. And now here she was, already old, but only a story. And Moll, not so old as she had thought, perhaps no more than a few years beyond her own age.

The past was suddenly turned the wrong way out, and Catherine could not find her way back to the present day. She felt around in her mind for a little pity, but when Connie swiveled in her saddle to stare at their misery, Catherine saw the hatred in her eyes and hardened herself against it. She would save her pity for her husband and her son.

That night, Benjamin was shackled to a bed in a common room. The men seemed to have decided that Catherine would not flee without him. Of the others, they took little notice, and everyone went sullenly to their chambers, the girls weeping a little when they kissed Benjamin. Ann held onto Alice, and Diana onto Veronica, as they went, but Catherine demanded to rest on a pallet beside her husband. It was unseemly, Connie sniffed, but Catherine insisted, and the men relented at last.

Catherine did not sleep, but she didn't care. She lay in the dark and watched the fire settle onto its deathbed. A log fell, quartering itself with a sigh, into the embers, and sparks lit up the hearth. Benjamin shifted and groaned. Catherine dozed and startled awake, dozed and startled awake, plagued by memory and visions of a past that now demanded revision. She grew bitter, thinking of Old Moll and her lies, then saw her in gaol, lying in her own filth, with no one for company but the rats. Then she saw Benjamin in a cell. Then Robbie. She rolled to her side and touched her husband's warm back. She would go directly to the queen, before Gardiner could punish anyone else. She would throw herself to the ground and Mary would show mercy. She would. And with that assurance, like a silent prayer thrown out to the shrinking flames, Catherine fell asleep.

# Chapter Fifty-Nine

Catherine thought she smelt London before she could see anything of the city. After five more days of riding, the villages were closer together, and she was sure they would see something, S. Paul's or Southwark, before nightfall. She'd gotten turned about in her head and could not determine their direction. The houses were still neatly laid out along the high road, but the stink of blood and men's guts got in her nose, and she began to plot when she would break off and search out the queen.

The girls all rode in a ghastly silence, Veronica tight-lipped with rage, Alice nestled against Reg, and Diana staring at nothing at all, her lips moving without making a sound. Ann kept all of them between herself and Reg, and Arthur Huff rode with Thomas Jones at Ann's other side. Catherine might convince them that they needed to go home, that there was nothing to be gained by marching children all the way to the queen's front door. Benjamin would understand and would go on without argument.

Reg probably still had the map, but, sleeping beside Benjamin every night, Catherine had not had a moment to consult with him or with Ann. There was no talking allowed among them, and every time she had gone near Ann in the inns, there Connie had been, as well. Reg and Thomas would know where they were by now. Ann might also know. But Catherine could only gaze at the slant of the sun and wonder how much farther it was, and when she might beg for release.

They rode on, the sun tilting above their heads, then descending behind their backs. Catherine pushed herself up in the stirrups once, trying to see ahead, but one of the men said, "Eager to meet your fate?" and she sat again without looking at Benjamin.

Still, London did not show itself, though the taste of blood was in Catherine's mouth. She thought she had bitten the inside of her cheek, but when she ran a finger around her teeth, she found nothing. Perhaps it was the taste of fear. But there was nothing to fear. The queen would let them go. It was Mary. She knew Mary. She had to find the queen. She glimpsed something before them, in the distance, the shape of a building, and she risked a glance at Benjamin. He did not seem to have seen anything and was ruminating privately, one hand on the empty sheath from which the men had removed his dagger. Before long, she smelt water, rank and fishy, and Catherine searched for a stream or a pond, but she knew that it was the river. They had come southerly the day before. If they meant to meet a barge, they would have to divide, and then Catherine might beg to be allowed to go on to Davies House. What need to pay to haul them all down the Thames? It was sound reasoning, to let her go with the others, and she was fitting words to her plea when they rounded a bend and she realized where they were. The red walls of Hampton Court were unmistakable, and in the lowering sunlight, the palace walls flamed.

Barges had pulled up on the other side of the palace, and Catherine could see the two men in front, sidling together and pointing ahead. Two more rode up, from behind, and joined the leaders to confer. They stopped, and Catherine heard Reg say, "Ho, there," to his gelding, and Ann said, "What is this?" but she didn't dare turn her head. She started forward, and Benjamin put out his hand. Catherine looked at him, but he was studying their captors.

The leader sent on the two who had come up from behind, and arched his arm for the others, still in the rear, to ride forward. These, he also sent before him, and one of them whooped a little, glad to be free of his duty. The leader, with his fellow, turned back toward Catherine and Benjamin. Connie was idling alongside, but they ignored her. Catherine steeled her tongue for her argument, but the two went on past her and stopped before Reg.

"Can you find your way back to London with these women?" he said.

Catherine now looked at Reg. He was looking at Benjamin. Benjamin called out, "He can. Thomas should go with him."

The leader said again, to Reg, "Can you make your way?"

"I can," said Reg. The serving men had circled around the back and now sat beside the older man. Reg indicated them with a flick of his reins. "These men will be my guides. They never get lost." He said nothing about the map.

The leader narrowed his eyes at Arthur Huff. "This one's a boy."

"With as good a nose for home as any hound," said Reg.

"Well, then," said the leader, as though that settled the matter. "Get you home, and take these women with you."

Catherine could not believe her good fortune. She would ride straight into the palace and ask for the queen. But when she nudged her mare forward, the leader held up a hand.

"Not you, Madam. These others will go on without you."

"But I am their mother. And I know the way home from here, as well."

The man's mouth moved under his beard. He might have been smiling. "I expect that you do, but they will have to find their way on their own."

"Wherefore would you haul me all the way to Winchester? Has the Lord Chancellor not seen enough of my face?"

"Winchester?" said the man. He was laughing now. "You think we came from Gardiner?" His partner began to laugh with him, and the leader wiped his eyes. "You think you will throw yourself on the mercies of that old lecher and be done with all this?" He sobered up. "I reckon I should be insulted, but I expect you don't know a bishop's man from a queen's." He gestured toward Hampton Court. "You're going there, Madam, and your rebel husband with you. And then my time with you is at an end. It's not the Lord Chancellor who wants to see you. It's the queen."

The separation was swift, though Veronica and Alice wept. Ann did not need to be told what to do. She bade the girls to kiss their mother and father and come away. Diana showed them how, embracing Catherine with a touch of lips on her cheek, and then hugging her father quickly. The girls followed suit, but Alice clung until Ann gently pulled her away. "Your mother knows what she does." Reg bowed to Benjamin, and then the two men grabbed each other for a moment.

"Have you money in your pocket?" said Benjamin.

"Some," said Reg.

"Have this. You'll need an inn before the sun's gone." Benjamin put a small bag into his hand. "Take care of my girls," he said, and Reg nodded, already turning away.

The two remaining men escorted Catherine and Benjamin as far as the inner gate and, finding a couple of palace guards, dismounted and walked their horses over to deliberate with them. Connie had ridden in behind them all, and when the guards came, guided by the two men—Lord Chancellor's men, queen's men, Catherine could not think now what to call them—Connie dashed forward. One of the guards took hold of her waist and pulled her from the small mare.

"Not me!" she said, dusting her skirt down. She pointed at Catherine. "She's the one you're to seize upon."

The guard turned and said, "Which one?"

"Both of them, for all my concern," said the leader of their group.

"But I am not under arrest," said Connie. "You must take me back to Lady Dudley's house."

The man scratched his nape and then up into his hair, under the greasy band of his hat. "That is not the direction I go, Madam."

"Who is this woman?" asked the guard.

"Informer for Gardiner," said the man. "She was sent to us. She's none of mine. I am for the queen." He swung himself back onto his horse, and his fellow did the same.

"You cannot leave me here alone," said Connie. "It is almost night time."

"You are not alone," said the man. "And I have done. Now God be with you, because I certainly will not be." He tipped his head toward the road, and the two rode away.

The guard had Connie's arm, and the other one took the reins of her mare. "You may leave your horses here," he said to Catherine and Benjamin.

"Or we may not," said Benjamin.

The guard did not answer, but stared up at the sky as though he were studying the growing darkness above him. "You will," he said finally.

Catherine slid from her palfrey. Benjamin could dash for the gates if he wanted. He was watching her, and she nodded slightly. The light was going fast, and she didn't know if he understood what she meant. But he dismounted after her, and stood before her. He could see her clearly enough.

"And what will you do with me?" Connie said. "My mother is dead, and I needs must bury her. Who will pay?"

Catherine turned. Connie was staring at her. "What?" Catherine said. "Do you mean to ask me?"

"We are kindred," said Connie. "Your children and I share blood."

"And your mouth may have shed quite a lot of it," said Catherine. "You may go bury your mother in a ditch and lie there with her. What do you have to do with Jane Dudley?"

Connie glared silently.

"Ladies," said the guard, stepping between them. "We are to bring you before the queen. Let's have no scratching before."

"Yes," said Catherine. "Take us to the queen."

"Not tonight," said the guard. "She's abed by this hour. You will have to wait until morning. All will be clear then. And we have beds aplenty."

Catherine took Benjamin's arm. "We will sleep wherever you put us, as long as you do not put us near that woman."

The guards seemed to care little where they lay, and Catherine was allowed a small chamber with Benjamin, and without Connie, who was carried off, squeaking her protest, down a hall. The room contained a soft bed, a small taper, and a jug of water, though there were no windows and the door was locked after them. It was cold, and Catherine only took off her outer garments. She laid them on the floor and Benjamin laid his jacket on top of them. "And now we will lie like our garments, at peace with the world," he said. Catherine climbed into the bed, and Benjamin put out the light before he lay beside her. The room was as black as the inside of a tomb, and they could both pretend to be sleeping.

# Chapter Sixty

Catherine knew it was morning when a threshold of grey appeared at the bottom of the door. Then the key turned in the lock, and a man stood, a shadow against the light, and said, "Get you out of there now."

Benjamin groaned and sat up. Catherine tumbled out the other side, but the man remained, watching at bored attention while she put on her outer clothes and let Benjamin tidy up the back.

"You might give my wife a moment to herself," Benjamin said.

"Must watch," said the watchman. "Get you dressed, sir, and come along with me."

They did so, and Catherine took a moment to splash her face with the slimy water. The man produced a large clout for her. "Enough bath," he said. "We must go now."

In the hallway, the light smacked Catherine, and she covered her eyes with her forearm. She felt grimy, underdressed. "Is there nowhere a woman can go to clean herself up for the queen?" she asked.

"Nowhere," said the man. "This way."

He led them along the corridor, already filling with men and women, some in grand costume, others looking as though they had slept there. One young boy held a piglet in his arms, and a couple of the palace guards were taunting it with their daggers. No one stared. No one whispered as Catherine and Benjamin passed, and then they were taken into a small room and made to sit on a stone bench.

"You will wait here. That one will be your guard." The man indicated another, dressed just as he was, standing beside the door. "We will fetch you when you're required." He nodded to the other man and went out.

"Perhaps we had better say our good-byes now," said Benjamin.

"None of that," said Catherine. "Mary will only want to see you penitent. Get on your knees and tell the truth." Her hands were shaking, and she put them under her thighs. "I will be beside you."

Benjamin swiped a spider's web from the wall. "Well. We can hope this loyalty of yours will pay off at the last." He raised his voice to the guard. "What do you say, man? Is the queen merciful?"

The guard kept his eyes on the air in front of him and said nothing at all.

It might have been an hour. It might have been three. But at last the door opened, and the first guard said, "Come you along now."

Catherine's thighs were numb and needled with pain, but she went without limping or complaining. Benjamin came behind her, and they followed the guard further down the hall. Catherine knew where they were going before he turned into the reception room, bowed, and retreated. They were left in the midst of court ladies and a few brightly dressed men. And on the throne before her was Mary Tudor.

"Come forward, Catherine," said the queen, "and your husband with you."

She stumbled across the floor and almost fell in front of the queen. She made a curtsey of it, more servile than was necessary, and the queen said, "Have you injured yourself?"

"No, Your Majesty," said Catherine. She hoisted herself to her feet and shook out her skirt.

Benjamin had bowed beside her and lifted his eyes only when the queen said, "Look at me, Master Davies. I've no need to see the top of your head all day." Catherine prepared her mouth to speak, but Queen Mary had directed her gaze over them. "Get the boy," she said to someone behind them, and Catherine almost turned her back on the throne.

Mary Tudor put her palms together. Her head tilted forward until her chin sat on her fingers. The movement pushed her mouth into a frown. "And what shall we do with you?" she said.

"He is scarcely more than a child, Your Majesty," said Catherine. "He is penitent. He has had his head turned by a gentleman, older and more cunning than he is. He was poisoned with honeyed words, but he is purged now and will be obedient."

"You are his mother. What else would you say?" Mary Tudor looked at Benjamin. "And you. You were at his side, and you are no boy. And I've never heard that anyone could persuade you to believe anything you were not inclined to believe already."

Benjamin hesitated, and Catherine could see a rope of anger twisting under the skin of his neck, but he knelt, looked up at Mary, and said, "I have acted as the boy's father, and as a father I felt it was my duty to bring him home. I have not joined the cause of the rebels, nor do I subscribe to their ideas or their methods. I think they were a pack of fools who wasted many a good horse and weapon, and I did not want my son among them, but I came upon him at an unfortunate time. I am no rebel, and that is the honest truth of it, by God."

He seemed unable to decide whether to remain on his knees or to rise, but Mary said, "Well spoken. That is the longest string of words I have ever heard come out of your mouth, but you were beside Robert Overton in the battle, were you not?"

Benjamin had hitched himself to stand, but now thought better of it and sank down again. "I was beside him only because I meant to get him by the collar and drag him back to his mother. I was the one dragged instead."

"Mm," said the queen.

The door opened behind them, and Catherine felt the current of cold air on her ankles. She was getting stiff in the joints. Her knees hurt.

"Here's the young one," somebody said, and then Robbie walked up and stood on Catherine's left. He did not look at her, and she did not embrace him. He should kneel, she thought. Or bow. At least drop his head. But he stood, gloomily glaring at the queen's feet.

Mary Tudor waited. Robbie Overton did not bend his knees. Catherine coughed gently, reprovingly. Benjamin made a move on her right, and the queen raised her hand to stop him. She said, "Your young man has no manners, Catherine."

Catherine turned full on her son. "Bow, Robert. Kneel to the queen. It is your duty."

But Robbie Overton remained on his feet.

Mary Tudor stood, and Catherine fell forward. "He is stubborn and froward, Your Majesty, but he means no harm." She glanced to her left. Her son remained where he had been.

"You are guilty of treason," the queen said. Catherine lifted herself to her knees. Mary was pointing at her son. "You will kneel." She snapped her fingers and two guards approached.

"My only treason is the guilt of good conscience," said Robbie. He backed up a step. "I never intended harm to your person."

"My person?" said the queen. "Who are you to speak of my person?" Her skirts trembled, and she stuck her hands among their folds. "I should have your head cut from your shoulders where you stand. Kneel."

The guards took Robbie Overton by either shoulder and slung him to the floor. His face smacked the pavers and he pushed himself up on his elbows. One of the men set his boot between the boy's shoulder blades and shoved him flat.

"No, Lady. Please, Your Majesty," Catherine said, but Benjamin stepped in front of her, and she scrambled backward, unsure whether to rise or remain on her knees. Benjamin said, "I beg you. He has been bewitched by the silver tongue of that Wyatt, and he will mend with time. He's a boy."

"He is enough of a man to hold a sword," said the queen, "and to disobey an order from his queen."

"He is green in judgment," said Benjamin. "He speaks out of books, and with other men's mouths. He doesn't know what he thinks."

"I do know what I think," said Robbie. He ventured onto his elbows. "I know that Rome is a whore and that the Spanish want our necks under their boots."

Mary's face was bloody-red, and she stormed forward, bowing to smack Robbie across the face. He took it with only a tremor, but the spot on his cheek flamed.

"You hear him?" said Benjamin. "He talks like a madman. He knows only what he's been told."

Catherine rose. Mary Tudor was in front of her, and she grabbed her sleeve. "Please, Your Majesty. Do not kill my son." She realized, horrified, what she had done and withdrew her hand.

"I will look after him," said Benjamin. "I will be his voucher. You may take from me what you would have from him."

Catherine said, "No," but it was too late. The queen had seized upon Benjamin's words. She turned to Benjamin. "So you will indeed vouch for him," she said. "You were with him in this, were you not?"

"I was beside him, but not with him, nor with any of them, I swear it." Benjamin extended his palm.

Mary did not take his hand. "Then your vow can be your punishment." She looked at Catherine. The queen said, "You and I have seen many years pass by us. I would say that I know you."

"Yes, Your Majesty," said Catherine. "A long time since."

"You have not always done well, but you have never betrayed me. And because of that, I will give you this much. Your son will live."

Catherine breathed the darkness from her chest. "I thank you, Your Majesty."

"But he will not live in England." She looked at Robbie. "Two days. You have two days to leave this island. You will not return, on pain of death, ever in your lifetime. Not one foot upon our shores. Do you hear me, boy?"

Robbie Overton had gone chalky around the jaw, and he whispered, "Yes." He swallowed and said, "Your Majesty."

"Get up," the queen said. Robbie got his feet under him, wary of the guards, and finally stood. His face was flushed. Mary said, "You will inherit no property. You will own no lands in this realm, ever. Your Yorkshire buildings, your fields—everything your father ever held in title—will be forfeit to your mother and her heirs. But not you or yours. Do you understand?"

Catherine felt the floor grow cold beneath her feet. The icy air crept up her skirt and her knees shook. She wondered if someone had opened the door again, but the room was still as a stone.

Robbie said, "Yes."

"And you," said Mary, turning to Benjamin. "You have stood beside this traitor, and you say you will vouch for him. Then you will go with him." Benjamin opened his mouth, and Mary held up her right hand. "You will go. Five years should teach you something. You will be gone with this son of yours. Your London house will belong to us. Your country house and its fields are also forfeit to the crown. You may take what you can carry and hope that your wife here can manage her own estate in your absence. Catherine and the daughters will remain in England. Neither she nor they may join you. And when you return, return with a more obedient spirit in you."

Catherine cried out, "No, Your Majesty, please. He is my husband."

Mary turned her fierce eyes on Catherine. "You have lived as a widow before. I expect you can do it again. Five years should be nothing to a woman of your age. Your blood could benefit from a period of cooling. You still have a household to manage. Manage it with better eyes. You should look more closely to your servants and your acquaintances."

"Your Majesty," Catherine began.

But Mary Tudor had already turned away. She put out her right hand and said, "You will have guards to see your men to their boat. Be sure they get on it. I have done. Now, out of my sight, all of you." She walked back up to her throne and leaned upon it. She put one hand to her forehead and said no more.

The guards prodded Robbie backward, and they had no choice but to walk out. Catherine turned and went, forgetting to bow and retreat. But no one noticed. The next penitents were already at the door.

# Chapter Sixty-One

Catherine stood in the inner courtyard, blinking up at the sun. It looked warm. Its light shone down on her, and she pushed back her head cover to let it touch her face. In the gravel next to the wall, a yellow flower had opened and Catherine wondered at it. Such a small thing, struggling to live there, wedged between stone and stone. "I cannot feel it," she said to the flower. She thought she should know what it was called, but the name eluded her, skidding somewhere in the back of her memory. The sun shone down, and she held out her arms.

"I'm cold." She pulled her sleeves back, but still her skin ached and tingled, as though she had plunged her arms into a winter stream.

"Banished," said Benjamin beside her. "I'm banished. I am bankrupt."

Catherine put her hand on his arm and he almost buckled. A couple of men glanced their way. They likely thought him a drunkard. They would go to the coast after all, she thought. She could slip onto a boat after them without being seen, or maybe she could get them to Yorkshire, where there were plenty of villages in which a man and boy might hide.

But the girls. What would they do with the girls? They would take the girls. But she had not been given permission. "Shall we sail together?" she said. "All of us? And not be found out?" She sounded mad, and she knew it.

"No. You cannot, not against her express word. We'll return to find she's taken your land in Yorkshire too, and then the girls will have nothing. She may arrest us all. Someone must stay and make money." Benjamin regained his feet. A man was bringing their horses, and he lowered his voice. "I will find me some markets. In Calais or Paris, perhaps Rome. There's good business in the Lisbon ports, I've heard." He burped up a nasty chuckle. "That would serve her nicely. I'll be selling Yorkshire wool to the Pope while she sits here in the cold with her barren body."

Robbie joined them. He was leading the gelding that Benjamin had bought for him. "I will ride straight to Dover and leave on my own," he said. "I have nothing at your house."

"Not on that horse, you won't," said Benjamin. "Not unless someone rides with you to take it for your mother to sell."

Robbie's face burned, then he sulked. "You have plenty. I have nothing."

"I *had* plenty. Before you rode off into their hands. Before you took up with that band of fops. And now my houses are gone. My family is gone from me. And your mother will have to turn her hands back to business to earn our keep. You have nothing because you have thrown it away and spat after it."

A cloud of guilt passed over the boy's face. "You can return."

"Oh, yes, indeed. In five years. No thanks to you. And don't turn a white eye on me, either. You wanted to go. You've been aching to go. Or was it only when you thought you could come prancing back into England whenever you wanted, like a little prince?"

"I never wanted to return. I was content in Wittenberg with men of conscience."

"Then why didn't you stay there?"

"My countrymen needed me," sniffed Robbie.

"Your countrymen are rotting corpses, and your country has just cast you out like the tail of yesterday's fish."

Robbie opened his mouth, but Catherine covered her ears and said, "Stop. Both of you. We must go home and gather what can be gathered. Most of the large goods were broken up by Gardiner's men, but there will be something. I have some ready coin hidden. That's what you need." She leapt onto her palfrey. "Come on then. It'll do no one any good to stand here casting blame."

Benjamin said, "Spoken like a scholar." He mounted and waited for Robbie to do the same, then threw a line over and strung it through the bridle of Robbie's gelding. "No running off again."

The boy bowed his head and let himself be led.

The two guards met them at the gate and agreed to allow them to stop for necessaries. Not for long, they warned, and Catherine's stomach turned over. These men would not be fooled.

They rode straight to the Davies house, but it was late afternoon before they arrived. The stench was impossible to avoid. Bodies still hung here and there, though mostly eaten to bone. A lone skeletal hand remained tied, inexplicably, to a wooden gate that seemed to lead nowhere. Robbie stared as they went, his face ashy and sick. "You see?" said Benjamin. He spat into the muddy street. "Any one of these might have been you." He turned to Catherine with a bitter look. "They fought for the devil, but your Mary is no saint."

"No," said Catherine, "she's not. She is Queen of England, though."

"Queen." Benjamin shook his head. "She's queen and pope. Judge and executioner. She's the Queen of Blood."

"And that appears to be true as well," admitted Catherine. She cast a glance at the guards, but they looked ahead, indifferent to bitter traitors.

At the house, everyone crowded around to hear the story. It had to be told quickly, and without Benjamin, who had little time to gather what he could. Reg went to assist, and the guards followed. Ann asked, "And where is Connie in all this?"

"I don't know. I fear it has something to do with Margaret," said Catherine.

Ann clenched her fists. "I should have known. I should have seen it."

"There was nothing to see," said Catherine, but a part of her wanted to see Old Moll's face one more time, to look into those mad eyes and see if the lunacy was, in fact, cunning.

Ann was alight to battle the decision, but Catherine took her hand. "The fight is over. They will have to go. Tomorrow."

Reg came into the entry way. "I should go with them."

"You will not," said Benjamin, behind him. "I need to know that Catherine has a steady right hand. And Ann might balk at it." "I will take Arthur Huff and Thomas Jones, if they are willing to go."

"No servants," said one of the guards, behind Benjamin. "You go alone."

"May I eat?" sneered Benjamin.

"You may," said the guard, without a hint of a smile.

Two of the maids brought in cold meat and wine, but Benjamin only ate for a few minutes, stuffing his mouth with bread. Then he said, "There is no time," and rose. "Robbie is pouting upstairs. You might tell him that it will do him no good. How much money is in the house?"

"More than you can put into your pockets," Catherine whispered, though the guard did not look her way.

Ann came in, with an armload of woven sacks. "Fill these with as much of your clothing as you can," she said. "I will begin stripping the house."

"Take only what belongs to your persons," said the guard. He leaned against the doorjamb, watching now. "The furniture and goods belong to the queen."

Reg went out to bring around a wagon for the journey to Yorkshire, and Diana, wakened by the noise, heard the news with a solemn face, and then held a lantern quietly while they loaded battered cases and old chests and dirty bags. But concealed deep inside them were some saleable goods—silver spoons and bowls, some silks and embroidered cloths, a few undented cups, everything that Gardiner's men had spared. It wasn't much. The linens from the beds and two of the feather mattresses were laid at the bottom of the wagon, purportedly to soften the ride to Yorkshire for the women. They hadn't been deemed worth stealing, apparently.

Catherine stole down to her accounts room and opened the bottom drawer of her little writing table. At the back was a bag full of coins. She let her wrist measure the heft of it. Not as much as she remembered. But it would have to do. Benjamin could easily conceal it in a pocket, after all.

Upstairs, Benjamin was ordering the men as though he was planning to go with them. "That's enough," he said. "You will be fine enough when you arrive. You don't want thieves upon you during the journey. Reg, you will ride beside this wagon yourself. Do you hear me? Take at least six men with you, and arm them. Take every sword and dagger in the house."

"I will do it," he said. He turned to Catherine. "What has become of Robbie?"

"Still upstairs," said Catherine. "He is probably sorting his books." She tucked the bag into his breeches and he nodded.

Reg said nothing, just slid his eyes past Ann's and bent to tighten the straps around the edges of the wagon.

The eastern sky was showing the first pink of dawn as they finished, and Catherine leaned back, holding her palms against her aching hips. She was wondering if they should go, go now, before the household stirred, when a window opened above her and Alice cried out, "Father! You're home!"

# Chapter Sixty-Two

They could not send Benjamin and Robbie off without giving the children their chance to say good-bye. Benjamin woke Veronica and took her with Alice into the dining gallery. Catherine stood in the doorway, unable to stop her hands from wringing themselves, as he explained that he and their brother would have to take a long journey, under orders from the queen. He did not condemn Mary, and he did not say that Robbie would not return. He did not say "five years," and Catherine was grateful that he knew the time would sound like an eternity to a girl Alice's age. They wept, and they clung to his neck and begged him to say the queen nay. He must stay with them, in England. But Benjamin was firm, patting their backs and promising to send gifts from everywhere he travelled. Catherine's heart clawed at her chest. She did not intervene.

Within an hour, he had calmed them, and Veronica had put on a face of resignation. Diana came down and shook her father's hand, presenting an image of stoic acceptance that Alice observed and then mimicked. Catherine wondered if she could be as gentle and wise as her stepdaughter.

Robbie showed himself when the crying had ceased and the room had gone quiet. He came silently down the stairs, a bag slung over one shoulder, and stood at the front door, gazing out at the horses and wagons and guards. Veronica said, "You will travel with Father?"

"He has kept me company, and I am bound to do the same for him," Robbie said simply. He was blinking back tears when he turned to his sister, and she looked into his eyes to read whether he spoke the truth. Finally, she let him put his arms around her and lay his face on her shoulder.

"Write to me," Catherine heard her elder daughter say. "And keep yourself among good men."

"Come, no long farewells," said Benjamin. He had Alice on his hip, though she was too large to ride so, and he threw his arms around her, held her tight, and then set her on the floor. "Keep to your lessons, and mind your mother."

Diana approached her father and gave him a dignified hug. "Be well, Father," she said. "I will look for your return."

He nodded at his slim, straight daughter. Then she backed away from him.

The younger girls insisted on standing at the door, waving, and Catherine almost felt that she would not return, either, so torn was her breast with grief. The tutor had not come since the house had been broken up by Gardiner's men, and she set them to their lessons. Diana took their hands and said, "We will be upon it, Mother."

Reg led out the men hauling the wagons, after the guards did a cursory search and granted them leave to take it all to Yorkshire. Reg appointed three servants to wait for the women, while Ann hugged Catherine hard and promised to be ready, with the girls, to depart when she returned. She would explain to them, once the wagon had gone, that their house was seized. Catherine got onto her palfrey and Benjamin, his big gelding, and Robbie, the roan. They walked out into the road, following their guards, and had not gone past three other houses before a woman came trotting around the corner on a little palfrey, almost a twin of Catherine's. She was followed by two serving-men, and Constance.

It was not Jane Dudley. Catherine yanked back her reins. Of course. It had to be Margaret.

She halloed, as though they were old friends, and jumped to the ground without assistance. The men sat their horses and looked at nothing. Connie stared ahead, impassive.

"Well, sister," said Margaret, leading her palfrey behind her. Her skirts dragged in the muddy gravel of the road, but they were already well-worn and did not suffer from it. She pushed her hood back enough to show her face to the early sun. She was still tall, but now so thin that the skin lapped around her mouth. Her bodice was flat, and the folds of her neck swung loose as wattles. Her eyes had grown sharp and angry, and her voice shrilled down the road. The hair that showed, falling from the hood, looked unnaturally dark. She must have dyed it. The colour made her pale skin look deathly.

Catherine said nothing. Margaret did not look at Benjamin, but picked her way past him, holding up the thread-bare skirt, and set her hand on Catherine's leg. Her touch was cold, the fingers fleshless and grasping.

"Sister," Margaret repeated, "it has been many a year. How do you?" She now cast a glance at Benjamin, who had turned in his saddle. "I hear that your family has got into some trouble with the queen. It is a sad day indeed, for us all. Why, this must be your son. How he has grown. He's big enough to carry a weapon, or so I hear."

"Margaret," said Catherine. The name scorched her tongue. "Let us pass. I had hoped never to lay eyes on you again. Go home, wherever your home is, and do not plague me."

"My home is with Lady Dudley," said Margaret. "Or it was. She is freed, have you heard? She is as free a woman as you or I."

"I'm very glad to hear it," said Catherine. "I hope she uses her newfound liberty to clean up her household of spies and traitors."

Margaret laughed a high squeal at this. "Spies and traitors? I believe I see before me the only traitors I know." She smirked at Robbie, but he did not look at her. "And the stain of your son's treason has splashed us all with mud. Connie and I are asked to seek positions elsewhere, after all we have done for her!"

"She might expect to be bitten when she has kept a serpent in her bosom," said Benjamin.

"You have a tongue in your head for me yet," said Margaret. "I hear that you are banished along with this boy for your own actions against the anointed queen. The serpent, I believe, is here among you."

"What do you want, Margaret?" said Catherine.

"I must needs have a roof over my head. I am still an Overton. I must needs be housed as befits my station."

"And you expect me to provide that house?" asked Catherine. "When you and that harridan you keep have taken our houses away from us?" She tried to point at Connie, but her finger shook and she tucked her hand under her arm. "What has become of your husband, Margaret? Let him give you a roof."

"I have no husband. I have been a nun, and you know it right well." Margaret sniffed. "It is against the law of England for me to have a husband."

"I heard that you had one despite the law. And a child of him."

"Rumour, no more." Margaret waved her hand. "You have seen children disappear before they breathe the air." She eyed Benjamin. "And husbands promised are not husbands won. It was only the idle talk of a moment. I have been required to take a position in service. That position has been lost. Now I must have a family."

Catherine pondered Margaret's speech. She had felt the child in Margaret's body with her own hands. It had been no rumour, but it was true that babies died. She had a moment of pity for the woman below her, but she looked up and saw Benjamin. She was losing a husband, too. And a child. "If you have lost your position, you may seek another along the road. We have long been strangers, Margaret, and I will not harbour you. You have betrayed your own blood."

"I have been loyal to the queen. The queen is the country. The queen must be obeyed."

"Then go to the queen," said Catherine. "I am sure she will give you a place among her ladies." She shook her reins loose and stepped forward.

Margaret was forced to retreat to save her skirt, and she slapped at the air. "You cannot refuse your kin. You cannot shut your door to us."

"I have no door in London anymore, and no furnishings, either," said Catherine. "Get you gone, Margaret. And take that creature with you. We must ride to Dover. You will not be welcome in any place where I bide."

She rode on, Benjamin beside her, and she heard Robbie spit upon his aunt as he passed her. Margaret shrieked a curse, but Catherine did not look back.

# CHAPTER SIXTY-THREE

The ride to Dover was dismal and damp. The rain fell soft at first, then became a chastisement, and the road before them washed into the ditches. Robbie rode proudly for a while, but was soon transfigured into an image of misery, bent over his roan's dripping mane and hugging his jacket to his chest. The guards rode side by side at the rear. They passed foot-travellers, who plodded through the mud without looking up to see whose way they might obstruct. The villages were shut against the weather, and the early blossoms drooped against the tender grasses. They stopped for food and drink, but the inns were dank and the ale was flat and weak.

"It is the punishment of the queen that has done this," said Benjamin, as they mounted again, after an early meal. There had been no beds available for a rest, and they were forced to continue into the storm. "The people here are all painted with the names of rebels and are filled with resentment."

"They will rise against her again," said Robbie, with a fresh note of anger.

"And they will be put down once more," said Benjamin. "They should keep their necks to the yoke and be quiet about it."

"Their necks may be shackled, but their consciences will not," said Robbie.

Benjamin turned, his gelding's hooves sliding in the muck, and faced Robbie. "Then she will cut the heads from their shoulders, and that will be an end to their consciences. Now be quiet."

And they rode on. Catherine's stockings were wet through, and cold, and she silently cursed the clouds, cursed Margaret and Connie. Almost cursed the queen, then crossed herself against the bad fortune she might bring on them. She ventured a glance at her husband, his pale, furious expression. Then she went ahead and cursed Mary Tudor. How much worse could their fortune become?

They were joined along the way by others on horseback, equally soaked and silent. From side lanes and alleyways, people headed to the coast, and Catherine wondered how many were fleeing Mary's reign, how many had been driven into exile.

But the boats would not sail, not in the relentless rain, and they counted themselves lucky to find an inn with empty beds. Robbie and Benjamin would have to share with the guards, and Benjamin would have to pay for them all. He ordered the roan to be tied to his own gelding and watched through the night.

"We are condemned to leave this island," Benjamin said, out loud for all to hear, "and this young man has disappeared in the night before. He must needs be watched."

The innkeeper held out his hand for more coin. "I can have the room guarded."

"We have guards for him," said Benjamin, but he paid again.

They ate without tasting the fish and bread, though both were fresh and hot. The fire in the hearth dried their clothing, but now they were stiff, and Catherine itched all over. She stank. She ordered wine for herself and Benjamin, but Robbie would not drink it. He accepted a mug of ale and drank it without complaint. There was little conversation and no mention of the queen at all.

Catherine washed herself before she said good-night to Benjamin. She would not weep, but she clung to him, listening to his breath. He said, "This is not for all time. It may not even be for a long time."

Catherine leaned back and looked into his face.

He whispered into her ear, "There are boats coming to England as well as going out. I will go, but do not think I mean to stay away. I will move quietly, and I will not put myself in any more danger than is necessary, but I do not mean to be gone for five years."

"And I will come to you. Be sure of it. I had never thought to cross the sea, but I will do it if I know where to seek you."

He set her away from him. "You will know." He was silent a moment. "I cannot swear to keep Robbie in my sight."

"You cannot do anything more for him at all," said Catherine. "You have done more than any man should be asked to do."

Benjamin held her again, leaning onto her shoulders, and said, "My wife." She let him weigh her down, committing the scent of his skin and the curve of his muscles to her heart.

The morning rose too quickly. Catherine awoke, wound in the sheets, to a pounding on the door. The sun glared in.

She dressed in a few minutes, barely presentable to the world, and came out to find everyone else ready to go. "The storm has passed," said Catherine.

"I fear me the storm is just beginning on this island," said Benjamin, "but the boats will sail and I must be on one of them."

Robbie sat dutifully at the table in the big public room, a plate of fish and cheese before him.

"You will need me to pay your passage, I suppose," said Benjamin, sitting across from him. He poured himself a large draught of ale and drank. "And give you pocket money for your travels?"

"I have a destination," said Robbie. "I will need to get there."

"Very well." Benjamin downed the drink and stood. He hadn't eaten. "I will book passage for us both."

"I go to a land of freedom. You seek business. We need not sail together," said Robbie, staring at his plate.

"No, we need not. And we will not." Benjamin took a chunk of bread from the platter and bit into it.

Catherine sat beside her son. She filled his cup again and he sipped at it. The innkeeper's wife brought a plate of hot, crisp fish, and laid it before her. She broke the skin with her knife and inhaled. It was fresh, and delicately seasoned. And yet her stomach would not ask for it. She said, "To Wittenberg, then?"

Robbie nodded, shrugged, shook his head. Nodded again.

"Letters will be watched for. They may be read," said Catherine. "I do not know if they will reach me."

Again the nod.

"You have sure companions? You will not want?"

"Yes," he murmured. He glanced up. "Your queen has done this."

Catherine watched her son. Such a young man. Not a man, still a boy, but headstrong as a prince. "No, she has not. You have done this thing yourself." She expected to feel a tempest of grief, but her son seemed to sit a long way off, an unreal thing, as though she were staring at a picture of him. She was calm. She searched inside herself for the love of a mother, and she seemed to stumble over it, like a small treasure hidden deep in her breast. She fancied she might draw it to the surface of her mind and examine it, like a curious stone, and then place it back in its niche. "If you find yourself without friends, you must write to me, whatever the risk."

"I will not be without friends."

"Very well." Catherine lifted a sliver of the fish to her mouth and tasted it. She was sure it was as fine as any she had ever eaten, and yet her tongue would not tell her if it was good.

Benjamin went out with one of the guards and returned within the hour. The boats would sail, while the weather held, and everyone was required to board at once. He rushed up to their room and got his bags while Catherine stood by, her mind confounded. He could not be going. He could not, but he was, and she followed him as he went out the door, pulling Robbie along with him. The docks were crowded and loud, men going this way and that, and Catherine stood like a post as Benjamin pointed westward. "That's yours, Robbie. Get upon it and keep your head down." Benjamin produced a small bag and shoved it into the boy's hand. "Do not let this be seen. There are men aboard already who will cut your throat for it."

Robbie tried to refuse it, but his hand closed over the fabric even as he thrust it forward.

"Take it," said Benjamin. "Now go."

Catherine hugged her son and tried to think of something comforting to say, but someone was ringing a bell and the noise was greater than her voice. She could not think of a word, anyway, and as she released him, Robbie was gathered into a group of men, headed toward his ship, and he disappeared.

"And now it is my turn," said Benjamin. The guards stood a few feet off. "No tears. I forbid them. Think of this as a voyage of fortune. You shall hear from me, and when you do, it will mean that I am shortly to follow. I may appear unannounced. I will not say when or where in writing, but do not despair of me. I will see how the wind blows in Calais. If they won't abide an Englishman, I will try further south, Rome or Lisbon. Do you hear? Catherine, do you hear me?"

She did, like a gale in her ears, and she held onto his forearms as he grasped her elbows. She nodded.

"Stay on the sunny side of your queen," said Benjamin. "Smile when she smiles, and put your head down when she frowns. She is not a young woman for bearing children."

"Not young at all," said Catherine.

"Keep your head. Do not anger her, against yourself or the girls. I have done this myself."

The words echoed in her mind, and Catherine said, "No. You have not been at fault. It is the queen. The queen has done this, with the power bequeathed to her by her father and her brother."

"Kiss me." He put his arms around her, and she was lost in him for another moment. And then he was walking away from her, the bags over his shoulders and his long, curly hair still ragged on his shoulders.

She stood, watching the men readying the sails for travel. She had seldom seen the sea. Twice she had come to wait at this very dock, as Benjamin prepared to travel to Calais, studying the ropes and broad sheets of the ships, wondering at them, like great tapestries against the sky. She had trailed her fingers in the water after he had gone, wondering about the lands beyond, but she had never gone with him. The children had been at home. The weavers and the accounts to look after. Now, she shaded her eyes against the rising sun, and waited while he went away from her again. He would be back. Of course, he would. He would not forget her. Would he? He said he would not, but didn't the queen claim to be a woman of God? Her breath tightened, and she put her hand on her breast to ease her heart. Her palm touched the beads she had taken to wearing, and she drew them out, stroking the figure that hung at the bottom. Then she yanked them off, shattering the thin chain. She heard the soft clatter around her feet, and then she lifted the Roman icon over her head and threw it, far away, into the waves.

# Chapter Sixty-Four

The ships were gone. The guards were gone. And still Catherine stood, watching the gulls and the wandering dock workers. She should retrieve the horses, sell the roan, ride back to London. Benjamin had forgotten to bring a man along for her, and she would need to hire a companion for the journey home. She felt her stomach grumble. It must be close to midday.

"Why do you wait here?" a woman said, beside her.

Catherine turned. Her tongue had sharpened to snap at the stranger, but she found herself looking at Jane Dudley, wrapped up against the sea-wind. The woman's face was chapped and lined, but she was smiling.

"Jane." Catherine almost reached out to touch her, to see if she was real.

"The same," said Jane Dudley.

"You are out of the Tower?"

"So I appear to be. The queen has shown mercy, and I am to be thankful for it."

"And are you?"

"Greatly."

"And what do you here? Are you banished? Like my husband?"

Jane turned her face toward the sea. The waves had whipped into white-caps under the wind, and she breathed in the air. "Not banished. Not even beaten. I am to return to my home and submit to the queen. And that I shall do."

"But your home is not in Dover."

"No."

"And you have your household. You have much to make you proud there." Catherine had also turned her attention to the water, and they stood, side by side, neither looking at the other.

"I did not know, Catherine; you must take me at my word. I do not hire the servants, and I have been much at fault in not noting who was among them. If I ever saw your Margaret, I did not know her. And I did not know of this maid of hers, or her mother, I swear it." Jane laid a bony hand on her chest, and Catherine glanced at the gesture. "Having laid eyes on her since my release, I can vouch for her unmarried state. The woman looks like a scare-crow. Has she grown taller since she grew so lean?"

Catherine knew she was supposed to laugh at this snippet of maliciousness, but there was no humour in her. "And you have turned her out?"

"On her ear. And the fat red-haired maid with her. I do not keep spies among my people. You must believe me."

"Well," said Catherine. "It is no matter whether I believe you or not. The damage has been done." She lifted an arm to the water. "As you can see, Benjamin is gone, as is my son."

"I saw. My husband and son are gone, too, but they will not be coming back," said Jane. She took Catherine's elbow and pulled her so that they were face to face. "We ordinary women must survive. Together. I am here to seek you."

"Ordinary? Well, you have found me," said Catherine, "and so you have done your service. The men are gone, so you may take your findings back to the queen."

"You will take them yourself," said Jane.

"Wherefore would I do that?" said Catherine.

"You are sought," said Jane. "Do not think that the queen bears you ill-will, despite your family's failings. She knows your skills right well, and she is a woman who determines to bear a child."

"She will need a man to make that happen, not me," said Catherine. She retrieved her arm and stepped backward.

"You must not say no," said Jane. "She wants a woman who knows how to make a woman conceive, to make a child stay seated in the womb and to bring it into the world strong. She prefers you."

"Prefers?"

"She orders you to be brought. She will pay you handsomely. Your daughters will have no worries. Her men are waiting."

So the guards had not gone, after all. They had simply retreated to lie in wait. Catherine was staring into the sun now, and her head ached. The water slapped the dock, and she thought for a moment that it was her heart, banging into her ribs. A gull shrieked overhead. The queen wanted her. The queen wanted a child. Her daughters would need tutors again, in the country.

She looked out to sea, where wild ducks bobbed and swayed on the waves, going where the current would take them. One dived and came up with a small fish, lifted its head and let the treasure disappear down its slender throat. What might come might also go away. A child might appear and then be gone, without the queen ever knowing what had befallen her. A woman her age, hoping for an heir. She would still be young enough to hope that her blood would knit into a child. But blood called for blood, and Queen Mary was already ankle-deep in it. She didn't know one herb from another. And she was aging. Every day.

"If the queen orders it, then I must go," said Catherine. "If you have men with you, I would be most grateful for a companion to take me to her."

"I have anything you need," said Jane Dudley. "The men have carried you here, and they will carry you back."

Catherine smiled. She already had everything she needed, back in her still room, for a woman who might be with child, or might believe that she could be with child. They would allow her to retrieve her herbs. Or they would let her go to Yorkshire, where her stores were fuller. She had long yearned for a community of ladies, and now she would have it. And she might have some power over one woman's body: Mary Tudor's. The breeze hit her skirt, and the scars on her knees itched. She thought she would never kneel in comfort again. The clawed thing that had been ripping at her breast seemed to grow wings and fly out of her. Catherine said, "Then let us go serve this queen as she deserves," and turned away from the churning sea, closing the heavy wrap tight, over her heart.

# THE END

# About the Author

Sarah Kennedy is the author of the novels *Self-Portrait, with Ghost* and *The Altarpiece, City of Ladies*, and *The King's Sisters*, Books One, Two, and Three of The Cross and the Crown series, set in Tudor England. She has also published seven books of poems.

A professor of English at Mary Baldwin University in Staunton, Virginia, Sarah Kennedy holds a PhD in Renaissance Literature and an MFA in Creative Writing. She has received grants from both the National Endowment for the Arts, the National Endowment for the Humanities, and the Virginia Commission for the Arts. Please visit Sarah at her website: http://sarahkennedybooks.com

# IF YOU ENJOYED THIS BOOK

## VISIT

## PENMORE PRESS
www.penmorepress.com

All Penmore Press books are available directly through our website.

# *Mistress Suffragette*

## *by*

## *Diana Forbes*

A young woman without prospects at a ball in Gilded Age Newport, Rhode Island is a target for a certain kind of "suitor."   At the Memorial Day Ball during the Panic of 1893, impoverished but feisty Penelope Stanton draws the unwanted advances of a villainous millionaire banker who preys on distressed women—the incorrigible Edgar Daggers. Over a series of encounters, he promises Penelope the financial security she craves, but at what cost? Skilled in the art of flirtation, Edgar is not without his charms, and Penelope is attracted to him against her better judgment. Initially, as Penelope grows into her own in the burgeoning early Women's Suffrage Movement, Edgar exerts pressure, promising to use his power and access to help her advance. But can he be trusted, or are his words part of an elaborate mind game played between him and his wife? During a glittering age where a woman's reputation is her most valuable possession, Penelope must decide whether to compromise her principles for love, lust, and the allure of an easier life.

PENMORE PRESS
www.penmorepress.com

# Assassins of Alamut
## By
# James Boschert

*An Epic Novel of Persia and Palestine in the Time of the Crusades*

The *Assassins of Alamut* is a riveting tale, painted on the vast canvas of life in Palestine and Persia during the 12th century.

On one hand, it's a tale of the crusades—as told from the Islamic side—where Shi'a and Sunni are as intent on killing Ismaili Muslims as crusaders. In self-defense, the Ismailis develop an elite band of highly trained killers called Hashshashin….whose missions are launched from their mountain fortress of Alamut.

But it's also the story of a French boy, Talon, captured and forced into the alien world of the assassins. Forbidden love for a princess is intertwined with sinister plots and self-sacrifice, as the hero and his two companions discover treachery and then attempt to evade the ruthless assassins of Alamut who are sent to hunt them down.

It's a sweeping saga that takes you over vast snow-covered mountains, through the frozen wastes of the winter plateau, and into the fabulous cites of Hamadan, Isfahan, and the Kingdom of Jerusalem.

"A brilliant first novel, worthy of Bernard Cornwell at his best."—Tom Grundner

PENMORE PRESS
www.penmorepress.com

# ROCAMORA

## DONALD MICHAEL PLATT

No man is closer to a woman than her confessor, not her father, not her brother, not her husband.

-Spanish saying

Vicente de Rocamora, the epitome of a young renaissance man in 17th century Spain, questions the goals of the Inquisition and the brutal means used by King Philip IV and the Roman Church to achieve them. Spain vows to eliminate the heretical influences attributed to Jews, Moors, and others who would taint the limpieza de sangre, purity of Spanish blood.  At the insistence of his family, the handsome and charismatic Vicente enters the Dominican Order and is soon thrust into the scheming political hierarchy that rules Spain. As confessor to the king's sister, the Infanta Doña María, and assistant to Philip's chief minister, Olivares, Vicente ascends through the ranks and before long finds himself poised to attain not only the ambitious dreams of the Rocamora family but also—named Spain's Inquisitor General

PENMORE PRESS
www.penmorepress.com

# Between Two Kings

## By

## Olivia Longueville

Anne Boleyn is imprisoned in the Tower of London on false charges of adultery, high treason, and incest on the orders of her husband, King Henry VIII of England.  Providence intervenes – she escapes her destined tragedy and leaves England. Unexpectedly, she saves King François I of France, who offers her a foolhardy deal, and Anne secretly marries the French monarch.

With François' aid, she seeks vengeance against the English king and all those who betrayed her and designed her downfall in England.  Henry must face the deadly intrigues of his invisible enemies, while his marital happiness with his third queen, Jane Seymour, is lost and a dreadful tragedy also strikes the king.  The course of English and French history hangs in the balance.

From the gloomy Tower of London to the opulent courts of England, France, and Italy, brimming with intrigue and danger – Anne Boleyn survives, becoming stronger and wiser, and fights to prove her innocence.  Her hatred of Henry is inextricably woven into her existence.

PENMORE PRESS
www.penmorepress.com